CW00403942

CHILD OF DESTINY

BOOK 1 OF THE RISING SAGA

M.K. ADAMS

For my parents, who believed in me even when I did not.
And for Rachel, always.

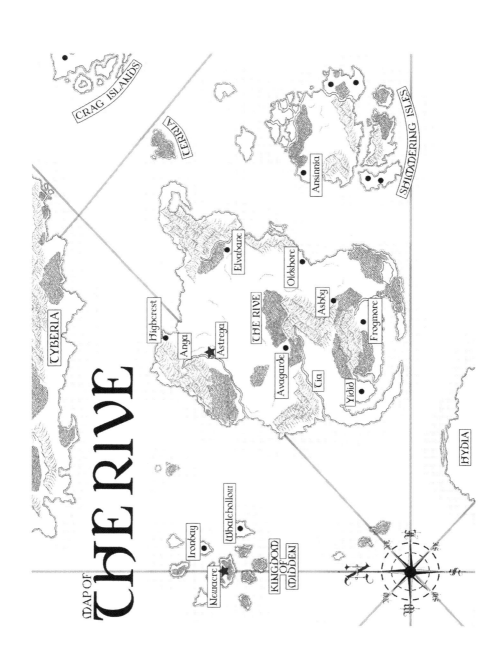

MAP OF

THE RIVE

CRAG ISLANDS

CERRIA

SHIMMERING ISLES

Arsinnia

CYBERIA

Elvabane

Oldshore

Highcrest

THE RIVE

Ashby

Frognore

Anga

Astrega

Avagarde

Cia

Ydid

LYDIA

Whalehollow

Ironbay

KINGDOM
OF
MIDDEN

Newacre

N

Contents

Chapter 1...1

Chapter 2...11

Chapter 3...20

Chapter 4...29

Chapter 5...35

Chapter 6...44

Chapter 7...51

Chapter 8...60

Chapter 9...66

Chapter 10...76

Chapter 11...82

Chapter 12...88

Chapter 13...97

Chapter 14...102

Chapter 15...109

Chapter 16...116

Chapter 17...122

Chapter 18...129

Chapter 19...135

Chapter 20...141

Intermission...147

Chapter 21...155

Chapter 22...161

Chapter 23 167

Chapter 24 173

Chapter 25 181

Chapter 26 187

Chapter 27 194

Chapter 28 200

Chapter 29 206

Chapter 30 212

Chapter 31 219

Chapter 32 225

Chapter 33 232

Chapter 34 239

Chapter 35 244

Chapter 36 250

Chapter 37 256

Chapter 38 263

Chapter 39 269

Chapter 40 275

Epilogue 282

Book 2: Betrayal of Destiny 289

CHAPTER 1

The carriage turned a corner and the polite chatter of Gemstone Avenue turned into a more raucous fanfare, signalling their arrival on Merchant Street. Lyvanne peeled back the curtain of the carriage ever so slightly for confirmation and proceeded to eye up potential targets down the street. The bakery was always a favourite, but the baked goods weren't the easiest to grab in a hurry. The fruit seller was easiest but least filling, and the butcher, despite having hanging meats outside for people to view as they pass by, had the hardest goods to conceal during her journey home. So more often than not, Lyvanne turned her attention to the wandering merchants, those who rolled trolleys down the street filled with different offerings. Usually from a store situated in the lower level of the city, trying to entice rich customers down to see their wares in person.

Lyvanne had spent most of her life invisible. Just another nameless urchin wandering the large and busy streets of Astreya stealing food to survive. But at only fourteen years old, Lyvanne was fast approaching the expected age where she would have to make a decision about her future.

"You can't stay here forever," her friends had warned after one particular encounter with a stubborn lord. She was becoming too old, growing too tall to remain invisible on the busy streets for much longer. Soon her unkempt clothing and ungainly nature would single her out among the wealthy and proud of the kingdom's capital.

Many children chose the path of least obstruction, to migrate towards the lower levels of the city, where blossoming gated communities and mansions were quickly replaced with sewage and slums. Others chose servitude in the gemstone mines below the city; it offered a small wage and warm food, but it was dangerous and there were more children who never returned from the deep underground caverns than there were those who did. Then there were those who fled the city entirely, escaping into the vast world that lay beyond the city walls and rolled with whatever cards life dealt them. Lyvanne had no doubt that some had gone on to lead peaceful lives, maybe even start families of their own… but maybe not. All she knew was that none had ever come back to help the other orphans, the ones remaining in Astreya.

Lyvanne didn't want to abandon the friends she had lived beside all these years since her parents died. She didn't want to simply give up on those who had effectively raised her. So every night before she slept, Lyvanne said a prayer, not to the Goddess of Creation or the God of Death, but to the Angel of Destiny.

Dear Angel watching over us, please lend me your sight. Please show me what I am to do, and show me what is to come.

Lyvanne lacked the upbringing to fully understand religion, nor did she know the formal pattern of prayer that the adults would talk about so nonchalantly on the streets. As in most situations in life, she did the best she could with what knowledge she had acquired from others. But the nights came and went with no sign or message from the Angel of Destiny. So Lyvanne had decided long ago that she would take things into her own hands, that she would be the master of her own destiny and forge her own path.

The carriage was steady, its large gilded wheels unfazed by the cobbled floor of Marchant Street. The aim was the same as usual: ride a carriage unbeknownst to the owner through the bustling traders, stick her hand out, steal as much food as possible, and then ditch the carriage at the earliest opportunity. Lyvanne had stolen from merchants thousands of times, but the older she grew, the harder it became. About a year ago, people had started to turn their heads with repulsion as she crept down the streets, her small burlap sack tied to her waist. Not everyone, but enough to warn her that she needed a new method, one with better cover.

Fortunately, there was a reason that Merchant Street was always so busy. It was as close to the centre of the wealthy sectors of Astreya as a high street could get. So Lyvanne hadn't wasted much time in figuring out her new way through. Just beyond the northern end of the street were gates that led into one of the many residential districts in the Upper layer of Astreya. A collection of glistening communities of polished white houses and spiked walls. An escape for the rich, noble, and lucky.

Luckily for her, the rich didn't like to walk anywhere they didn't have to, but they also didn't take too kindly to the smell of horses mucking up their picture perfect homes. So stables had been built. They were owned and funded by the king, a gesture of goodwill to those who contributed so much wealth into the kingdom's coffers. Just far enough away that a carriage could be summoned with relative speed and on a person's whim, but not close enough that it interceded with the residential gardens and water features. The quickest route for these carriages to get to and from the residential districts? Merchant Street.

She reached out her long skinny arm through the velvet curtain of the carriage and quickly grabbed a small cinnamon bun from one old man's trolley. For years Lyvanne hoped that the guilt would one day pass, but it never had.

"Sorry," she whispered under a breath as she watched merchant pass by. What made it worse was that she knew the old man saw her do it, but just like the rest he wouldn't say anything. Not if it meant angering whomever else was in the carriage with her, of bringing the City Watch down on their business for upsetting the wrong person.

Regardless, she still had to be careful. If she reached out too frequently then there was a chance the driver of the carriage would notice. She had to only take the risk when the opportunity was too enticing.

Just an hour previously, Lyvanne had wandered down to the Anya, the pale blue river that ran through part through the city. Whilst there, she had done her best to wash off the mud and clean up any cuts that adorned the olive brown skin of her arms. If merchants saw a battered and muddied arm reaching out from a carriage then they'd be more likely to question what was happening. If she kept herself clean, then it's just another spoiled rich kid taking what they don't own.

After filling her sack with just enough food to get by for a couple of days, Lyvanne took a moment to peer out of the corner of the carriage's curtained window. Her brown eyes and curled brown hair ever so slightly visible to the outside world as she peered out. Beyond her hiding place the street was littered with people who had never known a hard life. People adorned in coloured silk clothes, thick leather boots, and feathers gathered from exotic birds from far off continents. She was used to seeing the luxury of others by now, but to this day she struggled to understand how those with such money failed to help those without it. None of the street dwellers had enough money to get off the streets, and none of them were welcomed if they tried. Every year, Lyvanne would have to say goodbye to another friend, whether they were young and alone or old and weary. The streets of Astreya didn't care who you were, if you weren't careful they would claim your life without hesitation.

Lyvanne smiled as she peered out at the affluence of Merchant Street. She took note of every person that her carriage rolled by, their faces, their clothes. She made up their histories, their lives away from the street that they shared. One woman in particular caught Lyvanne's interest; she was unlike anyone Lyvanne had seen before, different even to the thousands of people she used to pass every day whist aimlessly walking the city streets as a young child. She had long flowing hazel hair and her coat was made of fur, as was common among the wealthy, but hers was colourful, as if made with the fur of a thousand different animals.

The woman's face told a different story than everyone else. She held her nose high in the air and had an aura of indifference to everyone else she passed, as though she despised the rich almost as much as Lyvanne did. Her exuberant and brightly coloured coat was a rare choice of clothing under the baking sun, but there was something else. The woman's gown, which fell gently beneath the coat, was cut short just above the knees, and Lyvanne noticed that hers wasn't the only gaze the hemline attracted.

As the carriage began to leave the woman behind, Lyvanne noticed two heavily armoured guards, walking 10 feet behind the woman with their eyes firmly fixed on her back. They weren't from the City Watch, which meant they were her personal security, a luxury even for the rich.

Who are you? Lyvanne wondered as the carriage carried on towards the end of the street. Her mind began to race with possibilities. She'd never seen a member of the royal council before, or maybe she was even a lesser-known member of the royal family?

Then Lyvanne made a mistake. She shifted on the backseat of the carriage, moving towards the rear window eager to know more about this extravagant and colourful woman. She wasn't discrete enough. The movement caused the carriage to shudder, not much but enough to catch the driver's attention. The driver called out to the horses and the carriage stopped.

Lyvanne knew that her time to make a decision was fading away fast. Like grains of sand trickling through a sieve the seconds washed over her with every step the driver took in her direction.

He sat on the right, Lyvanne told herself as she remembered back to first sneaking onto the carriage.

Giving the driver just enough time to make his way down from his perch Lyvanne opened the door to her left and darted out onto the busy street. Her sudden appearance drew the attention of a few bystanders. Some looked down distastefully, and others looked into the carriage quizzically. A glance to her right and Lyvanne caught the eyes of the woman who had thrown her off kilter in the first place. The woman and her two guards watched on, not with the distaste of the others, but with intrigue.

"Oi!" The driver called after her, spying her through the open doors of the carriage.

Not wasting anymore time, Lyvanne clung on tight to the straps of her sack and raced down the street. The quickest way to her hideout was back down Merchant Street, but for now, the focus had to be on finding somewhere less crowded. The driver gave pursuit, but after a few short metres, he was holding out a sweaty hand in a vain effort to close the distance. As he tried to push his weighty figure past a steadily growing horde of pedestrians the distance between them began to widen.

As suspected, the driver didn't bother chasing her for long, but up ahead there was a pair of City Watch guards who had noticed the commotion. Lyvanne knew she would have less luck there. Placing one hand on the hilts of their swords and another outreached as if to signal her to stop, they made for a formidable sight, but it was nothing that Lyvanne wasn't used to. Their steel-plated armour, brightly polished and adorned with gold and silver fortunately made them stand out like sore thumbs among the crowd. Lyvanne had ample time to plan her response.

The City Watch wasn't known for their mobility. The armour, whilst useful in a battle, was only a hindrance on the busy streets. Lyvanne dove to her left moments before running straight into the reach of one of the guards. She rolled under a market stall, making sure to keep her sack of food from being squashed underneath and carried on past the guards as if they were nothing. Unlike the driver of the carriage, these two did try and pursue, but it was wasted energy and before long the end of Merchant Street was in sight.

Another happy adventure, Lyvanne thought jokingly as she slowed her pace and moved out onto the quieter streets where she could more easily find a hiding place.

Lyvanne took the usual route home, the long way via the docks. Taking what food she felt could be spared, Lyvanne approached dock workers and crew from all manner of ships. Some were regular customers, others she risked approaching fresh. Every time she went to Merchant Street she would come back this way, sell small morsels of food here and there for horribly low prices. The people she sold it to knew that it was probably stolen, and so she didn't have much room to budge when it came to the price.

Tucking the bronze and silver coins away in a small pouch that she carried around her tattered cloak, Lyvanne counted as she went. Nearly enough to trade for a gold coin, she noted. The money wasn't for pleasure, and she'd had to keep it a secret from everyone else around her. It was her dreams made real. One day Lyvanne planned to make it out of the city, to bring her friends with her and to live their own life free from the city walls, and this small bag of savings was going to be how she did it.

It was a few hours before the young commoner made her way back to the dingy entrance of her hideout. The rise in guards asking around about "some street rat" had given her cause for caution, and she didn't want to bring any unwanted attention back to her friends. Moving aside the moss-covered wooden crate that hid the child-sized hole in the wall of a long abandoned house, Lyvanne began to hear the echoes of voices coming from within. Walking through the hole, Lyvanne glanced back into the damp and dilapidated alley that served as the front garden, just to make sure no one was around, and re-covered the entrance.

"I'm back!" she called down into the hideout.

The echoes of childish replies travelled from within in response. The house was small, but it had a basement and it was in there, she knew, that she would find the others. Upstairs was little more than charred wood and ash; a fire long ago had seen that there was no comfort left there and little in the way of viable living space.

Footsteps came racing up the hollow shell of a staircase that remained. Turning a corner and facing the descent into the darkness of the basement below, Lyvanne saw Oh's beaming face as he threw himself into her open arms.

"You were gone long, Lyv," The young boy said, as he bounced on the spot in eager anticipation. There weren't many people she would let get away with calling her that, but he was one.

Returning from her adventures out on the streets of Astreya was often the first time in the day that Lyvanne saw the others, and she usually arrived with food. Oh was younger than Lyvanne and significantly shorter. His skin was even darker than her own, a trademark of the people from the Shimmering Isles who lived their lives under the searing heat of the sun.

Kneeling down so that she was at similar height to the young boy, Lyvanne reached into her sack and pulled out the cinnamon bun she had comandeered earlier in the day. She handed it over to the boy who was visibly drooling at the mouth, whilst placing a single finger over her lips.

"Go share this with Lira, but keep it secret. You know Abella doesn't like you having sugar," Lyvanne whispered as she ushered Oh back down the stairs.

Lyvanne heard Oh announce her arrival as she followed him down the stairs, one hand on each railing as the wood creaked and bent under her weight. The staircase opened up into a large, dimly lit room. When the house had first been built there was no doubt in Lyvanne's mind that the basement had been the largest feature. Its stone walls and floor made it a cold room but sturdy. It had been virtually the only place to escape the fire unharmed, as the blaze had woven its way through the largely wooden house above. It was a sign of luxury and was no doubt a lifetime investment for the owner, whom just so happened to be sat in the centre of the room, candle by her side, asleep.

Abella was old, very old. She'd been old when the house had caught fire over a decade ago, and when Lyvanne asked why she stayed here, she had insisted that there wasn't enough life left in her to move elsewhere. So she sat here, every day, caring for and loving the young children who came and went, homeless and alone. Lyvanne had her doubts about why Abella remained. She would have had friends who could have helped her move. No doubt all those friends thought her long dead by now, the shell of her former home all that remained of her memory.

Oh had taken a seat on the floor by his toys, a pair of handmade wooden soldiers and a very poorly crafted horse, all of which Lyvanne had stolen to keep the young boy occupied. The fourth and final person in the basement made her way over to Lyvanne as she stepped out from the shadows of the stairs.

"I was worried," the young girl said flatly as she pulled Lyvanne in close for an embrace.

"No need," Lyvanne replied, a reassuring smile on her face.

Lira, who Lyvanne noted was now discretely biting down on a small chunk of cinnamon bun, was only a year or so younger than Lyvanne, but unlike her elder, she had yet to mature beyond her age. Lira helped where she could, especially when there had been more people living among the ruins of Abella's house, but in large the role of mother had been left to Lyvanne. It was she who went out to find food most days, and it was her who made every effort to keep their location hidden from those who would want to remove them from the city's Upper Level.

Deep down, Lyvanne knew that it was only a matter of time before some lord or lady complained enough that the king would actually take action regarding the ruined household. It was certainly an unwelcome sight in what was, for the most part, a ravishing sector of the city. If the wreckage had lain beyond the giant gateway that separated the rich from the poor, then no one would even cast a second glance. But they didn't live on the side of the poor. They made their home among the rich; they lived near the food. Their only reassurance came from the fact that Abella's home was in the furthest reaches of this sector of the city. The rear end of the house was built into the great stone wall that separated the Upper layer of Astreya from the lower, and it was likely the only reason that the entirety of the house had not completely collapsed in on itself during the fire.

Firm foundations but lousy neighbours, Abella always said.

"What happened?" Lira asked.

"I was seen, had to run and hide for a while."

Lira placed her hands on her hips and shot Lyvanne a stern gaze. "Why were you seen?"

"Got too caught up in the moment. There was this strange looking woman -

"A strange looking woman isn't worth your life," Lira interrupted as she loosened up her body and helped Lyvanne unpack the food.

Lyvanne wouldn't want to say anything that might upset her, but it was refreshing to hear the younger girl talk like the adult of the group for once. It had been a long while since Lyvanne had last slipped up, and it was reassuring to know that Lira cared enough to chastise her for it.

"I know. I'm sorry Lira," Lyvanne replied sincerely.

Lyvanne quietly tucked her savings away under her bed, and the four of them shared the food that she had brought home. Lira and Lyvanne stayed up long into the night after the others had fallen asleep. They didn't need to say much, but enjoying one another's company was still an easy task after all their years together.

"Don't go doing anything stupid next time, okay?" Lira said quietly as the pair lay side by side on the hard floor.

"I'll try not to," Lyvanne said with a smirk. Inwardly however, her confidence was quickly fading. If she'd learned anything that day, it was that she wasn't suited to the streets any longer. So closing her eyes, she turned to the only outlet she knew.

Dear Angel watching over us, please lend me your sight. Please show me what I am to do. Show me what is to come.

CHAPTER 2

It was a new day, and for once Lyvanne decided to take the day off. Unsure of whether or not the carriage drivers would be more perceptive of their surroundings following the incident the day before, Lyvanne made the call that it was probably best to avoid Merchant Street for the day.

Taking advantage of a rare day away from Merchant Street, Lyvanne laid in her makeshift bed of wood and fraying fabric until the sun began to beam in through the burned structure of the house above and down the stairwell into the basement.

After giving herself enough time to properly wake, she said her farewells to the others.

"I just need the time alone," she said as she ruffled Oh's shaggy brown hair as he asked to go with her for the day.

"Okay," he replied reluctantly before slouching his shoulders.

Lira was more understanding. "Everyone needs some alone time every now and then," she said to Oh. "Lyvanne's no different."

Abella had muttered a few words of encouragement in her half-dream state, wishing her to have a good time wherever she wandered before falling back to sleep. Lyvanne grew more wary of the old lady's health every day. A few years ago, she had been as spritely as someone twenty years her junior, but the past few years had taken their toll on her. Lyvanne missed the days when she would be up and about in the house, taking at least some of the responsibility out of Lyvanne's hands. Now, whilst she would have her good days, she slept most of the time and rarely had the energy to help in most matters.

Stepping out into the sunlight was like entering a different plane of existence. The light burned Lyvanne's eyes and forced a weary arm up in defence. At the same time, it was blissful. The warm rays beat down on her skin, which was a welcome change from the cold stone floor of Abella's basement. Astreya wasn't the hottest location on The Rive; the Shimmering Isles to the South were far hotter and less hospitable according to overheard conversations and hearsay. But the past few weeks had been hotter than any others Lyvanne could remember, and she wasn't the only one who had noticed. All the wealthy people seemed to talk about was the weather as they walked elegantly down the streets. Lyvanne pitied them if that was all they had in common to discuss.

Astreya itself was constructed as three circular layers, each with an increasingly imposing wall that watched down on the people below. The lower layer housed the masses, the people who couldn't afford the luxuries in life; the Upper layer was where Lyvanne lived, filled with the rich and every luxury you could imagine. The third and final layer housed the King, his family and his staff. The third layer served as a castle within the city. Only the exceptionally fortunate knew what the King's castle looked like, and Lyvanne could only dream of finding out as she walked along the curvature of the King's Wall, one hand gently brushing against the grey stone.

Lyvanne wasn't walking with the intention of finding her way inside, however; instead she was heading for her favourite part of the largest city in The Rive. The journey took her through winding streets of cobblestone, past busy streets of shoppers and professional socialisers and finally by the front gates of The Accord, the smallest yet most expensive of the gated communities which housed the wealthiest of Astreya's citizens. All the while travelling under the watchful shadow of the King's Wall.

Just beyond The Accord was Lyvanne's destination. The furthest wall of the gated community was built on the edge of a grassy slope, decorated with flowers and elaborate hedges, carved into the shapes of all manner of magnificent creatures. At the very bottom of the slope was the river Ayna. The Goddess of Creation had placed the river at the very heartland of her chosen people's empire, running through all three layers of Astreya the way a vein flows through a body.

Shuffling her way through a small gap in the connecting stone-work between the King's Wall and the rear wall of The Accord,

Lyvanne burst out onto the grassy slope. She had trod the path many times before, but regardless had to be careful where she went. If she caused too much noise or left behind too great a trace of her presence, then no doubt the King's gardeners would be on the lookout the next time she came along. So like always she took her time, carefully making her way down the slope. Taking in the strong and beautiful scents on offer before finding the world opened up before her as she walked out onto the quiet bank of the Anya.

To her left, the river snaked through a grate in the King's Wall where it flowed out of sight. To her right, the river followed along the grassy slope for about hundred yards before the scenery turned to buildings and stone. Further upstream beyond the first buildings the river bank was busier with other people going about their business. Handmaidens washing the clothes of their masters, optimistic fishermen standing on quays and even what looked like a young noble walking a pair of well-groomed dogs along a riverside walkway.

It was quieter here at Lyvanne's little hideaway on the riverside. The makeshift orphanage at Abella's old home wasn't exactly loud— it couldn't be if they wanted to remain hidden—but living with Oh at the age he was made life tiresome. She loved the young boy with all her heart. He was like a little brother to her, and it often made her sad that none of them knew where his parents were or what had become of them. It was rare for Islanders to live this far north into The Rive, it was rarer still for children from the Shimmering Isles to be here alone. Oh was a handful at the best of times, and downright tiring at the worst. She wanted a better life for him, for all of them.

Taking off her worn leather sandals, Lyvanne ran her toes through the grass and made the final few steps down towards the river. She swung a large bag she'd been carrying over her shoulder onto the edge of the river and began to unload a pile of dirty clothes. They didn't have much back at home, but what they did have Lyvanne was determined to keep as clean and as respectable as possible, even if it cost her a day off to do it. The alone time was worth it, Lyvanne told herself as she began to wash the clothes in the cool water of the river, occasionally splashing some water up her arm in order to keep herself from roasting in the mid-day sun. The only sounds were the continual chirping of small insects buried amongst the grass and hedges, the rippling of water and the distant clatter of citizens going about their day in the distance. That was, until she heard footsteps coming from the top of the slope above her. It was quiet at first, the gentle rustling as someone brushed against the shrubbery that formed a thin wall above. But it slowly grew in aggression as the person fought their way through the line and down onto the grassy slope.

Lyvanne knew that she would be less than welcome if someone found her here. It wasn't strictly breaking any laws, but the rich didn't take kindly to people like her being nearby, let alone so close to their homes and the areas of the city that they deemed their own. Instinctively, Lyvanne's hand gently brushed over a small scar that sat on her left cheekbone, the remnant of a punishment for being in the wrong place at the wrong time. Hearing the footsteps growing louder as the newcomer made their way down the slope and towards the river, Lyvanne scoured the area for the best place to hide. Running out of time, she threw the bag of washing out of sight and crawled under a large bush with heavy green leaves that was flourishing on the very edge of the river. She was hidden, but well enough? She didn't know.

To her surprise, it wasn't one of the nobles who stepped out into the clearing, but a young man, wearing the drab and torn clothes you would expect of a commoner, or worse, a Hemeti. He wasn't being as quiet as Lyvanne would usually be, which made her question whether he was just stupid or overly confident about the possibility of being caught there.

He was striking to look at. Most people in The Rive had dark skin and brown eyes, the result of thousands of years living under the intense sun. This person was pale, not just pale like the Southerners who lived in the White Mountains to the far south, but a sheer white, as though no sun had ever kissed his skin. Lyvanne had seen a Hemeti before, a race of greenskins who sat even below commoners when it came to their place in society, but he was not one of them. He was something different.

After standing at the edge of the river for what felt like an eternity, he took off his tattered shorts and worn down top and slowly began to wade into the river, not far enough that he had to swim, but allowing the swirling waters to rise steadily up until they covered his thighs.

Lyvanne lay silently underneath the thicket. She was entranced by what she saw. The young man couldn't have been any more than five or six years her senior, but he looked like a man returning from a far off war. His whole body was covered with scars, embedded deep into his gleaming white skin. They were all manner of size, some stretching an arm's length down his back, others barely visible to Lyvanne who lay only a few metres away. She had never seen someone like this before, and then he did it…

He began to weave his arms through the air, like he was conducting some elaborate orchestra or dancing among one of the eastern tribes as they called for water. At first it all seemed very strange to Lyvanne, like the situation wasn't abnormal enough already, but then thin streams of light began to pour out of his body. When they danced and swirled with the motion of his arms, Lyvanne realised what she was seeing. For the first time in her life, and what she thought would probably be the last, Lyvanne was witnessing the rarest of phenomena in the entire Rive: she was watching magic.

A few minutes later and it was over. Lyvanne wasn't entirely sure, but she couldn't remember breathing the entire time as she had lain there silently, her eyes following every movement.

He bent over, haunching his back and tightening his shoulders as if being riddled by the end of a sword. With time, it appeared to pass and he regained his composure and held out his right palm, revealing a key. As the young man stared at the key, his breathing becoming steadily more relaxed, Lyvanne wondered if that had been his goal, to conjure a key from thin air, and if so where did the key lead?

She didn't have to wait long to find out.

"You can come out," He said, his voice deep and jaded as if it belonged to a man three times his age. At first, Lyvanne dared not to move. He could be talking to someone else she told herself as she dug deeper into the dirt ridden ground beneath the bush.

"I know you're there," he continued, this time slightly inclining his head in her direction.

Lyvanne shifted uncomfortably, sweat slowly beginning to trickle down her forehead. He isn't noble, she told herself as she uneasily fidgeted. Which meant he would be in just as much trouble for being here as she would be, but that didn't make him safe to be around.

It was the lure of magic that won her over in the end, and equally the fear of what this person might do if she disobeyed. Crawling out from under the bush, Lyvanne nearly fell into the water, but managed to keep herself dry.

The young man smiled at her, his eyes a penetrating green and his hair almost as white as his skin. He returned to the shoreline where Lyvanne waited, placed his shirt over his body, pocketed the key, and dumped himself down on the grass.

"It's okay, you can sit, I won't tell anyone you were here," he said reassuringly, gesturing to the grass by his side.

Lyvanne was still reluctant. She wanted so badly to reach for the washing bag she had dumped behind the shrubbery as she hid and to make a run for it, but she figured that running from a warlock was probably futile if they really wanted to catch you.

"What's your name?" he asked, staring up at Lyvanne. The burning sun seemed to have little impact on his eyes.

"Lyvanne. Who are you?" she asked meekly, standing a few feet away from the stranger. Never before had Lyvanne felt so powerless, so immobilised by fear and intrigue at the same time.

"I don't give out my name easily, little one."

Lyvanne pouted. Despite her age, she had the responsibilities of a full-grown adult and didn't take kindly to being patronised.

"You're a warlock," she replied, growing in confidence as if to rival the patronising comment.

He nodded approvingly, "That I am, Lyvanne."

"You're rare, aren't you?"

She received no answer.

"Do you know a lot about magic?" he asked.

"Not really, only the stories that Abella used to tell us."

"Well, I'm sure that Abella is a very knowledgeable lady…"

"Not particularly, not anymore at least."

The warlock let out a genuine laugh, causing Lyvanne to recoil slightly out of fear of being heard by someone in the Accord.

"Well, this Abella was right about the fact we're rare. The scholars believe that there's only one warlock for every few thousand people born in the Rive."

Lyvanne took a step closer, her fear slowly being replaced with genuine curiosity. "What's the key for?"

Nodding, he reached into his pocket and pulled out the key. It was incredibly plain, no decoration or engravings, not even a fancy pattern that so many of the rich people seemed to enjoy. Whatever he was planning with it, he wasn't going to be selling it anytime soon.

"Straight to the point," he said, waving the key around gently. "This is the key to one of the houses up in the Accord. The house of a particularly nasty foreign dignitary to be precise."

Lyvanne didn't know what dignitary meant, but she could catch his drift. "Why do you want that?"

"Because I plan to rob her." Lyvanne was taken aback by his honesty. Robbing someone who lived in the Accord was as dangerous as it was foolish. You would have a hard enough time getting past the guards, and even if you did, if you were caught the punishment would likely be death for a commoner.

"Why?" Lyvanne pressed.

The warlock paused, seemingly conflicted on how much information to pass on. "You're an inquisitive one aren't you?" She nodded in reply. "This lady has something that I want, something that my friends and I need."

Lyvanne wasn't happy; he hadn't really answered her question, but she decided not to press the situation any further. Instead, she sat down beside him on the grass, bringing her knees up to her chest and staring out at the quiet waters of the Anya.

"Did it hurt?" she asked.

"The magic? Yeah, one of the pitfalls of having this gift, I guess. Maybe I'll tell you more about it one day"

"One day?"

"Yeah, I get the feeling this won't be our last encounter little Lyvanne." He turned to Lyvanne and offered a knowing smile. It annoyed her. "Why don't you join me when I go to the Accord?"

The question took Lyvanne by surprise. "Why would I do something that stupid?"

He shrugged his shoulders.

"You must have someone you care about, even if it's yourself. There will be a lot of things in this house that you could sell, might even keep you fed during winter if you wait it out. Besides, she won't be there. She's away on business, and it'll be a clear sweep."

Lyvanne heard the sense in his argument, and she couldn't believe that she was actually considering his offer.

"You'll be caught," she retorted.

"Maybe…maybe not. Only one way to find out I guess? Besides, I can protect you if things go south."

Lyvanne sat there in silence; she the gaze of this complete stranger boring into the side of her head, as if he was reading her very thoughts. She ignored him, her mind wandering back to the friends she had left behind at the house. She thought of the warm clothing, the food, and the proper bedding she could buy with the spare money. More selfishly she thought of the quiet and secure life she could buy for herself if she added more money to her secret savings. Then she drifted back to the performance she had seen this person conduct in the river, the magic that had swirled around him and the key that had formed in his hands. If he could form a key out of thin air then surely he could keep them safe?

"If I go with you, will you show me how to use magic?"

He laughed again. "It's not something that can be taught I'm afraid, you have to be born with it."

Lyvanne's face sunk. A few minutes ago her life had been so different, she'd barely given any thought to the existence of magic, but now that she had seen it first-hand it was engulfing her. She found that to her very core she needed to know more about it.

"I can show you more," he continued. "I can show you the limits, the drawbacks and the best ways to fight back against it."

"Why would I need to fight back against it?"

"As of this morning, I doubt you'd ever seen a warlock before, now there's one offering to teach you about the ways of magic. You never know what tomorrow holds, best not to live your life assuming you know every twist and turn it might take."

She tossed his words over and over in her head. It was dangerous, and she wasn't the sort of person to take risks where she didn't need to.

But the reward for her friends was too much to ignore, and to learn about magic first-hand, even if she couldn't do it herself, was something that many could only dream of.

"Listen," he said as he stood up. "I won't force you to do anything, but if you're interested then meet me back here tomorrow night once the sun has gone down. After the job, we'll talk more about my special gift."

"Why are you being so open with me?"

He shrugged, "Got a feeling, I guess."

With that he left, making his way back up the slope and through the shrubbery at the top that separated the Accord's rear wall from the banks of the Aya. Lyvanne immediately began to think of questions that she hadn't thought to ask. Why had he made the key there? Why not in the lower layers of the city? It frustrated her that she had missed her opportunity.

Lyvanne spent most of the rest of her day on the slope, finishing the washing and staring out at the gentle waters just beyond her feet. She pondered over the choice given to her, and by the time the sun was setting over the buildings to her right she had made up her mind. Tomorrow night she would return and meet the warlock again.

CHAPTER 3

That night Lyvanne didn't get back to the house until late. She took her time wandering home, stuck to the longer routes and continued to think over her decision as she went. She passed the occasional drunk and the odd lady of the night, but her journey back was largely uneventful. Upon her return, she found that Oh was already sleeping. He had apparently been out on the nearby streets with Lira, and she'd managed to tire him out. It was a welcome respite.

Lira and Abella sat around a small makeshift fire in the centre of the basement's stone floor. Lyvanne could tell by Lira's face that Abella had been sharing her stories of long forgotten wars and continents so far out to sea that you couldn't see them from the shoreline. Lira hated the stories; she was very much a city girl and had no interest in what lay beyond the walls of Astreya, but Lyvanne loved them. Saying her greetings to the pair, being careful not to awaken Oh, Lyvanne relieved Lira of her place by Abella's side and let her head to bed.

"You were out late, Lyv," Abella noted as she placed a delicate hand on Lyvanne's shoulder.

Lyvanne hated the nickname Lyv, but she always gave Abella a pass. Abella was old and her memory wasn't the best it had ever been anymore. She tended to forget simpler things like what people did and didn't like being called. Besides, hearing Oh use the nickname probably didn't help matters.

Kneeling down by the old lady's side, Lyvanne asked her what stories she had missed so far, and with startling accuracy Abella listed them all off one by one. During her youth, Abella had worked in the King's library, and had no doubt once been an incredibly smart woman. Now her mind failed her, but some of the knowledge she gained during that time in the library had stuck with her. Lyvanne admired her for that. The woman didn't know how to light a fire to keep herself warm during winter, but she knew the intricate relationships between the eastern tribes of the Rive and the Islanders who lived a short boat ride across the East Channel.

"Abella, what do you know about magic?" Lyvanne whispered, eager to have some of her questions answered.

Abella grimaced, "A nasty thing magic, only for bad people."

"Why?" Lyvanne asked quickly. Her heart sank slightly, not wanting to believe that the young man she had met was a bad person.

"The cost is great, and the power too terrible for people to wield responsibly," Abella made as if to spit on the floor, but nothing came out. "Warlocks are born once for every ten thousand people born in The Rive, and now the only ones left are under the control of the King."

That was new to Lyvanne. "Why?"

"So he can watch us," she said matter-of-factly.

"What do you mean? I don't understand." If the warlock she met by the river was under the king's control, then she needed to know now before she did anything stupid.

"The king had a vision many years ago that his bloodline would be deposed of power. Now every warlock in The Rive works for him round the clock. Always watching us, always watching for visions."

"Visions? As in… the visions granted to us by the Angel of Destiny?"

Abella's head slowly drooped into her lap before snapping back to attention, age and the late hour taking their toll. Let her sleep, Lyvanne thought, but she needed more information.

"A warlock by the name of Akira once discovered a way to use his power to watch the visions granted to others by the Angel of Destiny's good will. Now the king keeps every warlock in his castle, always watching for visions, always looking for the one who will depose his bloodline."

Lyvanne took that to mean that he wasn't under the king's control after all. Regardless, it was interesting to know. Her whole life she'd prayed to the Angel of Destiny, hoping to be shown the path she needed to take or to see a glimpse of what her future could hold. Now, even that was being thrown into confusion and put under threat.

She hadn't thought it was possible to watch the visions that others had. But the more time she spent that night thinking about magic and religion, the more she realised that there virtually nothing that she really knew about them with nay level of certainty. Religion wasn't something that Abella had ever spent much time talking about, let alone teaching to the children. On top of that, her whole understanding of magic had been completely reshaped in the space of one day.

That didn't stop her though. Later that night as she bedded down for sleep, Lyvanne said her prayers to the Angel of Destiny and waited for the day that she'd be shown her way out of the city. Determined to cast the thought of any prying eyes to the back of her mind as she slept.

The next morning, Lyvanne woke with a start. She'd dreamt that she was down by the river and that she'd been arrested by city watch for trespassing. In the dream, they'd taken her away to a dark dungeon beneath the city, before moving her into the mines even further below. It felt like a warning, a sign not to go to meet the warlock, not to break into this person's house, a person who had done her no wrong. Yet, she felt more determined than ever to go through with it. She had questions filling her brain, questions that Abella couldn't answer, and for some reason she couldn't yet figure out, she trusted this stranger.

She went out of her way to leave the house before anyone else woke up, not wanting them to notice that anything was playing on her mind. Abella she could fool, but Lira and Oh were much more likely to notice that she was out of sorts. From then on, she spent the day for the most part keeping her head down. They needed food, and she scrounged what she could from the fishermen at the docks. She gathered enough to last them all a day or two at best, and decided to call it quits before she drew any unwanted attention. Today of all days was not the time she wanted to be testing the City Watch.

The sun was still beaming down onto the city as Lyvanne passed through the hole into Abella's house. Making her way down into the basement, she was greeted with the usual sight. Abella was playing toy soldiers with Oh whilst Lira cleaned the basement as best she could.

"Welcome back child," Abella said as she opened her arms up to greet Lyvanne, no doubt having little recollection of their conversation the night before.

"Thank you," Lyvanne said as she leaned in for a hug from the old lady, passing off her sack of food to Lira as she did.

"Look!" Oh said, as he came bounding over towards Lyvanne, holding out what she recognised as brand new wooden soldiers, painted in the green and silver patterns of the king's royal army.

"Where did you get that?!" Lyvanne asked, more angry than confused as she knew full well where they would have come from.

Oh backed away slightly, surprised by the anger in her voice, and Lira stepped forward in his place.

"I heard you leave this morning," she said timidly. "I couldn't get back to sleep, so I decided to do something nice."

"Lira, you can't go stealing toys from Merchant Street. You'll be caught"

"No I won't I'm not stupi -

"Lira!" Lyvanne shouted at her friend and immediately withdrew as a pang of guilt overcame her. But she knew she needed to follow through "It was nice of you, but it was indeed stupid. Don't put yourself at risk when you don't have to. Okay?"

Lyvanne felt hypocritical, but her situation was different she told herself; Lira risked herself for a toy whereas she was doing it for something much bigger.

"Come now children, don't argue here," Abella chimed in, trying to quell the situation. It worked, but Lira was noticeably upset and Oh went surprisingly quiet for the rest of the afternoon.

Neither of them said goodbye properly when Lyvanne left later that day. She had wanted to say something, to hug them tightly like she usually would, but they felt distant and the moment she stepped onto the street she regretted not apologising.

The sun was beginning to set over the stone and wooden buildings that made up Astreya as Lyvanne arrived at the Accord, casting long and menacing shadows over the quiet streets of the residential district. Taking a deep breath, Lyvanne reminded herself once again why she was doing this, for the quality of life she could at least in the short term offer to the others and for the personal knowledge she could learn from the stranger. Then she made her way down the slope and out onto the bank of the Anya.

She waited there for hours, as the night sky grew darker and more beautiful as the stars began to illuminate the black canvas that loomed overhead. It was then that she realised she'd never been this far away from home this late at night, and for a moment she dwelled on all she'd missed out on. The stars were the most beautiful sight she'd ever seen, a concoction of white and blue miracles living in the sky and all of them reflecting perfectly in the running water of the Anya.

Before long, she heard the rustling of movement coming from above, and she caught sight of the stranger making his way down to her.

"I'm glad you came," he said, keeping his voice noticeably quieter than the last time they were here, for which Lyvanne was thankful.

"I nearly didn't. I had a dream that I'd get arrested," Lyvanne decided not to tell him about what Abella had said about warlocks, not yet anyway. It could wait until she knew more about him.

The warlock wore a dark hooded robe, but underneath she could see him incline his head. "Dreams can be powerful, perhaps you should have listened to it."

"Do you want me to go home?" she asked, almost playfully.

"We both know you won't," he said with a cocky smile.

He was right, she'd come this far, and she was going to see it through to the end.

"Besides, everything is a possible future, nothing in this life is certain," he continued, his confident smile protruding from behind his hood.

"Visions are certain, visions from the Angel."

Another incline of the head. "They used to be."

"Used -

"Come," he interrupted. "These are things we can discuss another time, we have work to do tonight."

The interruption annoyed her, but she couldn't help but admit that this complete stranger had entirely captured her curiosity since their first meeting.

Who are you? She thought as the pair made their way back up the slope until they reached the wall that guarded the Accord and the houses of the rich within.

"Do I get to know your name yet?" she asked as the pair made their way up to the Accord.

"If we get caught, I'd rather you didn't know," he replied matter-of-factly, but with a comforting smile that kept her nerves at bay. "I'll tell you after, okay?"

The wall of the Accord was a few feet taller than the Lyvanne was, and the top was lined with a row of metal railing and spikes to ward off would-be intruders such as them.

"Come on, I'll boost you over," The stranger said as he placed himself up against the wall, "Once you're up there, I'll need you to keep an eye out for any guard patrols whilst I climb up."

Lyvanne nodded and let out a small grunt as he lifted her up and onto the top of the wall. Being careful not to impale herself on any of the spikes, she began to squint her eyes in search of any movement from within the Accord. Thankfully, there was none, so as her new found acquaintance started to pull himself up, Lyvanne crouched atop the wall, in awe of the houses that lay before her. Having never been inside the Accord, she had never imagined what the houses inside would be like. They appeared as large as two or three regular houses from the Upper layer of Astreya combined, let alone the smaller homes found in the lower layer. Each house was built from a strong looking grey stone, compared to the sandy rock used throughout the rest of the city, and what Lyvanne envied most of all was that each one had a surrounding area of grass and shrubbery, much like her hideout down by the river. How could people own so much, she asked herself as the pair slowly began to make their way down the wall and into the Accord.

"Quite something, huh?" the stranger asked.

"Yeah, something like that," Lyvanne replied, words failing her.

The young man led her through a maze of tall houses and elegant gardens, his steps never faltering as if he had lived here all of his life. Off into the distance, Lyvanne could just about make out the fires that illuminated the guard posts at the gates and the smaller fire about ten feet further into the air which indicated a watchtower. Lyvanne gawked at the security, questioning what made these people so much better than everyone else and what they had to fear from the rest of the citizens. She blushed when she remembered why she was there.

"Here we are," the pale young man said as they turned a corner to find one of the largest houses in the Accord: an elaborate mansion of refined stone and glass windows.

"Who did you say lived here again?"

"A dignitary from the Shimmering Isles," he replied as the pair made their way towards the side of the house, always being careful to stick towards the shadows. As of yet they hadn't seen any patrols, but that didn't mean they weren't out there.

"You can protect us if things go wrong, right? With magic?" Lyvanne asked.

He nodded. "That is where this comes in," he said, pulling out the key which he had forged in the Anya the day previous. Motioning for Lyvanne to hang back momentarily, he crept up to the front door and used the key to unlock it.

"How the -

Lyvanne began to question aloud, before being beckoned to follow on. Passing over the threshold of the front door was like entering an entirely different world. Lyvanne had never known such luxury; she had never even known that it was possible to live this way. The house was decorated with the pelts of exotic creatures that Lyvanne did not know, from places that she had never heard of. The walls housed various paintings, some of beautiful landscapes, others of rich looking people with elaborate robes which would even put to shame some of the people she used to see on Gemstone Avenue.

"How can you live like this?" Lyvanne whispered, terrified of being discovered, but with a surge of pure adrenaline coursing through her veins leading her on.

"Not the time for questions," the young man replied. "I need you to stay here whilst I search upstairs, if you see a patrol coming then you need to let me know, I don't want us walking out of -

There was movement upstairs, the sound of footsteps against wooden floorboards. The stranger looked immobilised with shock and Lyvanne's face turned a ghostly shade of pale, almost akin to the warlock who had enticed her to come along.

"I thought they weren't supposed to be here?" Lyvanne whispered with ferocity, her natural instincts to be the grown up in any situation kicking into gear.

"They… they weren't," he replied, evidently trying to plan out his next move now that his whole mission had gone down the drain.

After a moment's hesitation, he pulled the hood up over his head and carried on undeterred, taking large but quiet steps up to the top floor. Lyvanne wanted to call out after him, to warn him that it was a bad idea, but she held her tongue. He can look after himself, she convinced herself as she turned her attention back towards the doorway, still ajar from their break in. Staring out into the cool night air, Lyvanne took in a deep breath of fresh air, using it to calm her senses, before quietly closing the door and using a nearby window to keep one eye on the outside whilst she began to look around for nearby riches. Just something small, she told herself, enough to help set up outside the city. Her search was cut short almost immediately. Three members of the City Watch caught her eye through the window as they passed by, inspecting each house as they went. The trio wore more mobile gambesons than the usual uniform would dictate and each with a long sword sheathed around their waist. She pulled herself away from her search and crouched down beside the window, keeping an eye on the patrol's movement. Lyvanne watched them intently. They weren't far from the house, but if they could just pass by then they wouldn't pose any immediate danger.

Lyvanne heard a scream, swiftly by the sound of breaking glass and the heavy thud of footsteps. Her partner in crime bounded down the stairs, a piece of parchment in his hands and a tear in his tunic.

"Let's go!" he shouted as his feet reached the final step down to the ground floor.

Lyvanne tried to signal for him to quiet down and to warn him about guards outside, but he wasn't in the mood for listening. There were a number of footsteps following him and after waving away her concerns, he crashed through the front door, alerting at the very least the three City Watch who were stood nearby. One after another, they drew their long swords.

"Follow me!" the young warlock shouted, darting off into the night. Lyvanne couldn't believe what was happening. Her dream was right, she was going to be arrested here and thrown into the mines to work the rest of her life, or if she was lucky, killed for her crime.

Deciding that she didn't like the sound of that fate her instincts kicked into action. Two of the patrol had followed the stranger into the far reaches of the Accord. She wasn't fast enough to catch up with him now, she would have to make her own way out and that meant getting past the guard who was now making his way towards her, sword drawn and blood pumping.

It didn't take long for it to dawn on Lyvanne that she had absolutely no idea where to go. She could run around the Accord all night and likely not find a safe way out. So, she decided to go straight, to make her way back to the wall that they'd climbed over and use the Anya as her escape. The only problem being that the guard was blocking her way.

She tried multiple times to find a way around him, trying to give him the slip as she ducked and weaved, running behind various houses and using bushes as a barrier. She was younger than the guard, who seemed at best to be twenty years her senior, and she had faith that given enough time she could tire him out.

She wasn't entirely wrong. After a few more minutes of playing chase the guard's strides became shorter, the swings of his sword became more wild than they were precise. *He's tiring*, Lyvanne observed.

"Stand still, you little bitch" The guard called out as he chased her all over the Accord.

At last she had her chance. Once again ducking out of his reach, Lyvanne made a beeline for a wall she could see in the distance, praying to any and all Gods that it was the wall she needed. She wasn't tall enough or athletic enough to scale the wall on her own, but fortune was on her side just this once. One of the elaborate houses had a small extension unlike the others, which was built into the side of the wall. Using some gaps in the stonework, Lyvanne began to climb up the extension. She was a mere few feet away from safety when the blade fell.

CHAPTER 4

Lyvanne rolled herself onto the stone expansion just as the blade came crashing crashed down, clattering against the building, sending fragmented pieces of stone flying into the air. The steel blade cut through her arm like paper, tearing through her skin and sending blood spattering across the wall. If she hadn't made the roll in time, the blade would have cut through bone as well and she may well have lost the arm entirely.

The pain rose up her arm. Lyvanne had been beaten by guards before, scarred and left bleeding at the side of the road, but never before had she felt pain like this. Time wasn't on her side, and the guard was already voicing his success and sheathing his sword so that he could climb up after her. Seeing her opportunity to escape slipping away before her eye,s Lyvanne used her one good arm to push herself back to her feet. She threw herself over the wall and out of the guard's reach, narrowly avoiding the spikes which lined the wall. She crashed down into the shrubbery below and began to tumble down the slope, leaving a trail of blood behind as she did. With every roll there was a fresh stab of pain injected into her body. She was convinced it would have rendered her unconscious if not for her desire to escape.

As she slowed to a halt at the bottom of the slope, she allowed the cold water of the Anya to run over her good arm. She'd made it, she told herself and with one final lunge, she rolled her body into the water.

Lyvanne noted that her escape had landed her further upstream than her hideout, which meant she had a route for escape once the current carried her the rest of the way towards the King's Wall. Sure enough, a few minutes of drifting, and the King's Wall began to loom large overhead, the small iron gateway preventing people from using the river as an entrance to the final layer of the city growing closer.

As she lay still in the water, blood pooling out around her, Lyvanne could make out the small open patch of grass that she would use to hide away. It was empty and the small opening by the King's Wall above was likely to be a clear route to safety. The guards from the Accord would have gone the other way around the wall to try and find her.

They weren't the brightest bunch and wouldn't have taken the river's current into account, Lyvanne told herself as she tried to distract herself from the pain. She figured that the guards would opt instead for the easier option of going down the manmade roads towards the river side on the other side of The Accord. That's even if they considered her worthy of chasing. The young thief who would likely die of her wounds anyway she mused.

Urging her body into action, Lyvanne pushed off from the King's Wall and made her way upstream towards the river's bank. It took all the strength left in her body to heave herself onto the grass, sodden and tired. A small part of her had hoped that the stranger would be there, that he could use his magic to heal her or that he could at least explain what had happened. Another part of her hoped he'd been caught. The anger was unlike any emotion she'd experienced, and in that moment, whether it was the pain, anger or the adrenaline, she felt both more alive and the closest to death that she had ever been.

She knew that if she chose to stand at that moment she wouldn't make it far, but equally she couldn't wait around too long in case the city watch did decide to search here. So she gave herself a few minutes of rest before using the shrubbery to pull herself back up the slope.

It was a long walk home, and everywhere she went a thin trail of blood followed. She wasn't a nurse; she hadn't known how to tend to the wound or even how to clean it before she set off. Instead, she said a prayer with every step that either Lira or Abella would know what to do. As she approached the turning that would lead her home, her eyes grew heavy. They began to open and close seemingly of their own will. Her legs grew weak, giving way every few steps, unable to carry her own weight. Worry gripped her. She was so close, but the final few steps seemed like an eternity away. One final prayer was said and she forced her body down the alley way, threw aside the crate that covered the entrance to Abella's home and collapsed.

• • •

Lira heard the clatter. At first she was scared that they'd been discovered, that the king would have them kicked out and sent down to the lower level of the city. But no one came and there were no more noises. She told herself that it was a wild animal, some kind of large vermin that had left the sewers, but then she glanced over at Lyvanne's empty bed and she suddenly had to know for sure.

Being careful not to wake up Oh or Abella, she started to make her way up the stairs and into the house itself, blackened and crumbling. There she was, Lyvanne, lying motionless at the entrance. Lira brought up her hands to her face in shock as she noticed the small pool of blood building by the side of her friend. Instinct quickly took over and she ran to Lyvanne's side.

"Lyvanne!" She shouted, not caring who in the vicinity heard. "Wake up!"

Lyvanne didn't respond. Lira quickly discovered the source of the blood, a wound on her right arm. Something had cut her, causing a deep and penetrating wound about two inches long.

Grabbing her by the good arm, Lira used all her strength to drag her into the house, placing the crate back in front of the entrance once she had. Lyvanne drifted in and out of consciousness, but never really acknowledged Lira or the fact that she'd made it home.

This was Lira's worst nightmare. Lyvanne was the one who was supposed to take care of them, not the other way around. As tears welled up in her eyes, she grunted and began to carry Lyvanne down the stairs and into the basement.

As she reached the halfway point, the commotion woke up Oh, who in turn shouted and woke up not just Abella but probably half the neighbourhood.

"What happened?"Abella asked whilst moving as fast as her tiring body would carry her.

"I don't know."

The pair carried Lyvanne over to her bed where they cleared out as much of the dirt as they could before placing her down, using her bedding as further support for her head after realising that her thinning pillow wasn't much good.

"What do we do?" Lira asked weakly.

Abella didn't respond immediately, instead she just began to work. Reaching for a nearby rag she used it as a makeshift bandage to stem the blood flow.

"She's going into a fever," Abella said, still half asleep. "Get me some water, child."

Lira was impressed with how alive Abella had become. It was the most spritely and engaged she had seen her in a long time. The two began to work in tandem, fashioning dressing and cleaning the wound. Oh sat on his bed gently sobbing and biting his nails as he watched his friend suffer a few feet away. Lira tried to keep her friend awake, tapping her cheek and calling out her name when she had the breath, but it didn't take long for Lyvanne to drift back into unconsciousness.

• • •

Lyvanne opened her eyes.

Something was strange, something was different.

The world around her was blurred, like a mist drifted through her own eyes.

It took a moment but she began to make out her surroundings piece by piece.

She wasn't outside Abella's house anymore.

She was somewhere… new.

A million questions raced through her mind, none of which came out of her mouth as she tried to speak.

You're dreaming, she told herself, you're unconscious and you need to wake up.

When she tried and failed to awake from this dream, she instead turned her attention to the world around her. Where am I? She asked herself as she began to walk forward, step by step.

Everything felt real. Every time her foot touched the stone floor it convinced her that it was real.

Her mind darted back to the robbery, to her escape, to the wound...

The wound was gone. Her arm was clean, unsoiled and lacking any of the pain she had felt moments before.

The mist began to fade away. What had once been blurred was becoming clear.

She stood in a grand room made of marble, stone, and wood.

The ceilings appeared as high as mountains, and the walls as thick as the trees from the Great Oak Forest in Abella's stories.

At the centre of this great room there was a long wooden table, with six ornate chairs on either side and a further one at each end.

Each chair was occupied. Lyvanne didn't recognise them, and judging by their clothing they certainly weren't Lords or of noble birth, as you would expect in a place such as this.

None of the people were moving; they remained utterly still as if paralyzed by some exotic poison.

Her attention was drawn to two individuals in particular.

Two Hemeti.

What are they doing in a place like this? Lyvanne wondered as she made her way over to the table, examining the strange looking people.

From what she could tell, this was a place of importance, and Hemeti would never be allowed such an honoured seat.

The Hemeti were how she remembered her one other encounter with their kind. They were both tall, with skin tinged green in colour and eyes a piercing blue.

One had iron piercings in both of his ears and scars down his cheek, the other was more appealing to the eye, elegant but stern.

The mists expanded further and something at the far end of the room drew her attention away.

The room was longer than she first thought, and everything appeared to be built towards its peak at the far end.

There, cracked and covered in graffiti words and symbols which she didn't understand, was what she believed could only be the Throne of the Rive.

The king's seat, the location of all power in the land.

In that moment, she understood what was happening.

This is a vision, not a dream, she decided.

The Angel of Destiny had granted her a gift, a vision of the future… of a possible future.

She considered what that meant.

It meant this scene was important to her.

It meant that a future version of herself was somewhere in this room.

Her eyes darted away from the throne and back towards the table.

Now that she knew what she was looking for, her eyes settled on her future self almost immediately.

Lyvanne drew in a deep breath, her hands were shaking as she stood there in silent shock.

The woman sat at the table wasn't herself as she was now. She was at least 10 years older and, more shockingly, battle scarred.

Her older self had a scar running down her right cheek, from the outside edge of her eye down to the tip of her nose.

Her clothes were in part shredded and a faint red could be seen through the holes left behind, signalling wounds still fresh from battle.

Lyvanne walked closer. The eyes of this future incarnation of her, they seemed tired and forlorn.

Why am I here? She asked aloud.

What happened?

Where is the king?

The king. Fear gripped her again.

If what Abella had said was true then the king's warlocks would be watching, they would have seen everything that she had seen.

Her eyes darted from left to right, examining every inch of the room.

If they were watching alongside her then she couldn't see them.

Her heart started pounding faster with every beat, sweat began to form on her forehead and her thoughts ran back to her friends.

The King would look for her… he wouldn't stop looking for her.

Panic took hold of her every fiber and she was thrown from the vision.

CHAPTER 5

Lyvanne gripped at the air as she jolted awake, the fear from her vision tightening around her neck like a noose. She couldn't breathe properly, each intake of air shallow and sharp. Lira had sprung to action, having been sleeping restlessly by her side.

"It's okay!" she called out as she tried to restrain her friend who was now clawing at her own neck. "Lyvanne, it's okay!"

Within moments, Lyvanne noticed the sudden presence of Oh by the side of her bed too. A small sense of relief crept back into her body and mind. A shooting pain ran through her left arm, causing her to yelp and reach for its source.

"It's okay, child," Abella said, slowly waking and making her way over to the commotion. "We've cleaned your arm up best we could. You're lucky it wasn't worse."

"Where were you? What happened?" Lira asked, her tone almost scolding.

Lyvanne looked down in shame. Her bed was a puddle of sweat, and her clothes saturated.

"How long have I been back?" she asked.

Lira shrugged her shoulders. "Not long, a few hours I guess."

"What happened, Lyv?" Oh asked, almost bouncing with anticipation. She ignored him.

"I need to leave," Lyvanne said, the words hurting her almost as much as they appeared to hurt the others. "I might have led people here. It's not safe for me to stay."

"What happened, child?" Abella asked, her voice quiet and calm, but more serious than she was used to from the old lady.

Reluctantly, Lyvanne spent the next half hour recounting the story of how she'd met a warlock by the river, how he'd enticed her with his powers, and how she'd hoped for a better life for the rest of them. It hadn't completely dawned on her until she repeated it all back that in the confusion she hadn't even had time to steal something they could sell. Part of her felt relieved by that, but a larger part was annoyed. Oh, had believed the story to be a tale. Lira had been awed by the fact her friend had met a warlock and Abella just sat there, silent and angry.

The others discounted her vision as a fever dream, something Lyvanne did not take kindly to. She'd suffered fevers before, but this was nothing of the sort. The Angel of Destiny had visited her and none of her friends wanted to believe her. No one said anything for the rest of the night. Oh was the first to fall back to sleep, Abella next, and after checking the makeshift bandages around Lyvanne's arm one last time Lira too fell asleep. Lyvanne just lay in bed all night, thinking about the pale-faced young man who had used magic to craft a key out of thin air, about the vision of the throne room and her future self, about the Hemeti who had transcended their place in society and sat where none had sat before. Hours later, exhaustion and the continuous stinging in her arm took her into a deep sleep.

The bells woke them all. The sound drifted through the creaking and broken house above and down into the small basement. Lira shot upstairs, followed by Oh.

"Be careful, children!" Abella croaked with her morning voice.

Lyvanne didn't need to see what was causing all the commotion, as she already knew. Her fears were confirmed shortly after when Lira and Oh came back down the stairs, noticeably slower than when they went up.

"It's the king's soldiers," Lira said timidly. "They're looking for a young girl with brown hair and olive skin… they're looking for you Lyvanne, aren't they?"

Lyvanne nodded slowly, the fear well hidden.

"You really did have a vision, didn't you?"

"Oh child…" Abella sounded distraught.

Abella had been right, the king had people who could see the visions of others. The king knew about what she'd seen.

"He'll never stop looking," Lyvanne croaked as she held back a flood of tears.

She had wanted to craft her own path; she'd wanted to get them all out of this god forsaken basement and now her chance had been taken away from her by the very being she used to pray to every night.

"I have to leave."

Abella moved over to her side and grabbed her wrist. "Not yet."

"Where will you go?" Lira asked from the stairs. She hid it better than Lyvanne but she, too, was on the verge of tears.

"I have to hand myself -"

Abella waved a finger in the air.

"No child, you will do no such thing."

Lyvanne looked up to her in confusion. "Why? I won't let them hurt you!"

"The Angel has granted you a great gift child," Her voice sounded sincere, almost pleased. Lyvanne looked on at her elder, confused as to how she didn't seem angry at their situation. "You've seen a better future for yourself, and I don't doubt it's a better future for us all. You're right, there's only so long that we can protect you here, but there will be others out there who can do so. You may have to travel outside of the city, but somewhere out there you will find safety. The Angel has shown you that. You're fortunate child, and I mean this without offence, but more than half the young girls in Astreya look as you do. The king will have a hard time finding you. You need to use that to your advantage."

Lyvanne had never heard Abella speak like this, especially not in the last few years. All she could do in reply was smile.

"Don't leave us Lyv!" Oh said as he ran over to her bed and threw his arms around her. He was irritating the wound on her arm, but she didn't mind.

"I'm sorry, Oh. I've got to." she returned the hug as well as her one good arm would allow as the boy started softly crying.

Lyvanne looked across at Lira who had sat down on the stairs. She too had tears on her face. The two shared a knowing look; Lira would be in charge now, it was down to her to look after the others. They had all known that this day would come eventually; she was growing up too fast. Not only that, but she hadn't been the first to come and she wouldn't be the last to leave. This basement was a safe place for people like them, and leaving was Lyvanne's last way of making sure that stayed true.

"Stay the rest of the day," Abella insisted with more determination in her voice. "The king's men are dumb, they won't come searching in this ruin, but you can't be seen just wandering the streets anymore either. Wait until it's dark, then head for the city's lower level, I can't advise you on where to go once you're there, child, but I have faith you'll find your way."

The hours came and went slowly. Every time they heard passing footsteps or a nearby bell of one of the king's criers, they tensed. Fortunately, as Abella had predicted, none searched the ruins. As the sun went down in the sky Abella applied a final dressing to Lyvanne's arm, it hurt a lot, but she was grateful. The old lady was trying to ensure that this child, who she had no true responsibility to look after, was sent off into the world with the best chance possible. That was more than most in the Upper Level would do if they found her. They let her keep her small sack that she would often use to bring them food, filling it with what they could spare; Oh even snuck in one of his toy soldiers.

"Are you sure you'll be okay out there?" Lira asked as the four stood at the base of the stairs.

"Yes, don't worry I'll be fine," Lyvanne lied. Abella knew that might not be the case, but she thought better than to interject the way she usually would.

Lyvanne wanted nothing more than to leave without saying goodbye, to sneak out whilst they slept like she would if she was just going out to find them food, as if she would be back that afternoon to see their smiling faces. But that wasn't going to be the case this time. She wouldn't be coming back, not unless she had a way of getting them out of there for good.

"Lira come here," Lyvanne said, pulling her friend upstairs into the hollowed core of the house above.

"What is it?" Lira asked.

Once she was sure that Oh hadn't followed, Lyvanne held out her hand, in her palm a small pouch that clinked as she passed it over to her friend. Lira's mouth fell agape as she slowly loosed the string that kept the pouch closed.

"What is -

"It's mine. It's not much," Lyvanne interrupted, trying to explain the sudden stash of money she had passed on to Lira. "But it will help you all if things get tough. Use it carefully though, you can make something of your lives if you keep saving."

It hurt Lyvanne to give up the money in this way. She felt as though she was giving up on a dream before it had had chance to blossom, but she cared about her friends and if this was the best way she could continue protecting them after she was gone then so be it.

Later that day after saying her goodbyes, Lyvanne set off up the stairs and out into the big world, alone for what felt like the first time in a lifetime. Abella had gifted Lyvanne with a travelling cloak she had stashed away in one of the few small drawers that had been brought down into the basement. Unlike the cloaks that Lyvanne had seen the rich wearing every day on the busy streets of the city, this one had no pigmented colour; it was a basic mix of brown and dark greens. Better not to draw attention with outward wealth Abella had argued when Oh had told her to give Lyvanne one of the cloaks with pretty colours. The cloak was now tied around her neck with a small pin; her arm had been washed and freshly bandaged and her clothes were in as good condition as she would ever get them. She was ready.

For the first few minutes, she barely made any distance. Too scared to move quickly, too unsure to walk with purpose. Unsurprisingly, the king's soldiers were still out searching, but there weren't as many as she expected. Every few streets or so she found herself changing direction just to avoid any confrontations, but aside from that she felt fairly certain that she could avoid contact. All the nobles and socialites were either tucked away safely in bed, or they were off galivanting among the wealthiest venues in the Upper level, far from where she was now. The streets were, mostly, her own. That was until she arrived within viewing distance of the Lion Gate. The gate which acted as partition between the Upper and lower levels of Astreya was swarmed with guards, more than she had seen before in one place.

Lyvanne said a little curse before manoeuvring into a position that gave her better scope for viewing the street ahead. Climbing up to the roof of a small blacksmith's, one of a few which lined the street she was on, she spied at least two-dozen guards around the gate. Some were stationed on the walkways of the wall, longbows in hand. Lyvanne knew that if she tried to run through the gate and past the guards that they'd be able to pierce her heart before she made it one hundred strides into the lower level. The king's soldiers were renowned throughout the Rive for their archery skills and it wasn't a story she wanted to test in person.

Most of the guards were City Watch, wearing the usual thick steel plated armour. A handful wore a more mobile gambeson. They would be the easiest targets to try and get past, she knew, but the king's soldiers who made up the rest of the group had her worried. Lyvanne made her decision; she was going to find another way into the lower level. Perhaps if she followed the Anya upstream she would be able to find an unprotected grate or similar which she could use to slip through, she thought.

Momentarily forgetting about her injured arm, Lyvanne placed her full weight down onto her right side as she began to climb down from the roof. The arm buckled with pain, and she fell to the floor below, crashing hard into a stack of crates she had used to climb up in the first place. Two of the guards closest to her looked up the street and in her direction. She didn't have time to think about what to do next as they saw her lying there at the side of the street.

"Oi, girl!" One of them called out as he placed a hand on the hilt of his sheathed sword.

She didn't wait for the pleasantries to be said, for the pretence that they meant no harm. Instead, she darted in the direction she had just come from and the guards gave chase. Some of them at least; she didn't dare to turn back to see exactly how many.

Her footsteps rang out from the cobbled streets as she bounded as fast as her feet would carry her. Every so often she would see the rich and indignant peer out from windows or doorways, inquisitive as to what all the commotion was about. She needed to be quick, before one of them tried to be a local hero and stop her for before the guards could.

She took a sharp turn to her right and down a narrow street, dimly lit except for the entrance to one of the rowdier taverns in the

Upper level. Even the rich, noble, and proud had worries that they had to drink away. Outside the entrance, as she had hoped, was a gaggle of drunkards, swinging from side to side in fine gowns and garments, arguing and singing as they drank the night away. They perfectly clogged up the entire width of the alley, so using her size and speed she barged through their legs, causing little to no commotion. The guards weren't so lucky. They had to shout and forcefully move the patrons to create a clear path through. She looked down at her arm as she ran; it stung from where she had forced through the crowd, but the bandages were holding up well and there was no sign that she had done any further damage to it. She hoped that the wound wasn't as bad as she had first thought; otherwise she wouldn't last long on her own. Her mission had been relatively successful; she'd put some distance between herself and the guards who had been quietly gaining on her for the past for few minutes.

"Get back here!" she heard as the first of those giving chase broke through the crowd. The clatter of steel echoing in her ears as the guard pulled free his sword, causing a phantom pain to crawl up her arm.

She was running out of options and fast. The river had been her first choice, but it was on the other side of the Upper level, and at this rate she would never make it, let alone find a way through to the lower level before she was caught. Hiding wasn't an option; they were too hot on her heels. She had one final chance she realised as she turned a corner onto a wide street large enough for carriages and at the far end saw a sharp dip in the ground. The sewers.

Her legs picked up speed; they were tiring fast but that wasn't going to stop them from getting to safety. More shouts sounded from the guards as they realised what her aim was. They weren't going to stop her now. She reached the dip to the side of the street and sure enough it lead down towards the sewers.

There was no time left to second guess her decision and she darted down the tunnel, only just large enough for her to fit in. To say it stunk, as her feet splashed down onto the currently shallow stream of sewage would have been the greatest understatement in the Rive for a century. Lyvanne couldn't help but retch, only just holding back the sensation to vomit.

"Come on," she told herself as she held a quivering hand up to her mouth. "Nothing you haven't seen before."

Pulling her hood across to her mouth, she began to forge ahead, further into the dark depths. The guards shouted down after her, but not even for a second did they appear as though they considered following after some street urchin who probably wasn't even the person the king was after. For now she was safe, but whether or not she would be able to pass through the wall and into the lower level from down under the ground was another matter.

Lyvanne felt like she was scrambling around in the dark for an eternity. She stuck mostly to the walls, where the flow of sewage was least troublesome She had no doubt that by now she was as foul smelling as the tunnels themselves. So much for clean clothes, she joked. The first light-hearted thought she'd had since leaving Abella's.

Time passed slowly down in the sewers. Lyvanne didn't know how long it had been when she finally found a tunnel system that provided with her with enough light to pass through relatively easy. The sun that gleamed in through small grates in the ceilings indicated that the morning was dawning on the streets above and soon the searches would begin again in earnest for the young girl who had seen the downfall of the king. She heard the king's criers, she saw the passing shadows of soldiers, but never once did Lyvanne leave the sewer. She hadn't thought it possible to live a harder life than the one she had known before, but now she found herself sharing accommodation with the city's rat population and human waste. It was far from ideal, but at the very least she was safe from those who hunted for her.

On an idle hour her mind drifted to the mines below the city. She wondered how much closer she could get to them if she took the right turns in the sewer systems. It was an answer that she didn't really want to find out, but she'd lived most of her life underground and found a certain irony in the fact that once again that's where she found herself, always one step closer to the mines than the average person.

Days came and went. Lyvanne began to catch rats when her stomach started to growl at her for sustenance. She knew it wouldn't be enough in the long term, and the search for the tunnel which would take her into the lower level became all the more pressing. Her arm had held up nicely considering; she daren't take off the wrapping in the sewers, but with every passing day it hurt less and less.

The tunnel roofs were littered with grates that led to the surface, providing her with just enough light to get by. She wasn't alone below ground, everywhere she went she was greeted by rats scurrying along the floor. At first she had tried all she could to avoid them, but once it became clear that food would be hard to come by she turned her attention to the vermin. They weren't scared of her like she had expected, and at times they even crawled up to her in curiosity. She cried for hours the first time she had to kill one, but her stomach hadn't stopped growling for hours and she couldn't see any other options.

After days of continually wandering through almost identical dark, putrid and twisting corridors of the underground maze Lyvanne finally took a turn that granted her some much needed relief. Passing an entrance much like the one she had used to first climb down into the sewers Lyvanne used the opportunity to survey where exactly in the city she'd wound up. An immediate sense of both relief and confusion washed over her. The buildings here were much smaller than she was used to, many with decaying walls and chipped doors. They were bunched together in a manner that indicated severe overpopulation, and some were no bigger than the stone extension she had used to escape the Accord. She'd never been here before, but the contrast to what she was used to seeing from Astreya was so strong that she immediately knew that at some point the underground sewers had passed her into the lower level.

CHAPTER 6

The situation in the lower level of Astreya was worse than she had hoped for. The crowds were so vast, the people so poor and bland in appearance that it would be easy for her to get lost and make her way towards the city's exit. But to counter the crowds the number of city watch and king's soldiers patrolling the streets were double, maybe even triple the number that Lyvanne had seen and heard in the Upper level.

It didn't pose too much of a mystery. Everyone knew that the people fortunate enough to live in the Upper level were treated differently by the king. So once he had been told about this young girl's vision, he would have automatically assumed that any resistance to his reign would likely come from the commoners. He wasn't entirely wrong, Lyvanne mused, but equally that wasn't a life that she wanted for herself. The pull to hand herself over and to explain that she wasn't going to revolt, had slipped further away with every hour that she'd been forced to spend in the sewers. She had little choice but to hide, and when the opportunity next presented itself, to run.

She dared not venture out of the safety of the sewers, choosing for the time being to stay safe and underground. At times, she called herself a coward for it, trying to convince herself that for her own good she needed to leave. But she had never been to the lower level before, not that she could remember anyway, and she was just as likely to end up back at the Lion Gate as she was the exit to the city. So over the next few days, Lyvanne ventured out into the lower level of the city, only ever at night and only when she was sure there was no one around to see her leave, which was rare. She scavenged through waste buckets, searching for any kind of food. It was a harder job than she'd had back in the Upper level, the poorer people of the city were evidently less likely to waste food, let alone throw it out. Yet, she managed to find enough to keep her going day by day.

Over time she began to regain strength that she'd lost wasting away in the sewers. The morsels of food were like feasting on a king's banquet compared to the skinny rats she'd had to feed on prior. As the nights passed by, she began to venture further away from the sewer's entrance, familiarising herself with the surrounding areas so that one day, when she felt confident enough, she could make her escape.

In the area immediately surrounding the sewer entrance, there was no fewer than three taverns, all of them more crowded and less hygienic than those she'd passed by in the Upper level. It made for good cover from guards if she needed it, but it also meant that she had lots of eyes on her if she chose to travel via those routes at night. It wouldn't necessarily be an issue, but she didn't like the feeling it gave her that her options for escape were almost immediately restricted the moment she stepped out of hiding. If she caught the attention of one wrong person outside the taverns then it might be game over.

Two more nights she told herself as she crept down a street packed to the brim with market stalls, a tavern, and small shanty houses that appeared strung together with some haste. Two more nights of exploring and familiarising herself with the nearby streets and she would make her grand escape from Astreya. Her theory was that if she never set herself a target then she would grow comfortable, she'd become the creepy urban legend that parents scare their children with. The rat killer who lives in the sewers.

Her time exploring the city streets came and went. Lyvanne had progressively spent more time outside the safety of her sewer tunnel, occasionally coming dangerously close to being spotted by the king's men, but always managing to stay one step ahead of the threat. Tonight was the night it mattered most though, either she made it out of the city or the chances were that her journey would end in the king's grasp, entirely at his mercy. After making sure that everything was safely packed away in her sack, she tied her traveling cloak around her neck and took the first step out of the sewer— and there he was. No more than five metres away with a hood over his head was the tall and slender warlock who had abandoned her in the Accord.

"Hello Lyvanne," he said as though they were long lost friends.

Lyvanne didn't reply, she only froze on the spot. She considered running, back into her tunnels or straight past him she didn't care, but it was too late to throw away her chance for escape. Equally, she wanted to speak to him, to ask him where he went, to ask him what happened on that night?

She did neither, instead she slowly walked towards him. He held out his hands to show that he meant no harm, but in doing so left himself unguarded. Once he was within her reach, she balled up her fist and punched him straight in the gut. She knew that her punch would do nothing, but it was more about the message it sent to this stranger.

"Did that help?" he asked as dusted off the impact of the punch.

Lyvanne scowled at him. "Let me do it again just to check?" Lyvanne replied sarcastically as she began to walk straight past him.

"Why're you living in the sewers?" he asked, following closely behind her.

"Can you be quiet and leave me alone? In case you hadn't worked it out yet I'm trying to stay low," Lyvanne scolded.

"Yeah… the sewer smell gave that away."

For a few minutes, Lyvanne walked on in silence, deciding that his company was not something she wanted, yet she didn't force him away. She felt unusually safe with him around.

"I saw you the other night, out on Creek Street. Decided to give you some space."

Lyvanne carried on walking, her hands balled up into fists and her frows burrowed.

The young man, whose pale skin almost shone in the night's sky, walked up to her side keeping pace stride for stride as she made her way through the streets.

"I'm impressed that you made it out of the Accord," he continued, evidently trying to make her talk to him. "Once you didn't follow, I thought for sure that I'd lost you to the guards. So… sorry about that."

The compliment didn't work; in fact, it only served to antagonise Lyvanne as she recalled the way he had run off without making sure she was with him.

The young man sighed, "My name's Turiel."

Lyvanne stopped on the spot, toying with whether this complete stranger telling her his name actually meant something to her or not. She decided it didn't and carried on walking down the street. This time it took Turiel a few moments to carry on walking behind her, almost as though the latest rejection had stung.

Voices, coming around a corner up ahead of her. Lyvanne froze, the clink of chainmail and the gentle swing of steel swords was growing closer. A moment later, Lyvanne realised that she had failed, she had let him distract her and three of the king's soldiers had now turned the corner, two with torches and the third, evidently in charge, with a sheet of parchment that Lyvanne had no doubt featured a rough description of her.

Turiel's arm landed firmly on her shoulder. He held her in her place as she attempted to shake free of him and to run in the direction she had just come.

"Don't move!" Turiel demanded.

"Are you crazy?" Lyvanne shouted as she tried once again to break free, only to feel Turiel's grasp harden.

"Do not move," he repeated, eyes never once leaving the dirty street that they were originally heading down.

It was then that Lyvanne realised that the soldiers hadn't said anything. They weren't chasing her, and they hadn't even acknowledged their presence. Lyvanne gazed up, the three soldiers were still walkingin their direction, but talking amongst themselves, completely unaware of their existence. Turiel, whilst holding her firmly in place with his right hand had outstretched his left, and around his open palm were the white streams of magical energy that she had seen him make use of down by the Anya. She looked up at his face. Was he hiding them? hse wondered. The look on his face indicated that he was in some level of discomfort, more so than when he had been weaving the key into existence the last time she had seen him use magic.

"Don't move," Turiel said once more, struggling to get the words out.

The guards grew closer; they were audibly discussing the search for "some nobody whore." The words stung Lyvanne more than she would have expected. She had never done anything to these people, but through the order of their king they already hated her. It was a painful yet revealing moment, she wasn't made for this city, for these people.

As the guards passed them by, no more than a few feet away, Lyvanne found herself naturally holding her breath. Glancing sideways at Turiel who was panting heavily, she grew embarrassed and started breathing again. The soldiers passed by and once they were out of sight and earshot Turiel released the concealing spell that he had weaved together the moment he saw Lyvanne freeze. Lyvanne watched as Turiel bent over in pain, the same way he had done in the Anya, but this time the cause was clear. As Turiel clutched at his body she watched as a small scar, the size of a thumb, appeared on his chin.

"Did… did the magic cause… that?" Lyvanne asked nervously, not wanting her safety to be the reason that he was in pain. Her mind raced back to that day in the river, all the scars she had seen across Turiel's body and wondered if they were the result of magic too.

Turiel let the pain pass before turning to face her. "I said I would teach you the way that magic works and there will be time to explain all of that, but for now… we need to get you to somewhere safe," he said, drawing one last deep breath mid-sentence as the pain finally subsided.

Lyvanne didn't really know who Turiel was, but in that moment she decided that he was worth her trust, despite all that had happened. Besides escaping the city would be easier with him by her side. She'd never had a big brother before, but she was almost certain that this was what it felt like.

"There isn't anywhere safe in this city though" she argued, hoping that he would offer there and then to help her escape the city entirely.

"I know somewhere," Turiel said softly as he grabbed her by the hand and led her through the city streets, swift and without hesitation. She could have fought his pull, to insist that he told her where exactly it was that they were going, but instead she just moved as he did, allowing him to take the lead. She had to admit, that despite her reservations, it was nice for someone else to be taking responsibility for once.

Turiel managed to avoid patrols for the rest of the journey, only ever taking them down quiet or entirely deserted streets. Lyvanne had grown used to the streets of the Upper level, where even at night there would be rarely be a soul to see outside of the taverns and Lady Houses. But down here, in the lower level, Lyvanne found that the deeper into this maze of houses, shops and blacksmiths that Turiel led her, the more frequently they crossed paths with people carrying on with their lives as if the sun had never set.

"Don't pay them too much attention," Turiel said as they passed a line of beggars who reached out with frail hands in the hope of being offered food, their bones showing through thin layers of skin. More than a few times Lyvanne had to look away in horror as she saw lifeless bodies slumped against buildings or signs. Whether they'd withered away due to starvation or been quietly put down she wasn't sure. What she had figured out however was that she would never have made it out of the city alone. The streets surrounding her sewer entrance were nothing like the streets a few hundred yards away, which were nothing like the streets another hundred yards after that, all of which were nothing like the Upper level of Astreya.

The amalgamation of cultures, structural design and variety of goods on offer astounded her. Even in the dead of night goods and wares belonging to Shimmering Islanders adorned far more stalls than would be commonplace in the Upper level. Then there were the goods and stall design that looked nothing like what she was used to. Wooden constructs with loosely hanging animals skins and decorative patterns replaced the bland and monotone style stalls that were rampant in the Upper level.

"Where are all these from?" Lyvanne asked quietly as the pair made their way through a quieter market street.

"People from all over the world come to Astreya to sell their goods," Turiel replied.

Turiel slowed his pace. They reached an alley, not unlike the one that been the location of Abella's home, only this one didn't have any burned down buildings. Instead, they were all just as equally unpleasant looking as one another. None of the buildings seemed large enough to house a family of any decent size, and all of them seemed poorly constructed. Some with misshapen walls, others with small holes in hastily constructed doorways.

Turiel stopped outside a bland wooden door, motioned for her to wait, knocked five times and stood there in silence, constantly flicking his eyes back to the alley's entrance as if expecting their luck to be bad enough that a pair of soldiers were almost due to arrive.

By the Goddess' fortune they didn't and a few moments later the door slowly creeped open, revealing the inquisitive face of a Hemeti.

CHAPTER 7

It had been years since the one and only time Lyvanne had seen a Hemeti in person. She had been wandering the small docks on the Anya in Asterya's Upper level and on board one of the merchant ships she had seen him... her... it, she wasn't sure. They'd had chains around their wrists, enforced into servitude for committing one crime or another. It was a nasty life to lead and it was reserved for only the lowest rung of society. Slavery had been abolished throughout The Rive and all subservient realms of the king's kingdom, but Hemeti criminals came about as close as you could get to the label.

This Hemeti however was very much a free person; their skin as was standard was tinged green and they had ink decorating their arms with elaborate patterns and symbols. The Hemeti appeared to be studying her just as much as she was studying them. But after sharing nods of approval with Turiel they were motioned inside.

"So this is her?" Lyvanne heard the Hemeti ask Turiel as they were led down a creaking wooden corridor. To their left were a number of doors, of equal looking poor craftsmanship, and to the right a staircase with no railing that led up to what Lyvanne could only assume was the only other floor of the house.

Turiel ignored the question, "The king's soldiers are all over the place, nearly didn't make it here."

"You weren't seen coming in were you?"

"No, we were in the clear" Turiel assured the Hemeti. "Is Jocelyn home?"

The Hemeti shook his head. "Left this evening. Gone to Avagarde on... business." The Hemeti glanced back at Lyvanne.

The corridor opened out into respectably sized living quarters. There was an assortment of chairs, a table for eating at, and some basic cooking equipment. Lyvanne had to admit that it was little better than the life she'd been used to at Abella's.

"Turiel, we need to talk."

"Yes, we can, but first I believe that proper introductions are required," Turiel beckoned Lyvanne forward. "Lyvanne, this is Sinjin, he is one of the few good people in Astreya."

Lyvanne cautiously walked over to the Hemeti. He seemed just as nervous about the meeting as she was. Her staring at the front door probably hadn't helped matters, but she reached out her hand regardless and watched as a relieved smile crossed his face. "Good to meet you, Sinjin."

"It is nice to meet you, Lyvanne. You are welcome here in my house. May Iridu shine upon your time here."

Lyvanne had only ever heard about the "strange and unwelcome" Gods that the Hemeti believed in, and this was the first time she had heard one of them named. More so than hearing the name of a previously unknown God, what surprised Lyvanne most was the way Sinjin spoke. The way that people in the Upper level spoke of Hemeti made them sound like creatures new to the idea of sentience. But to Lyvanne this person seemed no different to everyone else; he was just a man of flesh and bones with a peculiar coloured skin.

"Why don't you go and get some rest, Lyvanne?" Turiel continued. "Sinjin and I need to talk, and I doubt you've had a lot of rest since the last time we met"

Lyvanne nodded, but not knowing where to go just stood there awkwardly.

"I'll show you to your room."

Room? Lyvanne hadn't seen much space in the house, let alone enough for her to have a room all to herself. But she didn't question anything, bowed, and said goodnight to her new host and allowed Turiel to show her to a small bedroom located behind one of the closed doors to the left of the entrance. The room itself was far from special, it was barely large enough to house a small wooden bed and a chest of drawers, but it was far more than Lyvanne could have wished for.

"Get your rest, Lyvanne. We have a lot we need to discuss and tomorrow will likely be a heavy day for you," Turiel said as she stood at in the doorway, ready to depart.

Lyvanne didn't know what he was on about so just said goodnight and allowed him to leave. Turning back to her bed, she noticed that the blanket on top was much thicker than the one she was used to at Abella's, and whilst small, the bed itself was made of much softer material. She undressed, wrapped the blanket around herself and dumped her whole weight onto the bed.

Sleep came easily but it didn't last for long. What could only have been a few hours later Lyvanne heard a commotion in the corridor outside her room. After listening carefully, she determined that Jocelyn had returned, her trip to Avagarde a failure. Turiel sounded happy that she was there regardless.

"She's here," Turiel said, the noise filtering through to Lyvanne's room. In her half sleep state not realising that she was the subject of his comment and not Jocelyn.

Before long, the conversation was moved to the living quarters and out of Lyvanne's range of hearing. Without realising she was doing so, Lyvanne began to fall back to sleep shortly thereafter, wakinghours later to small streams of sunlight peering into her room through small holes in the wooden wall to her right.

There were voices coming from down the corridor, so groggily she got out of bed only half remembering the arrival of Jocelyn during the night. She went to reach for her clothes but recoiled when the smell hit her. Spending a whole night out of the sewer had made the smell foreign to her again, and she felt incredibly embarrassed that she was going to have to go and see the others smelling the way she did. Not making the connection that she would have smelt the exact same way the night prior.

She opened the door, and to her surprise, nearly tripped over a small pile of clothing that had been placed right outside her room. Not knowing whether to be ashamed or relieved, Lyvanne took the meaning of the pile and swiftly changed. Despite being tall for her age, the clothes were still too large for her, but she was grateful nonetheless. The new trousers were long and slender, the tunic woolen and about two sizes too large for her body. The boots, however, were the right size and she couldn't ever recall having footwear so well made before. Her gifts made her blush; she'd never had the luxury of having real presents before. Her friends had done their best. Oh used to share his toy soldiers for the day, but they always ended up back with him, which made the small foot soldier she'd found in her pack mean all the more to her. Lira had once brought her flowers that she'd stolen from a small gated garden, and Lyvanne had cherished them every day until they withered. Abella had never given gifts, otherwise she would have felt the urge to give them to every child who passed through her care, and that was too much to ask. But Lyvanne had treated her stories as the gifts she could give, the tales of far off lands and people. They were the knowledge that Abella had passed on to Lyvanne and the gift she would always have with her.

Lyvanne walked into the corridor and down towards the living quarters. The smell of food was strong, and it served as quite the motivation to overcome her nerves and to go and say good morning to the others. She'd always been sociable, she had to be in her environment, but it had been just Lira, Oh, Abella and her for so long that it felt strange to be under the same roof as complete strangers.

In the living quarters, she found Sinjin, Turiel and Jocelyn, who like Sinjin, was Hemeti.

"Good morning, Lyvanne," Turiel called out. "Come, sit"

"Good morning, everyone," Lyvanne said timidly as she made her way towards an empty seat next to Turiel. Her usual confidence and assuredness overwhelmed by the unfamiliarity of her situation.

Sinjin walked over to her, a bowl of hot broth in his hands. It didn't look like much, but Lyvanne was incredibly grateful when he handed it over.

"Good morning," he said with a smile.

"Good morning," she replied, unable to hide the smile as she took a deep breath of the broth.

Everyone turned their gaze towards Jocelyn. She looked of similar age to Turiel and was of similar height, which Lyvanne found strange for a woman. Her skin was green like Sinjin's, but she didn't have any visible ink on her body. Jocelyn was more obviously female than when she had first seen Sinjin. Her hair was longer, falling down by her shoulders, and her figure the same as some of the more strapping ladies Lyvanne had seen in the Upper level.

"Good morning, little one," Jocelyn said, offering out a hand to greet Lyvanne who made quick work to shake it in return. "My name is Jocelyn. Turiel has told me a lot about you."

Lyvanne shot a quizzical look at Turiel. *He's barely met me himself*, she thought.

"Well, as much as one could tell," Turiel interjected.

"Indeed," Jocelyn said, a curious smile on her face. Lyvanne noticed an obvious connection between the pair. She couldn't quite blame Turiel for being smitten, if that was the case. Despite the green skin Jocelyn was an undeniably attractive young woman, so much so that Lyvanne almost felt intimidated in her presence. "May Iridu shine upon your time with us."

"Thank you," Lyvanne replied, not knowing if there was some formal response she should be saying.

Breakfast went by fast. The others, not wanting to treat Lyvanne as an oddity, turned their attention to more mundane subjects: the weather, the food, and stories from Turiel's recent time in a tavern. Lyvanne knew that they all wanted to talk more openly about other matters, but whatever they were, her being there stopped it. The group finished their morning meal as though nothing was wrong, but once they'd finished, Turiel's face grew dark and he stood from his chair.

"I feel as though I have some explaining to do to you, Lyvanne."

"You do?" she replied with genuine uncertainty.

Turiel bowed his head and directed her towards the door.

"There's a space upstairs we can use," he said as he ushered her through the single corridor of the house. Once up the stairs, Lyvanne was surprised to find only a single doorway. It was heavily bolted, with the same numerous locking systems the front door was equipped with..

Turiel unbolted the door for her. The door opened out onto a rooftop, open and bland. To the left and right the roof was flanked by buildings, taller yet unimpressive, but directly opposite the doorway the view was quite something. The roof faced northwards, looking out towards the Lion Gate and the slums that lay between, separating her from the streets she had grown up on.

"That's quite something," Lyvanne had to admit. "How did they afford a place with a view like this?"

Turiel chuckled. "Sinjin and Jocelyn are brother and sister. This home belonged to their parents and their parents had a lot of friends who were willing to help them find their feet."

The answer was good enough for Lyvanne who simply grunted in approval and moved towards the edge of the roof for a clearer view.

"Sinjin and Jocelyn are good friends of mine," Turiel continued, not needing an invitation to begin his explanation. "If you're worried about them selling you out to the king, then you needn't be. I'm sure when I first brought you to this house that Sinjin was just as worried about you selling him out as you were him."

Lyvanne turned to face her saviour. "How do you know the king is after me? And on what grounds would I sell Sinjin out to the king?"

"Well, our escapades at the Accord weren't enough to warrant a search party the likes of which Astreya is seeing right now, let alone for the king to send out soldiers from his army into the streets. Heck, I doubt they remembered a robbery even took place by the time the sun rose. So, there must be a bigger reason, something else that happened to cause this kind of commotion, and you seemed dead set on laying low if you were willing to hide away in a sewer."

Lyvanne avoided his eye contact, embarrassed that he had sussed her out almost immediately. She wasn't surprised that the first warlock she'd ever met was smart, but the way that he had so quickly come to know her was almost unnerving.

"So what was it?"

She didn't understand. "What was what?"

"Your vision," he replied bluntly.

Lyvanne hesitated. She trusted Turiel enough, but she didn't know how he would react to the vision of a fallen king and her being in the throne room.

"I only had a fever dream, a result of the wound," she told him, trying her best to sound convincing. She couldn't work out why, but she trusted Turiel the same way she had trusted Lira and she didn't want to scare him away.

Turiel reached out and grabbed her hand. He moved quickly; if he had been an enemy she would have fallen. A flock of pigeons resting on one of the buildings above went scattering into the sky.

"Lyvanne, you need to be honest with me. The king wouldn't have his soldiers out looking for someone after just any old vision. It wasn't a fever dream. The Angel of Destiny visited you and whatever you saw, it was a real. You need to share with me if I'm going to help keep you safe." His voice was stern, but soft and caring at the same time.

Lyvanne hated this; she hated everything that had happened since she met him. She'd lost her friends, her way of life, and now she was being hunted through all of Astreya. The very thought brought bile up her throat.

"Why do I need your help? You've only caused me trouble," she argued. Her temper flaring as she tried to remember that she survived before she met Turiel and that she could do it again on her own.

Turiel seemed cut by the words, but he carried on regardless. "Because you're more important than you know, Lyvanne. I didn't just happen across you on the banks of the Anya. I knew you would be there."

Lyvanne's head turned dizzy, questioning everything as Turiel continued.

"I knew you would be there because I've had a vision too, and you were front and centre of it. Seven years ago, I lost my father and mother, but I gained something else because the Angel of Destiny visited me on the very same night."

Lyvanne was taken aback. The parallels in their life were glaring. It made him hard not to trust and even harder to stay mad at.

"What did you see?" The words trickled out of her mouth without her command.

"Yet you won't tell me yours?" A sly smile creeped into the corner of his mouth, they both knew that he'd won. "I saw a young woman as she stood at the head of a rebellion against the fat pigs who live in the Upper level, and the king beyond them. There were people like me, Islanders and even Hemeti, all rallied behind her as one. She stood there like a shining beacon of hope where before there was none. That person was you, Lyvanne."

Lyvanne almost buckled under the pressure suddenly placed upon her shoulders. Her knees quivered and her breath was sucked from her body.

"No," she replied with no strength behind her word. "You're wrong, you must be. How would you even know it was me? You don't know me!" Her voice was filled with desperation; this wasn't what she had imagined, it wasn't the life she had wanted.

As if he had been prepared to answer this very question his whole life, Turiel proceeded to remove his tunic and turned away from Lyvanne, leaving the scars covering his body to stare her in the eyes.

"Using magic takes a toll on the body, sometimes a great one." There was a real pain behind his words, and Lyvanne felt sorry for him as she studied each scar intently. "The unfortunate reality though is that to become better with my gift, I had to use it over and over again. I had to train my body so that I could cast with more power, more efficiency."

He tucked his arm behind his back and traced the outline of the largest scar, which ran nearly the entire length of his body. "This was the day I found you."

Lyvanne's stomach churned, why did this person have so much faith in her? Why did he have so much faith in what he had been shown by the Angel of Destiny?

"Why did you do this?" she asked as she reached out and traced the outline of his scar with her hand. Her cheeks flushed as she ran her hand across his body, but she was comfortable enough that it didn't scare her away.

"Because I want to live in a better world, I want my friends to live in a better world... and I believe that you can lead us to it," Turiel replied. "So, I spent my years training my body and mind. Then one day when I was strong enough, I reached out for the person I saw in my vision and I was shown you. I used my magic to follow you long enough that I could find you on my own, and sure enough, I found you by your hideout on the banks of the Anya."

Lyvanne wanted to believe him; she wanted to have someone she could trust, and yet there was still something pulling her back.

"Your friends, who are they?"

"Sinjin and Jocelyn are the ones who found and looked after me when I had no other family left. Together we started an insurgent group called The Spring. We all believe that there is a better tomorrow for us, for everyone, if we fight for it. Now here I am, quite literally scarred for the cause, a believer that there's a better tomorrow. I also believe entirely in what the Angel of Destiny showed me, which means that you're just as important to all of this as we are... no, you're more important."

"Killing won't solve The Rive's issues, it will only add to them," She said emphatically, trying her best to recall all of Abella's stories about the king's wars.

"Maybe so, but what if you're wrong?"

"What if you're wrong?"

"Then at least we will have tried," he sounded defeated.

Lyvanne shook her head, this wasn't what she wanted.

"I'm sorry, Turiel. I'm not the person you're looking for. I'm not a tool for you to use in your war. Thank you for the saving me and bringing me here, and thank you for your friends' hospitality, but I have to leave. The king is looking for me and I'm not safe staying anywhere in the city for too -

"You'll never make it out of the city," Turiel said, stopping Lyvanne in her tracks. "Jocelyn was supposed to go to Avagarde yesterday, she couldn't because the king has sealed off the city in search of you. Only traders, guild members and the rich can come and go as they please."

Lyvanne sighed. She struggled to believe the lengths that the ling was going to in the hope of finding her, a needle in a haystack. Did he truly fear her and her vision that much?

"Stay one more day?" Turiel asked. "I did, after all, promise to show you how magic works. I couldn't in good faith let you leave the city without sticking to my word."

It was a flimsy attempt to keep her around. They both knew it, but it made Lyvanne smile regardless.

"One more day."

CHAPTER 8

Sinjin and Jocelyn had more "business" talks to attend soon after, which meant Turiel and Lyvanne were free to discuss the intricacies of magic. Turiel wasn't the best teacher, Lyvanne thought, not the way Abella would have been, but he had clearly had to explain it all before which she figured was a positive. He started by explaining how the use of magic relied heavily on the user's body and spirit, with more intricate and powerful spells leaving a mark upon the user's body.

Lyvanne watched Turiel's eyes as he went on to discuss the different kinds of spells he had mastered and the ones he was yet to try. They almost seemed to gleam in the dimly lit house, betraying the happiness that talking about his gift brought him. Despite the pain it brought, it was both a gift and curse to him.

"When you first met me I was using a conjuration spell; it's powerful and left a nasty looking scar," Turiel said, appearing both proud and fearful of the memory. "I'd had to spend a few nights scouting out the woman's house first though. I needed as much detail about the keyhole as possible before I dared risk creating the fake key."

"You never told me what you needed from that house. Did you get it?" Lyvanne asked, thinking back to the countless questions she'd had that night.

"I did… but maybe it's something you're better off not knowing if you truly want no part in this game?"

Lyvanne nodded, her curiosity was getting the better of her, but she knew he was right.

"The spell I used to hide us from the soldiers last night was quite simply, an invisibility spell that cloaked our bodies and any sound we made," he continued.

"And I would have broken the spell if I moved out of your grip?" Lyvanne asked.

Turiel nodded. "You would have, so thanks for staying put/"

"I nearly didn't."

"I know; you're a tough one when you want to be."

Lyvanne smiled. "Thank you."

The conversation flowed easily after that. Turiel went on to explain the feeling that magic sends through your body as you use it, how tiring one prolonged spell can be and how he expects that he won't live as long as the average person simply because of the toll it has taken on him over the years. Then the conversation turned towards the thing Lyvanne had been most eagerly anticipating, how to defend against the use of magic. Turiel opted for a more practical demonstration for this part of her lesson and they retreated to the rooftop. To Lyvanne's surprise, they had been talking for so long that the sun had already begun to hide behind distant buildings, casting long shadows across the city ahead of them.

"Stand there," Turiel said, pointing to a spot on the roof a few feet away from him.

"I don't want you to hurt yourself just to teach me."

"Don't worry, I'll use a weak spell, one that won't scar." Lyvanne nodded her agreement and took up her spot on the roof. "Watch my eyes, watch my hands."

She tried, but he was too fast. His hands flew through the air like knives, and she had no idea if his eyes had given away any kind of clue before she was hit by something that felt like the sting of a bee.

"What was that?!" Lyvanne yelped.

"A weak spell. If you were in real danger from a warlock who wanted to hurt you then they would have used much worse"

"How in the God's name am I supposed to stop that?"

"Don't stop it, dodge it." Another blast came, another failure to dodge.

"At least give me some warning you mad man!"

"No," Turiel said firmly."The enemy won't."

"I am not their enemy! Need I remind you Turiel? I'm here to learn about magic."

Turiel's head dipped, but he accepted her decision.

"Okay, point taken. Regardless of that fact there is one kind of magic that I must teach you to defend against." Turiel sat her down on the roof, being careful not to touch anywhere that he had just blasted with magic, "The king has two kinds of warlocks working for him, those who are loyal and true to his cause lead his armies. They fight his enemies and ever push the boundaries of his empire. Although the king's armies are proud and won't ever tell you as much, choosing to keep the glory for themselves. The others are the enslaved ones, those who have been discovered, captured and forced into his work. He usually holds some personal leverage over them to keep them working. They're the ones who are taught to steal into the visions of others, an incredibly painful and taxing kind of magic. And just as I -

"Turiel," Lyvanne interjected "How do you know so much about the king and his warlocks?"

The question had been floating around for some time now, but she only just felt confident enough to ask it. The answer scared her, but she needed to know more about this person who was giving so much for her.

"My father was one of the loyal ones," he replied, a sadness growing behind his eyes. "Magic is rare in the people of The Rive, but it is more common among children with a magical parent. Once my Father had me he started to grow worried at the thought of me being forced into war after war if I showed signs of magic, and sure enough…" Turiel threw a small ball of light up into the air as demonstration "So he decided to help my mother and me escape the king's castle during one of his return trips from a foreign war, but he was caught. My mother was killed, and my Father taken into servitude, the king deemed him a resource too valuable to waste. I was the lucky one, I escaped. It was that night that I had my vision, and by the Goddess' fortune my father's betrayal had caused enough commotion that my vision had been missed… or at least that's the best explanation I could come up with."

Turiel looked out over the city as dusk slowly turned to night, Lyvanne could see that it had been some time since he'd had to tell the tale.

"Lyvanne, I know you want to leave, I know you want to get out of Astreya, but you're not safe. The king will never stop hunting you, and he has the means to find you"

"What do you mean?"

"The warlocks he keeps locked away at the castle are weak, their bodies are drained from constantly watching for visions. Eventually, one of his generals, the ones fighting his wars, will return to Astreya and when they d,o he will use their power to search for you, the same way I did. They will be able to see you no matter where you are."

Turiel backed away, giving the information time to settle in. Lyvanne couldn't believe what she was hearing. This was it now, this was her life, always running, always hiding.

"Is there anything I can do?"

"Yes. You have to let me help you, I can put a spell on you that keeps them out, but it's only a temporary solution and it will only work whilst I'm nearby." Lyvanne seemed dejected, Turiel took it as less a slight on him and more the past few weeks draining her of any mental energy. "I can train your mind to block them out, but it's going to take a long time, more than we have here."

"How long?"

"It depends on how well you take to the teaching… weeks maybe months."

Lyvanne frowned. "How can I trust anything you're telling me? How do I know you're not just trying to keep me around because you see me as some kind of hero?"

"I can only prove myself through my actions. The rest is up to you as to whether you believe me or not."

Lyvanne considered her options. No matter which route she chose to take, she felt entirely helpless. If she left Astreya behind, she might be able to lead a happy life somewhere out in the countryside, or on a far off continent like the ones Abella used to tell her about. But she would always live with the fear that Turiel was right and that one day they would find her. Or she could stay here, entrust her life into the hands of someone she's only just met and hope that the path didn't drag her into a war. Her mind drifted back to her vision, the battle scars on her face, her place at the table and the words of Abella who said that it was a better life being offered to her. What if this was what the world wanted from her? To be some hero.

"Teach me to block them out," she said, almost demanding. "Once it's done, I'm leaving."

"As good a deal as I could expect, but first, the spell. Stand up," Turiel said as he rose to his feet and raised his hands into the air. He angled them towards Lyvanne, and she flinched slightly out of fear he was about to attack her again.

"Will this hurt?" she asked as she too stood.

"No, just stand still."

Turiel closed his eyes, which didn't fill Lyvanne with confidence, but she did as he asked and remained motionless. The white streams of magic began to flow out of Turiel's body, a sign that Lyvanne now knew meant that a spell was strong enough to leave a mark on the caster's body. His hands began to dance in intricate motions and slowly the magical streams moved across from Turiel to Lyvanne. She wanted to move out of their way, scared of their power, but she stayed still. The magic swirled all around her, and after a few minutes, they nearly entirely surrounded her. There was a bang and a burst of light then the magic vanished.

"It's done," Turiel said as he fell down to one knee, clutching at his covered chest. The pain was etched across his face, and Lyvanne knew that the spell had cost him greatly.

"Are you okay?" Lyvanne asked whilst carefully making her way over to him, cautious not to get too close.

"I…will be," he panted.

"Let me help."

"Help me… downstairs."

Doing as he asked, Lyvanne lifted Turiel up by the arm and helped to carry him back down into the house. Once downstairs, she asked where his room was. She was surprised when he revealed that she had taken his the day she arrived. Knowing that fighting the issue would be fruitless, she resorted to resting him down on one of the chairs in the living quarters.

"Thank you," Turiel said as he slowly attempted to regain his breath.

"No, thank you," Lyvanne said, crouching down and taking his hands. "You've done a lot for me based on some foreign notion that I'm going to save you all. I'm sorry that's not who I am, but I want you to know that I am grateful for everything."

"You are most welcome, little one."

She found the pleasantries from both of them to be awkward and cringe inducing, but she knew no better way to express her thanks, so she just blushed, nodded her head and sat down on a chair opposite him. After giving Turiel a moment to recover, Lyvanne decided that this was as good a time as any for answers so she decided to do some more pressing.

"If you think of me as some kind of hero, then why did you take me to the Accord? I could have been captured or killed."

"I had to be sure you were who I believed you to be. I had to see you under pressure. Also, I'd seen how you were with the people you lived with, and I genuinely wanted you to have the opportunity to steal something valuable for their betterment. Given that you didn't have that chance, I'm truly sorry." His answer seemed sincere, and it was appreciated.

"So why did you run off without me?"

Turiel laughed lightly. "I honestly thought you were behind me; I didn't realise you'd been left behind. When I first realised that was the case, I blasted the two guards who were chasing me and went back to look for you but you'd vanished. I guess you're better at escaping than I am."

There was a pan of broth bubbling over towards the other side of the room, left over from their meal at noon. Seeing Turiel was still suffering from the pain of his most recent spell, Lyvanne walked over to the pan filled a nearby bowl and brought it over to him.

"Eat. Next time, perhaps leave the escape plans to me, okay?"

CHAPTER 9

As the days came and went, outside of the hours Turiel spent teaching her magic, and after the time spent learning how to block a warlock from entering her mind, Lyvanne started to spend more time with the others. The two were completely different by nature. Jocelyn was mature, confident, and carried herself with a certain gravitas that Lyvanne could only imagine having. Despite that, she loved the time they spent together. She found Jocelyn funny, and her constant quips about the stupidity of the men in her life were always amusing. Sinjin on the other hand was more serious. He was kind and caring, but often buried in his books or writing letters in a quiet corner of the house.

"Can I try to read one of your letters?" Lyvanne once asked once whilst she had time alone with Sinjin. The Hemeti was doing his best to teach her to read, and by his accounts she was a good student, but that request caught him off guard.

"They aren't for you, Lyvanne," He replied sharply. Seeing her take a step back he softened his stance and elaborated. "It's too dangerous to tell you too much, at least until we've got you out of the city and away the king, okay?" He asked, putting down the reading material and placing a calm hand on her shoulder.

It was refreshing being the least responsible in the group for once, but not having that responsibility did often lead her to missing those she left behind. Most nights she found herself sleeping with Oh's toy soldier in the bed, and others she would wrap herself in the travelling cloak given to her by Abella simply for the comfort of what she had once considered home. Jocelyn noticed this side of her more clearly than the others, and the small ways that she tried to make Lyvanne feel better about it all was perhaps the reason that Lyvanne had gravitated towards her. Simple things like bringing her new clothes from time to time helped her feel like the child she'd never been allowed to be, and even if only for a few hours detracted from the looming threat of the king's watching eye.

This particular day was a rarity for Astreya; the sky had been darkened with clouds and rain fell heavy onto the ground for hours on end. In the last hour, thunder and lightning had even started to occupy the sky, creating sights and sounds that Lyvanne had never seen or heard before. She had sat in the doorway leading onto the roof watching everything unfurl until Turiel had found her and told her off for letting the landing get damp from the rain.

Bringing her downstairs, he grabbed a tattered blanket from the kitchen and started drying her hair.

"How are you supposed to bring the people together in rebellion if you can't even dry a young girl's hair?" Jocelyn said sarcastically as she watched Turiel flail around, not really sure of the best way to approach it. "Give it to me," she continued before winking at Lyvanne and taking the blanket out of his hands.

"At least I tried," Turiel exclaimed innocently, holding his hands up in the air.

"Stick to the magic lessons," Jocelyn replied. Lyvanne couldn't see her face as she dried her hair, but the grin on Turiel's face was impossible to miss.

Sinjin was out on business and for the rest of the evening the three of them just sat in the living quarters, talking, laughing and pretending to be scared every time the sky roared. It was the most fun Lyvanne had had in a long time, but just before it was time to retire to bed, it all changed.

Someone knocked on the front door five times. The signal that it was safe to open, Lyvanne had figured out. Jocelyn went to open it, unbolting the numerous locks and opening it to find Sinjin, drenched from head to toe.

"You look rather wet, brother!" she joked as Sinjin pushed past her and into the corridor.

"Where's Turiel?" He asked, ignoring her joke.

Turiel didn't waste any time and went to meet him in the corridor.

"What's the matter Sinjin?" He asked. Lyvanne had followed Turiel and stood slightly behind him, just within sight of Sinjin and Jocelyn who remained in the corridor.

"The king's soldiers, they've gone to Udnak's home… searching for Lyvanne."

The three exchanged worried glances, but none of it made sense to Lyvanne. Why does it matter? she asked herself. As long as they aren't coming here then I'm safe. Turiel didn't waste time; he grabbed his own cloak that was hanging on a hook in the corridor and followed Sinjin back out into the pouring rain.

"Lyvanne, stay here! Bolt the door and only open it if someone knocks five times," Jocelyn said, holding out a hand to stop her from following before joining the boys out in the rain.

Lyvanne rolled her eyes. She knew the "five knocks rule" and didn't need reminding like a child. But something didn't feel right about letting the others go off on their own. Her instincts told her that she needed to look after them just like they did for her. Something like this had never happened during her stay here, but one thing was for sure, she wasn't going to sit around and wait for them to come back.

Quickly grabbing her cloak and tying it around her neck, Lyvanne made sure that she'd given Jocelyn enough time to put some distance between them. She couldn't let her friend notice her following, but she couldn't let her get so far ahead that she couldn't keep up. Lyvanne opened the front door, brought her hood up over her hair as the rain began to lash against her face, and gave chase after making sure the door was firmly shut behind her.

The storm made it difficult to keep an eye on where Jocelyn was and the direction she was heading, but it also meant that the streets were pretty quiet and that her footsteps couldn't be heard as she ran to keep up with Jocelyn's pace. It quickly became evident which direction they were heading in. Over the rooftops of the streets around her Lyvanne began to notice a plume of smoke rising high into the sky, and as Jocelyn ran down the twists and turns of the lower level the plume slowly grew closer.

Between the claps of thunder, echoes of people shouting and the clang of steel rattled through the streets. Jocelyn vanished from sight as the twisting roads and rapture of noises took hold of the world. But Lyvanne wasn't about to let that stop her; she'd grown up on the streets and if there was one thing it was good at it was this. Following the direction she'd last seen Jocelyn go, and using the plumes of smoke rising into the air as a marker she pushed onwards.

Taking one last turn the street opened out into a cobblestone courtyard. At the far end of the courtyard was the largest fire Lyvanne had ever seen. Even in the stormy rains the heat radiated in her direction as the flames licked high into the night sky. The courtyard itself was filled with people, some of them in the colours of the city watch and others were part of the king's army. Most were commoners, staring intently at the fire and even shouting abuse and throwing things in the direction of the city watch. Towards the back of the crowd she could just about make out Jocelyn, now stood by the side of Sinjin and Turiel.

She knew she shouldn't be here, it was dangerous for her to be around this many people, let alone the people who were out to look for her. But it was too late now and she wasn't about to go back without finding out what caused the fire that was engulfing what appeared to be a small house. Deciding that it was safer for her to be near people she knew and risk their anger she moved over towards Jocelyn and the others.

"Lyvanne!" Turiel scolded under his breath as he noticed her stood by their sides. "Go home, now!"

Lyvanne just shook her head, her eyes never leaving the blaze in front of them "What's happened?"

"Lyvanne!" His voice sterner than she'd heard it before, "Go back."

She was being pulled in two. Part of her was telling her that Turiel was right. But she didn't feel ready to leave yet; she wanted to see what had caused this. "I'm staying," she replied, her voice calm and steady. She knew that he wanted to be like a big brother to her, that he only wanted to protect her, but she needed to feel free if she was going to stick around.

All Turiel could do was gently let out a defeated sigh as he turned his attention back to the blaze. Seeing his silence, Sinjin answered for him. "The house belonged to a man called Udnak and his family; they had a small girl who fits your description. The king's soldiers came; it was her turn to go to the castle for questioning, but they refused to give her up."

Despite talking in whispers there was an unmistakable anger in his voice that Lyvanne suddenly felt responsible for.

"They wanted to take her?" she asked, not wanting to believe what she was being told.

"Yes," Sinjin nodded. "Been happening all over the city since your vision, young girls who could match your description being taken away to the king's castle."

Lyvanne looked to Jocelyn and Turiel for confirmation, but their refusal to deny it was all that she needed to hear. Mouth agape, she turned back to the wall of fire that was dangerously close to igniting the neighbouring buildings, the heavy rain throughout the day perhaps being the only thing preventing such a scenario.

Stood outside and closest to the wreckage were five of the king's soldiers stood in a semi-circular formation preventing anyone from approaching the burning building. They were the recipients of any objects being thrown from the crowd. At the tip of the formation was one of the king's criers, dressed in decorative robes that swayed wildly in the wind.

"Let this be a lesson to you all!" the crier shouted, his voice struggling to carry over the noise of the storm. "The king is searching for a traitor to The Rive, a villain of the worst kind. If your child is called for questioning then you would be doing them and yourselves a disservice by trying to halt the king's justice"

Lyvanne could hear shouts of dissent from within the crowd, but no one seemed willing to take any further action.

"Do not worry, the innocent have nothing to fear. This family sought to hide away their offspring, to what end is yet to be determined. If their child is the one the king seeks then your trials shall be at an end and you may return to your lives, if she is not then…"

Lyvanne stopped listening. The man had a long and sharp face; he was short and anything but imposing. He had the look of one that she would not associate well with and took the thunder that interrupted him as an opportunity to turn her attention to her friends.

"Turiel, what happens to the children they take?" She asked, hoping he would answer. When he didn't, she turned her attention to Jocelyn.

"From what we understand, their warlocks have ways of getting information out of people, a kind of magic that leaves no physical scars on the victim but causes great mental anguish." She chose her next words carefully, "some of the children have returned from questioning weaker than when they left, but they'll be alright. Others have not been so fortunate; their minds are weak due to age or illness and they have not returned as the same children who left."

Lyvanne thought back to Lira. What if they had found her? What if they had taken her in? Oh and Abella wouldn't be able to look after themselves and would she have been alright? She couldn't bear to think about Lira being put through such pain because of her. She wanted to go back, to find them, and bring them with her, but she knew that wasn't possible and the reality hurt. Her attention snapped back to the crowd who had suddenly started voicing their anger in unison.

"What did he say?" she asked as she turned to Turiel and Sinjin who had both balled up their fists, appearing only moments away from taking action against the soldiers.

"Jocelyn, take Lyvanne home now," Turiel said without removing his gaze from the king's crier.

Without needing to be told twice, Jocelyn put her arm on Lyvanne's shoulder and guided her away from the crowd and back towards the house.

"No, I don't want to go back. What happened?" Lyvanne pressed.

Jocelyn looked as though she was contemplating whether to tell Lyvanne, but something clearly made her decide that it was best not to hide these things from her. "Udnak and his wife were still in the house when they started the fire."

Lyvanne broke down. She cried for the rest of the journey home. She couldn't shake the feeling that these people had died because of her. Not for a cause that they believed in, not because they had made enemies of the wrong people, but because they didn't want to give away their daughter when it should be her who was taken in by the king. Because of her the king had created another orphan, another orphan for the streets of Astreya to swallow whole.

Jocelyn opened the door to their home, waited for Lyvanne to walk through, and then bolted it shut behind them.

"Please don't leave my home empty and unlocked in the future, Lyvann,e" Jocelyn said before turning to the younger girl and realising she was still crying. "Come here."

Jocelyn brought the girl in close and squeezed her arms around her tight.

"It will be okay," she said, her shoulder length brown hair dripping water onto the top of Lyvanne's head.

"I didn't want any of this," Lyvanne said between whimpers.

"None of us do, little one," Jocelyn said as she ran a hand through Lyvanne soaked and matted hair. "We've all seen trauma, that's why some of us have chosen to fight for what we believe will be a better world, to stop nights like tonight."

Things were finally starting to make sense to Lyvanne; she was beginning to understand why The Spring fought for a new world. Her mind wandered back to her dream of buying her way out of Astreya, of settling down, leading a quiet life with her savings. She wasn't ready to entirely give up on that dream yet. She wasn't ready to join their ranks, but understanding was a start.

"You may not be one of us, but regardless you will need to be strong. Can you be that for me?"

Lyvanne nodded her head.

"I need you to promise me, little one."

"I promise."

• • •

Turiel and Sinjin exchanged worried glances. The fires were ripping further into the sky and if something wasn't done soon, there was no telling if the rain would be enough to hold it at bay and to stop it spreading.

"Go find others," Turiel said as he placed a firm hand on Sinjin's shoulder. "I'll stay here and do what I can."

Sinjin nodded and darted off into the darkened streets they had just come from.

"I leave you now," The king's crier continued to the crowd. "Let the ruins of this house remain as a warning and a promise. The king will not abide criminals, but if you live within his laws then he shall be… generous."

Turiel balled his hands into fists, and his arm started shaking with adrenaline. Do something, he told himself, do something now. The magic had begun to course through his veins, flowing freely through his body until it reached his fingers. No, I can't. He told himself. If I reveal my powers now, I would be throwing away all I've worked for. The magic receded and any chance of saving his friends from the fire, he knew, was lost.

"Turiel," the voice came from within the crowd. "Over here!"

Turiel saw her, waving an arm in the sea of people that separated them. "Evelyn!"

"We have to do something," Evelyn said, as Turiel pushed his way through the crowd towards her. Evelyn had been a friend for years. She'd always offered a helping hand if he had needed it, and he wasn't surprised at all to see her out here in this weather offering to help once again. She was as much a part of The Spring as he was.

He shook his head. "We can't Evelyn," he said with remorse. "Not until the guards have left."

He knew it wouldn't be long now, but as the guards lingered, every second that passed grew more painful. "There'll be nothing left," Evelyn noted solemnly as the pair watched from the back of a thinning crowd as a charred ruin of a wall collapsed to the floor.

"I think that's the point," Turiel replied. "Come on, let's get closer."

"Scum!" A rogue voice from the crowd called out towards the guards. Seconds late,r a rock flew through the air and clattered against the helm of the man who had been on the receiving end of the insult.

"Who was that?!" The guard retaliated, drawing his iron sword from its sheath.

"Shit," Turiel said.

Another rock flew into the air, this time missing its target but only by a few inches. A third rock was launched, this time from a different place among the crowd and the remaining guards responded by drawing their remaining swords in unison. Seeing temperatures flare, Turiel pulled his hood up over his head and pushed his way through the rest of the crowd and threw himself into the small space left between the onlookers and the guards.

"Turiel, no!" Evelyn shouted after him, but it was too late.

Holding out his arms in both directions Turiel went on the defensive. "We don't want to do this!" he shouted.

"Why's that?" The guard who had been hit replied, pressing another step forward.

Turiel knew there had to be a way out of this. "The Crier, he's already gone, he doesn't know what's happened. You want to start a bloodbath without anyone around to back up your word?"

It was flimsy he knew, but there was no other choice. The crowd would calm down if the guards left, he could count on that, but getting them to leave in the first place could be troublesome. The guard looked around at the scene before him, the rain pattering against his armour, the fire reflecting back in the eyes of the crowd. Almost on cue, Sinjin returned from the side streets, a rabble of people at his back, all faces that Turiel recognised.

"Clean up this mess," the guard said stubbornly, waving his head in the direction of the burning building as he took two steps back and made to sheath his sword. His eyes carefully tracing the newcomers to the crowd. The other guards following suit.

Walk away, Turiel pleaded to himself. Hoping that no one else would do anything to agitate them.

The fire crackled and one of the last remnants of the roof fell to the floor below, causing a wicked crash and throwing dust and ash pouring into the air in front of the crowd. "Come on, let's go," one of the guards advised a cloud of ash settled around them.

"Let's get to work," Turiel called out to Sinjin and his following as the guards left the crowd to clean up the mess and to stop the fire from spreading.

"You sure know how to throw yourself into the mix, Turiel," Evelyn said as she drew up alongside him.

Turiel smiled. "Can't be helped sometimes."

The heat was unlike anything Turiel had felt before. A towering inferno whose roaring reach was only being held at bay by the downpour of rain falling from the blackened sky.

"Sinjin, find some pails!" Turiel shouted through the storm, but Sinjin was one step ahead. Forcing their way through from the back of the crowd, Sinjin and his followers arrived, pails of water in hand.

"Sent some others to fetch more," Sinjin said as he arrived by Turiel's side. "A lot of people saw what happened, but they're too scared to leave their homes."

"Let's get to work," Evelyn said as she stepped past Turiel and took a spare pail away from a bystander.

A warmth surged through his body that he was sure wasn't caused by the fire raging ahead of him. He looked across at all the faces of those who had gathered to help and knew that their time would come.

CHAPTER 10

Lyvanne intended to keep her promise. Sinjin and Turiel returned later that night. They had done what they could to put out the fire, but there was little but rubble left by the time they had finished, and no sign of Udnak or his wife. From that day on, Lyvanne worked twice as hard with Turiel to learn and understand magic, and she worked twice as hard to learn how to keep the king's warlocks from entering her mind. The latter was both taxing and difficult to understand. Turiel taught her how a warlock would try to invade her mind, to see things that she saw, and to use their power to determine where she was. He promised her that it could be stopped if the victim was strong willed enough. It couldn't keep them out completely, but if she could train her mind's defences to be strong enough, it would cost the warlock too much pain and time, turning their attempts into a race against time before their body burned out.

As time went on, Lyvanne's hosts began to talk more openly about their business, although they were still careful not say too much in her presence. Lyvanne picked up on tales of small groups of The Spring living out in the countryside, others in Avagarde and a large Hemeti colony living deep in the Great Oak Forest. She found it fascinating, much like the stories Abella used to tell, only these were real and happening right now. She dared not pry too far into what was happening, knowing that it wasn't her place and that they were already being generous enough by being more open around her. What was most amazing to Lyvanne however was how quickly she had grown accustomed to living with two Hemeti. She now found no trust in the stories that people told about them. In fact, she had decided that Sinjin and Jocelyn especially were nicer than any people she had come across wandering the streets of the Upper level. All but her friends from Abella's that was.

On the very rare occasions that she was allowed to leave the house, she often made note of people who cast her Hemeti friends unaccepting looks. Even the lowborn commoners who walked through various markets appeared to shun them as though they were wild animals. It wasn't as cruel or venomous as what she had heard in the Upper level, but that distrust was still there. The City Watch and soldiers from the king's army were the worst. She hadn't been there to see it, but Lyvanne had overheard Jocelyn telling Turiel about a particularly nasty brute who had threatened to beat her and leave her for dead in the sewers if she didn't apologise for walking into him. Lyvanne couldn't understand it and with each passing day she found herself growing a natural dislike for anyone who wore the king's colours.

The trips out into the streets had been a courtesy that Turiel had been reluctant to allow. The king's soldiers were still searching for the treasonous child who they feared would be the downfall of the monarch, but he knew that he couldn't keep her locked up forever. So once or twice a week, he would allow her to venture outside so long as she had at least one of the three with her.

Despite all her training with Turiel, despite her adventures out onto the city streets to visit markets and busy courtyards filled with people plying their trade and selling their wares, it was the time she spent with Sinjin and Jocelyn learning about their people that she enjoyed the most. Sat alone in the wooden rooms of their house, the Hemeti told Lyvanne about the Great War between their peoples many centuries ago. Some of the history she already knew, Abella had often told Lyvanne about how "our people" had conquered the great unwashed masses of the Hemeti. Having met Hemeti herself, it did somewhat tarnish her memory of Abella, the lady had been prejudice, just like the rest of them. Hearing the history from the point of view of the side who lost however she found genuinely intriguing. Whereas Abella had taught Lyvanne about the way that humans had sailed across the sea from their ancestral home to the South in Hydia, eager to help the Hemeti people, to make their civilisation better, to raise them up from the tribal wars that plagued the land of The Rive. Jocelyn and Sinjin laughed at the story and recounted it differently. According to them, humans had wiped clean Hydia of all its resources, and like locust,s they had to move on to their next dish. Viewing The Rive as a continent of great wealth and beauty the humans landed with warships, sending their troops to Hemeti tribes, offering them servitude or blood. The Hemeti had been a proud people, so when diplomacy failed they rallied together as one army, something that had never been done before, and they fought back. Although the tales differed, the outcome was always the same. The Hemeti lost the war and The Rive fell under the control of the Hydia Royal Family, the Greystones.

• • •

It was during one of these history lessons that the knock came. Three knocks rapped against the door, followed by the voice of a king's crier.

"Citizens of Astreya, open your door to the king's justice."

Turiel and Sinjin weren't home, it was just Jocelyn and Lyvanne. They were sat in the living quarters and exchanged terrified glances. Deep down, all four of them had known that one day it would be their turn to have the house searched so the king's men to ensure they weren't harbouring the child fugitive, but they had all hoped it would come long after she had left the city.

They had gone over the plan numerous times, but this was the first time they would have to put it into action. Lyvanne raced upstairs, not wasting any time, quickly followed by Jocelyn who did her best to keep quiet as her feet pressed against the wooden floorboards.

Another three raps on the door. Another summons from the crier.

Jocelyn loosened some floorboards on the landing, and Lyvanne crawled into the hole beneath. Once inside Jocelyn gently kissed her on the forehead before replacing the floorboards, taking extra care to make sure there were no signs that they had been moved. One of the king's soldiers was in the process of knocking for a third time when Jocelyn made it downstairs and started to unbolt the door. She opened it to find three large soldiers, fully armoured and each with a long sword hung around their belts. The fourth man in the group was one of the king's criers, adorning garbs that only the richest in the Upper level would be able to afford.

"Can I help you?" Jocelyn said as she opened the door. She could tell immediately that they were disgruntled to be stood facing a Hemeti.

"We're here on orders of the king, all houses in the city are to be searched," the crier said with venom behind his teeth.

"What for exactly? Maybe I can be of assistance?" Jocelyn retorted.

• • •

From her hiding place under the floorboards, Lyvanne could hear the sarcasm in Jocelyn's voice, but it appeared as though the soldiers were none the wiser.

"A citizen who seeks to bring harm to the king," the crier twirled his thumbs between one another, growing impatient. "I would ask if you had any children, but for once, this terrorist isn't of your kind."

The words made Lyvanne angry and she didn't dare think how they had made Jocelyn feel. She shifted uncomfortably in the dark, being careful not to make any noise.

• • •

"Please, come in," Jocelyn said defeated as she moved clear of the doorway.

The soldiers immediately walked into the house, splitting up and searching every nook and cranny. The crier hung back at the entrance by Jocelyn's side. He was staring at her in a manner that made her feel incredibly vulnerable.

"Do you live alone, Hemeti?" he asked.

Jocelyn shook her head, trying her best to appear confident and in control of the situation. "No, I live with two friends."

"Are they Hemeti like you?"

"One of them is."

The crier scowled. "So one of my own has chosen to live with your kind?" His expression changed and he moved a skinny and frail looking hand through Jocelyn's hair. "Still, I too have to admit that I have often wondered what it would be like to bed with one of you lot"

Jocelyn had to fight to hold back her body from shivering, and to prevent the fist she had formed with her left hand from striking him in the face. Upstairs one of the king's soldiers paced the landing, his feet falling heavy with every footstep.

Jocelyn turned her attention towards him. With every step, he took she watched as his feet sent specks of dust careening into the air. Don't cough, she pleaded as she struggled to peel her eyes away from the floorboard beneath which Lyvanne was hidden.

With there being so little to search upstairs, the soldier didn't spend long wasting his own time. He opened the door to the rooftop, had a quick search and then retreated back down the stairs. A few moments later and the other two soldiers reported in that the house was clear.

"Thank you for letting us into your house," the crier said, "We are pleased that you don't obstruct the king's justice…"

He noticed the multitude of locks and bolts on the back of the front door as they made to leave.

"Well, isn't that an awful lot of security?" He pried.

Jocelyn didn't have an answer ready, so she improvised. "My kind aren't liked much, even by the other commoners." She knew the word would please someone of such high stature "Have to look out for ourselves."

The crier seemed to contemplate her answer, deciding whether or not he found it satisfactory or not. "Yes… I guess you do."

The soldiers were the first out of the door.

"I hope to see you again, Lady Hemeti," the crier finished, offering her a sickening smile as he departed and made his way to the next house.

Her temperature rising, Jocelyn took a deep breath, allowed her fists to relax and slowly closed the door behind them, making sure to lock every single bolt. Turning, she immediately ran back up the stairs and helped to lift Lyvanne back out of her hole.

Letting out the coughs she'd been holding in ever since dust fell into her mouth, the young girl sounded as though she might choke. Jocelyn did all she could to pat her on the back and ensure her that they were safe now.

"No, we're not." Lyvanne replied. A sentiment that she echoed when Sinjin and Turiel arrived back at the house later that day.

After Jocelyn had recounted the story of what had happened in their absence, Lyvanne was adamant that she couldn't stay in the city, and for the first time everyone else appeared to agree with her.

It was time to leave Astreya.

CHAPTER 11

It was early dawn when Turiel woke her from her sleep. It was time to leave. Her things had already been packed for the past two days, all she had to do was slip on her travelling clothes, passed on to her by Jocelyn and grab the sack she had brought with her from Abella's. Evidently the others had already said their goodbyes to Sinjin, which left just her.

It had taken a week before Turiel could make the necessary preparations for them to get out of the city. It was to be Turiel, Lyvanne and Jocelyn who made the journey, leaving Sinjin behind to look after the safe house that they had called home. Lyvanne didn't know where they were going; Turiel had decided that it was on a need to know basis. Knowing how Lyvanne felt about the insurgency group known as The Spring, Turiel had offered to simply get her out of the city's walls and set her on her own path.

"No," she'd replied to Turiel's surprise. "My training isn't done yet." In truth, she'd grown closer to Turiel and Jocelyn than she thought would be possible in such a space of time, and she wasn't quite ready to say her goodbyes.

"Okay," Turiel said with a smile. "When your training is complete, we can talk again," Seeing it as more than a small victory Turiel was happy to accommodate.

"Thank you for letting me stay" Lyvanne said to Sinjin innocently as the pair said goodbye. Despite the danger, she really had enjoyed her time in the house and was sad to leave it behind.

"My pleasure Lyvanne, thank you for listening to the stories of my people… and for being a tidy house guest."

The two shared a quick hug and then it was over, her time in this small home in Astreya had ended. The three turned and waved as

Sinjin closed the door behind them, and they set off down the alley towards the busy streets of the lower level. Turiel made sure to bring Lyvanne's hood up over her head and always walked on the opposite side of her to Jocelyn, making sure she was protected from both sides at all times.

The three of them made swift progress through the streets of Astreya, never once stopping, never making any movement that might draw too much attention to them. It was early in the morning but there were already bakers, butchers, and smiths hard at work, ready for a long day of selling and working. The smells coming from one bakery in particular nearly made Lyvanne pause, only for Turiel's firm hand to appear on her back and keep her moving along the street. It saddened her to know that despite how long she had now spent in the lower level, she hadn't really seen much of it at all. It was all still a foreign world to her. Which caused a great deal of anxiety when it finally dawned on her that she was about to leave the entire city for what would be the first time in memory.

After a while, it started to become clear to Lyvanne which way Turiel was taking the trio. They weren't headed for the main gate as she had at first presumed, but judging by the sea birds who had suddenly appeared in the sky above them and the growing smell of salt, they instead were making their way towards a small harbour on the banks of the Anya. Upon arrival, Lyvanne marvelled at the sight of the river. It was so close to the space where she used to hide away from the world, and yet already the river appeared to be a completely different animal here. It must have been twice as wide as it was in the Upper level of Astreya, and with far more traffic than she was accustomed to seeing on the river. The harbour was filled with all manner of people. Fisherman were both venturing out for the first trip of the day, and others were returning from a long night of fishing. Merchants were peddling their wares to passers-by, and others were boarding boats ready to leave the city for pastures elsewhere. It amazed Lyvanne how much people in the city relied on one river. Without it, she couldn't comprehend how a city this large could keep going. Turiel ushered them both towards a boat on the furthest quay of the harbour. It wasn't small by any means, but neither was it the largest she could see.

On the deck of the boat was a large man, well-dressed but quite obviously sea-worn with a large shaggy beard. He was as wide as Lyvanne was tall, and he spoke unlike anyone she'd heard before.

"Bring ye'self aboard," he bellowed as he saw Turiel approaching his boat.

Turiel went up the ramp to the boat first, leaving Jocelyn and Lyvanne on land for now. The two men shook hands. Turiel had obviously planned this in advance, but nevertheless he appeared nervous.

"Do you know who that is?" Lyvanne asked Jocelyn as they waited for permission to board.

"I've met him once before, he's a good man and loyal to our cause. I shouldn't be surprised that Turiel thinks him our best chance at getting out of the city."

Lyvanne picked up on the wording. "But you aren't?"

Jocelyn remained silent as Turiel waved them aboard.

"Welcome aboard mi' ladies," The man said in a much more hushed tone than when he had welcomed Turiel aboard. No doubt having being scolded by Turiel for being too loud. Lyvanne risked a quick glance around the quay. There were at least three men from the City Watch out on patrol. Her heart beat just a little faster when she noticed them.

"Thank you, Trystan," Jocelyn said as she boarded the boat. Her voice was polite, but the discomfort she felt about the whole situation could be heard in her voice.

Lyvanne was just behind her. The first thing that caught her attention once on board wasn't the robust man who stood with arms out as if she was a lost cousin, but instead the multitude of different cargo that he had on deck. Almost immediately, Lyvanne could spy a number of different vegetables, spices, metals, and precious stones. Lyvanne had never seen anything like it before and drool immediately began to pool in her mouth.

She wiped away the trickle of saliva rolling down the corner of her mouth with embarrassment as the trio were taken straight below deck by Trystan. Like on deck, the hull was also filled with cargo, but most of it was locked away inside large crates. Beneath the stairs, Lyvanne saw an open crate of shining red apples, other crates were marked or labelled with the names of fruits, herbs and spices that she didn't recognise. Once everyone was downstairs Trystan showed them a small closet, barely large enough to house the three of them.

"We're staying in there?" Jocelyn asked Turiel critically.

"We don't have much choice if we want to get out of here safely," he replied.

Trystan pushed through to the front of the gaggle. He pointed at the inside of the door leading into the closet.

"Should be safe down 'ere. You can lock t' door from the inside. I'll come and get ya when we're clear of Astreya," Trystan promised, rubbing one hand across his abnormally large stomach for no discernible reason.

With that, he left them to lock themselves away. Turiel, it seemed, had left it as late as possible before leaving, not wanting there to be any spare time where something he hadn't accounted for could go wrong. The steady rock of the boat moments later signalled that Trystan had detached them from the quay and pushed out into the waters of the Anya.

"Are you sure we're going to be okay?" Jocelyn asked, "Trystan isn't exactly the most subtle of people and his business isn't considered large enough to be one of the merchants who is being let through the blockade."

Turiel nodded, "We'll be fine, Trystan had a long-term shipment scheduled in for Terria and the Shimmering Isles, and they won't halt that much cash flow from coming back into the city. Besides, if things are starting to look worrisome then I'll cast an invisibility spell whilst the boat is being searched"

Jocelyn and Lyvanne both cast him dubious glances. Neither wanted him to be hurting himself without it being absolutely necessary.

"I'll be fine," he said before locking the door and settling down into his spot in the closet.

Lyvanne was nervous, so much so that her hands shook. It wasn't just that she didn't want be caught, but she didn't want her friends to suffer for her in the event that things didn't go to plan. Her mind was plagued by the thoughts of the children who had been taken by the king because of her, to how her life had been back at Abella's, how safe and tame it had been without her even realising it. They may have struggled for food from time to time, but squatting in the Upper level made life far easier than if they'd been anywhere else. Now roughly a month had passed and she was involved with magic, insurgent groups who were fighting to dethrone a king and now she was stowed away on a complete stranger's boat as they all tried to escape the city she had grown up in all her life. She found it funny, and at the same time entirely terrifying.

The boat rocked towards its destination. She couldn't hear much from below deck, but the steady sound of sea birds and gentle waves bounding against the hull were beginning to cause nausea in the pit of her stomach.

"I don't feel well," she whispered to Jocelyn as the boat continued to rock along the river. She'd never been in a boat before, and she'd certainly never expected it to cause her stomach to flip and twist like a travelling circus performer.

"It will pass, little one. Most people feel ill their first time on the water."

Jocelyn smiled down at Lyvanne. It was an infectious smile, and after glancing between both of her newfound friends, Turiel too was hiding a smirk of his own; a rare sight, Lyvanne had never seen him so tense and quiet as he had been on the journey to the quay.

Time began to meld into a blur. Having never travelled by boat before Lyvanne wasn't sure what to make of their speed, but with each passing minute a palpable tension began to form in the air.

"How long until we make it to the checks?" Jocelyn asked as they swayed side to side in their closet.

Turiel glanced across at her. "Not long."

He wasn't wrong, a few minutes of holding her hands tight across her churning stomach and Lyvanne felt the tug of ropes slowing the boat to a standstill, and voices beaming out towards Trystan, who in turn bellowed back.

"Keep quiet," Turiel whispered, raising one hand to his lips and using the other to make sure the door was properly locked.

The obvious sound of footsteps echoed down from the deck. There were quite a number of people on board now, and Lyvanne was starting to get a curious sense of deja vu after having to hide under the floorboards of Sinjin's house not too long ago.

Voices and footsteps came down the stairs leading up to the deck. The trio all looked at each other as if to say it would be alright. On deck an inspector was audibly checking all of Trystan's goods, and Lyvanne could have sworn she heard them stealing and eating one of the apples she'd seen stored beneath the stairs.

Scoundrel, she thought to herself.

Then the moment came, the inspector walked towards the door. It was after all his job to not just make sure all the cargo was correct, but that there was no smuggling taking place either. He placed one hand on the doorknob but it wouldn't budge. He tried again, nothing. Turiel's hand reached over and rested on her shoulder. He was preparing to cast a spell, she knew, but by the Goddess' fortune the moment never arrived. As the inspector was about to make his third attempt at the door, and the one that would probably cause him to raise some alarm among his peers, a chorus of laughter came from on deck. Lyvanne could make out the deep belly laugh of Trystan, and she figured that the rest was coming from the City Watch who had boarded the boat to inspect the cargo. The laughter bought the attention of the inspector, and he turned, leaving his work unfinished. Turiel and Jocelyn let out a collective sigh of relief, whilst Lyvanne closed her eyes and brought forward memories of simpler times as she felt her heart beating furiously in her chest. The boat began to rock again, they had been let through the Water Gate, and sure enough Trystan appeared moments later to let them out of the closet.

"Told you my boy! Trystan'll keep you safe!" he bellowed as he swung the door open dramatically.

The four of them made their way back above deck after Trystan assured them that they were far enough away from the city's external wall for it to be safe.

"How did you manage it?" Turiel asked, his expression visibly more relaxed than when he had been in the city.

"Cost me a good whiskey! Opened it up to soften 'em up to me"

The merchant had kept his word and they were safe Lyvanne thought as she looked back over the stern of the boat and for the first time in her life saw the dominating walls of Astreya from the outside.

CHAPTER 12

What Lyvanne saw outside Astreya amazed her. She knew, through Abella, that there were millions of people living throughout The Rive, and even more if you counted the lands outside of the king's Empire, but to her untrained eyes it appeared as though every single one of those people were either entering or leaving the capital city. To the right of the riverbanks, some few hundred yards away, was the main gate into Astreya. From the boat alone the area outside of the large steel gateway was completely filled with people, some camped out in small makeshift huts, others sleeping rough and even more pleading with the guards to let them in.

"How long has it been like this?" Jocelyn asked Trystan as the four of them stood at the side of the deck, watching as people climbed over one another to try and make room along the giant walkway which lead to the city gate.

"Been bad since the king shut the gates. First time I've 'bin out personally, but word among circles is that this is the best it's been, thousands gave up weeks ago. Gone back to whatever hole in the ground they came from," Trystan replied, waving an arm through the air nonchalantly.

The remark earned him a sneer from Jocelyn before she turned to face Lyvanne. "These people come to the city because their lives have been ruined elsewhere. Some people travel across the sea to get here because their homes have been destroyed, sometimes by war, sometimes through disease. Others may have just wanted to make a life for themselves in the capital, but I would put money on those being the ones who left when the king first shut the gates."

Lyvanne wondered what the lands had been like where they came from, what horrors they had seen that drove them away from their homes and towards this city of all places.

"Is there nowhere else for them to go?" she asked.

"Yes, but I doubt the situation in those places is much better. The more you travel little one the more you will learn that we are too many in number. The rich hide away behind their big walls, and fancy houses, but the poor are left to suffer, treading on one another for the last scrap of food."

Lyvanne's eyes wandered from the horde of people trying to enter the city and to the lands that surrounded them. She realised that this was the first time she was seeing what lay beyond the walls that had encapsulated her throughout her entire life. It wasn't what she had expected, the land was well trod and people threw up dust everywhere they went. It wasn't dead, as of yet, but the sun had baked over it for so long that any grass had withered and turned brown, leaving little in the way of beauty.

Turiel was watching her. "It's not all like that, don't worry."

His words were reassuring but Lyvanne, as was second nature to her now, was sceptical. As the Colossal, Trystan's boat that did anything but live up to the name, made its way down the cool and calm waters of the Anya, Lyvanne began to examine the various vessels that they passed. More than a few times she spotted others merchants, travelling to far off places to trade their goods. Some of the ships they passed were symbols of luxury. Overly sized personal ships that the rich used to host parties and gatherings of a less than savoury nature. There were military ships too, those she saw more often than the rest. Some were heading in the direction of Astreya, filled with men who appeared tired of life entirely. Their armour muddied and broken and their faces often scarred or as bloodied as their armour. More than a few times Lyvanne had to stop herself from heaving as she saw men with slings holding up stumps where their arms should be, or crutches holding them tall where their legs had been taken away. The other ships were heading away from Astreya, their large masts sailing them down the river faster than the Colossal could ever dream of. The soldiers aboard those looked eager, driven even to be heading off to war, but even they weren't immune to the sights of their comrades returning from the front lines.

Realising that the information that Abella had passed down to her was likely out-dated, and having never paid much attention to the biased words of the king's criers, Lyvanne moved towards Jocelyn who had taken up a seat on the deck of the ship near the bow and asked her for as much information as she knew about the king's current wars.

"How much time do you have?" She replied jokingly. "The king is greedy in every sense of the word. His uses the wealth of the nobles to fund his bloodlust and in return he offers them sanctuary from the starving masses. That I know of we are at war with currently two other kingdoms -

"Three," Turiel said from further down the boat as he slowly made his way over to join them.

"Three?" Jocelyn asked, evidently unaware of the latest addition.

"Three," Turiel confirmed. "About two weeks ago, the Mountain tribes of the South caught wind of Astreya being on lockdown. They took it as a sign of weakness from the king and declared independence."

Jocelyn looked at him quizzically, not believing that this news had passed her by. Lyvanne listened intently to the conversation. She knew that the others had been trying to shield her from the larger problems in The Rive ever since she met them, but she was determined to get the information out of them regardless. Astreya had been her entire world for as long as she could remember, but that world just grew infinitely and she wanted to know what was waiting for her.

"Don't worry, it hasn't reached the criers yet, but you can count on my word," he said as he took a seat by their side, "Wouldn't worry too much. The Mountain tribes won't be allowed any semblance of independence for long, and they don't have the military power to maintain it either. Probably just hoping they can negotiate some better terms out the end of it."

"And the other two?" Lyvanne enquired, her interest piqued. "Who else are we at war with?"

"The Kingdom of Middin, an island chain far off the western shore of The Rive. They've been at war with the king for pushing three years now, but I dare say it's not really much of a war anymore. The Kingdom used to consist of many islands, but the king has claimed all but the one that remains."

Turiel nodded his head in agreement. "Most are aware that the king could have finished it by now, but he's waiting. He wants their total surrender, he wants that justification, but the Queen of Middin is stubborn, and I doubt she will budge easily."

"But those soldiers you saw returning to Astreya, I would put money on those to be returning from the front lines of Tyberia," Jocelyn added.

Now that was a name Lyvanne recognised, Abella had told her about the strained relationships with the Northern continent of Tyberia on numerous occasions.

"Relationships with the Tyberians have always been tense, but the two kingdoms have been in open war for the past half-decade. The losses to both sides have been overwhelming at times, but the king has nothing to show for it. No matter how hard he pushes his men, no matter how many warlocks he throws at the front lines, he has not once claimed any significant land there."

"Why?" Lyvanne asked, her eyes growing larger, this was the stuff that interested her, hearing tales of far off countries, of landscapes completely different to the one she knew. This was where she found her enjoyment.

"If you want the real answer you'll have to find a place on the king's royal council," Turiel joked. "We know little more than rumour and whispers."

Lyvanne felt somewhat deflated. "Can I hear the rumours at least?" she asked. Lyvanne watched as Jocelyn shared a look with Turiel and smiled.

"I suppose sharing some rumours wouldn't hurt any of us," Jocelyn said as she nudged up closer to Lyvanne. "Besides, if I've guessed where we're going correctly then we have enough time to talk things through."

Lyvanne noticed that her last comment was made with a sly grin and knowing look in the direction of Turiel, who in turn scowled.

"I heard a bard sing one time about how the land of Tyberia is, for the most part, covered in snow," Jocelyn said as Lyvanne's eyes lit up again. "Their winters are longer than ours and more intense, making it difficult for the inkg's men to maintain a foothold for long"

"How do people live there?"

"That I don't know, little one."

Lyvanne leaned back against the railing of the deck and sighed with happiness. She wasn't aware of when it had happened but she had grown fond of Turiel and Jocelyn calling her "little one," and it was refreshing to hear new stories that Abella had never told her before. It set her mind racing, how much more was there out in this world beyond Astreya's walls that she was yet to learn about? And importantly, it took her mind off everything that was happening in Astreya.

Turiel stood again, "I'm going to get some rest, I suggest you two do as well at some point, we won't arrive for another couple of days, no point baking in the sun above deck all day."

The two smiled and waved as he wandered off in search of somewhere to rest his head below deck. Jocelyn followed along shortly after, but Lyvanne opted to stay above deck, saying that she would sleep once night fell. Until then, she sat staring out at the lands beyond the river. She watched as arid and desolate dry lands turned in luscious and vibrant countryside, her jaw agape for nearly the entire time. They passed all manner of creature, some herded in fences, farmed for their meat and milk, others roaming the wilds, free from Human or Hemeti interference. Some of the animals she was familiar with: cows, chickens and horses she had seen within Astreya, whether at a market or towing along the carriages that transported the rich. Others she was less familiar with, only having a passing knowledge of them from the stories that Abella used to tell her. At times Trystan would come over to keep her company and she would ask him to test her as she named the various animals they passed by.

"You'll learn, kid," Trystan would say as he laughed at her third incorrect guess at naming a gaggle of geese that were sunbathing by the banks of the river.

As day drew into night the countryside grew denser. The trees edged closer to the river and as they began to tower higher into the sky, the animals Lyvanne saw although less frequent, became more exotic. By now the sun had long been hidden behind the encroaching trees, with only thin veils of light breaking through the canopy but she didn't care, nor did she plan to rest anytime soon, despite her frequent yawning.

One creature in particular caught her attention. It was larger than anything she had seen before, grey in colour and walked on all fours. Trystan told her that it only ate the plants and trees of the jungle and that it wouldn't harm them. Before adding that their tusks were a valuable commodity among merchants. Lyvanne for one couldn't imagine anyone wanting to harm such a beautiful animal and she found herself waving as the boat slowly drifted by and off down the Anya, leaving the animal to bathe in the shallows.

Despite her reluctance tiredness eventually took hold. Lyvanne was still too stubborn to fall asleep below deck though where she might miss something, so instead Trystan offered her a pair of blankets which she could use to rest her head on, and before long she fell asleep on deck. But not before warning the boat's captain that he was to wake her if he saw anything interesting.

• • •

Jocelyn tossed and turned on a small wooden bed and thin mattress that had been set up at the aft of the ship. She knew that she should try and get some sleep, but her mind couldn't relax. There were too many questions she had, too many plans that she was being left out of. At first she had let it slide. Sinjn and Turiel had always played a bigger role in The Spring than she had and she was fine with that, but to still not know for certain where they were going itched away at her like a bad rash.

Rolling out of bed and taking a second to steady her feet against the gentle rocking of the boat as it made its way slowly down the river, she pulled herself up and set off to find Turiel. Out of courtesy, they'd refused to use Trystan's bed, which meant there had only been the one spare. She'd smiled when she came below deck to find that Turiel had left the bed for her or Lyvanne to use, but lying against a sack of potatoes she doubted that Turiel was having any better luck sleeping that she was.

"Turiel?" she whispered as she entered the main cargo hold. "Are you awake?"

A ruffling from among the sack of potatoes gave away his answer. "Jocelyn? You should be resting," Turiel replied, unflatteringly stumbling up to his feet. "Everything okay?"

She considered lying, trusting that he knew what he was doing and going back to sleep. "Not really."

"What is it?" he asked groggily, wiping away sleep from his eyes.

Jocelyn walked over to him. Everything had always been a various shade of awkward between them, if The Spring wasn't a thing she often wondered how differently their lives would be, how different they would be together. "Are we going to meet up with The Spring?" she asked, not wanting to beat around the bush at this hour.

"Yes," Turiel replied flatly. "Why?"

It was the answer she had been expecting, but her heart sank slightly regardless. She had never mentioned it to Turiel, but she had been hoping that the three of them could escape together alone, that Turiel had found a quiet village where they could live together away from the watch of the king. "Is that really what's best for her right now?"

"What do you mean?"

"She's a child, should we really be throwing her into all this already?"

Turiel seemed conflicted; all Jocelyn could do was hope that he saw her way of thinking. "She may be a child, but you know how important she is to our future, everyone's future."

Hemeti didn't believe in an Angel of Destiny, she wasn't sure what validity there was to Turiel's vision, or if he'd really ever had one. But she trusted him as a person, and wanted to believe what he said.

"But still... she's still a child, don't forget that okay? Let her live a little before it's too late," Jocelyn said. She let the words settle for a brief moment before raising her hand up to his elbow. "You can trust me with anything, you know that right?"

Turiel smiled and nodded, "I know."

"Good, next time let me know where we're going then... enjoy your potato sacks," she said, deciding that any lingering questions could wait until they'd reached their destination, in the hope that Turiel would naturally divulge more once they were there.

She woke early the next day, the sun rising in the distance over a hilly meadow. The thick jungle was long behind them Trystan said and Lyvanne wasn't sure if he'd slept at all. Turiel and Jocelyn soon rose as well and after sharing some of Trystan's cargo among themselves to break their fast, they began to watch the horizon with Lyvanne, teaching her about the different farms and crops as they passed by. There were small idyllic villages, some larger than others, some more obviously densely populated.

"Life doesn't seem so bad out here," Lyvanne commented as they passed by one particularly beautiful village, where the occupants were out at work in the fields and some were even washing clothes in the Anya, a mere few metres away.

"This is only one part of the story," Turiel replied. "You might see a village like this and think they have a perfect life, but you don't see the hunger in their stomachs, you don't see the overcrowded houses or the refugees who wander here looking for a new home. You don't see the predator who eats the livestock at night. Try not to forget all that, like the king has."

Lyvanne nodded. She started to realise how much she had learnt in such a short time. She felt like a completely different person to the one who had spent her days scavenging for food in the Upper level of Astreya.

"You never told me, were you both born in Astreya or did you move there?" Lyvanne asked, turning between Jocelyn and Turiel.

Jocelyn answered first. "I moved there, my parents bought the house you stayed in when Sinjin and I were only very young, but originally we came from a small village to the north of Avagarde. My father worked as a smith and my mother a teacher," Jocelyn was proud of her parents, her eyes gleamed as she recalled their memory. Lyvanne didn't want to ruin the moment by asking what had happened to them, so instead she turned towards Turiel.

"I was fortunate enough to be born there," he dutifully answered "My father had already enlisted with the king when he had me, I spent the first handful of years growing up in the king's castle, a real honour," he twisted the last word with sarcasm. "After that... well, you know the rest."

"You turned out alright for a man of the king," Jocelyn said playfully to some laughter. Lyvanne watched the pair share a smile.

Cute, she thought simply.

The rest of the day went slowly, Lyvanne kept watch of the surrounding countryside, but even she had to admit that after a few hours of seeing nothing but grassy hills and wheat fields, it began to feel all too similar. Before long, the sunset behind the horizon and Lyvanne decided that it was time she got some proper rest. Following Jocelyn and Turiel below deck she found what would have to pass as comfy flooring and settled down for the night.

She didn't wake again until she heard Trystan bellowing from from above deck, "Destination in sight!"

CHAPTER 13

S ure enough, as the trio woke themselves up and made their way above deck, Turiel let out a spry smile as they beheld a small quay off in the distance. The surrounding areas seemed like nothing special to Lyvanne as she tried to figure out where their end destination was. The quay itself was too small for more than one boat, and it wasn't well constructed like the ones in Astreya, so it couldn't be a heavily populated area. Similarly there were no visible roads or dirt tracks that could signal a nearby town or city. It was just as much countryside as the past day's journey had provided.

"This the place?" Jocelyn asked Turiel for confirmation.

"This is the place," Turiel replied as he went below deck to gather the few belongings he had brought along for the journey. A few minutes later and the Colossal had been docked alongside the small quay. Trystan helped each of them off the boat before bringing up from below deck a small satchel of food that he had prepared for their departure.

"You're too kind," Jocelyn said as she accepted the parting gift. Despite her initial doubts, Trystan had delivered them safely out of Astreya, and Lyvanne could see her friend's recognition of that.

"My honour, mi lady. Be sure to say 'ello to t'others for me," Trystan continued as he turned to Turiel ,"has been too long."

"I will," Turiel said as he moved forward and shook the merchant's hand farewell.

"And to you kiddo," Trystan said as he turned his attention last to Lyvanne "T'was a joy to watch you experience this world for the first time, glad I was around to see it."

Lyvanne blushed, gave the giant man a hug as well as the length of her arms would allow and stepped away from the boat. "Good luck on your journey, Trystan," she called out as the merchant began to untie the Colossal.

He waved his thanks and moments later he was off down the Anya, seeking destinations so far away that Lyvanne struggled to comprehend it. A part of her, although she wouldn't admit it to the others, wanted to go with him.

"How did Trystan become involved with The Spring?" Lyvanne asked as they gathered up their things and began to set off into the countryside.

Turiel smiled. "I do believe that's the first time you've used our name."

Jocelyn jokingly punched him in the arm. "Stop being self-proud and answer her question."

"Alright, alright. He was a friend of my father's back before he was captured, drinking friends by all accounts. It was a complicated relationship given the vast difference in social standing between the two, but it was there. When my father vanished, Trystan presumed my family to be all dead. When he discovered I was alive and well, and I explained to him what had happened, he was quick to change sides. Never openly acknowledging his association with The Spring, but always helping where he can."

Jocelyn grimaced. "You don't trust him still?"

"Find it hard to trust a man who changes allegiances so easily," she replied.

"He did it for my father," Turiel reminded her.

"I know... I hope you're right."

Lyvanne wished she hadn't pressed; it was obviously a sore issue between the two and was likely why Turiel hadn't shared the plan for escape, even with Jocelyn. The sun was high in the sky by the time the three made any significant traction into the grassy meadow before them. It was hot, but noticeably cooler than it had always been at Astreya. Lyvanne would take that small mercy she thought as they trudged through long grass and overgrown meadows, making it difficult to make any decent time on their travels.

"Who were the others that Trystan mentioned?" Lyvanne asked, too bored to keep silent anymore as she fought off small flying insects that had followed them since the river.

"You'll find out soon enough, little one," Turiel replied in his ever mysterious way.

"How soon is soon enough? Because it feels and looks like we could be walking forever before we find any signs of civilisation."

Jocelyn chuckled and Turiel tried to hide the fact that he wanted to do the same. "You see that tree line?" he said, pointing off into the horizon where the meadows gave way for a small woodland area.

"Yeah."

"Our destination is in the heart of that wood. No doubt we'll be met at the edge though, we're expected."

Lyvanne nodded and with a newfound determination pushed on, striding ahead of both Jocelyn and Turiel, although the speed didn't last for long. The trio stopped shortly after for food and some rest. Sitting in a small clearing to the side of a meadow, they shared a loaf of bread and some salted foreign meats that Trystan had gifted them. Conversation had been infrequent since they left the boat, and everyone seemed eager to just make it to the woods. The rest, however, afforded Jocelyn the chance to do some prying of her own.

"You know all there is to know about us, little one, but you've never really told us about where you came from," she inquired, as she nudged some more bread in Lyvanne's direction.

Truth be told, she didn't really know much about where she had come from, she had been a street urchin for about as long as she could remember.

"I really don't know. I have a small memory of my mum, she seemed nice, but I don't know what happened to her and I don't know how old I was in the memory." Lyvanne chewed on some food as she strained to make some memories appear. "I guess I was born in Astreya, but Abella's house was the closest thing to a home I knew."

"Did you live there alone?" Jocelyn asked and Lyvanne suddenly realised that through all the talk of magic, insurgencies and escaping the city she had never really sat down and told Jocelyn about herself.

"No," Lyvanne said, shaking her head ."A lot of orphans came and went, but towards the end it was Abella, me ,and two others, Oh and Lira."

A sadness overtook her as she talked about them. She missed them more than she cared to admit and rarely a day went by that she didn't worry about them. Her mind also drifted even further back, to the orphans she had known years ago, who had left to make their own lives, Merry, Took and Issy to name a few. She wondered where they were now.

"You must miss them?" Jocelyn asked, as Lyvanne started to fight back tears.

"Yeah." The one word was about all Lyvanne could manage without crying.

"We'll go back for them one day," Jocelyn said.

"Promise," Turiel chimed in. The words meant the world to Lyvanne. She'd always planned on going back for them, to find them and free them from Astreya's grip, but knowing she had people who would help her do it gave her a hope she'd never had before.

After the meal, the three appeared more refreshed than they had done in a long time. Turiel was back to his jovial spirits of old, and Jocelyn was frequently joking at his expense. Lyvanne figured that he liked having the attention from her. As they grew closer to the woods the sun slowly began to make its descent down from the sky. In its place Lyvanne found the most dazzlingly and beautiful array of stars, reminding her of her hideout on the banks of the Anya back in the Upper level of Astreya. She found solace in that moment and everything felt right.

She became less optimistic as the stars slowly became shrouded by cloud. The moon vanished behind a dark behemoth in the sky, and no sooner had she been admiring the beauty of the night sky than had she begun to feel the first drops of rain falling from above.

"Rain's more common this far south," Turiel warned as he drew his hood up over his head, his red travelling cloak becoming spotted as the falling water found its mark.

"Last one to the trees has to buy drinks the next time we find civilisation," Jocelyn said jovially as she sprinted ahead of the others, hood drawn and doing her best to beat the rain.

Turiel and Lyvanne both laughed but quickly followed suit. Lyvanne didn't want to admit that she was far too tired to be running anywhere at this point, but she was having fun and that made a lot of difference. The tree line grew ever closer, they were only a few hundred feet away when Lyvanne made out the first signs of life. Small fires flickering along the edge of the wood. Jocelyn had slowed to a walk, easily beating the other two who eventually fell in behind her.

"They're here," Turiel said as he took the lead and walked towards the fires, his voice muzzled by the patter of rain on their clothes and the grass surrounding them.

As they walked closer, Lyvanne began to make out the faint outlines of people under what she now considered to be torches lining the woodland edge. *Ten, no twenty*, she thought as she tried in vain to count their numbers through the rain.

"Who are they?" She asked to either of her companions who would listen.

"The Spring," Jocelyn replied.

CHAPTER 14

Turiel was the first to enter the line of trees. Three men with drawn swords immediately swarmed him, their eyes trained on his every move.

"Why are they threatened?" Lyvanne asked Jocelyn as they hung back just beyond the edge of the wood awaiting Turiel's signal to join him.

"It's part of the life they've chosen. They have to be constantly aware, constantly on edge. Many of them will have never met Turiel, just like I have never met any of them."

"How are you on the same team if you've never met?" Lyvanne quizzed, the intricacies of the situation escaping her.

"It's not as simple as saying we're on the same team, little one," Jocelyn replied, putting an arm around Lyvanne's shoulder and drawing her in close "We fight for the same cause, but as a whole, we lack the funds or organisation to stay in constant communication, let alone to meet face to face. Turiel will have had to pull in quite a few favours to get this particular branch to let us stay."

Lyvanne was trying her best to understand, but it all felt very foreign to her. This was a world apart from the life she had believed she would lead. The two watched as Turiel spoke with various members of The Spring, before at last one put his arms around Turiel like a brother and the two began laughing together.

"Looks like we're all good," Jocelyn said, the green skin around her eyes loosening with relief.

Turiel motioned for them to come forward. Lyvanne had been right, there were at least twenty people stood just behind the tree line, all of them armed. Immediately she noticed a mix of races; there were three Hemeti, green of face the same as Jocelyn, five Islanders whose dark skin reminded her of Oh and the rest were similar to her, residents of The Rive.

"Jocelyn, Lyvanne let me introduce you," Turiel said as they entered into the wood, the leaves of the trees somewhat shielding the gathering of people against the rain "This is Kwah."

Turiel held his arm out towards the man who he had embraced. He was one of the Islanders, his skin darker than Oh's and he towered over even Turiel who Lyvanne had thought to be tall. He was clothed in a basic brown gambeson, leather boots, and a hooded cloak for protection against the weather.

"It's a pleasure to meet you both," Kwah said, making sure he welcomed each individually. "As fellow members of The Spring you are welcome among my band of brothers."

Lyvanne wanted to tell him that she wasn't a part of their insurgency, that she was here to be with her friends rather than any great cause, but thought better of it when she felt Jocelyn gently squeeze her shoulder. Instead, she nodded and thanked him for the welcome, before turning to as many of the others present as she could and thanking them too.

"How do you know Kwah?" Jocelyn asked Turiel as the company made their way further into the shadowy cloak of the woods, the only illumination coming from the torches carried by a handful of men surrounding them.

"A couple of years ago when I journeyed The Rive in search of allies, Kwah saved me from a slaver ship just off the coast of the Shimmering Isles. I haven't seen him much since then, but he's been working for our cause ever since. I owe him two favours now," Turiel replied, occasionally batting away a rogue branch before it could rake at his eyes.

Lyvanne found herself surprised. She struggled to believe that there was anything this pair didn't know about each other, but more than that, she was surprised at how active in this organisation Turiel was for his age. To journey The Rive at such a young age would have been daunting for the bravest of men.

"You didn't tell me you were nearly caught by slavers," Jocelyn scolded him.

"I figured it best to leave out. You were so happy to see me return after all."

Jocelyn grinned but tried her best to hide it beneath a scowl. "Next time you tell me, buffoon," She turned to Lyvanne who was walking on her other side. "Never let men get close, they are stupid in many ways."

The comment drew more than a few laughs, even from nearby members of The Spring who had overheard the conversation. Hearing the laughter Kwah slowed his pace and backtracked to walk with the trio of newcomers.

"Turiel has told me a lot about both of you," he said gesturing at Lyvanne and Jocelyn.

"I am saddened to say that I cannot say the same about yourself Kwah," Jocelyn replied.

"I cannot say that I am surprised. Turiel was always ashamed that without my aid he would currently be watering the plants of some far off foreigner's garden, praying that the lashes were only minimal today."

Turiel scoffed, "I would have made my own way off that ship eventually."

"Yes, the chains seemed very flimsy," Kwah joked.

The company travelled deeper and further into the wood than Lyvanne imagined they would have. The faint rays of moonlight that had been trying to break through the clouds were now entirely hidden above the canopy of trees. But through the trunks of the trees, there was light.

"We're here," Kwah said as they made their way into what turned about to be somewhat of a clearing within the wood. The company were greeted by a sizeable grouping of people. Between forty and fifty additional insurgents were spread out among the clearing. Tents and makeshift huts had been constructed throughout, enough to house most if not all of the party. There were a number of fire pits, some with food still being roasted above, others encircled by people trying to keep warm. Lyvanne noticed that the rain had stopped; a manmade canopy had been constructed high in the trees, siphoning and collecting the rain water in a series of wooden troughs around the edges of the camp.

"Clever," she said as she stood in amazement.

"Thank you," Kwah responded from a few feet away. "The woods are good for protection, and the animals are just about enough to keep us fed, but the nearest stream is half a day's walk from here. Not very practical for people who are trying to stay hidden."

"Come, I'll show you to your hut," one of the men said, he was of a similar height to Turiel, but where Turiel's skin was a sparkling white, this man's was more similar to her own. He led the three of them through the camp. As they passed one of the fire pits the smell of roasting rabbit sent her stomach growling. She'd had more food over the past few weeks than she could have ever dreamed of having back at Abella's, let alone during her time in the sewers, and she was starting to think that her belly was growing greedy because of it.

Their hut was far from special. A conglomerate of branches, leaves and rope, but it would do Lyvanne thought as she stepped through a small fabric doorway and saw ample room for the three of them. Claiming a small sleeping area furthest away from the entrance ,she immediately dumped her sack of belongings, took out the small toy soldier that Oh had given to her and placed it where her head would be when she slept. Soon after Kwah appeared at the entrance to their new home.

"Turiel, it's time we spoke my friend," Turiel nodded, said his goodbyes to the others and made his way to follow Kwah.

"Come on," Jocelyn said to Lyvanne, "Let's go get some food!"

"Don't you need to be at those talks too?"

The question surprised Jocelyn, and appeared to give her some food for thought. "Soon. Our allies are slow to trust newcomers, but Turiel will introduce me over time. He might even involve you if that's the path you choose." She knew that the comment would draw a weary look from Lyvanne, but she laughed all the same. "Let's eat."

Making their way back out into the encampment Lyvanne was surprised to find that she had either not noticed before, or had given it no thought, that there were as many women in their ranks as there were men. Women from The Rive, Shimmering Islands and Hemeti all the same.

"Do they fight too?" she asked.

Jocelyn looked on proudly at the women around them, most of whom were armed, and those who weren't seemed capable of taking on any man in hand to hand combat if the situation called for it.

"They do. If you believe in the cause and you have something to offer then you can join The Spring. Some women choose not to fight, to help in other ways; at Avagarde, I met a woman from the Shimmering Isles who is one of the best medics I've ever seen."

Lyvanne smiled, she had not seen or even heard of such a fighting force before.

They took a seat around a fire pit with four other members of The Spring.

"So, you're the new blood Kwah's been going on about?" one woman said as she offered out a hand to Jocelyn. "The more the merrier, going to need a lot of bodies for what's to come."

Lyvanne watched the creases form in Jocelyn's forehead. For now they held their tongues, but she knew that Turiel would be asked a series of questions later. Instead, they said their pleasantries and moved off to a quieter area of the camp to eat the cooked rabbit and boiled vegetables.

"What do you think she meant by what's to come?" Lyvanne asked Jocelyn when they were alone.

"Not sure yet, little one. We can ask Turiel when he comes back."

Lyvanne nodded and went back to her food. "Do you think we'll be safe here?"

"Yes, at least for the time being. I don't know an awful lot about these people, but I do know that they've been out here for a couple of years now and they've faced minimal resistance from the king. The important thing is that we keep you out of his reach until you're strong enough to stay hidden without us, and then you can do as you please."

"Will Turiel really let me leave?" Lyvanne asked, the question burning in the back of her mind to stay quiet for any longer. She had been worrying about how much stock Turiel was placing in his vision. If he really saw her as some kind of saviour then why would he let her just walk out of camp?

Jocelyn put down her food and stared at her friend "Of course, he will. Turiel often finds himself caught up in the vision the Angel gifted him; he forgets that people still need to lead their own lives. But he's a good man and if when the time comes you decide that this isn't what you want from life, then he will accept that... and if he doesn't then I'll make him."

The two laughed together quietly, neither liked the attention and they were already drawing enough eyes as people walked by. As it turned out they didn't get the chance to speak to Turiel. They weren't sure where he had gone, but Turiel didn't return to their hut until late into the night, by which point both Lyvanne and Jocelyn had already bedded down to sleep.

Lyvanne fell asleep surprisingly easily given the constant commotion of people in the camp, and the pattering of rain on the canopy above. But once she did sleep her dreams swiftly turned into nightmares. She dreamt about her vision, that rather than being sat around a table at the centre of the room she was instead on her knees before the throne, upon which was sat a faceless king. To her right was Turiel, motionless and devoid of life on the cold stone floor. To her left Jocelyn, hands bound and mouth gagged. She looked up at the king defiantly before an unseen man brandishing the largest sword Lyvanne had ever seen brought it swinging down and through her friend's body. She was then snapped into another dream, where she found herself wandering around the camp. The huts were on fire and there were bodies all around her.

"Help!" she cried out into the darkness of the night, but no one replied. She ran to the hut where she had been sleeping, but that too was on fire. "Help!" she cried out again.

Movement to her left. Turiel stumbled out of the woods, she ran over to him but she was too late, he fell at her feet, two arrows embedded into his back. In the distance she could hear the clang of steel on steel. Running in the direction it came from she found Jocelyn, two swords in hand duelling with the same creature that had cut her down in the dream before. It was a goliath of a person, a good two heads taller than Jocelyn and bearing down on her quickly with their monstrous sword.

"Run!" Lyvanne screamed at Jocelyn, but her words had not been heard. The two continued to duel and Lyvanne wanted to run to her friend to try all she could to help, but her feet wouldn't move. Then it came, the giant knocked Jocelyn's swords from her hands and in one fell sweep, he sliced at her throat.

Lyvanne sprung awake, panting and sweating the way she had the day she'd had her vision. She checked around her, Turiel and Jocelyn were both there, sleeping and safe.

"It was only a dream," she whispered to herself, before lying back into her sleeping area, damp from the sweat. She grabbed Oh's toy soldier and held it close, the sight of her friends being killed replaying over and over again in her head as she slowly drifted back into a deep sleep.

CHAPTER 15

Lyvanne woke up late the next morning. Jocelyn and Turiel had already left the hut by the time she woke, and the sun was beaming down into the camp site. After changing into some fresh clothes packed away into her sack, Lyvanne left the hut and sought out her friends. All the time she searched for them, she contemplated whether or not to tell them about the dreams. The images of Turiel lying dead at her feet, and of Jocelyn being slain twice by the behemoth were still burning into her mind.

"Morning Lyvanne," a voice called out from across the camp. It was Kwah, and with no need for a hood under the morning sun, Lyvanne realised that he was bald. A common fashion among Islanders she had been told, but a rare sight back in the Upper level of Astreya.

"Good morning," she replied, doing her best to shield the sun beaming through the trees from her eyes as she stared up at him.

"Your friends went for a walk, that way," he said as he pointed off into the woods.

"Thank you."

"Would you like some food before you follow?"

Lyvanne was unsure. She didn't yet feel entirely comfortable around these people, but that wasn't going to change if she kept clinging to Turiel and Jocelyn.

"Sure," she replied before following the Islander over to a large cauldron situated near the centre of the camp.

"It's not much," Kwah said as he poured a ladle of what looked like a vegetable broth into a small bowl and handed it over to her, "but it's warm."

Kwah was right it wasn't much. The broth had virtually no taste, and lacked the meat that would make it a satisfying dish.

"I promise to find more rabbit for your dinner," he said, nudging her with a fist and taking a seat down in front of her.

"Thank you, it's good," she lied.

"So, I presume that Turiel has explained why he has such interest in you?" Kwah asked nonchalantly.

Lyvanne was taken aback and her face immediately flushed red. She hadn't realised that Turiel had told anyone outside of Jocelyn and Sinjin about her role in his vision, but now that she gave thought to it, it made sense in helping convince The Spring to take them in.

"Yeah, he mentioned it."

Kwah could hear the trepidation in her voice, "Don't worry, we don't all feel the need to put such pressure on the shoulders of a young child the way Turiel does."

"Hey!" she shouted playfully, "I'm fourteen you know? I can make decisions for myself."

Kwah raised a hand up in innocence. "Forgive me, Lyvanne."

The pair laughed together. Lyvanne toyed with the idea of telling Kwah about her own vision, he seemed nice enough after all, but before she had the chance she spotted Jocelyn making her way back through the tree line and into the camp. She was walking with pace, without Turiel and headed straight for their hut.

"Excuse me," Lyvanne said, finishing another mouthful of her food and chasing after Jocelyn.

Lyvanne found Jocelyn in their hut, knelt over her sleeping area packing up her belongings. Her face was flushed with a tinge of red and her eyes were puffy. It didn't take much for Lyvanne to work out that she'd had an argument with Turiel.

"What are you doing?" she asked, her voice shaking.

"Lyvanne… I just need some time to myself. I'll be back soon, okay?" Jocelyn replied as she carried on packing her few belongings into a satchel.

"What did Turiel say? What did he do?"

"Nothing to concern you, little one." As she finished packing, she turned to Lyvanne and brought her down onto her knees before squeezing her arms tight around her.

"I can come with you?" Lyvanne pleaded, not needing to know what was wrong, only wanting to be there for her friend.

"Not this time. You need to stay here where it's safe."

"I would be safe with you."

Jocelyn shook her head, "Turiel's spell can't protect you from the king's warlocks if you're too far away."

"I'm nearly strong enough though. Turiel tells me that soon I'll be able to remove his spell and keep them out on my own."

The comment wasn't entirely a lie. Turiel had told her that she was getting stronger, but he had yet to insinuate exactly when she would be ready which as she came to think of it led Lyvanne to believe that he may just be delaying the inevitable.

"I won't be long. Just stay close to Turiel and try and make some new friends. These people seem nice." Lyvanne nodded. Whilst she enjoyed no longer being the responsible person of a group, she was beginning to feel as though no one saw past her age and that if the time came she wouldn't be relied upon to do anything that could help her friends.

With that Jocelyn departed. She didn't say where she was going, and Turiel wasn't yet around for her to ask. At first Lyvanne didn't leave the hut, she didn't understand what was going on and she wasn't even sure if she wanted to. She obsessed over whether she should have told Jocelyn about the dream, about whether that would have made her stay, but it was too little too late. Sometime later Lyvanne emerged from the hut. The camp was busy, everywhere she looked there were people going about some kind of work, whether it was collecting water from the troughs, preparing food for later in the day, patrolling the perimeter or sharpening a large pile of weapons. For a group of people who lived in little makeshift huts in the middle of the wood she found them all to be quite charming. They clearly co-existed well and everyone seemed happy enough with their manmade home out in the wilds. It made her smile trying to picture the people from Astreya's Upper level trying to live in such conditions. She wasn't sure that any of them would last longer than a single day.

Her eye was drawn to one particular sheltered area of the camp. It was a wooden structure, slightly larger than the huts everyone used to sleep in. The structure was open on one side, and on the inside Kwah, Turiel and a few others stood around a circular wooden table. She was too far away from the table to discern exactly what they were all looking at or talking about, but she could make out various sheets of parchment, and what appeared to be wooden figures similar to the toy soldiers Oh had used to play with back in Astreya. Reluctance held her back at first, but Jocelyn had left for a reason and she wanted Turiel to tell her why. Straightening her back and quickening her pace Lyvanne strode into somewhat of a march, aimed directly at Turiel.

"Turiel!" she said, almost shouting, as she declared her arrival.

The warlock seemed taken by surprise. Unsure of what had caused, or how to deal with, her newfound attitude.

"What's the matter, little -

"Why has Jocelyn left?" Her hands shook so she hid them behind her back. Anger and nerves pulsing through her blood in equal manner.

"It doesn't matter she'll -

"It does matter, to me."

Lyvanne spared her gaze from Turiel for a split moment, the others around the table were all looking at her wide-eyed and engrossed. Kwah had a half-smile; she thought he was enjoying the scene more than the others. There were three other men in the structure besides Turiel and Kwah. Lyvanne could tell by the olive colour of their skin that the first two were natives of The Rive. One of whom was a bulky man, both in height and width, a small giant in comparison to Lyvanne. His hair was black and cut short to his scalp, and his strong jawline traced by a hard line of stubble. The other was lean, of average height for a man, and as he smiled Lyvanne noticed that he was missing at least half his teeth. The third man stood with a straight back, his hands clasped behind his back, like Kwah he was an Islander, black skinned and regal looking.

"We disagreed on strategy, that's all. She'll just be blowing off steam," Turiel raised his hands as if in surrender.

"What strategy?" Lyvanne snapped back, not happy with his answer.

"Turiel!" The lean man shouted, cutting off Turiel before he could answer. "She ain't one of us. Be grateful that we let her stay here, but don't push our generosity."

"She's only a girl, Drystal," Kwah intervened, holding a hand up to calm the situation.

"Drystal is right," The other islander spoke and all of a sudden Lyvanne regretted her abrupt entry. "She should not be in here. The Annex is for the Council, no others."

Lyvanne looked around the wooden structure. She should have paid more attention before she confronted Turiel. This was clearly a structure for the leadership of The Spring, or at the very least where they co-ordinated their plans. She couldn't read the parchment in full from a distance, but she knew a map of The Rive when she saw one and there was a large one sprawled across the table with the wooden soldiers dotted vicariously across it.

Turiel didn't wait for the rest of the argument to unfurl. He waved a hand in the air and moved around the table to stand face to face with Lyvanne. "That was unwise," he said as he rested his hand on her shoulder and ushered her away and back out into the camp. The two returned to their hut, where Turiel hoped they could talk in peace.

"Jocelyn is stronger than you know. She'll be fine, trust me. I wouldn't let her put herself in harm's way," Turiel promised as he knelt down in front of Lyvanne and took both her hands in her own.

The images of her dreams swirled around at the forefront of her mind. It took all the strength Lyvanne had to try and push them away.

"What are The Spring planning Turiel? What are you planning?"

"That's something you need not worry about. Until the day comes that you choose the same path as these people all you have to do is stay here, do your bit to help out, and stay safe. Can you do that for me? We're nearly there with your training. It won't be long before you can leave if you choose to."

Lyvanne stared into his eyes for what felt like minutes. She trusted him, but she didn't know how much longer she was willing to be left in the dark. "I can do that," she said reluctantly.

And she did. The next few days she made a point of not keeping to herself, not to please Turiel, but because she had told Jocelyn she would. At times she would help gather firewood or collect the rainwater from the troughs, neither was that stimulating but she enjoyed finding more out about the people she shared a camp with. Most had horrible stories of how they found their way towards the open arms of The Spring. Others were only there to fulfil a sense of justice.

She appreciated that every person who took the time to speak to her did so as an equal and not the child she knew she was.

The days began to blur into each other. She even took up reading again. Using abandoned notes and recipes lying around the camp, she took them back to her hut at night knowing that Turiel wouldn't return until late and studied them over candle light. She was surprised how much came flooding back to her from Sinjin's lessons once she put her mind to it.

As reading became more natural, Lyvanne in turn became more adventurous with what she chose to read. Finding carelessly placed letters from around the Annex, or on the tabletops within a hut, before quickly putting them back before anyone woke up. Details of trade routes, the names and locations of other people associated with The Spring, what little information they had on the king's forces both within The Rive and abroad. She was hooked, not just by the fascination of being able to read but by the contents of what she was finding.

Gradually she saw less and less of Turiel, who became distracted by meetings and patrols. They would still hold regular lessons as Turiel endeavoured to teach her how to strengthen her mind against invasion, but she often found the lessons had grown stale, disinteresting and all too similar to the last. At times, she thought about saying something, but there was a nagging feeling that even if she did Turiel would only brush it off before disappearing again.

She found some joy in watching two particular men sing songs around the fires at night. One wore a red cloak, not too dissimilar to the one Turiel would often wear, and a matching red hat. The other was more neutral in his clothes and less dashing to look at.

"I'm Greyson," the one in red said on the night she finally plucked up the courage to introduce herself.

"And I'm Davidson," the other echoed in a joyful tone. "In case it wasn't obvious, we're brothers."

She found herself gravitating towards them as Turiel slowly distanced himself, but just like everyone else, they had jobs and duties too, so her time around them was limited. One person who did find the time for her, however, was an extremely round Hemeti chef called Oblib.

"Not trying to take my place as chef are you, kid?" he said jokingly one night after catching her trying to steal a recipe to read.

Rather than look unfavourably on her taking what was his, he instead shared what he had and thinking her to be an innocent child often shared more rations with her than he perhaps should have. Lyvanne found him funny to look at, white tufts of hair sprouted out from his ears giving him a peculiar similarity to a night owl, but she loved their time together.

However, it wasn't all positives. The nightmares only grew with intensity.

"It's only a dream," Lyvanne reminded herself as she strode through the burning camp. She no longer needed to call out for help; she knew it would pass eventually, but the scenes she saw were never easy to watch.

Davidson was slumped against a palisade, his chest lacerated and his eyes devoid of life. Oblib ran through the woods in the distance, his clothes were on fire and before she could reach him he fell. She didn't need to check to know that he was dead too. This time was different to the other nightmares though, this time Jocelyn never appeared. In her place, she found Kwah, fighting the behemoth of a man who a broadsword the size of a small person. Just like Jocelyn, Kwah too died at his hands. She watched them all die time and time again, each more gruesome than before and every time they fell, her heart broke ever so slightly more than the last.

CHAPTER 16

As had become common, Lyvanne woke with a start. Her heart beat rapidly in her chest and sweat poured down her cheeks. It had been just over a week since Jocelyn left the camp and there was still no sign of her return. The nightmares had been getting worse and with Turiel becoming increasingly distant she felt as though there was no one to turn to. But she wasn't ready to quit just yet. She'd been determined to make this deal work. Until she knew for certain that she would be strong enough without Turiel's magical protection, then she wasn't going to leave and put others around her in harm's way.

The day started as it usually did. Some bread and weak stew by one of the readymade fires in the morning, followed by helping where she could in the gathering of wood and others essentials. The camp ticked along nicely, everyone knew their job and they all seemed to be good at it. At times, she would see larger groups wander off into the woods with swords and bows; she often wondered whether they were hunting food or… other prey. As dusk fell she started to become faint. Turiel had been hard on her during training - a welcome change from the nothing lessons which Turiel had crammed into what little time they shared together recently - but whilst the magical onslaught often left her feeling drained it wasn't anything like how she felt tonight.

After dinner had been served and portioned out, she took her bowl and retreated back to her hut, much earlier than was usually the case, and whilst the isolation may be frowned upon by some in the camp she wasn't of the mindset that she wanted to socialise. Unfortunately, the peace and quiet that her solitude brought didn't help at all. Her head pounded, like one of the smiths back at Astreya were swinging down on her with an iron hammer. Sweat had begun to form on her forehead and at the base of her neck and a shooting pain clawed at her right arm. At first she thought her old wound from her escape at the Accord had festered, but taking a quick glance down there was nothing there.

The pain grew and grew until she thought she might scream or cry out for help, but just before the breath left her mouth she was flung from the world she knew and cast into one of flame.

Lyvanne opened her eyes. This wasn't like the nightmares, this was something else, something more sinister. All around her, the world was on fire, like an eternal furnace burning in her mind.

She cried out for help, none came.

"Wake up!" she shouted as she tried in vain to force herself back to the camp. "Wake -

The pain seared through her body like the dying curse of a scornful demon. Her scream echoed around the wall of flames that surrounded her and as she lay contorted on the black and lifeless floor, a shadowy figure stepped through a parting in the fire.

"My, my... you are an interesting one," the shadow hissed.

The creature was faceless and twice the size a normal person should be. Lyvanne wanted to escape, to claw, and scratch her way back from the oncoming monster, but she couldn't move.

"Get away!" she snarled back through gritted teeth as the shadow took another step in her direction.

"Do not resist me child," the shadow was only a few feet away from her now. "You have done well, but it's time for you to rest."

Lyvanne tried to remember how Turiel had cast his spells. She didn't know if there were any secret mental incantations he did, and she didn't have time to worry about that. Instead ,she prayed to any God who would listen that if she had dormant magical powers that they would surface now. They didn't, and the demon stepped closer.

Looking down on her, the shadow, faceless and cursed, appeared as though it was looking into Lyvanne's soul. All the while drawing closer towards her.

The pain seared again, and again, she screamed. This time louder than she had ever heard anyone scream before. The flames appeared to recoil from the noise, and the creature, showing its first sign of weakness, clawed at its own chest.

"Lyvanne!" The voice was like an echo, not just through the flames, but through time and space, so distant that she wasn't even sure if it was real. "Lyvanne!"

"Tell me child, who taught you?" There was venom in the creature's words, a frustration that hadn't been there before.

"I...don't... know what... you're on about," Lyvanne sputtered as she tried to regain composure through the constant swell of pain coursing through her blood.

"Focus Lyvanne! Focus!" There was the voice again.

She did as it asked, trying to focus not on what she saw in front of her, not on the creature who by now was leaning down towards her, but on where she knew she really was, back at the camp, back in her hut.

The flames spluttered, their heat diminishing.

"Come back Lyvanne!" She recognised the voice now. Turiel's voice. It was stronger and clearer than it had been before. The wall of flames subsided, leaving only her and the creature alone in an entirely vast and empty black space.

"No!" The creature howled as Lyvanne was torn from the realm it had stolen her away to.

Lyvanne thrashed wildly as she awoke in the hut. She nearly caught Turiel square in the jaw with a flailing fist, but he was astute enough to dodge it and restrain her until she gathered her surroundings.

"You're safe now," he said, looking down at her as though he had been about to lose a loved one. His pale skin was covered in sweat, and his eyes appeared to be holding back tears.

"What...what was that?" Lyvanne asked as she tried her hardest not to cry.

"They're looking for you."

"The king?"

Turiel nodded. "Whomever you saw in there -

"The shadow?"

"Yes, the shadow, was whichever of the king's warlocks who has been tasked with finding out where you are."

"Did he succeed?"

Turiel smiled. He looked proud, despite the obvious worry. "No, you would know if he had broken through to your mind."

"It sure felt like he did. Why didn't all that happen when you used your power to find me?"

"When I used my magic to search for you, you were defenceless. If you'd had training back then, it's entirely possible we would have been taken to whatever realm you just saw."

"Why didn't you tell me that might happen?" she asked, her voice turning dark "Why didn't you warn me?" Turiel's words left her feeling entirely vulnerable.

"I'm... sorry," he replied, shaking his head as if disappointed with himself. "All the training we've been doing, it's been to get you to that realm and to help you defend yourself once you're there. You just didn't realise it because you never distanced the concept of your mind from your actual body."

"Because you never taught me too!" she replied viciously.

Turiel's face turned sour. "That's in part my fault, I admit. I should have been tougher on you in training; I underestimated what you could handle because you're only a kid. I'm sorry, we won't make that mistake again, you're nearly there, the fact that you were able to hold off that warlock long enough for me to get here to help was amazing, Lyvanne."

"What did you do?" she asked, her temper slowly subsiding, unsure of what had actually fought off the invader.

Turiel pulled down his rough spun tunic around his neckline and pointed at a fresh scar, as long as one of her fingers running from the base of his neck and across to his shoulder.

"When I heard you scream, I came running, but by then you could have been in there alone for nearly a minute for all I knew," he tapped her on the shoulder as if to say well done. "Whoever it was is clearly powerful, they must have broken through the protective spell I put around you. It can't have been easy; they must have been working on it for some time. But once I got here I was able to put it back up, it helped me to talk to you through your mind."

So he had saved her then, she realised. "You've been distant recently/ I feel like I can't talk to you anymore," Lyvanne finally admitted. Turiel looked saddened. He was tough, but hurting Lyvanne had been the last thing he had ever wanted to do, only he was too proud to see that it was happening.

"I'm always here if you need me, little one. I'm sorry for how I've been lately. I've just been caught up in all of this," Turiel replied, waving an arm around the hut, but she took his meaning to be The Spring.

She sat there in silence for a minute, contemplating what to say next, but with a lot of hesitation she finally told him about the nightmares. She recounted every detail, every time she'd seen her friends die.

"How long have these been happening?" Turiel asked, his tone more serious than it had been before.

"A while, long enough that I'm running on pretty much zero sleep."

He drew a hand up to his mouth, Lyvanne thought it made him look funny the way he cupped his own chin, but she knew it meant he was in deep thought.

"Okay, I have a plan."

"Go on," she said tentatively.

"You and I are going to go on a little trip out into the countryside. It's obvious that the king is on to you and so are his servants, so it's time to step up your training. We won't be coming back to camp until I'm sure that if you were attacked again, you'd be able to fend for yourself. Deal?"

"Deal," Lyvanne said determinedly, but at the same time she felt utterly scared. If that was true, then she could be leaving to forge her own path in a few days, what if Jocelyn hadn't returned by then? Where would she go? What would she do?

"I have to warn you though, our methods are going to become more extreme. Do you think you could handle that?"

"I'll do anything."

"Okay, well try and get some rest. Hopefully, if all this works then you'll not only be able to defend your own mind, but if luck is on our side then it will do something about those nightmares too."

Turiel made to leave the hut after giving Lyvanne a quick kiss on her sweat-covered forehead.

"Turiel!" she called out, causing him to duck back under the entrance.

"Yes?"

"The nightmares… they're nothing to be afraid of right? They're only dreams?"

Turiel faced her in silence for a moment. "They're just dreams, nothing to be afraid of. Goodnight," He said quietly as he left the hut.

• • •

Outside, the hut was surrounded by just about every person in the camp. From Kwah, to Oblib, Drystal and Greyson all waited intently to hear what had become of the girl whose scream had echoed through the wood.

"She'll be fine," Turiel said after making sure he was out of Lyvanne's earshot, before collapsing by one of the fire pits. Grabbing a satchel of water from a nearby wooden store, he forced a swathe down his gullet to try and ease the pain caused by his shouting.

Most of the onlookers dispersed, going off to bed or back to their final chores for the day. The drama seemingly over, a mere nightmare to the untrained eyes and ears. Drystal was the last to leave the scene, his face twisted and scornful. Turiel caught the onlooker in the corner of his eye, skulking in the shadows of the fire. He knew that Drystal didn't trust him, didn't trust any warlock in fact, and that he didn't feel safe with Lyvanne around. But that battle would have to wait for another day.

Turiel saw movement to his side. Kwah nervous and eyes full of worry appeared, taking a seat by Turiel's at the fireside.

"Is she going to be okay?" he asked.

Turiel nodded. "Yeah, she'll be alright," he said, his every thought spent on trying to untangle the meaning of her nightmares, "but double the guard."

CHAPTER 17

The memory of the night before was still burning bright in Lyvanne's memory as Turiel brought her an early breakfast.

"Are you still sure you want to go through with this?" he asked as they ate quietly in the quiet of the morning.

"Yes," she replied assuredly. In truth, she just wanted Jocelyn to be here with them, to know that she was there to lean on when things got tough.

Lyvanne found the journey out into the countryside beyond the woodland to be much easier than the journey they'd undertaken to arrive there in the first place. Turiel and she had set off at the first sign of dawn as the sun, blotted by a spattering of grey clouds, began to peer in through the dense thicket of trees that surrounded them. Kwah had been gracious enough to lend the two a horse for their travel. The Spring didn't have a large number of horses, enough for a dozen riders, kept in a small fenced area to the rear of the camp. So it was a commodity that he hadn't had to share.

"Thank you," Turiel said as Kwah walked over with a black stallion in tow.

"Thank you, Kwah," Lyvanne echoed.

Taking the reins of the horse Lyvanne watched as Turiel tied a large backpack onto his saddle. Turiel hadn't told her how long they would be gone for, but she had seen him packing a substantial amount of food and water satchels into his backpack. There was enough to last the two of them a few days out in the wild, Lyvanne had concluded.

"Why do we need to be so far away from camp to do this?" Lyvanne asked as she struggled to keep herself perched on the back of the horse, holding tight onto Turiel's waist as he led the horse through the countryside. Her experience of learning how to ride a horse was limited to the few days she had spent with more than enough spare time on her hands at camp, watching those richer than herself ride back at Astreya, and the few hours they had been journeying that morning.

"Fewer distractions," he replied as he brought his hood further up over his head in a futile attempt to fight away the heavy beats of the sun as it began to soar high into the sky. "Besides, these next few days aren't going to be pretty for either of us, we don't want the others getting itchy feet around us."

All in all, they were journeying by horse back for half a day before Turiel pulled up in a small clearing at the base of a large rocky hill, a rare landmark among the dominant meadows of the countryside.

"We go up there," Turiel pointed up towards the summit of the hill.

Lyvanne nodded and Turiel spurred their horse into action. The hill itself was an easy climb, especially for the broad and strong legs of the horses, but finding a place to set up a camp was less so.

"What is this place?" Lyvanne asked with childlike glee as their horse reached the summit of the hill.

Where Lyvanne had expected a simple rocky outcrop, she instead found the relics of a by-gone age. Ruins littered the land before her, small and large, stable and broken. Walls with ancient carvings that she couldn't read, a gorgeous archway of meticulously carved stone half collapsed in on itself and the remnants of a long fallen column broken into pieces where it fell along the summit.

"Depends who you ask," Turiel replied as he gazed at the physical remnants of forgotten memory. "Some say that they were made by the first men to set foot on the Rive, others would argue that it's a fallen Hemeti watchtower and some may even tell you that it pre-dates them both. No one really knows."

A small grassy patch of hillside revealed itself as Turiel led their horse through the ruins. It was only a few square metres in space, but it was more than ideal for the two of them and had enough ruins on either side that the horse could be tied up with some ease.

"Can you read the writing?" Lyvanne asked as she dismounted the horse and ran over to a series of intricate markings on the side of a crumbling wall.

"Afraid not, I don't know of anyone who can."

At first, Lyvanne was crestfallen, but a sudden surge of determination warmed her blood and quickly turned into a promise, not to Turiel but to herself. "I bet I could learn."

"I have no doubt"

After unpacking a pair of basic bed mats from his backpack, Turiel threw one over to Lyvanne and told her to find her spot, not that there was much variety to choose from she thought. With the horse safely tied up, Lyvanne parked herself onto the damp grass around a fire that Turiel had started crafting. It had rained lightly on their climb up the hill but nothing too torrential, at least not yet, and Lyvanne was grateful for the chance to dry off among the shelter of the ruins.

Peering out from their perch high up above the countryside Lyvanne had an almost perfect view of everything that lay beyond the foot of their claimed hill. The woodland area that she knew housed the other camp took up a large portion of the world before them, the wood evidently being larger than she had first realised when they arrived in the dark. Down to the north, she could make out the feint shimmering of a small river, a divergent arm of the Anya. As her gaze followed the river toward the horizon she could make out the signs of what appeared to be a small village. The location, she assumed, where The Spring would restock their supplies when needed. But looming once again above it all were the threatening grey clouds she had learned to loath in such a small amount of time. Especially now that she didn't have the protection of the canopy above the woodland camp. Watching the low rumble grow closer Lyvanne began to seriously question why she'd agreed to come along.

The duo didn't do much for the next couple of hours; Turiel cooked a late lunch of sausages, tomatoes, and the usual small loaf of bread split between them both. The sun was beginning to set when Turiel finally slapped his knees and stood. The grey clouds had fortunately avoided them, but from her lookout position Lyvanne watched the rain falling heavy over some mysterious land off in the distance

"Up!" Turiel commanded with a playful gusto. Lyvanne did as asked and joined him back in the small clearing. "One last chance to back out, little one. Otherwise, there will be little rest between now and our return to the woods"

"What exactly are we going to be doing?"

Turiel's face turned dark, and not just because the sun was lowering in the sky behind Lyvanne, casting her shadow out across her pale friend.

"We need to revisit the place where your mind took you last night. Can you describe it to me? The more I know beforehand the more efficient I can be once we're there."

Lyvanne was unsure how much she wanted to share, the memory was still too vivid and too painful, but seeing the look in her friend's eyes she relented. "It was like an eternal darkness, completely surrounded by a wall of fire. It felt like the fire could burn the both of us at any minute, but the shadow... they didn't seem to be affected by any of it."

Turiel nodded his head. "Never been a fan of flames, but I guess it's a good defence mechanism."

"Is this going to hurt? Like the way it did last night?" Lyvanne asked, petrified of the answer.

"It will hurt, but not the way it did last night. For this to work, I'm going to have to try and invade your mind the same way the king's warlock had, but considering it's my own spell that was helping to protect you, I should be able to work my way through without causing too much distress to your body."

Lyvanne nodded, she felt ready, scared, but ready. "Do it."

"Steady on, Lyvanne," Turiel said through a curling grin. "There's a few things we need to clear up before we start. Firstly, you will be in pain whilst we're in there. I don't know the extent as it can change from person to person, but I know that it will be less than last night. Whatever you feel in there, whatever your body is telling you, none of it can follow you out, none of it will return here. If your body starts hurting before you're taken there then don't worry, it's just your body warning you that something it deems to be bad is about to happen, admittedly in a rather inconvenient manner.

"Secondly, once you're in there, once the fire builds up and it feels like there's no escape, that's when it's going to be just you and me, that's when you've got to force us both out of the defence your mind has built up. The place we'll be taken to is your own creation; it's your mind. I'm not in control there, nor anyone, None but you. Thirdly, and likely the most important, once we're in there the invader can do very real damage to you. Do not let me, or whomever else it is get close, do not let them touch you or their strength will only increase. They won't be fast. You're trained up well enough that at the very least that's something you won't have to worry about, but it's crucial that you stop them before they can connect with you physically. Do you understand?"

Lyvanne took a moment to try and take in everything she had been told, but quickly nodded her reply, followed - as usual - by a question. "Turiel… how do you know all this?" The words escaping her mouth unbidden, but she had to know. "You said your Father helped you escape once you started showing magical talents, but you never said he taught you anything he knew."

Turiel smiled, bringing back memories of the childhood he so nearly had. "You're right, it wasn't my father. He was an especially gifted warlock, but our time together was too brief and too fragile to train me. But, like all good students I did at some time have an even better teacher stood behind me… maybe that's a story for another time though. For now, focus."

The white streams of magic began to ebb and flow through Turiel's raised palms and fingers. Standing only a few feet away Lyvanne could now sense the presence of magic, something that she had not been able to do when she first came into contact with him. She put it down to growing accustomed to him using her as a theoretical punching bag back at Astreya. The two were stood apart from each other for a handful of minutes, with every passing second the sensations of the night before returned. The sweating, the pain…

"Stop!" she shouted and Turiel broke off his spell.

"Are you okay?" he asked, rushing over to her.

She nodded, embarrassed that she had chickened out before the real test had even begun. "Just… remembering last night."

"We can wait a little longer if -

"No, let's start again. I'll be ready this time."

And she was ready. Lyvanne didn't flinch as the pain soared through her arm and she wasn't fazed as her world turned to darkness again. It was a different story once they were back among the flames however. The pain was unbearable, true it wasn't as torturous as the night before, but it was still more than she could bear. Her screams reverberated around the emptiness beyond the wall of fire, and before he'd even had time to materialise Turiel broke off the spell and pulled them out.

That was the pattern they followed for the rest of the day until the sun had vanished behind distant hills and light had turned to dark. Turiel would invade Lyvanne's mind, Lyvanne would try her best to resist but the pain would steadily overcome her. It had become obvious that without Turiel's aid the night prior she wouldn't have withstood the invasion alone. Her friend never materialised in her mind's world the way the shadow creature had, instead he opted to hang back, watching as Lyvanne tried to master her surroundings. It caused him more personal pain than it would have done to materialise, and often dragged out a scenario that he could have ended himself in a matter of moments. But Lyvanne knew what he was doing, and whilst she appreciated it, she was also very conscious of the ever-growing cascade of scars that were climbing up his right arm.

Seeing the scars she squirmed uncomfortably in her place. The two shared a knowing glance. "Are you okay?" she asked after a particularly nasty looking scar climbed up the base of his neck.

"We both knew this would be tough," he replied, any pain well hidden. So, they continued.

After one particularly daunting episode within the fiery walls, Turiel took a step back. "We can finish for the night now if you wish?" he asked, beads of sweat pouring down both of their faces.

"No... not unless you need to?" Lyvanne replied, nodding her head in the direction of his newly formed scars.

"I'm good, suffered worse."

Back into the cycle they went. Lyvanne felt as though she was getting a handle over the pain as the night drew on. The flames still licked at her face, but she felt more comfortable in their presence, less scared by the opposing force she had to contend with every time.

"I can beat you," she said defiantly as the flames surged all around her. Her senses overloaded by the smell of burning ash, the sound of Turiel's shapeless form egging her on from a place of hiding and the daunting presence of the vast emptiness which lay beyond the wall of fire.

"Nearly," Turiel's replied, his body hidden beneath flame.

By the time they decided it would be best to finally get some rest, Lyvanne thought on the day to come as one where she would finally master the art it took to be able to lock her mind away from the invasion of others.

"Wake me up if you have the nightmares again," Turiel said as the pair settled down on their bed mats, nothing but the nearby fire and small thin sheets of fabric to keep them warm.

"I will," Lyvanne replied as she feasted on the last of a quickly made rabbit stew which Turiel had thrown together for the pair to eat before they slept. There wasn't much meat to be found on most of the rabbits, but it was better than nothing.

The night came swift and carried her off into sleep. The Goddess looked down on her kindly and for the first time in what felt like forever Lyvanne slept soundly through the night without even the smallest inkling of a return to her nightmares.

CHAPTER 18

L yvanne wondered exactly how much food Turiel had stashed away into his overly large backpack as she watched him cook a morning feast of watered oats and honey.

"You should have been a chef," She commented.

Turiel laughed, "Yes, I'm sure Father would have loved that. Turiel, son of Frandil, Weapon of the King… a chef"

"Weapon of the King?" Lyvanne asked.

"Well… yes. As you know my father was a loyalist and when you pair that with magical abilities then the king is oft to find a suitable place among his armies for you."

Lyvanne knew this already, but she felt as though there was more Turiel was yet to share. "Did he tell you much about the wars?" She asked, trying to choose her words carefully as the smell of oats wafted through the air and filled her senses.

"Not too much, enough to keep a young boy enthralled for an hour or two when he came home, enough to make me idolise him as some kind of hero. Doubt too much of it was true… hope the rest of it wasn't."

"Did he fight in Tyberia?" She knew that the years didn't quite match up for this latest conflict with the people to the north, but the two kingdoms had been warring hot and cold for decades now, he might have been there at some point.

Regardless, Turiel shook his head. "No, afraid not. My father had a specialty; he made for an exceptionally good Captain at sea, and so he was put in charge of the king's royal fleet."

"Who did he fight?"

"Tyberian fleets if they ever dared to venture too far south, which they rarely did. Pirates mostly, raiding and pillaging towns and cities along the Eastern shoreline. But he made his name in the Battle of the Winter Winds."

Lyvanne's eyes lit up. "I know that one!" she exclaimed, nearly jumping up from her seated position on the cold floor. "Abella told me about that one," she continued. "It was a convoy of five war galleys from the king's royal fleet facing off against three times their number from the Crag Islands! The winds were said to have been so strong, the rain so icy, that the captains had little control over their vessels. Your father fought in that battle?"

Turiel nodded, a thin smile giving away how impressed he was with her knowledge. "He didn't just fight in it, he won it."

Lyvanne's jaw dropped, "He did? I don't remember Abella mentioning anything about a warlock."

"She wouldn't have known, the king didn't like his victories to be blamed on the use of magic alone, so their work was often scratched from the official records. But yes, my father had seen their odds of survival were so thin that the only reasonable option would have been to run. But the king wouldn't have taken too kindly to that. So instead he conjured a spell so powerful that it shaped the very weather around them, he sent winds hurtling against the enemy and caused their ships to careen into one another. The royal galleys then swept in and finished what was left of the enemy."

Lyvanne smiled, she appreciated him sharing some of the few memories he had of his father with her. "Thank you."

Turiel smiled and soon after the pair returned to business. Off in the distance Lyvanne made out a herd of cattle, roaming what she assumed must have been farmland. She doubted they minded too much when she screamed in anguish. Turiel was being less forgiving today, manifesting himself into a creature similar to that of the shadow that had invaded her a couple of nights ago. He repeated the invasion over and over again until she was able to maintain some level of composure as he made his march through the flames and towards her.

"Focus," he said through a ghoulish grin. "We can do this all day if we need to, it's only going to cause us both more pain. You need to focus."

Lyvanne tried to recall how she had cast the demon from her mind the other night, what it had felt like, how her body had reacted. Even if it had been with the help of Turiel's spell, it had to be a good place to start. Turiel was striding in her direction, his every step a warning that if he touched her, she'd lost this horrific game and it would all be for nothing.

Come on, think! She told herself as the flames licked at her face.

Then, as if struck by a moment of genius, it all started to come to her. The feeling of power over this god-forsaken realm she'd felt when she banished the flames and pulled herself out. The feeling of anguish and frustration the shadow creature had experienced as between Turiel and herself they extended his stay, increasing the pain and stress on his real body, wherever in The Rive that may be.

She opened her eyes, not being entirely sure when she had closed them, saw Turiel's demonic shadow advancing on her, and as if she'd just snapped her fingers in banishment, the whole world began to vanish around her. Sinking in on itself until there was nothing left. Suddenly, she was back on the small clearing, high above the Rive's countryside.

"You did it!" Exclaimed a grinning Turiel. "I knew you could do it," he said as he wrapped his arms around her.

She returned the hug, although weakly, already exhausted from their day's work.

"Come on, let's go in again," Turiel insisted.

Lyvanne frowned, her arms heavy and her legs weak. "You don't let up, do you?"

They repeated the exercise three more times until they were both sure that her control over her mind was complete. Each time, Turiel took them into that realm of shadow and fire Lyvanne forced them from their prison quicker than she had done before.

"I think you're ready," Turiel said as if he was speaking to a student of years. "I'm going to leave up my spell just in case, but don't forget it will only work whilst I'm nearby, so if you choose to leave us you'll be on your own. If you don't mind?"

She didn't. Although she wouldn't admit it, having that extra bit of protection did make her feel more secure and she wasn't quite yet ready to make her decision as to what she wanted to do with her life. Not before she'd seen Jocelyn again.

They spent the rest of the day just enjoying each other's company. It had been far too long since they had spent any real time together, alone and without the worry of having to train her mind to defend itself.

"Do you like The Spring?" Turiel asked her as they sat around the campfire, the horses neighing calmly to their right and the sun setting off in the distance.

She had to think about her answer. She certainly liked some of them, Greyson and Davidson, Oblib and Kwah most of all had been especially nice to her when she let down her walls to let them in. But there were others who seemed distant, who didn't want her there and that made it difficult for her to outright say she liked the insurgency. As childish as she thought Turiel might find that. The one called Drystal had made her feel particularly unwanted and ostracised, but he himself seemed out of place among the others.

"Yes," she decided. "I don't think they all like me though."

"Yeah, some of them are like that. They weren't all overly fond about me bringing someone being actively hunted by the king into camp."

Lyvanne nodded, that seemed fair enough. But at the same time she couldn't help but feel a bit bitter over the fact that she would never have turned away someone from Abella's, even if they were being hunted the way she was.

"You enjoy learning about our world, don't you?" Turiel acknowledged as a period of silence grew between them.

"Always have done, the person whose house I used to live in was once a librarian in the king's library. She knew all sorts."

"I wish I'd met her, but I dare to say that the king's library wasn't exactly my scene. I always preferred to learn things through experience, so I guess I didn't learn too much whilst I was in the castle. But I learned a whole lot in the years after I left…"

Lyvanne nudged closer, she could always sense when a good story was about to start.

"As you know, Sinjin and Jocelyn were the ones who looked after me, without them I'd probably have ended up in the same place you did. After a while, I wanted to see what else lay beyond the walls of Astreya, and as part of The Spring I had my excuse. I travelled through The Rive like I owned it, like it was mine to learn and study, and in a sense I guess it was," he continued. "Once or twice, I even found my way to countries further abroad, searching for allies who felt the same way about our great monarch that we do. I had to be careful of course, sometimes I wasn't and got into trouble for it. Believe it or not, not all of these scars are the result of magic."

The two laughed together, of course it was no laughing matter, Lyvanne stared at the scars and not for the first time. At first they'd both fascinated and scared her, but looking on them now she saw that they were a part of Turiel as much as anything else. They were his own story written into his body, and once she saw it that way the fear began to drift away.

"Then one day I was rifling through a tomb I discovered up in the White Mountains to the South, don't ask why I was in a tomb, some adventuring just seemed like a necessary part of the job," He said, waving an arm in the air like it was the stupidest decision he'd ever made. "And buried deep in this tomb, after all the skeletons who came back to life to try and kill me, after all the booby traps…"

Lyvanne wasn't quite sure if he was joking or not.

"… I found the person whom the tomb belonged to. Rachel Goldheart, the brightest person of her age and buried alongside her body was a pile of books. Turned out they were her personal journals," he said with a smile on his face. "they documented everything she knew about magic and its uses."

"That's where you learned it all?" Lyvanne asked, it felt obvious but she just wanted to be sure.

"Yes. Over the past few years, I've learned everything there is to learn in those books. They were my teacher, and I consider myself lucky to have had them. Many warlocks are born and die without ever knowing how to control what they have."

"Do you still have them?"

"Not anymore. As I said, I learned everything there was to learn, so about a year ago I went travelling and put them back where I found them. Hopefully some other warlock will find and use them in the future."

For the first time since knowing one another, Lyvanne truly admired Turiel. Despite his age, he had seen and done things that some men wouldn't even be able to dream of in their entire life. But more than that, he'd had the will power to leave it all behind for someone else to use in the future. They spent the rest of the night with Turiel teaching Lyvanne about the various stars, their constellations and where they lay in relation to the landmarks on The Rive. Climbing to the other side of the rocky hillside, Turiel pointed at one star in particular, it shone brighter than any of the others.

"That star there is Icrayus, and it lies directly above Avagarde," He moved his hand down to point towards the vague shadowy outline of a valley far off to the South. "I would bet you a large wager that if you were to travel to Avagarde you'd find Jocelyn."

Lyvanne's ears perked up. "Jocelyn? How do you know?"

"She's always loved Avagarde. It's a city entwined with nature, where Astreya is all walls of stone, dust, and sun; Avagarde is filled with trees, the houses encased with vines, the river Tia that runs just outside its wall a home to all manner of creatures that I couldn't even imagine until I saw them in person. She has friends there, and she's gone there before to blow off steam when we've fallen out."

"Why did you fall out? You still haven't told me what about your strategy you disagreed on."

Turiel placed a hand on her cheek and made to walk back towards their camp.

"Not yet, that's for members of The Spring only I'm afraid," he said cuttingly. "She never disappears for much longer than a week, so she should be back soon. Maybe then we can speak, when we're all together again."

Turiel's eyes averted her gaze and flickered out towards the countryside surrounding them. Lyvanne's mind began to wander as she pondered what exactly had driven her friend away.

CHAPTER 19

"I will come back," Lyvanne whispered quietly to the carvings on the wall as Turiel readied the horse.

A heavy downpour of rain forced the pair to pack their belongings in a hurry, and it didn't appear as though it was going to relent any time soon. The wet ground underfoot made it more difficult for the horse to travel back down the hill and Lyvanne was scared that she might die of pneumonia before they ever made it back.

"This is your fault," she shouted through the rain toward her friend.

"Mine? I don't control the weather."

"Your father did!" She replied, proud of the joke, even if she had spent the past hour coming up with it.

She could just about make out Turiel laughing underneath his hood. "Well played. Guess Rachel Goldheart never took the time to learn how to control the weather."

As they made their way through the meadows and plains, they passed a herd of cattle; cows of varying sizes, colours and patterns. They were just lying on the grass, as if the rain had no effect on them. Lyvanne wasn't sure, but she felt pretty confident that it was the first time she had envied cows. Even in the rain though, she had to admit that the countryside was endless times more beautiful than Astreya had been. Whilst she admired the work that had gone into building such a city, and especially some of the larger or more ornate structures, she had never deemed it to be particularly beautiful. There were too many people crammed into too small a space, and seeing the open world around her Lyvanne wondered why anyone would ever want to leave.

As the day drew on, they grew steadily closer to the edge of the woodland area that concealed the encampment. Lyvanne welcomed the return to her hut and the canopy that kept away the rain, but at the same time she was going to miss spending time alone with Turiel. Despite the pain he had put her through, she dared say it had been fun.

"Promise you won't become distant again?" she asked him as they approached the edge of the woods.

Turiel looked over at her, "I promise. You know I have business to attend to whilst I'm here, fighting against the king doesn't come easy, but I promise that I'll make more time for you and for Jocelyn when she returns." The additional comment about Jocelyn made her happy; she wanted the two to be happy and hadn't enjoyed the idea of them being anything else.

The pair passed through into the threshold of the wood early in the afternoon, waving at the various guards on patrol at the woodland edge as they did. Both of them noted that there were more than usual.

"Why so many?" Lyvanne asked, noting at least half a dozen armed men and women spread sporadically throughout the tree line.

"Just a precaution, I guess," Turiel said limply.

Upon entering the woods, one guard spotted them and ran over in their direction. He was shorter than most in The Spring, but his shoulders were wide and strong. Lyvanne thought he had the look of the Dwarves from the old stories, but figured it polite not to mention it.

"Turiel, I'm glad you're back," The man said, barely acknowledging Lyvanne. "Kwah wants to see you immediately. There's been news from Astreya."

Lyvanne's stomach sank.

"Don't play games, man! What news?" Turiel replied.

"I don't know, been kept between the Council, just know it's important."

"Thank you," Turiel replied before spurring his horse on into the trees.

Lyvanne tried to spur her horse on in the same manner, but it was more timid and her control less profound. She ended up falling significantly further behind Turiel, but never quite out of his sight. The pair made good time through the rest of the woods and soon broke into the clearing.

Lyvanne dismounted her horse shortly after Turiel and watched as Kwah put an arm around his shoulder and guided him to the larger wooden structure towards the edge of the camp. After tying up her horse and making sure everything was in order, she quickly followed the pair. The structure was filled with the same people it had been the last time she barged in, evidently they were the people considered leaders. Seeing her making a bee-line for their table the lean man, Drystal, who had been quick to voice his concerns over her place in the camp during her last visit moved to intercept.

"Hold there kid, this ain't for you," Drystal said, holding out a strong arm to prevent her from entering.

"I want to know what's going on. I have friends in Astreya!" She said as forcefully as she could, hoping it would help her cause.

"It's okay, Drystal, let her in," Kwah said, but the man wasn't about to listen.

"What's the point, eh?" Drystal shouted back, not caring that he was causing a scene and numerous people around the camp were pretending not to listen in. "Why keep this from the others but let this child know?"

"Precisely because she isn't one of us," Kwah said, his voice deep and commanding. "She has a right to know."

Neither broke their gaze from the other. Drystal licked a venomous looking tongue over the few teeth he had left and cursed before letting Lyvanne into the structure.

"She's trouble," he said bluntly, before taking his leave.

Lyvanne noted that Turiel had stayed out of it this time, probably for the better to let Kwah fight those fights she thought. Her hands shook, she didn't know why Drystal hated her so much, but she wasn't about to let him get in her way.

"What's happening in Astreya?" Lyvanne asked, turning her attention to Kwah.

The other Islander, whose name Lyvanne didn't know strode to the front of the structure where she was stood. Using his height he reached up to the roof and unleashed a small hook, which sent a sheet of leaves tied together with twine tumbling to the floor, closing up the open wall of the structure.

"Welcome to the Annex, Lyvanne," The Islander said. "If you are to be in here and to share in our secrets then you may as well know its name. My own is Shri'ook."

Shri'ook stretched out his hand in offering and Lyvanne shook it, more confidently than she thought she would have done. The Islander didn't exactly seem pleased to be permitting her into their circle, but he wasn't arguing the point either.

"The man who just left is Drystal, and this here is Tublik," Shri'ook said pointing towards the final man in the structure.

"Pleased to meet you," Lyvanne said.

Tublik didn't say anything, but he nodded and showed the briefest of smiles. She would have to determine his stance on her later, but she didn't get the warmest of vibes. Besides, as far as a "leader" went Shri'ook appeared to hold the most seniority, so she'd passively decided to try and win him over the most.

"Together with Kwah whom you seem well acquainted with already, and Turiel when he leaves Astreya to pleasure us with his presence," Shri'ook shot a short and well-hidden smile in Turiel's direction. "Together we make up the Council of The Spring, the leaders of this branch if you will."

Lyvanne looked around at the mass of men around her and nearly keeled over as a sudden purge of nerves swept through her body. "Now that the pleasantries are out of the way, Turiel this is why I asked for you to come and see me immediately," Kwah said, holding up a short piece of parchment that had once been rolled and adorned the remnants of a small wax seal. "Whilst you were gone we received word from Sinjin. Things in Astreya have turned sour."

Kwah passed Turiel the letter. Rathe, Turiel snatched the letter from Kwah's hands.

"Turns out the king did find new depths to sink to," Kwah continued as Turiel read over the letter. "What do we do?" Kwah asked as he saw Turiel finish reading the letter.

"We have to stop them," Turiel replied, putting the letter down on the table. "They're killing people. If there's anything we've stood for, if there is any reliability in what we stand for, then we can't let the people of Astreya continue to suffer."

Turiel had an anger in his voice that Lyvanne had never heard before, but the glint in his eyes told the same story of the night the king's men burned down Udnak's house.

Not wanting to play the waiting game anymore ,Lyvanne reached across the table and picked up the letter for herself. The handwriting was untidy, but she thought she could just about make out what it said.

Dear Jocelyn,

I hope this letter finds you well. I am pleased to hear that you made it to The Spring with little trouble, I am sure they are treating you well. Please do send my regards to both Turiel and Lyvanne, the house is quiet and lonely without you all here, but I do often enjoy being able to focus on writing my book in my spare hours with little noise.

I wish I had good news to convey regarding the situation in Astreya. My contact in the king's Castle has gone quiet over the last few days, the last I heard was that a warlock - unsure which - had arrived back from the front lines and had been tasked with finding Lyvanne. I hope that she has handled that okay.

I presume their efforts were in vain because ever since then things in the city have only grown worse. The king has started taking in adults as well as children for questioning. None of the adults that I know of have come back. Hangings have grown in frequency as well. I've seen at least four over the past week alone. Three of which happened over the past two days.

The king is convinced that the girl is in Astreya, and it is starting to seem like he is willing to burn the whole lower level to the ground in order to find her.

I asked some friends to keep an eye out for Lyvanne's friends in the Upper level like you asked, but as of yet, nothing. I will write again if I hear more.

For now, I'm going to go dark for a while. Hemeti are being brutalised on the streets simply for not knowing anything about Lyvanne's whereabouts. It appears that the ling's patience grows thin and I don't fancy making myself a target should someone see me sending a carrier pigeon again.

Look after one another. Stay safe. May Iridu shine upon you all.

I love you,
Sinjin

A steady stream of tears made their way down Lyvanne's face as she finished reading the letter.

"All of this… to find me?" Lyvanne said through the tears, interrupting the conversation that she realised she had stopped paying attention to long ago.

The four men looked down at her, a mixture of sympathy and resentment etched across their faces. All but Turiel, who seemed angry more than anything else.

"The king is a cruel man, child. He will do what he pleases if it means he gets his own way," Shri'ook said, leaning down to match Lyvanne's eye level.

She ignored him and turned her attention to Turiel. "You have to do something, we have to do something. We can't just let those people die"

"I agree, but there is only so much we can do with short notice, and even if we gathered all our numbers in one place, we wouldn't have anywhere near the strength needed to take Astreya," Turiel replied, sympathy and desperation finding their way into his voice.

"You're all supposed to be smart aren't you? The people who fight for the little people? Why aren't you fighting?"

"You speak of things you know nothing about child," Shri'ook said, his voice growing firm. "The Spring already have plans in motion that cannot be altered. Now, please leave the Annex. We have granted you a decency by allowing you to see the letter, but do not pass on this information to the rest of the camp. That is our duty to do," Shri'ook pointed her towards the exit, lifting aside part of the hanging wall for her to pass through.

"I'll be with you soon," Turiel said as he watched her turn to leave.

Lyvanne didn't want to concede. Every bone in her body was crying out for her to do something, but looking around at the Council of leaders she knew that it wasn't a battle she was going to win. Find another way, she told herself and stormed out of the Annex. Tears welling in his eyes and anger flushing her cheeks red.

CHAPTER 20

L yvanne wandered aimlessly through the camp. A few opportunistic men and women tried to get info out of her, but in her trance she just ignored them all. Eventually, she found herself back at her hut. Even there she didn't feel isolated enough, so she went back to wandering, allowing her feet to guide the way. She didn't think too hard about where she was going—anywhere but the camp would do.

Her thoughts slowly turned from sorrow to confusion and through to anger. Her whole life had trained her to be invisible, to find her way when others couldn't. Now, being invisible was the last thing she wanted. She couldn't help the people of Astreya if she was invisible. She knew that something had to be done, but nothing came to her. She thought about leaving, about going back to Astreya and finding her friends. At the very least she could get them out of there if she worked hard enough. But she knew that on foot, without the proper supplies or ways of getting into the city, that it would be a futile journey. Besides, if she went back to Astreya and was caught then everything the others had done for her would have been in vain.

The rain lashed against her face as she passed from the safety of the canopy and out into the woods. She wondered how far she would get before Turiel came to find her, or would he break his promise this soon and forget about her? She pushed the thoughts to the back of her mind, it wasn't important right now. What did matter was that she needed to find out a way to save as many people in Astreya as she could. She wasn't going to accomplish that by feeling sorry for herself.

Her feet carried her further out into the woods, and her brain failed to come up with ideas. Feeling desperate, she knelt on the wet woodland floor. Closing her eyes, she proceeded to do something that she hadn't done in what was beginning to feel like a lifetime.

"Dear Angel watching over us, please lend me your sight, please show me what I am to do, show me what is to come."

The prayer felt foreign and nostalgic. Her prayers had been answered once before, and whilst it hadn't been a vision she'd thought she had wanted to see, maybe this time would be different?

As she had expected, nothing happened. *Fool*, she thought. No one has ever been visited twice. Regardless, she spoke again.

"Dear Angel watching over us, please lend me your sight, please show me what I am to do, show me what is to come."

Nothing. She changed her approach.

"Help me!" she shouted, demanding from the Deity just loud enough that any wandering members of The Spring wouldn't hear her.

She moved her attention away from the Angel of Destiny, praying to any other God who might be listening. She started with those she was familiar with: The Goddess of Creation, even the God of Death, but neither answered her plea. She wasn't aware of the formalities of the religion, but she even attempted to reach out to Iridu, the God of the Hemeti people, but again she found herself pounding the ground in frustration.

Then the idea came to her. She didn't need the help of anyone else; she could do this entirely alone, without even having to venture back to Astreya. The thought was dark and dangerous. Turiel would be furious if he found out, but she would need to tell him if she pulled it off successfully.

If they know I'm out in the wilds, she told herself, *then they will stop the searches in Astreya.* At least she hoped. Either way, she didn't have many other options. She wrestled with the idea; it was dangerous and would mean that she was putting the lives of the people in the camp in danger. The memories of her nightmares resurfaced, the images of Jocelyn and Turiel being struck down among a burning wood.

You have to, she told herself, trying to banish away the memories of her nightmares. She knew what she had to do. She was going to open her mind to the king's warlock, let them see her, let them find her.

Neither option was pleasing, and neither would end without some form of struggle, but Lyvanne had made her decision. This was her fight, not the innocent people living in Astreya. Once the King knew where she was, once the grip on Astreya had been loosed, she could leave the Spring and lead the King away. She could draw the king out into the countryside, sparing everyone.

The memory of Turiel's protective spell tickled the back of her mind. She would have to put some distance between them before she could attempt to summon the invader. She wasn't sure exactly how far she would need to be, but she hoped that there would be some kind of sign or feeling that gave it away once she had gone far enough. Springing to her feet, decision made, she ran further into the woods. Keeping a careful eye on her surroundings, she avoided any sign of patrols throughout the thick grouping of trees, hoping to skip by un-noticed before anyone could stop her or warn Turiel that she was seemingly running away.

Then she felt it. As she drew deeper into the woods, near the woodland edge Lyvanne stopped as Turiel's spell disintegrate around her. It was a subtle but new and unmissable feeling. She was free, but Turiel could have felt it too. She needed to act quickly before he came looking for her.

Taking a few more strides into the woods just to be safe, she cleared away a small patch of leaves and dirt and sat down, legs crossed. The rain had lightened since she left the camp, but it was still coming down, sending trickling streams of water across her face. Closing her eyes, she focused. She had no idea how to do what she wanted, but she knew there must be a way, and so she searched her memories for the feeling that had surrounded the shadow creature. She searched for the energy his magic had exuded, the smell, the sound, everything she could think of. Then she reached out, not with her hands, but with her mind in a way that she wouldn't have even conceived to be possible a few months ago.

Her eyes opened in the otherworldly realm she had become so used to over the past few days. Only this time, there were no flames, and she was there alone. The complete darkness surrounding her was foreboding, but there was an element of confidence she had this time that had not been there before. The flames, she presumed were a part of Turiel's spell or the usual result of someone invading her mind. Regardless, they weren't there now and everything felt far calmer.

She sat there in the dark, her every thought reaching out to the being who had only a few nights prior caused her such pain that she thought she might not wake or recover. At first there was nothing there, she was alone in her void. But as she continued, as she strained her mind to find this individual, a response reached back. She couldn't tell if the response had come from the real world or this one of emptiness, but it was there, small but growing in strength.

The pain returned with a vengeance. Her instinct was to scream out, but she bit her tongue, knowing that screaming might attract too much attention in the real world and this would all be for nothing. Flames erupted all around her, the heat searing against her exposed skin and she knew she had succeeded.

Still, she sat there as calmly as the pain would allow, waiting to be joined. Then, like a snake appearing from among the grass, the shadow formed ahead of her.

"Child," the shadow spat. "You are foolish to invite me here."

The shadow wasted little time advancing on her position, moving faster than it had done the last time it was here.

"You give yourself up so easily? Why?" it continued.

There was trepidation in the voice of the shadowy figure as it loomed over her. It was wary of a trap, and rightfully so. Even Lyvanne thought what she was doing might be the worst decision she'd ever made.

"The king is hurting people," her voice filled with anger. She wanted to fight this monster, she wanted to cause it pain. "That shall not continue in my name."

"Save your king the trouble, hand yourself in," the demon hissed. It could reach Lyvanne if it wanted to, but chose to glean more information as she seemed willing to give it.

Lyvanne shook her head violently, tears hiding in the corners of her eyes. "No! I nearly did once, but I've seen what your king does, and I wouldn't want to give him the satisfaction."

The demon roared with laughter. "Oh child, you are a true fool if you think you can evade us once we know where you are. We will find you, and I promise you myself that we shall kill every person you're with."

Lyvanne nearly broke off the connection, the vivid memories of her nightmares screaming at her to break it off before it was too late. But she resisted, and the demonic human figure reached out and placed a single finger on her forehead.

Her world spun out of control, and she was thrown from the fiery void. She awoke in the wood, face first in a pile of leaves and mud. She had done it, she had let in the enemy.

She looked about her to make sure no one else was around. Nothing felt different, there was no obvious presence watching over her, but she knew it would be there. She didn't know exactly how the magic worked, or for how long it would continue its hold over her, but there was no going back now. Her only hope now was that the warlock hadn't been able to see the others, that they were still blissfully unaware of The Spring further back in the woods. It was a fool's hope perhaps; Turiel had certainly seemed to know a lot about her after he had seen into her mind. But right now that hope was the only thing keeping her from going entirely insane.

Goosebumps prickled her arms. What if she really had just caused her nightmares to come to fruition? Had she just thrown away the lives of Jocelyn, Turiel and the others? All to save strangers who she didn't know in Astreya?

They aren't strangers, she corrected herself. *Your friends live there,* she thought, *and the people you grew up beside, whether you knew them or not they were your people.*

She wondered if she had even done enough, had the warlock seen enough that he could tell where she was? How did that part of the magic even work? There were so many questions that she now realised she should have asked Turiel before she attempted this. There was still time, she believed, if she was going to leave the camp once Jocelyn returned she could lure the king away from The Spring and if Turiel would teach her she might have all the knowledge she needed. But she would be alone and after what she had done she wasn't even sure if Turiel would want to teach her.

The thought of being alone in the world was a sobering one. Her time in the sewers, on the run from the king, was the only time she could ever recall being truly alone, and it wasn't exactly a memory she was fond of. She wondered how she would fair out in the wilds without Turiel and Jocelyn by her side. The thought was intimidating, but at the same time the idea of having adventures similar to the ones Turiel had been on excited her. Maybe she would be able to fight the king in her own way?

The journey back to camp was a quiet one. The rain continued to fall, causing a pitter patter on the leaves and ground, but other than that all was quiet. Lyvanne had purposefully walked slow, hoping that any remnants of the warlock's presence would have drifted away, leaving her free to re-enter the camp. Either way she wasn't sure.

Back at camp everyone present had been gathered around the various campfires with the Council spread out to match.

Lyvanne stumbled slowly through a thicket at the border of camp. Turiel was the first to see her. He met her eyes and as a single tear rolled slowly down her cheek. Through welling eyes the concern spread across Turiel's face.

INTERMISSION

T he king was not a cruel man. At least not in Merrick's view of the world. Yes the king had his significant flaws, but what rich snob living in luxury across The Rive didn't? Heck, as far as Merrick was concerned, the commoners, and worse the Hemeti, were plagued with flaws. If he had the power the king had then there would have been a culling of some kind a long time ago. That would solve any supposed hunger issues.

Merrick was known by many names throughout the king's Castle. His proper title of Royal Advisor perhaps being the least used of them all. Some called him Weasel, others joked that he was the king's "petty assistant" who was only around to do his dirty work, whilst others whispered less savoury comments in the shadows of the castle walls. But one thing he was not known as, was someone who would be late and that wasn't something that was about to change as he purposefully strode through the various corridors of the palace. The antechamber of the throne room was accessible by two doors, the first of which was most obviously via the throne room itself, but the king was less than happy with anyone other than guards being present in that room if he was not there himself. A fact which had always made Merrick chuckle, as he thought about the peasantry who kept the room clean, who to the king must have been little more than fairies and pixie dust.

"Good morning, my Lord," a few people mused as he passed them in the corridors. He ignored all but the nobles, to whom he returned their gesture with a slight nod of the head and a feigned smile. He had nothing to gain from their friendship; he would never rise higher than he already had done. To properly piss off a noble was often worth more trouble than the seemingly polite gesture would cost to keep them at bay.

The king had called an emergency meeting of the Royal Council, not a rare occurrence anymore, but Merrick's personal chambers and working chamber alike were on the other side of the castle's central palace. Residency in the palace itself was about as much clout as he could boast, many more people who worked within the king's castle had to journey in from the Upper level of Astreya. A tedious and time-consuming effort, Merrick had decided a long time ago, but the more council sessions that were called, the more frustrated he grew with even his accommodation.

This will have to change soon, he thought to himself as he turned onto the final corridor that would lead him towards the antechamber. The door that led inside, a large oak door reinforced with iron as was the case with most doors in the palace, was guarded on either side by two men in elaborate red and gold plated armour. The pair were wielding large halberds that reached almost to the ceiling above their heads. "Impractical" was the word Merrick had used when the king first installed the order for halberds to Sir Peribald, the Commander of the Dauntless, the king's personal regiment of soldiers.

Seeing Merrick's arrival one of the guards, likely the junior of the two, turned and unbolted the door, allowing the Royal Advisor to pass through.

"Welcome, my Lord," The other said, as though he was passing into some kind of welcoming party. Merrick ignored him.

Making his way into the antechamber Merrick was pleased to find that, as usual, he was the first to arrive. As a result of his unfortunate working accommodation, Merrick made it his mission to figure out the quickest routes through the Palace, even through the greater grounds of the entire castle itself. So far that mission had proved more than fruitful.

The antechamber was small, built entirely for private meetings such as these. Enough room to fit maybe a dozen people in, including the six seats that surrounded the large mahogany table in the centre of the room. Like everything else the king owned, the antechamber had been elaborately decorated. The mahogany table was encrusted with gold trimmings, and the surface was engraved with an old and outdated map of Astreya (An aged gift of a previous monarch). It gave the king great pleasure to repeatedly point out that the boundaries of his Kingdom has seen much expansion since the map was first made. Upon the walls were hung the skins and pelts of various animals from far off countries and paintings crafted by the finest artists the Kingdom had to offer.

"Good day Merrick," said the ancient and ragged voice of an old man.

Merrick turned and sure enough there was Lord Bullard, Commander of the king's Army and the only man on the royal council who Merrick could just about stand, making his way into the room.

"Good day, Lord Bullard," Merrick replied with his distinct high voice. The two were on first name terms, but Merrick always showed respect to his elder of many years.

"Any idea what we're doing here?" Lord Bullard asked as he made his way around the table towards his usual seat. It amazed Merrick how the man could wear chainmail armour and carry around his famed long sword at all times. At times these meetings would go on for hours and he became uncomfortable even when wearing the city's finest robes, let alone dressed ready for combat.

"Afraid not."

"It's never a good sign when you of all people don't know something," Lord Bullard chirped. Merrick was known for his network of spies who worked throughout the various cities of The Rive; his similar network of assassins was less widely known. Only a few days prior, he had needed to silence someone who he believed to be sending information out of the king's castle and into the streets of Astreya. He had taken great pleasure in doing so. The little bird had been chirping secrets for far too long and it was about due time his troubles came home to roost.

The other members of the Royal Council trickled in slowly but surely after that. Firstly, there was Lady Eastbridge, the king's Treasurer and direct point of contact for the nobles of The Rive. Merrick always thought her to be the most intimidating member of the Council, and yet stunningly beautiful at the same time. Her late husband had been the old Treasuer, but he was bad at the job and she was good. So when a terrible accident befell him, she was ushered into the role as quickly as one could snap their fingers. Merrick admired that quality about her.

Secondly, came Lord Pencival. Where Lord Bullard took charge of the king's army, Lord Pencival was head of the Royal Navy. The two often greatly differed on their approach to matters of war, and their endless bickering was the subject of many jokes among the other members of the Council. Unfortunately the king's lust to expand his ever growing empire gave Merrick great cause to believe that the two would have matters to argue over for many years to come.

The final member of the Royal Council to arrive, other than the king, was Lady Avina. If Lady Eastbridge was beautiful, then Lady Avina was nothing short of the Goddess of Creation herself. Her role was that of Ambassador to Foreign states. She entered the antechamber wearing a golden gown that was cut short around her thighs, something that would be deemed inappropriate if it wasn't for her high standing. She was also the youngest member of the Council, being no more than twenty-eight years of age. An honour that highly infuriated Merrick, who himself was only a few years older. Merrick found himself staring as she glided into the antechamber, her hazel hair falling gracefully below her shoulders. Idle chatter filled the room as the Council awaited their liege. To Merrick's right sat Lord Bullard, to his left Lady Eastbridge. As usual, all of Merrick's conversation was very much focussed to his right. A few minutes later the king stormed into the room, flanked by a man whom Merrick didn't recognise. The king appeared tired, as was usual these days.

Is your anxiety still keeping you awake at night? Merrick wondered to himself as he recalled the rumours of how the king grew more paranoid by the day. The king's hair, cut short to the scalp, had greyed significantly over the past two years. His eyes that still shone an unusual bright blue for someone from the Northern parts of The Rive - a result of his mother being from the far reaches of the South - now had a never vanishing ache behind them.

"My Liege," The council spoke in harmony as they stood to welcome their monarch.

The king waved a sleeved hand and everyone took his or her seat once again. The king was clothed in silk robes of green and silver with a golden belt adorning his waist, from which hung his ceremonial rapier.

"I have news which you should all know," The king spoke, his voice raspy and deep with age. "This is Melruin," he said, signalling to the tall and weathered looking man who stood behind him. The man's face, the only evidence of skin visible with his arms being hidden away behind long sleeved military robes, was covered with scars.

Merrick had heard the name before; this man was one of the king's secretive warlocks. Fantasy and children's stories, Merrick thought.

"Melruin has at last been successful in discovering the location of the traitorous child who has been plaguing my mind for far too long," The king carried on.

Merrick couldn't show it outwards, but he was eternally grateful for the news. He was far from the kind of person who would believe in eternal deities, who lived in the sky, but his king was and it was his moods to which he had to cater. The trouble surrounding this young girl who had supposedly seen the downfall of the king's reign had been a serious thorn in Merrick's side. It was highly embarrassing that his network of spies couldn't find one child, let alone when they had the backing of the city watch and the king's soldiers. The issue surrounding the child had been distracting the king from real issues for too long now and it was about time it stopped, a sentiment that he was sure the rest of the Royal Council echoed.

"Lord Bullard," The king turned his attention towards the Commander who sat to attention in his chair "I wish for you to send word to whomever you please that a platoon of our men are to go in search of her. Melruin will provide you with the necessary location. We are currently unsure as to how many people are with her but she isn't alone. Regardless, your orders are to kill everyone you find alongside the child. I don't want any connections to her to be left once you're through"

The king turned towards Lady Avina "My Lady, I wish you to send a message to every country under our rule."

"What message would that be my Liege?" Lady Avina replied, her voice like silk.

"I grow tired of hearing murmurs of opposition to my rule. If these issues cannot be stemmed at their core, if I continue to hear of foreign populaces taking up arms, then I shall be forced to deal with the matters in a manner more suiting to the crime," Merrick recalled the desolate ruin of civilisation which the king left in his wake on the Crag Islands after they chosen independence over subservience. "I don't know where this girl came from originally, but I don't want any more like her."

Lady Avina bowed her head, "Of course, my Liege. I will ask for a greater security presence where resistance is most common. With your command we can root out opposition like the plague it is," Merrick couldn't see but he doubted that Lady Avina's eyes conveyed the same agreement that her mouth had. The king had been pretty vague in his instructions to Lady Avina, and knowing her the way he did Merrick knew that it was likely something she would take advantage of. For all his military prowess the king had little skill in diplomacy, and much of The Rive's success Merrick had to begrudgingly admit was a result of Lady Avina's hard work behind closed doors.

"Lastly," The king said, turning towards Merrick. "Lord Stonecross, I wish for you to use your network of rumours and whispers. Discover if this child was acting alone, or if there is a greater threat out there which we need to be aware of. I don't want to have to find out about terrorist groups via the deeds of my warlocks again. Do you understand?"

"Entirely my Liege," Merrick also bowed, and internally he sighed. This would mean more time devoted towards the study of who this girl was and whom she might have known. It was a waste of time he believed and one of those orders that he simply wished he could ignore. She was a nobody, and this entire scenario with the vision had been a nonsense and unwelcome distraction. But, like most who found themselves in the presence of the king, their ability to remain there was dependent upon compliance.

"That's it then, back to your work," The king ordered as he rose from his chair.

With that the Royal Council adjourned. Lord Bullard and Melruin stayed behind to discuss coordinates. Merrick assumed the two already knew one another, if this truly were a warlock from the front lines of the wars. Something to discuss with Lord Bullard in more detail, he noted. And so Merrick set back off into the corridors of the Palace, with the aim of finding out as much about this little urchin as he could. If he had anything to do with it she wouldn't stay a mystery for much longer.

• • •

With his robes billowing behind him Melruin strode through the marble archway that separated the king's castle from the adjacent Warlock's Tower.

"Send for Kyvna," Melruin commanded a nearby apprentice.

"Yes, my Lord," The apprentice replied as he rose from a reading bench and strode off in the direction of library.

Whilst the castle was filled with all manner of servants, the Warlocks were more particular about who they allowed into their presence. They had adopted apprentices, young men and women who wished to study the ways of magic, but did not possess the gift themselves.

Climbing the multitude of stairs that formed the tower had once been tiring to Melruin, back when he had first joined the ranks of warlocks working for the king, but not anymore. The years of working his way through the ranks, with each passing achievement he was gifted a chamber higher and higher within the tower. Now his legs were iron, and his gift was death.

"My Lord," Kyvna said with the decorum expected of the king's warlocks. The warlock was fresh faced, a new recruit who was eager to please. "You summoned me?"

Melruin looked up from his reading material. "I did."

The girl will be a good test for him, Melruin thought as he studied the novice. "Our King has identified his next target, a group of insurgents located in the countryside to the South. Lord Bullard is in charge of their elimination, but he is prone to... underestimating."

Melruin watched the facial movements of his junior. He sought out weaknesses or doubt. There were none. He's confident, Melruin mused. "I am charging you with being my presence on the battlefield."

Kyvna appeared pleased, his face grew noticeably brighter and he held his chin in the air. "Is there a particular target, my Lord?"

Melruin nodded. "A young girl." Again Melruin watched for a reaction, to question the legitimacy of sending a warlock after a girl, but to Kyvna's credit there was none. "The king sees her as a particular threat. She holds no magical ability that we know of, but she's strong nonetheless. A fire is growing within her, either a warlock is training her, or she's exceedingly smart. Either way that fire needs to be snuffed out."

"Anything else?"

"Don't let the girl distract you from the insurgents. None are to survive. Do all that you must to wipe them from The Rive. We have enough to worry about without a rebellion from within."

"If that is your command, my Lord, then I will see it done. The girl will die, and those who fight by her side will fall with her."

CHAPTER 21

"What's wrong?" Turiel asked as he rushed over to her side. "I felt the spell dissipate. Where did you go?"

There was genuine concern etched on his face, but Lyvanne knew it wouldn't last. She had to tell him what she had done; she had to warn him about what was going to happen.

"Talk to me, Lyvanne. What happened? he continued.

The way in which Turiel had hastened over to Lyvanne's side had drawn the eyes of others in the camp, and more and more heads were turning in their direction.

"Not out here," she replied, her eyes surveying the prying faces.

"Come on then" Turiel said as he wiped the tear from her eye and escorted her back to their hut.

"I'm sorry," she said as they entered the hut, her eyes no longer filled with tears, ready for the accusations to start flying.

"What have you done?"

Lyvanne recounted the story of what had happened. How she had felt helpless, how she couldn't bear the pressure of all those people in Astreya and other far off cities suffering because of her. Of how she had thought through every possible action and that the route she had chosen was the only one which might actually work.

"Fool!" Turiel shouted as Lyvanne revealed that she had let in the king's warlock, that they now knew where she was. "You don't know how much you've ruined."

"I'm sorry, Turiel, but it was the only way. You can't force me to stand by and watch as my people are killed."

"Our people! Our people ,Lyvanne, and yes I can, because it would have kept you safe."

"I'm not more important than them! That's what you don't understand -

"No, you're the one who doesn't understand. You might not want to believe it, but the Angel of Destiny doesn't lie. She doesn't show futures which don't have a chance of coming true, and between you and I we've seen the downfall of the king and how it needs to happen."

"No, we've seen how it might happen. You can do this without me ,Turiel. You're strong enough to do this without me."

"It's not all about strength," he replied, his voice now calming, almost defeated. "It's about giving people hope. I've seen the way people are when you let down your guard around them. They can't help but like you, they cling to you despite your age. You're what our movement needs. You're what I lacked."

"What do you mean you lacked?"

Turiel tossed his hands in the air like the answer didn't matter.

"Turiel, tell me," Lyvanne pressed.

He relented. "I travelled across The Rive searching for allies. Sure, I found some, but I didn't have whatever it is that you possess. I didn't have that natural ability to make people follow, to make people like me or listen to what I have to say."

"Then try harder. Would Rachel Goldheart have given up?"

Turiel raised an eyebrow. "You didn't even know who she was until last night."

"Yeah, well the sentiment still counts. You've laid all your hopes on my shoulders because of what you saw in a vision, but you've not actually put into action anything or anyone who could take my place if something happened to me. Or what if I choose to leave? What would you do then?"

"That's because none of this would be here without you. If I hadn't seen you in my vision then I doubt Sinjin, Jocelyn, and I would have ever started The Spring. We never would have reached out to others like us, but we had faith in what I'd seen. We had faith that one day we'd find you and you would lead us to some kind of victory, no matter how small."

The words echoed through her brain. She'd never thought of it that way. Was she really that important? Was there a way she could help?

Would these people have ended up fighting side by side if Turiel had never seen her in a vision?

"I'm sorry, Turiel, but I'd made up my mind and I don't regret what I did. I will leave the camp as soon as Jocelyn has returned so that I can say my goodbyes -

Turiel waved a hand in her face. "Don't be stupid... you don't need to leave, little one."

"But the king will co -

"I don't care what the king will and won't do. I haven't put myself in harm's way for this long to just let you wander off on your own with the ling's soldiers following your every step."

"The others though, they didn't ask for this."

Turiel smiled briefly, the first since she'd told him what she had done. "Yes they did, nut just leave the others to me. Come on, I don't imagine we want to be wasting any more time."

The world was colder than usual outside the hut, like all the warmth had been sapped from the air in a winter storm. Most of the eyes in the camp were drawn in their direction,n and Lyvanne knew that one way or another her future would be sealed that night. Either they accepted what she had done and they allowed her to stay, or she had to leave.

Turiel approached Kwah and Shri'ook first, drawing them off to the side of the camp. Lyvanne was still by his side, something she soon regretted when Turiel told them what had happened.

"She did what?!" Shri'ook shouted behind gritted teeth.

"Breathe, Shri'ook. She is only a child, and she didn't know what she was -

"I did know what I was doing," Lyvanne interrupted, much to the surprise of the others stood around her. "Turiel has explained why I did it, don't presume that because I'm younger than you all that I'm not aware of how my actions impact others. I have become very aware of that over the past few months"

Her strength caught the others off guard, but to Lyvanne's pleasure all three of them smiled back at her.

"You show courage then, child" Shri'ook said, "but unfortunately you may have brought the enemy down on our heads -

"What was that?!" Drystal's voice interrupted the conversation. Seeing the commotion he and Tublik had made their way over with some haste. "Did I just hear that the little rat has led the enemy to us?"

The word both shocked and stung Lyvanne.

"What did you call her?" Turiel said, making his way over to Drystal, his hands balled up into fists and his chest puffed out.

"You heard me," Drystal replied, squaring up to Turiel, egging him on to do something in front of the whole camp.

"This is a matter for everybody," Kwah intervened, putting his body between the two more hotheaded members of the Council. "Start behaving with the responsibility we have been given and stand with me."

Tempers calmed if only momentarily as everyone made their way over to where the rest of the camp waited patiently, gossiping among themselves as they watched their leaders squabble over her actions. Lyvanne's eyes flicking back and forth between the waiting crowd and Turiel, whose gaze rarely left Drystal. Lyvanne could still feel the heat emanating between them both, like their tempers were ready to flare at a moment's notice.

"Friends, it appears as though we have a great dilemma," Shri'ook said, standing elegantly over a fireplace as he looked out at everyone who had been gathered. In the crowds, Lyvanne could make out her own friends. Oblib, Greyson and Davidson, but still no Jocelyn. "Turiel, I leave to you to explain in detail."

Turiel did as he was asked. There were audible gasps from the crowd as he explained the more worrying aspects of Lyvanne's story. With every sentence he told, Lyvanne quivered as more and more eyes began piercing her mind from the crowd. Things did not look good. Turiel was trying to explain away her misgivings, but was fighting a losing battle.

"Send her away!" One woman called out from the crowd. "She will lead the king's men right to us," Another declared with a quaking voice. Glancing across the line of bodies as panic flooded through her veins, Lyvanne caught a wicked grin cross Drystal's face as the tide turned in his favour.

Oblib spoke up in her defence, his voice deep and commanding. "Lyvanne is one of us, since when have we left our own to fend for themselves?" She could see some faces of sympathy in the crowd, but they were outnumbered by those who were being won over fear. So she took a step forward, bringing herself in line with Turiel, ready to fight her case herself.

"I didn't ask for all this to happen to me, I didn't ask to see the things I saw and for the king to see them too. I didn't want to become a symbol for a movement that I hadn't even heard about at the time. But all that did happen, and I ended up here with all of you."

The leaders on either side of her allowed her to continue, this fight was hers to win.

"I like to think that I've learned a lot from you all in the time that I've been here. But the thing that's perhaps stuck with me the most is that we don't leave people to suffer without even trying to help. There are people in Astreya suffering because the king is looking for me, they might not be people you all know, but some of you will. They are still your people, they have struggled through life the same way I am sure many of you have. You're good people, so why were we just going to let those people suffer?"

It was in that moment, Lyvanne realised two things. The first was that these really were good people, they had risked a lot by allowing her to stay and for that she was grateful. She enjoyed being around them all, learning from them and befriending them. Something she regretted not doing more of in her time here. The second was that these people had likely only found out about the suffering in Astreya mere moments before her arrival in the camp, but she figured her words would still have the wanted impact.

"I am happy to leave you, if that's what you want, if that's what keeps you safe. I can lure the king away by letting him in again; I can take him elsewhere -

Drystal interrupted, "And so she should! We aren't playing games 'ere, we're fighting for The Rive, for your children's future!" He shouted, waving his arms in the air for theatrics and casting a finger of accusation in Lyvanne's direction.

Turiel made a move to silence him, but a steady had from Kwah stopped him in his tracks.

"Do you really want to risk our future for some clueless little bitc -

Kwah's hand couldn't react fast enough. Turiel's arm was raised quicker than the eye could easily keep up with and a stream of magically energy flew from his fingertips. Lyvanne could tell that it was little more than she had experienced countless times back in Astreya, but the blast met its mark and Drystal seemed to jump five feet in the air from shock before landing flat on his face.

"See, even the magician is corrupted by her! She needs to leave!" Drystal shouted through gritted teeth and red faced, as the crowd erupted into a mix of laughter and shouts of agreement.

This isn't what I wanted, Lyvanne thought as she watched Turiel prepare for another blast, only to be subdued from either side by Kwah and Tublik. Noise rose from the crowd, but amongst all the commotion she could no longer make out what they were saying. Drystal continued his tirade to anyone around him who would listen, whilst continually rubbing the small of his back where Turiel had hit him.

Everything blurred together, every mistake she had made all piling up on top of one another. So she ran. If all they were going to do was squabble like children then she was going to take the choice out of their hands. She didn't stop to get her supplies, she didn't turn and say her goodbyes. Instead, she focused her eyes on the line of trees a few yards away and made her escape.

Turn around, she yelled at herself as she ran. *You're being stupid.* The words came and went through her mind the way water flows through a sieve. She wasn't going back, not when they couldn't even decide if she was wanted, not when her mere presence resulted in what she had thought was like a family turning on each other with violence.

CHAPTER 22

S he barely made it to the edge of the camp before someone grabbed her by the scruff of her tunic's neckline.

"Where do you think you're going?" It was Drystal. The man seemed incensed, his eyes were bloodshot and there was drool forming at the corners of his cheeks.

"Why do you care if I leave?" Lyvanne replied, struggling to get free of his grip. Her eyes darted left and right, she'd gone too far to be seen by the others who she presumed were still arguing around the campfires.

"Don't bother looking girl. They ain't comin' for you, and I don't intend on letting you go so easily for the bother you've caused me." She looked up at her captor. He had a sick grin on his face and a foul stench escaped his toothless gums.

Drystal was not to be considered a strong man by any means, but he was much stronger than Lyvanne and he put that to use by dragging her by her neck out of the camp and into the woods. She tried to scream for help, to somehow make Turiel notice what had happened. But the cracked and dry fingers of Drystal's hand slid over her mouth and before she knew what was happening it was too late. She didn't intend on being taken easily; every step of the way as Drystal pulled her through the wet floor of the woods she scratched and clawed at his arms. Satisfaction filled her as her nails pierced his skin and blood appeared over her hands. But it wasn't enough.

"Ah you bitch!" he said, throwing her across the woodland floor and into the base of a large tree trunk, her head hitting the wood hard and leaving her dazed.

"Screw you," Lyvanne said before spitting in the man's direction, an act which only served to entice him, even please him. "You're deranged!"

Drystal looked down at his arm where Lyvanne had left scratch marks and wiped the small stream of blood on his ragged gambeson. "Aye, maybe, but I had life easy before you showed up didn't I? King weren't ever goin' to find us here," he said, waving his undamaged arm around the woods. "Even got to have some fun playing with the king's soldiers from time to time. Then you turn up and change all that."

Drystal's hand moved steadily down his gambeson until it rested on a sheath around his waist. Lyvanne's dazed eyes widened. She hadn't noticed the knife hung around his belt until now, and suddenly the danger became much more real.

"If you kill me then they'll kick you out," Lyvanne argued, trying to make him see sense before he'd gone too far.

"Hah! Too late for that kid. Nah it's back to the harder life for me now… may as well make you suffer for that before I go."

He carefully unsheathed the knife. a large serrated blade with a nondescript wooden handle. Lyvanne's eyes were drawn to it, she tried to scream again but Drystal was prepared and covered her mouth once more, whilst using his forearm to hold her firmly in place against the tree.

"I'll give you credit, kid. That was some speech you gave back there… shame it won't matter for ya."

He raised the knife towards her cheek; she tried to scramble her way free but she was pinned against the tree and there was nothing she could do about it. She tried lashing out with her fists and feet, but Drystal just took everything and the knife kept advancing. Drystal pressed the knife against her cheek and began to apply the pressure, creating a cut the size of her thumb across her right cheek. A thin and steady stream of blood oozed out onto her face and trickled down her cheek.

"You not goin' to cry, girl?" Drystal said with a genuine look of surprise as Lyvanne sat there, gritting her teeth and accepting the pain. She gave him no answer, telling herself that she didn't want to give him the satisfaction of seeing her cry out in pain. Besides, she'd felt far worse recently.

Drystal raised the knife again, this time moving it away from her cheek and towards her throat. This was going to be it, this would be how she died. Then she saw movement, out of the corner of her right eye, coming from further in the woods. It was a Hemeti, judging by the feint shimmer of green skin Lyvanne could just about make out as they ran through the woods at a break neck pace. The knife grew closer, and stopped. The person was now close enough that their movements could be heard over the pattering of rain against the canopy of trees above. Drystal heard them too. He balled up his fist and punched Lyvanne hard in the side of the face where moments before he'd cut her with his knife.

"I'll be back for you," he said as he rose to his feet, ready to fend off whoever was coming to her aid. The blood from her cheek smeared across his knuckles. But it was too late, by the time he'd rose to his feet they were already on top of him. Lyvanne's entire face was in pain, and her vision had been blurred, but she could still just about make out what was happening in front of her.

"Jocelyn!" she called out as she slowly regained her senses and recognised her defender.

Jocelyn didn't react to her call, her eyes were deadlocked on Drystal who had managed to scramble back to his feet after being initially knocked down to the floor. They stood a few feet apart, Jocelyn unarmed facing off against Drystal with his serrated knife in hand.

Lyvanne wanted to help, she tried to stand using the tree as leverage, but her vision turned fuzzy, her body turned suddenly light and seconds later she had collapsed back by the side of the trunk.

• • •

"Better go back to wherever you've been hiding Hemeti, this ain't your concern," Drystal spat with venom in his words as he tried to circle Jocelyn.

"Yes it is," Jocelyn replied, matching his steps but making sure that at all times she was stood between him and Lyvanne.

Drystal lunged. The trees didn't give very much room to manoeuvre, but it was enough that Jocelyn had to think on her feet to avoid being out-stepped in this dance of life and death.

Fortunately, she found Drystal was very much the kind of fighter who relied on berserk rage and wild swings to win the fight, something that in the confines of the woods wasn't going to help his cause.

She easily dodged the first lunge, and using the space created on his open side she threw a stiff punch to his rib cage. The encircling trees had worked against her, preventing her from putting any real power behind her fist. It was far from a fight-ending blow, but it was enough to tell him that she meant business.

Drystal rocked back a few steps, placing his free hand on what was sure to be a bruised mid-section. He gritted his teeth, grunted and lunged again. This attack came closer to the mark and Jocelyn had to use her left hand to forcibly hold back the knife. The two were entwined and Jocelyn took advantage, slamming the man's head into the trunk of a nearby tree, before following it up with a swift knee to his mid-rift and releasing her hold of his arm.

She wasn't going to win a contest of strength for long, she knew, so her attacks had to be mobile, in and out quickly before he had a chance to react.

She chanced a glance back towards Lyvanne as Drystal recovered from the two-hit combo. The girl was dazed, but it appeared as though she'd be alright. *Good*, Jocelyn thought, she could afford to focus solely on her opponent.

This time Jocelyn moved first, acting before Drystal had the time to move away from the tree which had limited his range of movement. She feigned an attack to his armed side, waited for him to lunge in retaliation and swirled in the opposite direction. Cutting into the open space she delivered three swift punches, the first two to the same spot on his rib-cage that she had hit previously, the third a vicious uppercut to his jaw which sent him rebounding into the tree.

Drystal staggered, his legs growing wobbly beneath him. She doubted that he had expected this much of a fight from a woman, let alone a Hemeti. It was an underestimation that she planned on taking full advantage of.

Seeing the weakness in his legs Jocelyn saw her opportunity to finish the fight. She kicked out, hitting his left kneecap hard, forcing the man down to one knee as his yelled out in pain. She was pretty certain she had broken something in his leg, but just to be safe she stamped down on the other kneecap, immobilising him on the woodland floor. Next she grabbed the hand he was using to hold the knife, still firmly grasped between his fingers, and swung it back into the tree trunk, breaking his wrist and sending the knife flying in the process.

Drystal yelled out in pain. Jocelyn had heard enough and brought her knee up, smashing it onto the bridge of his nose. Drystal's head whipped backwards as blood spurted out of his nose and onto the forest floor. The trunk of the tree behind him was waiting and the double impact of knee and trunk left him unconscious on the floor.

The fight was won. Jocelyn turned her attention back to Lyvanne who was lying still against a nearby tree, her eyes wide and her jaw agape.

"I didn't know you could fight like that," Lyvanne stammered as Jocelyn made her way over to her.

"You should see me with swords. Are you okay?" she asked, leaning down towards her friend and running a thumb across the cut on her cheek.

"I think so, banged my head on the tree," Lyvanne replied, motioning to the back of her skull.

Jocelyn checked, there was a small amount of blood but nothing too bad.

"Come on, let's get you back to camp," she said, pulling all of Lyvanne's weight up and onto her shoulders.

"What about him?" Lyvanne asked, nodding her head in the direction of Drystal who still lay silent on the floor, covered in an unflattering mix of mud, leaves and blood.

"He won't be going anywhere any time soon. I'll send someone to come and collect him," Jocelyn said, her face stone cold as she considered the felled man.

Thankfully Drystal hadn't taken Lyvanne too far out into the woods, and Jocelyn found that the girl's weight wasn't too taxing as they slowly approached the border of the camp.

"Lyvanne?" Jocelyn heard a familiar voice call out.

"Over here," she replied.

Moments later, Turiel appeared at the edge of the trees. Upon seeing Jocelyn with Lyvanne hoisted up, her arms draped over the back of her shoulders, he came running over.

"Take that arm," Jocelyn said as he ran up by her side.

Turiel did as he was asked and helped Jocelyn carry her the rest of the way.

"What happened?!" he asked, his eyes filled with terror and a complete lack of understanding.

"Some prick had a knife to her throat. Turiel, you nearly lost her," Jocelyn replied, her voice cold and unforgiving.

"I'm fine," Lyvanne tried to intervene, but her voice was weak and barely audible. Her entire body was drained of energy, but in a manner that it never had before. She wanted nothing more than to fall asleep.

"Drystal," Turiel said as he slowly began to realise what must have happened. "I'll kill him, where is he?"

"Already dealt with him, few hundred yards back that way," Jocelyn replied as Turiel stole a glance back over his shoulder.

"Is he dead?"

Jocelyn shook her head as they entered the camp proper. It didn't take long before others noticed their arrival. Two men whom Jocelyn didn't know ran over.

"Drystal did this," he told them as he motioned into the woods. "If he hasn't taken his last breath already... make sure he does."

CHAPTER 23

When Lyvanne awoke to find herself in what passed for a medic's hut, Tyler, The Spring's resident medic, informed her that she probably had what was likely to be the "world's worst hangover." She had never experienced a hangover before, but it was certainly not something she ever wished to have again. Her head throbbed in multiple locations, sending constant waves of pain from back to front across her scalp, perfectly accompanying the constant dull ache that was growing outwards from a large lump under her right eye.

Raising a finger to her right cheek Lyvanne found a number of stitches where Drystal's knife had pierced her skin, and just above those was the swelling caused by his fist.

"Try not to touch," Tyler said as he passed her a small goblet of water. "Not the best work I've ever done, but then again I don't have the same kind of equipment out here."

Lyvanne studied him, the camp's resident medic. He was middle aged with slightly greying hair at the fringes. He was quite tall, taller than Turiel but not quite the same height as Shri'ook or Kwah. He had a certain charm that was rarely found in men younger than him. Lyvanne tried to hold it back but as butterflies tumbled in her stomach a hot red flush grew in her cheeks.

"Thank you for your help," she said, before realising that the swelling was somewhat impairing her voice.

"No need to thank me, it's my job. Just try not to talk too much, and definitely don't put any strain on that head of yours for the next few days okay?"

Lyvanne nodded, sending another wave of pain wracking around her brain that made Tyler slightly chuckle when he realised.

"How about you just do a thumbs up or down for the rest of the day, eh?"

Lyvanne gave him a thumbs up. "Okay."

She was asked to remain in bed for the rest of the day, over which she was visited by a handful of people. Jocelyn and Turiel came first, they pandered to her, making sure she was okay and that Tyler was treating her okay. Lyvanne had so many questions that she wanted to ask both of them, but she was still tired and struggling to keep her eyes open at times, so decided they could wait until later. Kwah was her next, albeit brief, visitor.

"I'm so sorry for what he did to you Lyvanne," he said as he placed a hand on her shoulder. "I long suspected him of having ulterior motives, of using us to fulfil his lust for… well, you don't need me to tell you. To his credit there was no better thief when you needed one, but I should have seen that he was using us sooner. No man should find joy in stealing, or hurting others. I was blinded by his usefulness, as were we all," Kwah appeared downtrodden by his own poor judgement. "I promise you that someone like him won't be welcome into our family again… speaking of which, I look forward to discussing her future when she felt fit enough."

The last to visit that day was Oblib; he came later on into the evening after he had finished cooking that evening's meal. Lyvanne was pleasantly surprised to see the large man wade his way into the hut, and even more pleased once she saw the bowl of steaming hot broth he was carrying with him. Unable to contain her grin, she gobbled up the food before he even had time to say his goodbyes. As he stood at the door a smile crossed his face and reaching into the pocket of his apron he pulled out and offered her an extra piece of bread he had stashed away.

Lyvanne spent the rest of that night in the medic hut, just to be on the safe side. She didn't mind too much, Jocelyn and Turiel probably needed the time alone, and after how her last appearance in front of a crowd had gone she wasn't too eager to be seen around camp any time soon. Unfortunately that wasn't to be long lived.

Tyler visited her early in the morning. The swelling on her cheek had gone down somewhat, meaning her speech was no longer impeded.

To finish the job Tyler gave her a wet piece of cloth and told her to hold it against the swelling whilst he went to fetch Turiel. The warlock arrived with her breakfast in hand and sat by her side on the edge of her bed, neither saying anything. Lyvanne had noticed the day before that Turiel had seemed quieter than usual when he and Jocelyn came to visit. She didn't know why; he wasn't to blame for what happened to her.

"Come on," he said as she finished her food and placed the empty bowl on the floor nearby. "Time we got you out of this hut."

Turiel took her by the hand and guided her outside. Even through the trees and canopy above their heads the sun was still bright enough that she had to cover her eyes, the bright light sending another twang of pain down her body.

"Don't worry, that'll go away in a day or two," Turiel said as he saw her shy away from the sun's rays.

She had assumed that they were going back to their own hut, but was surprised when Turiel began to lead her towards the Annex where she could see Tublik, Kwah, Shri'ook and Jocelyn waiting for them. The men and women they passed along the way all in some way acknowledged her, most by the polite nod of their head but some came up to her, stopping the pair in their tracks and themselves apologising for what happened to her.

"Why does everyone keep apologising?" Lyvanne asked Turiel as they made their way through the camp.

"Because we all blame ourselves. It's easy to forget for us all sometimes, but you're still a child. We shouldn't have let Drystal attack you the way he did, we should have been there to stop it," he replied moments before waving his greetings to the others waiting for them in the Annex.

Kwah was the first to walk over to her as they entered the Annex and pulled the loose wall down behind them. "How are you Lyvanne?" He asked, his voice calm and soothing. She had grown to quite like him.

"Better. Thank you, Kwah."

Shri'ook moved over to her side, thanking Turiel for bringing her over as he did. Soon after followed Tublik, both of whom offered their sympathies for what had happened and their apologies for letting it happen in the first place. Lyvanne was certain it was the first time she had heard Tublik speak more than one or two words in a row.

"I hear from Tyler that you are recovering quite well?" Shri'ook asked.

Lyvanne nearly gave him a thumbs up out of habit, but quickly stopped herself. "Pretty well I think."

"Good. Unfortunately the time for rest has come and gone, we are all aware of the situation we find ourselves in and we have much to discuss."

Knots formed in her stomach. Couldn't she just have a few days without having "much to discuss" she asked herself as she watched the glances being shared between the others.

"Turiel, I start with you first," Shri'ook continued, turning his attention to the pale faced founder of The Spring. "Without you none of us would be here. Many of us would still be struggling to make our way back at our homes with the king's noose always around our necks. For that, you hold the thanks and respect of everyone in our camp and of even more people across The Rive."

Turiel bowed his head. "Thank you, Shri'ook."

"Do not thank me," Shri'ook replied as he waved away the gesture. "It is a respect and gratitude that you have earned, perhaps more so than you know, so do not say your thanks for it. With that being said, we here are not ones to make decisions that could put our people's lives at risk without their say on the matter. Which brings me back to you, Lyvanne."

Jocelyn moved a step closer to her and put her arm around her shoulder.

"I know what you did and I know why you did it. In fact, in some ways I even commend you for your actions. But what you have done means that sooner rather than later the king's men will find us here."

Lyvanne nearly interrupted. She wanted to tell him that she could leave and draw them away, but something held her back. Unlike before, the more she thought about that route of action, the more she realised that she didn't want to leave.

"What to do about that will, no matter the response, require the thoughts of everyone in this camp," Shri'ook continued. "Fortunately for us all, Tublik, Kwah and I saw that all opinions on the matter were gathered last night."

Surprise dawned on the faces of Jocelyn and Turiel. It appeared as though they had been left out of these discussions.

"Don't worry, I'll go with you if I need to," Jocelyn whispered in her ear.

"Do not fret, Jocelyn. The decision was fairly unanimous. Besides one or two of our people, who will come round with time, we have all agreed that you are welcome to stay with us and together we shall overcome any obstacles that the king places in our path."

A torrent of relief coursed through Lyvanne's body. Her head turned giddy, unsure of whether it was a result of the knock she had taken the day before or a result of pure joy. It wasn't until the words had been said that she realised exactly how much she wanted to stay. The relief was shared. Jocelyn knelt down beside her and wrapped her arms around her, whilst Turiel went around the Annex shaking the hand of all three men stood before them.

"Thank you," Turiel replied with sincerity.

"You're welcome," Shri'ook said with a smile on his face, this time feeling it right to accept the thanks rather than cast it aside. "However, this is all dependent on whether the lady will have us?"

All eyes turned back towards Lyvanne. *This is it*, she thought, her decision had to be made now. Was a life of part of The Spring really what she wanted? Was the young girl who wanted to start a quiet life of her own beyond the walls of Astreya really gone? In the end it turned out the decision was an easy one to make.

"I want to stay here. I want to help."

• • •

Shortly after the meeting, Shri'ook grabbed Turiel by the arm and took him aside to one of the quieter corners of the camp. The two had a fond respect for one another. They had known each other for a number of years by this point and Turiel considered the older man a crucial cog in the establishment of what had been the early days of The Spring.

"Turiel, listen," Shri'ook said. "We have done all of this for the girl. I need you to understand that."

"What do you mean?" Turiel asked, matching the hushed tone that the Islander had adopted.

"Many of us are aware of your vision, the vision of a woman leading an army into battle against the king, but that is not why she stays, she stays because she is liked among our people and because we do not want to cast her off into the world alone."

Turiel understood. It was famously difficult to make people believe in the visions granted to others by the Angels of Destiny. He wasn't going to assume he would be one of the lucky ones.

"She will be a part of The Spring. We will teach her our ways, but I do not want you to put undue pressure on the girl," Shri'ook continued. "She is not a war leader."

"Not yet," Turiel replied with a knowing smile.

CHAPTER 24

"What made you want to stay?" Jocelyn asked as she and Lyvanne walked through the woods, collecting firewood for camp.

The rest of the day before had been spent celebrating the fact that Lyvanne was sticking around. More than once did people reassure her by saying that this was the life they chose and that danger was part of the package. Greyson and Davidson even wrote her a song. It wasn't the best that Lyvanne had ever heard, but it was a nice gesture nevertheless.

Jocelyn, Turiel and Lyvanne hadn't spent too much time talking about the ins and outs of the past few weeks over the course of the day. Instead, they had opted to simply enjoy their time together— the first chance they'd had to do so in quite a while. But today was different, today all the questions came flooding out.

"I don't know. If I'm honest, I didn't think I would until the chance to leave really started to open up," Lyvanne replied, struggling to keep hold of the large pile of tinder which had accumulated in her arms.

Turiel had told Jocelyn about everything that had happened whilst she had been gone. About the warlock invading her mind, their training out in the countryside, the letter from Sinjin - which had made Jocelyn cry when she read it - and how Lyvanne had felt responsible and drawn the king's gaze away from Astreya. But no one had yet told Lyvanne why Jocelyn had left in the first place.

"Why did you leave? Turiel told me it was something to do with strategy."

Jocelyn looked rueful, like she didn't want reminding of what it had been that caused her to leave for so long.

"Yeah, strategy," she replied. "Unfortunately, part of being an insurgent means that fighting is going to come part and parcel with the job. We try and minimise that where we can, and I know for a fact that it's especially the case if there's a civilian population involved. But eventually if we're going to oust the king then one day we're going to have to make a march on one of the cities."

The cogs in Lyvanne's brain started turning. "Someone wanted to attack Avagarde?"

Jocelyn seemed surprised. "How'd you know that?"

"Turiel said that's where you'd be, that it's where you go when you need to blow off steam. He said that you love it there. The way he described it... it did sound beautiful."

Jocelyn smiled. "Yes, you're pretty much right. It wasn't an attack though. Our numbers across The Rive are growing, but we're still not ready for an attack on a city. A large town, maybe?"

The joke didn't land, but Lyvanne didn't blame her for trying to lighten the conversation.

"No. The idea was put forward from one of the other branches that we could instead suffocate Avagarde, cut off the trade routes, harry the smaller armies as they try to put an end to it all. If the plan was... if the plan is successful, then the king would be forced to call out his real troops. Our scouts would be able to see where they came from, count how many there are and what routes they used to travel. We would disband before they reached us."

"To what end?"

"We'd have more information than we did before, and when you're playing a game as dangerous as the one we're in, information can be more valuable than numbers."

"So why did you disagree?"

"Because of what it would mean for Avagarde. Other cities like Astreya, Yidid and Elvabane are too big to try and suffocate, especially with our numbers. But Avagarde is perfect, it's a relatively small city located in the dip of a valley. We'd be in perfect position to cut it off from the rest of The Rive, but I don't think the city would survive, at least not enough to carry on as it is now. The king isn't the type to divert extra resources towards one of the lesser cities if he could avoid it through a show of strength."

Lyvanne tried to understand, to wrap her head around what the plan would mean for both sides of the conflict and for those caught between. "So the people there would suffer?"

Jocelyn nodded. "The nature within its walls would wither and die first as the people looked for ways to cook their foods and feed their fires... then the weak and vulnerable would begin to pass on."

Lyvanne wanted to throw up, this wasn't how she had imagined The Spring waging war. Then again, she'd never really thought about the intricacies of warfare before now. She decided not to press the matter any further. It was obvious from the sorrowful look on her face that Jocelyn truly did love this city, and of all the places across The Rive that Lyvanne had dreamt of exploring, Avagarde was all of a sudden at the top of her list.

"Do you think they'll still go ahead with the plan?" she asked.

"We'll see, little one. I think someone might have placed a few bumps in the road whilst I was away," Jocelyn replied playfully, nudging her friend in the arm with her elbow.

Lyvanne tried to nudge her back, but tripped on the root of a tree and ended up sending her pile of wood flying through the air, much to Jocelyn's amusement.

"It's not funny!" Lyvanne shouted through a laugh as she scrambled to pick up all the wood that had been dropped.

Jocelyn promised that she wanted to help her, but couldn't do so without dropping her own gatherings. The two laughed it off once Lyvanne had managed to gather up as much as she could, being lucky that it hadn't rained that day and the floor was pretty dry meaning that what wood had hit the floor hadn't been ruined.

There was no doubting that gathering the firewood was considered a chore, but today she hadn't minded. In fact, she'd enjoyed it. It had been too long since her and Jocelyn had been able to spend time together, and after all that had happened in the time that she had been gone, it was good to have another familiar and friendly face around.

• • •

Turiel found her along the edges of camp, a mallet in her hand and a pool of glistening sweat gathering across her forehead.

"Making yourself useful I see," he commented as he walked up behind her.

His arrival caught the attention of the crowd Lyvanne was amongst.

"The kid's got a knack for building barricades it seems," Greyson said as he put aside a large wooden stake that he had been sharpening the tip of.

"This is my fault, least I can do is help us prepare," Lyvanne replied as she finished hammering a smaller stake into the ground alongside a series of others.

Turiel smiled. Lyvanne was starting to let her guard down around the others and it was good to see. No one would have blamed her for shying away after what had happened, but if anything it had only made her bolder.

"Besides, here I get to listen to these two sing," she continued, smiling gleefully at Greyson and his brother Davidson who was a few feet away checking the quality of the barricade.

Turiel looked on at what they had built. It looked strong, he thought, hopefully strong enough. Shri'ook had ordered the construction of their defences as soon as they knew that the king was coming for them. The final touches wouldn't be finished until the enemies were within sight, but the islander had been eager to get things started.

"Mind if I borrow her for a while?" Turiel asked innocently.

"By all means," Davidson shouted over from the wooden construction. "But bring her back by nightfall, this barricade won't build itself!"

"I promise. Come on, little one."

"Where are we going?" Lyvanne asked as she wiped the sweat from her face.

"You like to learn, don't you? Well, I figured it was time to teach you something more... tangible, than magic," Turiel replied, a smirk hidden from Lyvanne's view as they walked side-by-side back into camp.

Pulling down the loose wall of the Annex felt like shutting themselves away from the outside world. Inside, alone, it almost felt peaceful and calm like a lone oasis within a raging storm.

"You sure I'm allowed to be in here?" Lyvanne asked as she looked around at the letters and maps stored throughout.

"For the purpose of what I have to teach you, yes it's fine, but don't worry I asked the others first," Turiel replied as he watched her eyes flit back and forth from paper to paper. "Come here," he continued. "This is what I wanted to show you."

Turiel waved a hand and signalled for her to join him in the centre of the room where he was stood around a large detailed map of The Rive. His eyes slowly gazed over every detail, it wasn't as intricate as the maps that he had seen stored away in the king's collection years ago, but for it was more than suited to their needs. "This is how we plan our moves, how we organise the various branches of The Spring."

Lyvanne wandered over, her eyes studying the map with every step. He admired that about her, her desire to know everything there was to know about the world they lived in. "And the wooden soldiers, they're the king's men?"

Turiel nodded. "Or at least where we think they're stationed," he elaborated as he picked up a wooden swordsman and passed it across the table to Lyvanne. "The king has been pushing the boundaries of him empire for years now, and whilst that means that the majority of his forces are abroad it also means that specific information is more difficult to find. The king might be cruel, but he's smart. He knows that if an enemy nation were to get their hands on documents detailing troop movements or stations then they'd have the upper hand."

Turiel turned his attention away from the map and towards a pile of parchment stacked on a small wooden stool to the rear of the room. All the while Lyvanne looked on in wonder, her attention utterly captured. "That parchment, pass it to me," he urged.

"This paper here," he continued as he picked out a ragged piece of parchment from the pile as Lyvanne lifted it onto the map. "This is what I stole that night in the Accord. Here, read it."

Turiel watched as Lyvanne's eyes began to light up with anticipation as he passed her the parchment. "Can you read it?" he asked.

"Yes," she replied as she scanned each and every line of information like a thirst she had not known she needed to quench until now. "Troop numbers... Officer names... Turiel, this has everything."

The pair smiled at one another. "Nearly... nearly everything," He replied, blunting the enthusiasm. "This document belonged to a foreign dignitary, specifically one from the Kingdom of Midden. They stole it from the king during a series of diplomatic talks, and one our sources within the castle caught drift and let us know. With the timing of it going missing, it wasn't hard to figure out where it had gone. That's when you and I stepped in, the night before the dignitary was due to head back to Midden. The only thing that it doesn't detail is where the troops are based."

"Which is why there's a plan to use Avagarde to draw them out?"

"Exactly," Turiel confirmed. The memory of his argument with Jocelyn came rushing back to him, and he had no doubt that Lyvanne had noticed it when he bit his lip in guilt. All he could do now was thank the Goddess' fortune that Jocelyn had made her peace with what needed to happen, and more importantly, had forgiven him.

"Turiel... what happened to Drystal?" Lyvanne asked, her eyes never leaving the wooden soldier as she spun over and over again high above the ground.

"He..." Turiel started to reply, careful to find the right words. "We couldn't keep someone like that around, not after what he did to you."

"Is he dead?"

"Yes," he replied, not wanting to keep the truth from her. Tears began to well in her eyes as she held her head up high and forced the water to stay hidden. He was more surprised to find his own vision blurred as water slowly forced its way across his eyes. "Come here," Turiel said before walking around the table to her side and placing both his arms around her shoulders and bringing her in tight to his chest. "You're growing up too quick."

• • •

Later that afternoon, Lyvanne found herself sat around a large cauldron that was bubbling over with water and vegetables as she helped Oblib with that evening's meal prep. Apparently her talents weren't as a future chef, as Oblib was quick to jovially chastise her for the multitude of mistakes she was making.

"It's not my fault this rabbit has no meat on it!" she replied one time, earning a few cheers of encouragement from passers-by.

Shortly after, she was relegated to washing pots and pans. Not the most thrilling of past times, but she was happy to be helping out where she could. It was in the middle of her washing up that Lyvanne saw Kwah rush into the Annex with Turiel in tow behind him. Something's happening, Lyvanne thought as she watched the pair shifting around figures on their map of The Rive. They were shortly joined by Tublik and Shri'ook who appeared from differing parts of the camp.

"Eyes down kid," Oblib said, as he turned her head back towards the dishes with a forceful hand. "Not for our eyes and ears until we're told it is."

Lyvanne grunted her reluctant acceptance. She knew Oblib was right, she'd been fortunate to be involved in conversations that she shouldn't have been before, but if she was going to fit in then she had to know her place alongside everyone else. Fortunately, she didn't have to wait long. A few minutes later, Kwah appeared from within the Annex and started rounding up various men and women from around the camp. Not everyone, Lyvanne noticed, but a sizeable number.

"What's going on?" Lyvanne asked Oblib, all the while making sure she kept scrubbing the dirty cooking utensils.

"Looks like someone's found us a new target on the North Road," Oblib replied as he nonchalantly carried on mixing in ingredients into a large cauldron.

Lyvanne's mind raced with possibilities. She remembered Jocelyn saying earlier in the day that the reason for the camp's location wasn't just that it was hidden among the trees, and hard to get to with a sizeable troop. But that less than half a day's ride to the east was a fairly significant road, which connected Avagarde with the northern reaches of The Rive, including Astreya. From this location, The Spring could carry out strikes along the road against the king's convoys; whether they were carrying food, money or weapons and not be in the immediate vicinity where the king would search if he ever grew tired of their attacks.

Spread throughout the camp, Lyvanne could make out men and women sharpening weapons at a much faster rate than was usually the case. Others had begun prepping gambesons and stray pieces of leather armour, washing it and testing that it was fit for purpose.

"Will people get hurt?"

"Depends what the target is like," Oblib replied, clearly not taking much notice in what was happening. "If there's a big security detail then yeah maybe, but that's what we've got Tyler for."

One medic between a camp of over fifty didn't seem like great numbers to Lyvanne, but she bit her tongue. She just hoped that Tyler wasn't the only one who knew how to knit stitches.

Moments later, much to her surprise, Kwah came over in her direction.

"You want to see what we're all about kid?" he asked, a toothy smile on his face.

She didn't know what to say or what to expect.

"Go on kid, gotta be around this stuff eventually," Oblib said, egging her on from his cauldron.

"Yeah… yeah okay then," she replied, putting down the washing. "I won't need to kill anyone will I?"

Kwah burst out in laughter as he ushered her over towards where the weapons were being prepped.

"No kid, no you won't. We leave at first light, how about you help this lot sharpen weapons and clean up the armour until evening meal?"

She nodded and immediately found a spot to sit down and help out. The armour smelled, and the swords felt unnatural and heavy to hold, but she didn't let that deter her. Instead, she just gritted her teeth and kept working. Those around her helped when they saw her struggling, but she was doing a decent enough job that she could handle most of what was needed on her own.

Turiel emerged from the Annex shortly thereafter and passed her as he made his way over to their hut. He looked down at her as he passed by and gave her a wink. She returned the gesture. She hated to admit it, but she was excited.

CHAPTER 25

O blib hadn't been wrong. The North Road stretched out before Lyvanne, almost as far as the eye could see before it followed the curvature of an outbreak of hills in the distance. As the company had gathered to leave, Lyvanne had done a quick head count. *At least half,* she thought to herself, half of the camp was being taken.

"Our scouts report that the security detail is large enough to signal a worthy target," Kwah had said during his briefing the night before. Lyvanne recalled the feeling of nausea she'd had whilst listening to the plan. "One convoy heading south from Astreya, we'll be split into two teams to handle this one. A prime team, and a second hidden from view… there for emergencies."

Lyvanne had asked why that was the case, and Turiel had been forthcoming. "If we start showing our real numbers then it's more likely that the king will start to take notice. The Spring has always tried do things with the fewest people involved that the situation will allow," he said as they walked towards their destination.

The flatlands themselves save for the occasional small hill that was dotted across the landscape, were not ideal for ambushes. At least not at first glance, which was probably ideal. The particular section of road that Lyvanne now looked over was at the bottom of a small ridge, not taller than seven feet high and only three or four carriages long, but it was enough to hide some of their troops. On the other side of the road was a field of crops grown tall, that's where the other half of The Spring had hidden, the half who ideally wouldn't be needed.

The journey to the spot had gone quickly, but long enough for Lyvanne to bite off half of her nails with nerves and anticipation. She'd never dreamed of being in a situation like this, and now here she was, laying down on the top of the small ridge, eagerly waiting the signal from Turiel to retreat further into the field behind her with Jocelyn and to hide. She wasn't to take part in the mission, which she was thankful for, but everyone had agreed that the sooner she was around situations like these the sooner she'd be able to handle herself when the right time came.

The plan seemed simple enough. There were enough weapons at camp for everyone who went on the mission to be armed, and should everything go smoothly, they wouldn't have to use any of them.

"Are you nervous, little one?" Jocelyn asked, as she lay beside Lyvanne on the dew covered grass.

"Yes," she wasn't afraid to admit it.

There was something else that had added to Lyvanne's nerves. Upon leaving the camp at daybreak, Jocelyn had readied herself for a fight, just in case she was called upon to protect Lyvanne. Around her waist, she'd hung two swords, both identical and as basic as they came.

"They might not look like much, but they suit my style of fighting," Jocelyn had said. But it wasn't Jocelyn's ability to fight that had Lyvanne worried. It was the burning memory of her nightmares, the reminder that she'd watched Jocelyn die so many times, and many of them with twin swords in hand.

"Just try not to get into trouble if you don't have to, okay?" she said as she turned on the grass to face her protector.

"That's the plan," Jocelyn replied, a playful grin peering back at Lyvanne. "Chances are that they'll surrender once they see they're outnumbered anyway," Lyvanne wasn't sure how it was that easy, but she nodded along and hoped for the best.

It wasn't much later that they caught the first signs of the convoy in the distance. The king's silver and green banners were flying high from two carriages, and Lyvanne could make out at least five or six heavily armed guards riding alongside.

Turiel came up behind them. "Time for you two to disappear."

Without needing to be told twice, they crouched and retreated back to their hiding spot a few metres away and off to the side where they had a clear but hidden view of what was about to unfold.

From her spot in the tall grasses of the field Lyvanne saw one of the singing brothers. Greyson, she thought, but couldn't tell from that distance, step out onto the road, a bit further down from the ridge. He had his lute in hand and began playing. Lyvanne was sure that he had been a bard before he and his brother joined The Spring.

The convoy grew closer. Two carriages and six guards, all adorning the king's colours.

"What do you -

"Sssh," Jocelyn interjected, holding a single finger up to her lips.

She heard shouting from the convoy, someone was calling out to Greyson to step out of the way. Unsurprisingly, he ignored them and carried on playing. Just as they'd planned the convoy began to slow down, eventually stopping right where Turiel and the others were waiting; at the bottom of the small ridge.

"Greetings, gentlemen," she heard Greyson saying, but the response from the guard was muzzled by his steel helm.

The guard who was at the front of the convoy was becoming highly animated, waving his arms in erratic fashion as if it would magically cast Greyson to the side of the road. Then came the whistle, and as if perfectly rehearsed all of the men and women lying flat against the ridge rose in unison, each of them with a longbow in hand. All together they knocked an arrow into their bow and aimed them down at the convoy. The horses jerked as the figures rose like shadows from the dark, but the guards kept control. She was surprised to see how calm everyone in the convoy looked. They were easily outnumbered by nearly two to one just by the people on the ridge.

She spied Turiel among those on top of the ridge. He seemed quite in control of the situation, his voice commanding and stern as he shouted down his conditions to the convoy.

"Place your weapons on the floor and drop to your knees!" he shouted.

After a moment's hesitation, it became clear why the king's soldiers appeared so calm. As four more heavily armed soldiers exited the front carriage and piled out onto the road on the opposite side of the ridge, putting the safety of the lumbering carriage frame between themselves and the archers above. Lyvanne knew that they'd inadvertently put themselves closer to Kwah's troops hidden in the crops behind them, but they wouldn't appear unless absolutely necessary.

Suddenly the odds seemed far more even than they had before. Twelve lightly armed soldiers on the ridge facing off against ten fully armoured soldiers on the road, as well as two drivers. Greyson, still stood in the road beyond the carriages tipped the odds in the favour of The Spring by one person, but even with the archers trained on their prey Lyvanne didn't trust the arrows to pierce the plate armour of all their targets, and that still left the four other soldiers who were hidden behind the carriage.

The nerves made her feel sick, but at the same time she was entirely enthralled. Her mind was racing with numbers, possibilities and strategies.

Turiel began shouting at the convoy again, ordering the hidden soldiers to come out from behind the carriage. But they weren't about to budge and the parley didn't appear to be going well.

Lyvanne's eyes drifted to the second carriage, the one that was obviously carrying the cargo. What have they got in there? She wondered. She was no military genius but it seemed like a significant security escort for whatever it was inside. Jocelyn moved beside her. Looking across she noticed that the Hemeti had moved her hand down by her side, hovering ready over the hilt of one of her swords.

This isn't going well, Lyvanne thought as she saw the concerned look growing in Jocelyn's eyes. She moved her attention back to the road. The person who was talking with Turiel had begun to remove his sword from its sheath, she could see Turiel commanding him to stop, but it appeared a lost cause.

There was movement in the field opposite the ridge. Tall stems of wheat began to move, rustling as if blown by a wind and as she had expected, Kwah and the rest of the men and women who had been brought along from camp emerged out onto the road, swords in hand. They immediately took hold of the four soldiers who had used the carriage as cover from the archers on the ridge, and the game was won.

"Surrender!" she heard Turiel shout down from the ridge as Kwah appeared around the side of the carriage with his prisoners in hand. No doubt the soldiers would still be able to take a few of The Spring with them into the next life if they chose to fight, but it was no longer a fight that they could win.

Jocelyn breathed a sigh of relief as they watched the rest of the convoy place their weapons on the ground, swiftly followed by Turiel leading the archers down from the ridge to procure them for better use. The convoy had been taken and not a single person had needed to lose their life. Lyvanne felt pleased, almost proud even, knowing that if it had been the other way around then the king would have ordered men to kill first, ask questions later. But they were better than that.

The pair waited, they knew the drill; once the king's men had been dispatched they could join in. Turiel hadn't wanted to risk Lyvanne being out in the open, even after the battle had been won. So they watched as one by one the king's soldiers were bound and placed into the first carriage, whilst Kwah and three others worked on breaking open the rear carriage. Once the soldiers had been squeezed into one carriage, Turiel gave one of the driving horses a slap across the rear and set it off back in the direction of Astreya. Lyvanne wasted no time in running over to the road once the coast was clear, Jocelyn taking a more relaxed approach to her walk over.

"Well done!" she shouted at Turiel as she ran over and jumped into his arms. She hadn't known what to expect from the ambush, but she'd never felt adrenaline quite like it.

"Thanks, little one. It nearly didn't go so smooth. We have Kwah to thank for that," He said beckoning over to the muscle laden islander who was currently contending with a particularly stubborn rear door of a windowless carriage.

All in all, The Spring had commandeered a selection of well-made Palace steel longswords, two longbows fashioned from some kind of animal bone and most importantly nine of the king's royal horses, strong and beautiful Destriers taken from the Eastern Plains.

Crack! Kwah and his companions had broken into the carriage.

"Turiel, you better come see this," Kwah said from behind the carriage.

Turiel, Jocelyn, Lyvanne and few more curious men and women who were keen to see what the prize for the ambush would be made their way over to Kwah. What Lyvanne saw made her sick to her stomach. The carriage wasn't filled with money, food, or any other goods that could be put to purpose by The Spring. It was filled Hemeti.

Mostly everyone stood there in stunned silence. One Hemeti woman to the back of the crowd started crying, and the look on Jocelyn's face turned ice cold. Slavery was common among pirates off the coast of The Rive, it was even known to take place in some of the richer households on the Shimmering Isles. But it was a strictly forbidden practice on The Rive.

"Are they prisoners?" she asked, hoping that her initial reaction had been wrong.

Turiel shook his head. "No need to transport prisoners," he replied, his eyes moving to watch Jocelyn. Lyvanne thought that it looked like he wanted to say something to her, to comfort her perhaps, but the words were lost in the gravity of the moment. There were ten Hemeti in total, two of whom were no older than Lyvanne was. Sat in their own squalor each of them looked deprived of nutrition, their ribs showing through their skin and barely enough energy to raise their hands as Jocelyn took the first steps up into the carriage to help them.

"Get in and help them," Kwah ordered to a handful of people stood around him.

"Why?" It was about the only question Lyvanne could feasibly put together. She had no idea that this sort of thing was happening in The Rive, let alone under the orders of the king.

"I don't know, Lyvanne. I'm sorry," Turiel replied, his face forlorn and haggard.

Lyvanne stole a look back at the carriage as the first of the Hemeti was helped out and onto the road. They looked drained of all life, and she wasn't even sure if they were aware they had been rescued.

You made the right decision, she told herself as she watched more of the captives being brought out into the light. *This is where you belong.*

CHAPTER 26

Despite tasting victory, the journey back to camp was a sombre one.

"Give them the horses," Kwah demanded, signalling towards the fragile and vulnerable bodies of the rescued Hemeti as the company prepared for the journey back to camp.

Turiel had wanted to go off and find some food for them, but Kwah had emphasised caution, opting to wait for Tyler to check them over first back at camp. So after putting some water into their bellies, they had set off.

"Which way are we going?" Lyvanne asked Greyson, who had just finished helping her set one of the Hemeti steady on horseback. She knew the way they had taken to arrive at the North Road, and she was sure that it wasn't the same way they were now travelling back to camp.

"It's only cautionary, kid," Greyson replied, an impressed smile hidden beneath his shaggy beard. "Always take the long way home, just in case anyone is tracking us."

• • •

Once they had been journeying long enough to be confident that wasn't the case, they changed course and made directly for the woods, travelling at the fastest pace possible so that they could get those they had rescued into some modicum of safety.

Lyvanne found herself walking alongside Turiel the rest of the way back. Jocelyn had distanced herself from the rest of the group, choosing instead to scout ahead. Lyvanne knew that seeing her people thrown into the back of carriages like slaughter animals had pained her, but she the best thing for her right now was probably time and space.

"Why couldn't you use your magic?" Lyvanne asked Turiel, trying her best to start thinking about anything other than the almost lifeless Hemeti riding on horseback only a few metres away.

Turiel didn't particularly look like he wanted to talk much but Lyvanne was ready to the force the issue if it kept him distracted from what they'd seen.

"We try not to kill people when it's not absolutely necessary. They might be fighting for the king, but for most of them it would just be a job, they have families back home somewhere. If I used magic in front of them, then we'd have to kill them. I can't risk the king finding out about me. Otherwise, he'd send a warlock of his own to come and find me and it might mean the deaths of everyone else around me. It's not worth the trade off, I would rather risk showing more of our numbers."

The answer seemed fair, but the similarity to her own position made Lyvanne feel guilty. She had had the choice to hide, but she had chosen to lure the king towards them regardless, putting those lives that Turiel chose to protect, in danger.

To her right Lyvanne could see Kwah and one of the Hemeti men from the camp talking to one of the captives. Upon their initial rescue, none of them had been forthcoming with any information about who they were, where they were heading or why they had been taken. But it appeared that Kwah was having slightly more luck now, with one of them at least: a tall Hemeti man, who had grey hair and a long scraggly beard.

"What will we do with them?"

Turiel looked over at the same Hemeti that Lyvanne found herself watching. "Not sure, I don't think there's ever been something like this before. We'll help them get better, find out what they know and then if I had to guess Shri'ook would want to offer them the choice to join us or make their own way, the same way you had that choice."

Lyvanne nodded. She liked that idea.

One of the rescued Hemeti caught her attention. He appeared to be a similar age to Kwah, older than Turiel but not as old as the aged Shri'ook. His ears were pierced in multiple locations, and for some reason she couldn't shake the feeling that she knew him from somewhere.

• • •

Back at camp, the returning men and women were greeted with quite the fanfare. No injuries and a good haul often called for an evening of celebration around the campfires. Any chance of that was quickly diminished as Lyvanne watched as one by one people began to take note of the Hemeti riding horseback.

"What is this?" Shri'ook asked as he paced across the camp towards their arrival.

Kwah ran over to greet him. "We need to talk."

Shri'ook nodded and the pair turned towards the Annex with Turiel not far behind.

"Come with me," a Hemeti woman from camp said delicately as she led the rescued captives towards Tyler's medic hut.

Deciding that her help wasn't needed anywhere, Lyvanne decided to find Jocelyn. It didn't take long, her friend had stayed at the edges of the woods nearby some guards patrolling the perimeter, choosing not to follow everyone else back into camp.

"Are you okay?" Lyvanne asked, as she approached her friend who had sat down at the base of a tree looking out over the countryside that lay beyond the woodland's edge.

"Been better," Jocelyn replied truthfully as Lyvanne sat cross-legged beside her. "I knew that my people were treated like savages by many of your kind, but I never expected to return to the ways things had been centuries ago. Even under a king like this."

Lyvanne's eyes met the floor. "Your kind." The words had made her realise how strong the divide between their two peoples could be at times. It made what The Spring fought for all the more clear. This group of fifty or so people fighting for what they believe in were living proof that Hemeti and Humans could live cohesively together. Proof that not all humans were like those who lived in the Upper Level. They just needed to make the rest of The Rive see it that way.

Lyvanne put a loving arm around Jocelyn's shoulders. "We're not all like that."

Jocelyn smiled back. "I know you're not, little one... has anyone ever told you that you have the heart and head of someone three times your age?" she asked, putting her arm around Lyvanne's waist in return.

Lyvanne chuckled and shook her head. "Well, you do," Jocelyn confirmed with a smile.

"I read the letter from Sinjin," Lyvanne said out of the blue a few moments later. "Thank you for asking him to look out for my friends."

The fact had escaped her mind with so much going on, but now as she sat here consoling her friend she was reminded of everything Jocelyn had gone out of her way to do for her.

"You're welcome. They sound like nice people and they don't deserve whatever future Astreya has for them."

Lyvanne couldn't hide the grin as she watched the sun slowly begin its descent into the rolling hills along the horizon. "No one ever came back for us. Not that we expected them too, you know? But we hoped. I plan to go back for them one day."

"I know you will. I'll help you if I can."

"Before we do that though, I have one more favour to ask," Lyvanne couldn't believe what she was about to ask for, but as well as to check on Jocelyn's well-being it had been the other reason for her venture out to find her friend.

"Anything," Jocelyn replied as she looked at her friend quizzically.

"I would like it if you could teach me to fight,"

Jocelyn rose to her feet and stared down at the motionless Lyvanne. "Lyvanne, you're too young."

"No I'm not," she replied, her answers already pre-planned in her mind. "Abella told me about young lords who start to learn when they're much younger than I am."

"I can't, it's too dangerous. Besides, you don't need to learn. You have a whole camp of people here who would be willing to protect you if you needed it."

"That's just it Jocelyn, I don't want protecting anymore. If you hadn't been there when Drystal attacked me then I would dead by now, and back at the road I could see that you wanted to go and help when you thought a fight was about to start. I can't keep being a burden, I need to be able to look after myself and I'm going to have to learn eventually anyway."

Jocelyn stood there, hands on hips. The cogs turning in her brain obvious to see. "I don't suppose there's much point in me arguing with you is there?"

"You said it yourself... heart and head of someone three times my age."

Jocelyn nodded in defeat. "If I do this for you then you don't tell Turiel, leave that to me okay?"

Lyvanne's eyes lit up and she nodded wildly. "Thank you Jocelyn," she said as she rose to her feet and wrapped her arms around Jocelyn's chest.

"Don't go thanking me yet," Jocelyn said, gently pushing her away. "If we're going to do this then we may as well do it properly, no half-hearting it."

"Of course!"

"I'll warn you now, I'm pretty tough. It won't be a pleasant experience."

Lyvanne had expected as much. Jocelyn had always had an air of confidence about her, especially for a Hemeti, but the way she carried herself both during her fight with Drystal and the calmness she exuded as she prepared herself for a fight on the North Road told the story of someone experienced with violence.

· · ·

Jocelyn paced back and forth, the wet leaves of the canopy grinding beneath her feet as she began to work out how exactly they were going to do this without worrying Turiel. The answer was that it wasn't going to be easy.

"We'll start by using our free time when we get any. If Turiel goes out hunting, or off on a mission with the others then we'll stay behind and train in the woods, away from too many prying eyes."

"Why does it need to be such a secret?"

Jocelyn thought back to all the times that she and Turiel had talked about Lyvanne, even before they'd met her. All the conversations they'd had about the one who would lead them to victory and the certainty in Turiel's voice.

"Truth is, although you might not act like it most of the time, you're still a kid," Jocelyn said as she knelt down and took Lyvanne's hands in her own. "Don't get offended, it's the truth," she continued as Lyvanne's face flushed red. "The problem is that Turiel doesn't always see you that way, and I just don't want him getting ahead of himself. In fact, I don't think he even fully understands how he sees you anymore. Some days he acts like he wants to protect you because you're younger than us, other days he wants you to be our saviour. So telling him that you're learning to fight might be a strange conversation to broach. Understand?"

"I think so."

"I promise that when I get the next chance I'll speak to Turiel alone, explain what we're doing and why we're doing it. I'll try not to let him get too excited and hopefully he won't send you off into battle the first chance he gets," Jocelyn said jokingly. "For the record, I'm still not 100% okay doing this with you… but you at least deserve the chance if you're going to join us. No point treating you like a child anymore."

"Why not start now?" Lyvanne asked, her voice brimming with eagerness.

Jocelyn grinned. "No time like the present, I guess. Come on then."

The pair headed back into the depths of the woods, looking for somewhere where they could train without being seen by people in the camp and without running the risk of a patrol walking past. Not that it really mattered, but Jocelyn wasn't fond of the idea of Turiel finding out about this from anyone but her. The place they settled on was a small clearing between four large trees, which Jocelyn noted they could use as a perimeter.

"Give me one then," Lyvanne said, motioning towards the two swords hung around Jocelyn's waist.

Jocelyn had to stop herself from laughing in the girl's face.

"No way. They come into it much later down the line. For now, we'll start by teaching to evade."

Lyvanne's face was etched with disappointment, but this wasn't a game and whilst she'd never had to train anybody before she wasn't stupid enough to start her off with sharpened blades.

Jocelyn taught Lyvanne how to "dance" during a fight as she called it, ducking and weaving out of harm's way. Something that she proved quite capable at after years of doing the exact same on the streets of Astreya. Whenever they found the chance the pair would escape to their small patch in the woods, and there they would train, often until long after the sun had set and the moon had taken into the sky. After a few days, Lyvanne felt comfortable enough to dodge Jocelyn's hits without instruction, after a couple of weeks she had begun to strike back. That's when Jocelyn started taking things seriously.

CHAPTER 27

T he sun was setting on another hour of training with Jocelyn. The smell of whatever it was that Oblib was cooking for that evening had long since started drifting through the trees, making it nearly impossible for Lyvanne to concentrate.

"Can we go back now?" Lyvanne asked as she knelt over and leaned her body weight onto her knees.

"Not until we finish the routine," Jocelyn replied, barely even panting or showing signs of any kind of fatigue.

Lyvanne grunted and from her bent over position lunged a surprise attack at Jocelyn, vying for her with a balled up right fist. As always seemed to the case Jocelyn saw the attack coming and easily dodged, grabbing Lyvanne by the wrist and using her own momentum to throw her to the floor.

"What do I keep telling you? Stop being so wild with your attacks, keep them measured."

Lyvanne could have quite easily stayed on the floor, let the insects come and make their homes in her hair, but she was just as stubborn as the Hemeti who was causing her this torment. So, she pushed herself back to her feet and readied herself for another round.

Lyvanne dived to her right, hoping to see some kind of opening in Jocelyn's defensive stance. When one didn't appear, she resorted back to rushing her, trying in vain to tackle Jocelyn to the ground.

"You fight like Drystal," Jocelyn mocked as she held the much lighter Lyvanne against her waist, locking her arms in place and not letting her go.

The insult was meant to goad her into losing concentration and historically it had worked quite the treat, but Lyvanne was prepared this time and had wanted Jocelyn to lock her in close. She was inside her defences now and releasing his own right arm from trying to tackle Jocelyn to the ground she balled up her fist and threw all her remaining strength into a punch that connected squarely with Jocelyn's side, sending her staggering back a few steps and forcing her to release her hold of Lyvanne.

Jocelyn rubbed the impact zone and looked across at her student with a measure of pride. "Well done, little one."

Lyvanne grinned like a child, her white teeth on show for the world to see.

"Now can we go back?" Lyvanne asked exasperated.

Her task of striking Jocelyn complete, the pair started their trek back to the camp. It had been three weeks since the incident on the North Road and the camp had been subdued ever since. Many were angry over how the Hemeti were being treated by the king and tempers had come close to bubbling over more than once. Unfortunately, none of those rescued had been able to supply any real information of value, they neither knew why they had been taken from their homes nor where they were headed. As Turiel had suggested, they had been nursed back to some semblance of health and were given the choice as to where they wished to go from there. Those with children opted to return to return to the world, to try and build new lives for themselves. There were two families, six Hemeti in total including the two children. Shri'ook and the other leaders had taken pity on them and given both families a horse each and some supplies to help them along their way. They were pointed in the direction of a nearby village that The Spring used to resupply and set off on their way.

A Hemeti by the name of Ronnoc spoke on behalf of the other four. His voice was foreign to her, but she refused to let go of the notion that this wasn't the first time she had met Ronnoc. The others shared no such familiarity, but they seemed nice enough and Lyvanne took some childish delight in not being the newest member of camp anymore.

The older Hemeti whom Lyvanne had seen talking to Kwah on the return journey from the North Road was one of them. The other two were a pair of twin sisters, and they told a gruesome story of how their family had been all been killed when they resisted arrest. As such, they had no one left to go back to and decided to fight back against the person who had caused their suffering. They didn't talk an awful lot, but Lyvanne didn't blame them for that, she hadn't exactly been the most open person when she first arrived either.

The camp was busy when they returned. Everyone was there, there hadn't been much traffic along the North Road in a few days now and it had given everyone a chance to relax and regain themselves after what had been some turbulent times. The camp being busy also meant that Lyvanne had enough cover to go and wash herself down before joining the others for their evening meal. Jocelyn had still yet to tell Turiel about their training, and it would raise suspicions if she turned up covered in mud. The bruises she couldn't do much about, Jocelyn had a tough punch. Her long sleeved tunic, which she now opted to wear on most days, did a decent job of covering them up, but the charade wouldn't last for long. The once oversized clothing that Jocelyn had gifted to her back in Astreya was already beginning to conform more tightly to her body.

After cleaning herself down, Lyvanne grabbed a plate of food: a mix of vegetables, rabbit meat and a homemade sauce as accompaniment. She found her friends sitting around one of the smaller fires off to the edge of the camp. Kwah had already finished his meal and was tending to the fire, but Turiel it seemed had waited for Jocelyn to return before he started eating, so the pair had just started digging in when Lyvanne appeared by their sides.

"About time you joined us," Kwah said as he motioned for Lyvanne to take a seat among their circle.

Despite his age, Kwah had started treating Lyvanne like a little sister. He often looked out for her and took her along on his daily chores. She was even sure that he had cottoned on to the training she was doing with Jocelyn, but he was yet to say anything about it.

"Where've you been?" Turiel asked through a mouthful of food.

"Don't talk with your mouth full," Jocelyn scolded before jabbing him in the rib cage so that Lyvanne had an opportunity to ignore the question.

The meal was good. She had started to find even the rabbit meat more refreshing than usual once the training with Jocelyn had started in earnest. She ate faster than before and more heartily, as though each meal might be her last. She just hoped that no one noticed too much.

The four remained around the fire long after they'd all finished their food and taken back their plates to the washing pile. Lyvanne couldn't remember a time where they had all just sat up together talking late into the night, and now that it was finally happening she couldn't stop yawning.

"So we finally make it off the ship," Kwah said, halfway through telling them the story about the time he rescued Turiel from slavers. "And the first thing this Tikah does is trip over his own feet and fall backwards into the ocean!"

The group burst out laughing, all of them with the exception of Turiel who sat there red faced and embarrassed.

"Needless to say I wasn't happy, the kid was too weak to swim out on his own so I had to go in after him, all the while we had slavers shouting and throwing spears at my brothers."

"It's not like I fell in on purpose," Turiel tried to defend himself. "We got away didn't we?"

Kwah patted him on the shoulder, "That we did friend, that we did."

"What happened to your brothers Kwah?" Lyvanne asked. This was the first time she'd heard him mention brothers, in fact any family in general, but the jovial tone with which he spoke about them signalled that it was a safe topic to broach.

"They stayed behind in our village. There are many places among the Shimmering Isles which work differently to The Rive, our people live mainly in tribes and my brothers were needed to both defend and inherit the tribe which my ancestors have governed for centuries."

"You're royalty?" Lyvanne exclaimed innocently.

Kwah laughed, as did Turiel. "No I wouldn't call it that. Governing and defending a tribe in the Shimmering Isles is no different than being a farmer in this countryside. It is just a job, one that is passed down from one generation to the next."

"So why didn't you stay behind as well?"

"Because of my Father. He was a great man, he loved the tribe and he loved his father the way I love him. But he knew how to live his life too; he travelled all over the world, earning his living as he went. He visited the more civilised areas of the Shimmering Isles, the big cities and such. Then he sailed across the sea and wound up here in The Rive. Eventually he went back to our tribe, met my mother and had my brothers and I. But just like him, I wanted to do something with my life before I go home and settle, I wish to grow up like my father, so that I in turn can be just as good a man for my children to one day look up to. Turiel gave me that opportunity to do something with my life."

The story was touching. Lyvanne could hear the love that Kwah had for his family in his voice, and the way in which his eyes brightened as he talked about them. Hoping for a similar story she turned her attention to Jocelyn.

"So, Kwah wants to grow up to be like his father… who do you want to take after?" She asked, nodding her head in Jocelyn's direction for all to see.

Jocelyn twisted and contorted in countless different ways, as if mulling over the meaning of life itself before answering.

"Well, it may be the current trend, but I would have to say my father too," The rest of the group booed playfully, egging her on to shake things up.

"I'm sorry but it's true, he was a good man and I hate to admit it but I was his favourite!" The others laughed. "And let's face it that was the best choice he could have made. I have no doubt that if you ask Sinjin the next time we see him he'll say he wants to be like our mother."

"The answer is fair," Kwah said passing his judgement and turning the attention toward Lyvanne. "Go on Lyvanne, what about you? Got any heroes you want to emulate?"

Lyvanne mulled it over, she didn't have any parents that she could remember or look up to. She could say any of the people sat around the fire with her but she would just be too embarrassed.

"Well… growing up on the streets of Astreya you don't tend to have many people to look up to other than physically. But if I had to grow up to be like someone… I guess it would have to be Abella, the lady who took in the orphans. She was smart and she knew so much about the world beyond the walls. That and she actually cared what happened to the children."

"A good answer," Kwah said from across the fire.

"What about you Turiel?" Lyvanne asked excitedly, expecting him too to say his father also.

"Rachel Goldheart," he replied, not really lending any thought to his answer. "She taught me everything I know and without her many of us, including myself, wouldn't be here anymore."

"What a lovely thought," Jocelyn joked as she tucked her arm under Turiel's and rested her head on his shoulder. Lyvanne hated to admit it but the answer had been somewhat cold. Then again, that's Turiel's nature, she thought as she watched on as Turiel tried to shake Jocelyn off his shoulder like a tired brother.

It came as quite a surprise to Lyvanne when she looked around after nearly an hour of more talking and realised that nearly everyone else in the camp had gone to sleep. There were the usual glimmers of torchlight coming from within the woods as people patrolled through the trees and Greyson was still sat outside his hut, writing on a piece of parchment what Lyvanne presumed to be his next big song. But apart from themselves and the distant hoot of an owl, the camp was silent.

"I think it's time I head to bed," Turiel said before gently pushing off Jocelyn who was still leaning on him.

"Me too," Kwah echoed. "Make sure you don't stay up too late ladies, you still have to do chores even if you're tired," he joked before setting off for his bed. They didn't stay up for much longer either. With the conversation all but gone, tiredness swept in quickly.

"I'm going to tell Turiel about our little training sessions tomorrow," Jocelyn said as the pair gathered up the mess they had made and headed over towards their hut.

"Just make sure you tell him how good I am," Lyvanne said through a yawn. "That way he can't be mad."

Jocelyn laughed and put an arm around Lyvanne's shoulders as they walked. "I hate to admit it, but you are pretty good."

CHAPTER 28

Jocelyn grabbed Turiel mid-way through the morning. She didn't have much of a reason to take him away from helping around the camp, but no one seemed to mind too much when they grabbed a pair of horses and set off through the woods.

"Where are we going?" Turiel asked as they guided their horses through the maze of trees and shrubs that encircled the camp.

"Nowhere in particular," she replied, "but I thought it was time we had some time alone for once"

Turiel seemed pleased with the idea and said little more until they'd passed the guards patrolling the borders and broken through the final line of trees.

"So… which direction then my lady?" Turiel asked, feigning nobility as the pair mounted their horses.

Jocelyn didn't reply, instead she kicked her heels into her horse and galloped away, leaving Turiel both literally and metaphorically in her dust. Smiling, he gave chase. The pair travelled north, winding their way through a series of meadows, fields and eventually even passing into the rolling hills that lay on the horizon if you were to look out from the woods encasing the camp. They had no real destination, and no real need to consider how long it would take them to make the return trip to camp.

"How long do you think we've been gone for?" Turiel asked as the horses came to a stop by the edge of small stream. The water wound its way down from one of the nearby hills before disappearing back into a rocky outcropping a few metres away.

Jocelyn looked up at the sky. "Probably a few hours. It's well past noon at the very least." It was hard to judge properly, given the overcasting clouds that had formed above, but when the sun did poke through it was far past its pinnacle.

"Maybe up there is a good place to camp? We don't have to head back tonight if you don't want to?" Turiel replied, pointing up the stream and towards the summit of the nearest hill.

Jocelyn nodded, dismounted her horse and led it up the hillside, occasionally stopping to allow it to drink from the stream. Turiel followed suit and grabbing the reins of his horse he guided it along path of the water.

"I'm pretty certain I won that race you know?" Turiel said as the pair made their way up the hill.

Jocelyn scoffed. "You call that racing? I could have gone twice as fast if I needed to."

"Sure you could have, and my horse is actually hiding wings that could have flown us the distance if you'd only given me the chance and not gallivanted off right from the start."

The two enjoyed their professional rivalry. They were both competitive people, and it often lead to them bringing out the best in one another. Jocelyn thought for a long time that it was part of the reason that she found Turiel strangely attractive and endearing.

The two sat together on the hillside for the rest of the day. They reminisced about older times, happier times when all they'd had was themselves and Sinjin. They laughed when a toad leapt up onto Turiel's leg, sending him jumping into the air and squealing like a child. Finally, they sat and watched as the sky turned a pale shade of red, the sun setting far off along the horizon giving way to night.

"Why did we stop doing this?" Jocelyn asked as she gazed upon the glowing sky. Turiel's hand was in her own. She wasn't sure when it had happened, but she wasn't going to complain.

"When we started focusing on things larger than ourselves, I guess," Turiel replied, his eyes transfixed on the burgeoning night sky.

Jocelyn didn't want to think of anything being more important than they were to one another, but she knew he was right. As children, they'd had more time to spend together, then Turiel started travelling the world in the hope of starting The Spring and everything had changed. She had told herself that she would do everything she could to keep things the way they had been, but maybe she too had lost sight of that along the way.

"What do we do when all this is over?" The thought of what was going to happen after their ultimate victory or defeat had never really occurred to Jocelyn before. She'd always been someone who tried to live in the here and now, but sitting there with Turiel, really alone for the first time in a long time, it felt like the right time to start thinking about it.

Turiel turned his gaze from the sky and looked into her eyes. Jocelyn guessed that he too had never really given it thought before. "Well… it depends, I guess."

"On what?" Jocelyn replied, half expecting him to say on whether they won or lost.

"On whether you want to live in the North or South… heck, we don't even have to live in The Rive," Turiel said, a smile on his face the likes of which Jocelyn had never seen from him before and one that she couldn't help but replicate.

There was no point hiding it anymore she decided, no point teasing tension where they both knew it existed. "Settling down to one or the other sounds like a mighty big commitment."

"Maybe so. What do you suggest then?"

"Well Mr. Grand Adventurer, why don't you show me around the world?" In her heart, Jocelyn had wanted to suggest Avagarde, but the thought of what it might become once the war had come and gone only brought up pain that she didn't want to ruin the moment.

"I could do that," Turiel said with a gleeful smile, "I'm sure there are at least a few places in the known world that you'd like as much as Avagarde."

The two hadn't broken from each other's gaze since the conversation started and Jocelyn had decided that she didn't want to wait anymore. She pulled Turiel in gently by the hand and for the first time in their lives, and long overdue by both their reckoning, their lips touched.

Not even a legion of the king's soldiers could have separated them for the rest of that night. They quickly decided to spend the night on the hilltop and enjoyed each other's company in ways that they had only ever been able to dream of before then.

When they awoke in the morning everything was different. They didn't feel like the friends they had been the day before, instead to her they were... something more. Her stomach filled with a thousand butterflies when she saw him lying there next to her, his clothes scattered across the hilltop. At first she felt open, vulnerable, and wondered whether she should put her clothes back on before he woke up too. But as she lay there watching him sleep, the cool morning air blowing against her bare skin, she decided that this wasn't unnatural at all and instead enjoyed the moment.

"Good morning," he said when he awoke at long last.

"Good morning," Jocelyn replied, a childish grin on her face.

The conversation was awkward and stifled at first. Neither of them could stop giggling like children who had just discovered some forbidden secret that they couldn't share, but as the morning drew on, they settled back into their old habits and relaxation appeared to set back in for the both of them.

"Come on, we better get back otherwise they'll have Kwah out looking for us," Turiel said as he gathered up the final remnants of his clothing.

Urgency struck Jocelyn. Her brain reminding her why she had brought him out here in the first place. She was scared to say anything, not wanting to ruin what had been a perfect night.

"Turiel... I need to speak to you about Lyvanne before we go back."

Turiel turned and faced her. He had admire how beautiful she looked standing there, her hair ruffled and the morning sun beaming onto her green skin and hourglass figure.

"What about her?" he asked, his head only half in the conversation.

"I've been training her to fight. We haven't moved on to weapons yet and she has good reason to want to learn -

"I know," Turiel interrupted, his expression and voice deadpan.

"You... you know?"

"You aren't exactly the most subtle people in the world Jocelyn. Kwah knows too. We joke about how we know whether Lyvanne's had a good day training or a bad one based off the mood she's in when you get back."

Jocelyn just stood there, her jaw agape and her mind empty. *All this time, all the secrecy because we thought he wouldn't approve*, she thought.

"Why didn't you say something?" she asked, raising her voice.

Turiel shrugged, "It wasn't my place to say anything. I knew you would tell me when you were ready"

Jocelyn couldn't believe it, but she couldn't have been more relieved. She wasn't sure that she would have been able to continue the training without him knowing if Turiel taken the news the wrong way she would have, so a very real weight had suddenly been taken off her shoulders.

"She's learning fast," she finally said as the pair stood there silently.

"I don't doubt it with you as a teacher. I imagine she'll be the best swordswoman in the camp before long."

"We're yet to train with weapons -

Turiel pushed past her with some haste, his gaze caught by the horizon. "What is it?" Jocelyn asked as she followed him towards the edge of the hill that overlooked the series of rolling hills and small valleys to the North.

Turiel pointed to the summit of one particular hill in the far distance. Banners gleaming silver and green in the morning sun.

"The King's soldiers," Turiel said, before hastily grabbing any of his remaining belongings and untying the reigns of his horse. "Take your horse and get back to camp, you need to warn them."

"What are you going to do? You need to come with me!" she exclaimed.

Turiel shook his head, "We need some idea of how many there are if we're going to survive."

"We can scout them when they're closer," Jocelyn argued, trying her best to tug the reigns out of his hands.

"Listen to me Jocelyn," Turiel said, his voice stern and his eyes serious. "You know what Lyvanne has seen in her dreams."

"She's seen us die," Jocelyn replied, the words coming blunt like a dulled blade. She recalled the way Turiel had recounted Lyvanne's sleepless nights and vivid blood-filled nightmares. She understood.

"I can't leave this to chance. We need a strategy, and if we're severely outnumbered then we need to know that so we can give ourselves time to run."

Jocelyn nodded. He was right, and this wasn't the time to argue. "Don't be long, we need you back at camp."

Turiel nodded, grabbed her around the waist and brought her in for another kiss.

"Don't let that be the last one."

CHAPTER 29

Turiel pushed his horse as fast as it would go along the North Road. He knew that soon he would have to veer off into the countryside around him to avoid being seen, but until then he intended on making up as much distance in as short a time as possible.

His thoughts were on Jocelyn, for every stride his horse made towards the enemy, she would be making a stride towards camp. He tried to do the calculations in his head. The hilltop where they had spent the night had been a few hours ride out from the woods, and the banners he had seen were maybe another few hours, even half a day out if the terrain and weather was against you. The king's soldiers would be slower, they were likely on foot given how long it had taken for them to arrive after Lyvanne gave away their location. That meant they had somewhere between one and two days before they would be at the camp.

It's enough time to run, Turiel thought to himself as his horse bounded along the road. But he knew that wasn't the course of action they were going to take, not unless the odds were heavily weighted against them.

The Annex had been filled with discussions over what to do in the days after Lyvanne's admittance to luring the king's men directly to them. Arguments had been made for both sides; Turiel himself had wanted to pack up there and then. Relocate the group to somewhere else, far away from where they were currently.

"The king only knows where Lyvanne was at the time of her exchange with the other warlock and they wouldn't be able to track her if we fled," He had argued, but Shri'ook had turned him over to the other way of thinking. Lyvanne had done what she did because she didn't want people dying in Astreya on her behalf.

"We can't argue with that wish, and if the king's soldiers arrive to find no one here then they would just start all over again until Lyvanne reveals herself," Shri'ook had said firmly.

So instead, they had agreed that they all face the threat together, and by hook or by crook the rest of the camp had agreed, claiming that this was what they had signed up for in the first place. Now that the moment was here, the glimmering banners in the distance caused him to doubt.

He knew that everyone was ready for the fight; they had trained for more than enough years now. But what this day meant for the larger picture in The Rive sent butterflies tumbling in his stomach. If blood and flame did encircle the camp over the next few days then it would be the first time that a non-state actor from within the Rive had risen up in armed rebellion against the king's army in centuries. There would be no going back and everything he had worked towards since leaving the king's Castle would be on the line.

There was also the nagging worry that the fate of those in Astreya might not be so easily fixed. Lyvanne letting in the king's warlock had been more significant than even she realised. Not only did she draw out the king's forces, but if the king was smart enough to realise then she also exposed one of her weaknesses: her empathy.

Turiel's heart beat faster as he contemplated the ramifications. If she was willing to expose herself to save strangers living in a distant city, then she would be the king's to control if he found any kind of leverage over her.

Turiel pushed the thoughts to the back of his mind. Concerns for another day he told himself as he pulled his horse off the road and deep into the fields and hills that ran adjacent.

• • •

Jocelyn raced back towards camp. Her mind swam with worry for Turiel. They had finally come together in a way that should have happened a long time ago, and he'd immediately been put in harm's way. Deep down, she knew that he was more than capable of looking after himself, especially when there was no intention to fight. But being that close to the king's soldiers when he was all alone filled her with dread. She had been riding for just shy of half the day when the sun began to hide behind a dark grey cloud that covered most of the sky. The woods were coming into view as she galloped through a grassy meadow that bordered the tree line off in the distance.

Get in, warn them, and get back out she told herself as her horse neared the edge of the woodland. She didn't intend to stay here long, not whilst Turiel was out there on his own, she couldn't in good conscience.

She dismounted her horse as it slowed down to a canter at the edge of the trees, passing the reigns off to an unsuspecting patrolman. "Bring her back to the camp for me!" She shouted as she darted off into the trees, knowing that she would be quicker on foot trying to navigate the trees.

"What's happening?" The patrolmen shouted after her, his words falling on deaf ears.

The woods were thick with people, some gathering firewood for that night, others collecting water. She studied them as quickly as she could whilst darting towards camp. Did they have what it took to battle the king's soldiers in numbers? You have to hope, she told herself, and we've already lost if we don't hope.

"What's going on?" Kwah called across to Jocelyn as she broke into the camp with some speed.

"King's army, they're coming. Maybe a day, two days out," she shouted back across the camp, loud enough for everyone to hear. There was no point hiding this from them, everyone deserved to know at the same time.

"Damn," Kwah said as he started moving people to previously assigned jobs. "Everyone you know the drill, we work as though we have one day before they arrive, I want everything in place by then."

Jocelyn called after him, "Kwah, I'm going back out there."

"Why?"

"Turiel has gone to scout them. He said we'd need to know how many there are."

"He is right, but you stay here," Kwah said, surprising Jocelyn who made to continue towards where the horses were kept regardless of his order. "Jocelyn! We need you here, not out there looking for Turiel. He will be fine, he knows what he's doing."

Jocelyn turned, ready to argue her case, but then she saw her standing no more than a metre away from Kwah. "Lyvanne," The word almost seemed to trickle out of her lips. Her heart was torn.

• • •

Turiel crept over the hillside; his horse tied up at the foot of the hill so as to avoid it making any noises or movements that might give him away. He'd been able to hear the enemy before he saw them, their footsteps falling heavy on the North Road and their armour and weapons rattling with each step like a cacophony of war and death.

As he reached the summit, he pressed his brown and green tunic into the grass and began crawling. It was slow work, but the hill would give him a good view of the North Road below.

Turiel cursed when he saw the throngs of soldiers marching along the road. Steel plated armour of green and silver glimmered under the few strands of sun that hadn't been covered by the overlooking clouds. Ten, twenty, thirty… in total Turiel reckoned he could see at least sixty or seventy men, all heavily armed and ready for battle. At the front of the column was a sole soldier riding on horseback, a rapier hung around his waist where otherwise there would have been a long sword. Turiel racked his mind back to the days of talking war and politics with his father as he studied the decorative shoulder-wear that indicated the officer's rank. If his memory served him correctly the two red stripes and one white indicated a Major in the king's Army, which meant that the men following behind was likely an entire company.

This isn't looking good, Turiel thought. At best they were out-numbered and out-matched in armaments, at worst they were fighting an entire Company who were experienced in the field together.

• • •

Jocelyn found herself in the Annex alongside Tublik, Shri'ook and Kwah. Not so much through choice but out of necessity. With Turiel currently occupied, they had requested her to stand with them in his stead. Apparently, her name carried more weight than she realised.

"I've sent Ives and Togo out to scout the surrounding area. If Turiel can make it back and let us know their numbers then Ives and Togo will let us know when they're here," Kwah said as the four of them scrambled to make preparations. "Unless Turiel comes back and tells us that we're hopelessly out matched then we stay and fight, or risk the king turning his wrath onto innocents in the cities."

"I'll take half," Tublik said, referring to what Jocelyn assumed was half of their companions. "Run through final drills, training, make sure they're ready. Kwah, you good to take the other half?"

Kwah nodded his acceptance. Slow progress had started on plans and general defences the moment that they'd found out the king would be coming for them, but now was the time to really start the cogs turning.

"Jocelyn, we need you to look after the girl," Shri'ook said in his ever regal manner.

"Surely you want me in the thick of it? I'm one of the best fighters we have," Jocelyn replied.

"As much as I would like to have you fighting by our side, Lyvanne is the only person among us who cannot protect herself and as we are all quite fond of the girl I am eager to give her the best protection we can afford to spare."

Jocelyn nodded. She wasn't entirely pleased with the concept of leaving the others behind to do the fighting, but she knew that what Shri'ook was saying was right.

"Good. I shall make preparations with our defences, I will take as few people as possible with me, the rest I leave with the both of you," Shri'ook continued, nodding at Tublik and Kwah. "Make sure they are ready to fight, none of them will have seen anything like this before. Once we have sights on the enemy then we shall reconvene here to discuss final plans. If we are lucky they will arrive at nightfall, but if the Goddess does not look favourably upon our cause then I expect them to arrive during daylight hours. Jocelyn you are welcome to join us, regardless of Turiel's return or not, just ensure you give yourself and Lyvanne enough time to get out of the woods."

After the meeting had finished and the others had all gone off in their own ways to prepare for the fight to come, Jocelyn went off in search of Lyvanne. *One, maybe two days*, she thought to herself, *plenty of time for some last minute training*. She may not be able to teach Lyvanne much in the space of that time, but it would certainly help to keep her mind focussed on the fact that Turiel wasn't back yet, and at best wouldn't be expected back until nightfall.

• • •

Turiel scrambled back down the hill and towards his horse, his travelling cloak billowing as the updraft beat against his body.

Seventy men. He considered the odds. This is a fight that we can we win, he thought to himself as he kicked into the sides of his horse to spur it on, but only with my help and the kind of luck that only the Gods could provide.

CHAPTER 30

Lyvanne had been one step ahead of her friend. As soon as she had heard what was going on Lyvanne had gone out to their training patch in the woods alone, something that Jocelyn criticised her for quite heavily when she found her. Lyvanne didn't know how to fight with weapons, she didn't know how to kill someone or even if she would be able to if she was given the chance. But she did know that she didn't want her inability to look after herself to be the reason that someone died.

"How're you feeling?" Jocelyn asked, sitting Lyvanne down on a nearby rock as the leaves gently swayed around them in a cool breeze. Lyvanne found it surprising how at home she had come to feel about the woods, how quickly she had adapted from city life.

"I don't know. How am I supposed to feel?"

Jocelyn shrugged her shoulders. "Couldn't tell you, never been in this situation before either."

Lyvanne hadn't realised it herself but everyone else at camp, with the rare exceptions of one or two people, all felt the same way she did. They were all waiting for their first battle like helpless lambs waiting to be taken to slaughter.

"I'm scared," she decided.

"So am I, but don't worry. You don't need to be scared; I'll keep you safe, I promise."

Lyvanne looked down at Jocelyn's waist. She wasn't sure when but she had at some point since arriving back at the camp picked up her twin blades, Lyvanne doubted that her friend would be without them at any point between now and the inevitable battle.

"Where did you learn to fight?" Lyvanne asked. The question had been simmering away at the back of her mind for a while now, but she'd never found the right moment to ask. With this potentially being her last chance it felt like the right time to find out.

"My father taught me. Remember on Trystan's boat how I told you that my father was a smithy before we moved to Astreya? Well, he didn't just make the weapons. Being a Hemeti in The Rive can be quite dangerous at times, so he liked to practice with them too, to keep us safe."

"Was he good?"

"Yeah, he spent a few hours every day training with them before we moved, but I'm better," Jocelyn said with a cocksure grin firmly attached to her face.

"How do you know if you've never been in a real battle?"

"Huh. I guess that's a good point. Well… consider me the best at training and small scraps. I'm not entirely inexperienced like you are."

"Hey! How do you think I got this scar?" Lyvanne joked, pointing at a small scar the cut given to her by Drystal had left behind. Before more seriously unfurling the sleeve of her tunic to reveal the scar of an old wound. A wound she'd received the night Turiel had taken her into the Accord.

Jocelyn nodded and rose to her feet. "Come on, no point wasting anymore time, it's not like we have a lot of it anyway."

Lyvanne reached up and grabbed Jocelyn's hand, using it to pull herself to her feet.

"So, what do you want to practice?" she asked, eager and ready to distract herself from the fear.

Jocelyn looked around. There wasn't much point in teaching her swordplay, if it came down to that then she'd already run out of any option other than to run.

"Stay here," she said and began to run back towards camp. "I'll be back soon, work on evading until I get back!"

She wasn't gone for long.

"Take this," Jocelyn said, handing a small wooden bow over into Lyvanne's outstretched hands. "It's not the best quality, but it was the smallest one I could find, didn't think a long bow would suit you quite yet."

"You think I'm going to learn how to use this in time to help?" Lyvanne asked, staring wide-eyed at the craftsmanship of the bow. Jocelyn had been right, it did fit nicely for her size and despite Jocelyn's comment about the quality, something about it felt right as she grasped the curved light wood tightly and held it up into the air.

"Honestly, I was thinking more long term. If things go south and you end up on your own for whatever reason -

"Why would I be alone? I'd have you."

"Just… just in case, okay? I can give you some basic knowledge of how to use this thing, and then at the very least you might be able to catch some food for yourself. We probably should have taught you to hunt a while back, I guess we've failed you on multiple accounts of what we should have started teaching you sooner, but it's a start."

Lyvanne didn't like the idea of being left alone. These people were fighting a battle on her behalf and she wasn't in the game to just abandon them if things looked tough.

"I've got to admit," Jocelyn continued, pacing around the clearing and studying the bow in Lyvanne's hands. "I'm not exactly the best shot myself, but I know the basics."

Jocelyn dumped a quiver of wooden arrows with steel tips onto the ground by Lyvanne's feet and they began. The two spent the rest of the afternoon training with the bow reusing the arrows until they'd gone blunt. Lyvanne's aim wasn't the best, but by the time the sun had started to set beyond the trees she was capable of at least hitting a tree each time— even if she never came close to hitting the intended target Jocelyn had set. They called it a day when word reached them that Turiel had returned to the camp.

Running back into camp, Jocelyn launched herself at Turiel, wrapping her arms around him and squeezing him tightly.

"Don't ever do that again!" she shouted.

Lyvanne watched them from a few feet away. Something about them seemed different she thought as she watched the pair holding each other.

"What did you two get up to last night?" she asked inquisitively.

The pair blushed, but it was Turiel who walked over ruffled her hair and promised that it was a conversation to be had at another time.

"Where's Kwah?" Turiel asked as he made his way over to the Annex, the time for reunions over with.

The atmosphere in the Annex was tense. Lyvanne wasn't sure whether they just hadn't noticed her, or they'd decided that it didn't really matter who was present anymore, but regardless she stood quietly by Jocelyn's side as Turiel relayed to Tublik, Kwah and Shri'ook what he'd seen of the enemy.

"Sixty to seventy men, likely a company from the king's Army."

"Any cavalry?" Tublik asked, his large round face noticeably red from sparring with the others all day.

"Just the officer in charge. If I had to take a guess I'd say that whoever organised the attack has deemed us not worthy of too much focus. Perhaps reluctant to send men at all and only doing it because it's a direct order from the king."

"Well, we can say our thanks to the Goddess once we're out of this alive," Tublik replied.

"Can we win?" Jocelyn asked from the corner of the room as Kwah moved around wooden soldiers on the map to reflect the new information.

The eyes in the room all turned to Kwah. He had the most experience of fighting out of them all, if anyone knew it was him.

"If the numbers Turiel have given us are accurate… then yes, maybe. But we'd need to hit them with an ambush, and we'd be relying on a whole lot of luck," Kwah said as he studied the map.

"Are our people ready?" Shri'ook asked Tublik and Kwah in stereo.

The two shared a glance. "As ready as they're going to be. Everyone appears willing and they're all capable of taking one of the King's men down with 'em, regardless of their fancy armour or not," Tublik answered for them.

"I gave Ronnoc and the other North Road Hemeti the option of taking some supplies and leaving. To their credit, they all chose to stay," Kwah added.

"Good. Then let everyone rest now. I shall continue to oversee the construction of our defences, and we shall meet again upon first sight of the enemy. Thank you for the risk you took Turiel, you again earn our respect," Shri'ook continued. "I recommend you all get some rest too. We will need leaders in the days to come and I don't want you all walking around like the living dead of Akaratosh"

With a wave of Shri'ook's arm the meeting was over. Turiel came over to Lyvanne and Jocelyn, taking each of them by the hand and leading them out of the camp and towards their hut. The camp was busier than Lyvanne had ever seen it; the usual steady pace with which everyone lived their lives had been replaced by a sense of urgency. Even people who had nothing specific to be doing appeared to be pacing back and forth with agitation.

"Where are we going?" Jocelyn asked as Turiel guided them through the crowds.

"For now, to the hut," he replied.

Once inside, Turiel sat them both down and lingered by the entrance.

"What's going on Turiel?" Jocelyn asked, her voice steady but she could sense that something was playing on his mind.

He turned and faced them, his eyes flicking back and forth between them both. "I want you both to leave the camp tonight."

"What? Why?" Lyvanne asked, her voice high and agitated. She knew that something like this would happen.

"The enemy could arrive at any point over the next day. They were marching, but that doesn't mean they couldn't pick up the pace and arrive quicker than we were hoping. I don't want you two here when they do."

Jocelyn shook her head. "Do you really think that we'd abandon the camp? That we'd abandon you?"

"It doesn't matter what I think, it's what needs to hap -

"These men are coming because of me!" Lyvanne shouted, interrupting her friend dead in his tracks. "I'm not running off and leaving you all to fight this battle without me."

"No offense, Lyvanne, but whether you're hiding in a field nearby or you use the extra time to make it to one of the nearest villages... we'd be fighting without you either way."

The words hurt. Lyvanne looked to Jocelyn for reassurance, but there was none to be found. "I hate to admit it, Lyvanne, but he's right.

We're not helping anyone by sticking around where it's most dangerous."

Turiel shared a look with Jocelyn that told his thanks without him having to say it. "Jocelyn will look after you, Lyvanne. I'll send for you in a couple of days once this is all over… if you don't hear from us then you know that things didn't go according to plan and you'll at least be safe for a little longer. You're strong enough to protect yourself from being found without my help anymore. I believe in you."

"But I've been training, I can help you fight," she tried to argue but she could see that her words were falling on deaf ears.

"Here, take this," Turiel said as he pulled an ornate looking dagger from a sheath around his belt. The pommel was ebony and engraved with words that she couldn't understand. It felt light, even in her hands. The blade itself was short, but looked menacing.

"What is this?" she asked.

"A gift from Kwah," Turiel replied. "He thought it better to come from me. It's a dagger made by his tribe for the governing family. He wanted you to look after it for him until this all blows over."

A tear swelled in Lyvanne's eye.

"You better make sure you look after that, little one," Jocelyn said, kneeling beside her. "Kwah won't be happy if you've lost it when you next see him."

That was when Lyvanne realised the enormity of the situation around them. She might not see Kwah again to give him back the dagger, she might not see Turiel again, all because she wanted to draw the king's gaze away from Astreya.

"I'm sorry for all of this," she said quietly.

"Don't apologise, little one." It was Turiel who knelt down this time and took Lyvanne's hands in his own. "This would have happened eventually. You just sped things up a little bit, that's all."

The smile on his face was genuine, and for a brief moment, the weight of the world slightly lifted off her shoulders.

"Come on then, if we're going to leave tonight then we better eat before we do," Jocelyn said, guiding her out of the hut, swiftly followed by Turiel.

The three ate together for what they all knew could be the last time. After their bowls had been emptied Jocelyn packed an empty backpack with bedrolls, some food and a water satchel for the pair to share.

• • •

Lyvanne said her goodbyes first. Kwah had already head to bed for the night, but she asked Turiel to wish him good luck before she departed. Jocelyn was the last to say goodbye to Turiel. They didn't share a kiss this time, instead opting just to hold one another close.

"Promise you'll come back to me," she said quietly, her face pressed against his chest.

"I promise. Look after her, okay?" Turiel replied. Jocelyn nodded, and with that they separated again. The pain of being drawn away from Turiel again was almost too much to bear, but she refused to let it show.

Jocelyn had sheathed two swords around her waist, and Lyvanne had swung her short bow over her shoulder, and pocketed Kwah's dagger in her tunic. So they pressed on, neither talking, both unable to tear their minds away from the people they were leaving behind.

CHAPTER 31

The night came and went, slowly giving way to the morning sun. Despite the warnings from Shri'ook, Turiel had not slept. Instead he found himself standing at the edge of the woods, staring out into the flatlands beyond, waiting for the enemy to arrive.

The crack of wood and the rustling of leaves floated on the wind as the final touches were put onto the defences. Volunteers had taken it in turns throughout the night to work with Shri'ook as they organised. The final touches were made to pitfalls were made throughout the woods, their spiked holes covered by leaves and branches and their location marked by a white concoction on nearby trees. They had even taken to chopping down trees in order to turn them into wooden palisades which could be used as defence should they have to fall back into the camp. Their last line of defence if it came to it. Turiel had wanted to help, but thought it better not to risk being told to go back to his hut by Shri'ook.

He went over the plan in his mind. It was simple enough, but so much depended on when the enemy arrived, and what the weather was like. If the Goddess blessed them with good fortune then the enemy would arrive at sundown. If they did, it meant they would likely hold off on their attack until daybreak, which would give Kwah and himself enough time to take the fight to them. As the sun rose gently into the sky, Turiel bemoaned their lack of luck. The storm had broken overnight, which meant that the sun had free reign to rise come the morning, casting bright rays of light across the flatlands. If the king's men were to arrive before the sun hid beyond the horizon then it meant that even the weather had refused to grant them cover to move.

His gaze was unmoving from the horizon, but Turiel's thoughts drifted towards Lyvanne and Jocelyn. They were safe, but even he had to wonder exactly how long that would last with the king hunting them. His only hope now was that they had done enough to win this fight, so that he could find them again, so that he could continue protecting them.

"You're going to drive yourself mad standing out here waiting for the horns to sound," said a voice from behind him.

Turiel chuckled and turned to face the approaching Kwah. "I'm starting to think that the waiting is the only thing keeping me sane. You couldn't sleep either?"

Kwah shook his head and kicked the ground beneath his feet, bringing up a clump of sodden mud on his leather boot. "The rain has made for a lovely fighting stage. The Goddess has been kind."

"Kind isn't the word I would use. I bet if you had your way then the enemy would arrive as the sun reached the highest point in the sky with not a single cloud in slight, just for the sake of a fair fight."

"Hah! If I had my way friend then the enemy wouldn't arrive until I was grey and old, weary of the world and ready to move on to the next," Kwah replied as he walked up alongside Turiel.

The two stood in silence for a few more minutes, staring out across the countryside, watching as cattle rose with the morning sun and made their way out across their fields.

"Did she like it?" Kwah asked, breaking the silence.

"Your dagger?" Turiel replied, a grin on his face. "Yes, she liked it. Better watch out otherwise she might not give it back to you the next time you see her."

"Ach! We both know that many of us will not see another morning sun like this one."

Turiel turned his gaze from the horizon and watched the ever-present smile fade from his friend's face. "Some of us will… if we fight this battle the right way."

Kwah turned to match Turiel's gaze. "In that case, let's make sure that we're part of that some."

The two shook hands and made a silent promise to one another.

"Who knows," Turiel continued, "by tomorrow you might have some scars to match my own?" he said, running a thumb along one of the magical scars which adorned his face.

"I would prefer not. Your skin is pale, the scars suit you. Scars would not suit me, I have already been kissed by the sun, you cannot better perfection."

The two laughed. It felt good to lighten the mood of what was no doubt going to be a day of anxiety and dread.

"We'll see just how pretty you are come the morning," Turiel replied before turning his back on the flatlands and towards the woods. "Come on, let's head back, see where we can help out and get something to eat."

The two made their way back through the woodland, and as Kwah had mentioned Turiel found that the ground had soaked through from the night's downpour of rain. He wasn't battle savvy enough to know if that would negatively or positively impact them, but he decided that ignorance might be bliss just for this one day. They passed the defences as they walked: pitfalls hidden among the ground, trees which had been cut down to narrow the paths the enemy could take to advance on their position and wooden palisades as they grew closer to the edge of the camp.

Upon arriving back at the camp, Turiel was somewhat surprised to see that Shri'ook had ordered the deconstruction of some of the huts in order to use their wood for further barricades placed around the edge of the camp itself. It hadn't occurred to Turiel up to this point, but it was obvious now that they wouldn't be able to stay here after the fighting was done.

You've got to get through the fighting first, he warned himself as the pair approached the Annex where they could see Shri'ook waiting.

Kwah and Turiel had been armed for hours now. Both of them were already wearing their gambesons and each had a longsword hung around their waist. So Turiel, at least, was taken aback when they found Shri'ook wearing the same muddied tunic he had worn over the night and no weapon in sight.

"Are his eyes closed?" Turiel asked quietly as they approached.

Kwah grinned. "He's not asleep if that's what you're asking. Greetings Shri'ook! Sorry to disturb."

Shri'ook slowly opened his eyes and regarded the others.

"Greetings," he replied, appearing to take a moment to center himself.

"Young Turiel here believed you to be asleep," Kwah said, ratting out his friend without hesitation. Turiel thought to object but knew it was pointless.

"Not asleep, I have found little time for that over the past few days. No, I was undergoing something our people have been studying for many generations now called Physical Memory," Shri'ook explained.

"Can't say that I've heard of it," Turiel asked as he took his place around the table in the center of the Annex.

"It has been many years since I have had to partake in a real fight," Shri'ook said, taking Turiel's ignorance as a call for explanation. "But our tribes believe that something such as warfare is not a skill that the body easily forgets. You only have to spend the time letting your body remember it."

"Does it work?"

Shri'ook studied Turiel for a moment. "Ask me again tomorrow," he replied with a grin.

The rest of the morning passed slowly. Turiel finally managed to steal an hour of sleep as the waiting game began, but even then it was restless and he woke multiple times, dreaming that they had been attacked whilst he slept. As morning turned into the afternoon, and the sun finally began its descent from the sky, Turiel started to believe that maybe their luck had turned. Then the horn blew in the distance, causing everyone in camp to freeze. The horn blew for a second time, and like clockwork everyone suddenly picked up the pace of whatever it was that they were doing.

Turiel looked around the camp. He found the gaze of Kwah and in tandem the two darted off in the direction of the horn. At the edge of the woodland they found one of the patrolmen, a young woman, not much older than Jocelyn, who had been on the afternoon shift. Turiel regretted the fact that at a time such as this he realised he didn't even know her name.

"Did you blow the horn?" Kwah asked as the pair approached.

"Yes," she spluttered as she threw a scrawny finger out across the flatlands beyond and in the direction of the horizon.

Turiel saw them immediately, the same green and silver banners that he had seen flying before, dimly lit against the evening sun. The enemy was here. Immediately, he turned his gaze towards the sky. The sun was falling, and given the distance that the enemy still had to cover it would be near enough dark by the time they arrived. Whether they would choose to attack immediately or not though could still be decided.

"What do we do now?" Turiel asked Kwah, who likewise had been studying the sky.

"Not much we can do yet. For now, we will sit here and wait"

Kwah hadn't been exaggerating. After thanking the woman for spying the enemy so far out Kwah sent her back to camp, to make ready for what was to come. Word also reached them that the scouts who had been sent out by Kwah had returned and confirmed the numbers that Turiel had passed on. Some blessing at least, Turiel mused, at least they hadn't met up with a secondary force at any point.

Turiel watched as the banners grew steadily closer, the butterflies in his stomach gradually turning into stampeding elephants. Shri'ook sent word shortly after the horns had been blown that all the defences had been finished, and later that evening Tublik sent a runner to say that everyone in camp had been prepped for battle.

"That's it then," Kwah commented. "Nothing left to do but to watch and see what move they make."

The inability to proactively take the fight to their enemies was painful in of itself, but Turiel realised that if they abandoned the safety of the woods, where it would be more difficult for the enemy to advance in formation and where the archers would have more difficulty hitting their target, then they would effectively be throwing away hope of victory.

As the enemy drew closer, the gambeson felt as though it was tightening around Turiel's chest. His breaths became more frequent and shallow, and sweat pooled in his palms as he gripped the hilt of his sword.

"I take it back," Turiel began, turning to Kwah at his side. "The waiting is very much driving me insane."

Doubt crept into Turiel's mind. He knew that there were many among their numbers that were better with a sword than he was, Kwah and Jocelyn to name two. Until now he'd always considered himself at least perfectly capable of putting up a fight. That confidence had completely dissipated now, and in its place he was left with a crushing anxiety that maybe he wasn't good enough to make it through the night.

As the evening drew on, the enemy became more clear among the grassy fields beyond their woods. Each individual soldier from the king's army was now visible, and Turiel almost felt like he could see their eyes watching him, hidden among the trees.

"Come," Kwah said in a deep and serious voice. "It's time to go back."

CHAPTER 32

Turiel wasn't sure what he would let pass as "good fortune" in a situation such as this, but when scouts among the woodland edges saw the enemy begin to set up a base camp of their own, he considered it about as good as his fortune could get. The plan was on, and as day turned into night Turiel found himself sat at camp for what could be the last time.

"They underestimate us at every turn," Kwah said mid-way through delivering what he hoped would be a rousing speech to all that had gathered. "They send one company to deal with us. I fought worse odds in the Tribelands of the Shimmering Isles."

A cheer went up from the gathered crowd of men and women, Hemeti and Humans.

"I am proud to fight alongside you all for this cause that we all hold dear," he continued. "We may not all see the light of another day, but do not think that means you fall in vain, because tonight is the beginning of a new history."

Turiel watched on in awe. He knew that everything Kwah was saying was the sort of cheesy wording that bards would use to rouse drunk tavern goers into a frenzy, but for some reason the way he delivered the lines were drawing him in. He believed everything that Kwah was saying, and for the first time since the horns had blown, he was starting to regain his confidence.

The speech ended with a bang when Kwah promised a brighter tomorrow in return for lordship blood tonight and the Islander was met with a chorus of cheers and the waving of swords in the air. But for once Turiel saw through his words. He knew that many of the people who would fight against them tonight weren't the evil figures that filled the halls of the king's castle, but they were his tools for destruction and that left them with little choice.

The camp split into two parties. The first of which was to remain behind, waiting in the shadows of the trees for the enemy to advance. The second was to be led by Kwah and Turiel, with the aim of prodding the snake into action. They had the smaller group of men and women, but their aim wasn't to be a devastating initial blow, but instead a more mobile and agitating one. Rather than walking straight out of the woods and directly toward the enemy, Turiel and Kwah took their small squad of fifteen out of the eastern border of the woods and made the long way around to the enemy's encampment. Under the dark night sky, Turiel and the others were nearly invisible as they crept slowly towards the burning torches that had been pitched around the camp's perimeter. The light of the full moon beaming high in the sky the only real source of illumination. The flatlands provided Turiel with a clear line of sight into the enemy camp. A small number of soldiers were walking around the circular perimeter, but the company were largely tucked away in their pitched tents.

Maybe they really did underestimate us, Turiel thought as he signalled for the others around him to stop where they were.

They had crept about as close as they could hope for without serious risk of them being seen. So, as planned, the group of fifteen split up once again, this time each group circling to an opposite side of the camp. Kwah, being more skilled at fighting this guerrilla style of warfare took the opposite side of the camp, leaving Turiel and his six to remain where they were, waiting for the Islander to make the first move.

Turiel loosed the longbow that he had slung over his shoulder for the crawl towards their enemy. Its weight felt unnatural in his hands, he'd always preferred a sword, but accuracy wasn't an issue for this particular mission. They just had to make a nuisance of themselves. Turiel glanced at the men and women around him, six in total, and sent a silent prayer to whichever God might be listening that they all made it back to the tree line without being felled.

Then he saw it, the first flamed arrow flying high into the sky and toward the enemy camp. Turiel threw a hand up in the air and he and his six knocked arrows of their own and in tandem released them towards the enemy.

Kwah's flaming arrow landed plum through the fabric of a tent, sending out a muffled scream as it hit the mark within. Turiel knew that the others wouldn't be so lucky, but regardless he watched in pleasure as the rest of the arrows flew high into the sky and cascaded down onto the enemy camp.

Shouts of alarm rang out from within the camp as bodies began to scramble out of the tents and into the open.

"Move!" Turiel shouted after his group had loosed their second arrows into the night's sky. They had opportunity for two more maximum, he knew, before the enemy would be organised enough to start their retaliation and a battle of archery against some of the finest archers in the land was not one he wished to be a part of for long.

Relocating to a position closer to the tree line, Turiel knocked his third arrow and let it fly. This time, he had aimed directly for one of the patrolmen who had ran towards the camp's edge to try and pinpoint the source of the attacks. Turiel's arrow flew through the air and cut directly into the man's armour. The impact wasn't enough to kill, nor was the positioning as the arrow lodged itself into the man's shoulder, but it was enough to have him down momentarily and that gave them enough time to fire off their fourth and final volley.

The enemy camp, being attacked from two sides, lurched into a fully frenzy. Shifting shadows of soldiers reaching for their weapons behind the flaming torches signalled that it was time to flee. Turiel's thoughts were confirmed when he spied the feint outlines of figures running towards the woods. *Kwah,* he thought to himself as he watched the figures dart through the field. *It's time to move.*

"Run! Now!" Turiel shouted as he and his six turned their backs from the enemy camp and made a straight line for the cover of the trees.

A smart commander would react to such a hit and run attack by doubling the guard and doing all that he could to make sure that it didn't happen again, Kwah had told them all. But the manner in which this assault from the king had been approached, the small number of men sent and the fact they felt confident enough to set up camp for the night outside the location they knew their enemy waited signalled overconfidence and inexperience. Kwah had been hoping that those traits would win out the day and that instead of doubling down at their camp, the king's commander would instead give chase.

The sound of whistling filled the air, and moments later the whistling was followed by an echo of thuds as one arrow after another penetrated the ground around them as they ran. A yell came from Turiel's left, and out of the corner of his eye, he watched as a Hemeti was brought down, an arrow protruding through his chest.

No time to stop, Turiel told himself as he urged his legs to run as fast as they could back to safety.

Turiel didn't dare turn back to see if Kwah's theory had been correct about the enemy, but it didn't take long for the answer to present itself. Turiel and his remaining five reached the tree line without further loss of life, and he finally risked a glance behind him. Sure enough, as Kwah had hoped, the enemy were forming up and making their way across the field that would lead them directly into the woods.

"Goddess' fortune," Turiel whispered to himself as he beheld the enemy. Despite the early hour of the morning, their formation was tight, as though it was the middle of the day and they had been prepared for this fight all along.

Damn it, Turiel thought. Hoping that their attack had done enough to rattle them regardless.

"Turiel! Come!" Kwah shouted through the trees. The islander was stood about ten metres behind him. Turiel realised then that he was the only one left standing at the edge of the trees, staring out at the enemy as the rest of his troop had followed the plan and made their way back to a defensive line further in the woods.

Avoiding areas that were marked with white X's the pair made their way through the trees before finally arriving at the pre-planned defensive line. There they were, the rest of the camp, spread out in two defensive walls through the woods. This was where they were going to make their stand against the enemy. Shri'ook and Tublik stood waiting for them.

"Did everything go according to plan?" Shri'ook asked.

"Think we riled them up good," Turiel replied, "but I lost Gindrak."

The Hemeti had been with The Spring for a long time. Turiel struggled with the loss, and just hoped that maybe he had somehow survived and that they could rescue him in the morning.

"We mourn our dead tomorrow," Shri'ook insisted. "Come, to our positions, and may the Goddess' fortune bless you all."

Kwah and Turiel took their place at what they hoped would the centre of the fighting, directly in line from where the enemy would be heading. Whilst Shri'ook and Tublik each took a wing of the defensive lines.

"See you on the other side my friend," Kwah said as the two stared out from the wall of men and women stood alongside them at the approaching enemy who had just breached the tree line.

"See you on the other side," Turiel replied as the first of the King's soldiers fell victim to one of the pitfalls. That was their signal.

"Charge!" Kwah shouted as man and woman alike along the first line of the defensive wall rushed toward the enemy. At the same time, the second wall pulled up long bows that had been nestled at their feet and in unison sent a volley into the sky and then a second. Each landing mere moments before Turiel and the first line reached the enemy.

Not many of the arrows hit their mark, but that was to be expected among the grouping of trees and the limited light that poured into the woods from thin veins of moonlight that broke through the leafy canopy above. It did enough to disrupt the movement of the enemy, and the first line of the defensive wall was nearly upon them.

The plan is working, Turiel thought as he charged toward the enemy and saw two more groups of men fall victims to hidden traps in the ground.

If they could keep them penned in to these first few tens of yards worth of woodland, where pitfalls had been constructed in earnest, then they might have enough of advantage to hold out for a victory.

At last Turiel was upon the enemy. They were fully armed and staring him down, bracing for the impact he and the rest would make when they hit their lines. Turiel took in a deep breath, and threw himself into the fight. His sword arm swung freely as he fought not to push deeper into the enemy ranks, but to hold them where they stood.

If all went to plan then they would be able to hold them long enough for the second line of Spring soldiers to be able to make their way around to the sides and catch the enemy in a pincer.

Turiel faced down the mystery opponents. Two armed soldiers were stood in his way, and his blood began furiously beating through his body.

Fight, he told himself and he did.

No longer could he see the battle raging on around him, instead the only people left in the world were himself and these two men who wanted so badly to kill him. Odds he fancied. The first lunged for him, sword in hand but unsteady on the sodden woodland floor. His blow was easy to dodge, and using the weight of the man's armour Turiel let him fall forward before sticking a leg out and tripping the man.

The second wasn't so clumsy and his strike was measured. Turiel met each attack with a parry, but seeing the man he had tripped attempting to regain his footing he knew he was running out of time. Another strike, another parry, each easier than the last, the man's cumbersome armour was tiring him quickly. The next attack came slower than the others and Turiel decided to put him on the back foot.

He pressed the attacker. After parrying a shot across his shoulder he feigned right with a strike of his own, only at the last second to pull out of the attack and thrust the hilt of his sword up into the cheek of his opponent. Discombobulating him and leaving his chest vulnerable as he staggered backwards. Turiel took advantage and plunged the tip of his sword through the weak part of the man's armour beneath the shoulder, ripping his arm completely from his body. The man was finished.

Turiel turned back to the first, his sword covered with the red blood of his victim. The adrenaline surged through his veins like he'd never felt before. The other attacker didn't last long either. Turiel danced around the slower man, using the weight of his armour and the muddy ground to his advantage, before finding an opening round the man's back and stabbing his sword deep into the steel plating. The man gurgled as blood came pouring from his mouth. A sight that Turiel believed would have made him throw up in any other situation, but there was no time for that right now.

Turiel looked for his next opponent. The battlefield was chaotic once he opened his gaze up long enough to take it all in. All throughout the wood there were soldiers fighting. The defensive lines had broken down and he wasn't sure if there was any semblance of order left. Then it dawned on him what that meant. He looked across to where Shri'ook's wing of fighters had been; it had completely collapsed. The enemy had broken through and were rounding on the rest of their men, cutting off any chance of a pincer against that side. He spotted Kwah a few metres away, his gambeson was covered in blood and there was a visible tear through the sleeve on his right arm. But it was the look on Kwah's face that worried him the most.

They were losing the battle.

CHAPTER 33

"Fall back!" Kwah commanded as he swung his sword at an oncoming attacker. The tactic had failed, and if they stayed where they were then they weren't going to see the light of another day.

The ground around them was littered with bodies from both sides of the fighting, and the trees had been stained red with blood. This is madness, Turiel thought as he swung his blade in defence of an overhead shot from an onrushing soldier whose eyes had turned red with frenzy.

Turiel was on the backfoot. He couldn't turn and flee or his attacker would strike a killer blow, but he couldn't stick around for too long or he'd be left alone whilst everyone else made for the palisades and barricades. The attacker pressed and Turiel's feet began to give way beneath him as he back peddled as fast as they would allow, swinging his sword wildly from left to right as he tried to hold off the attacks.

I can't do this, Turiel panicked.

The enraged attacker swung up high, ready to bring his sword down in a killing blow, but the attack never came. A sword drove into the man's side, piercing his rib cage and sending him careening into the floor, lifeless.

"Come Turiel, we must go," Kwah said, wiping his blade against his gambeson.

Turiel wanted to say thank you for saving his life, but there was no time. Instead, the pair turned and ran as fast as their boots would carry them. Turiel couldn't make out how many men had fallen, but he didn't think the odds had become any better for them. Fortunately, however, seeing the left wing collapse so quickly the second defensive wall had stayed their hand. Rather than rushing into battle for the sake of it, they had held their ground and formed up around the defensive structures, calling for the remaining two sections of soldiers to fall back onto their position.

The defensive wall held its ground as Turiel and the others fell back into safety, before reforming and aiding their friends at the barricades. Turiel looked around him; he tried counting as quickly as he could but the chaos made it impossible to tell how many remained of the first line of people who had charged the enemy ranks. Tublik was fighting on the right, Kwah had taken the centre again, but there was no sign of Shri'ook anywhere. Turiel pushed it to the back of his mind, but feared that the old islander had fallen with his wing.

The enemy pushed on their position, but they too had taken significant losses. The traps had done their job, and the barricades could hold for a short while longer, but regardless it looked like their numbers would be too much as they swarmed like locusts over the wooden structures.

I have to do something about this, he thought as he watched the king's soldiers push against the fortifications and his friends fall.

"Kwah!" Turiel called out.

"What?" Came the reply as Kwah tried to divert his attention from the front line of the defence long enough to converse.

"I need you to buy me time. I'm going to try and even things up."

Kwah didn't need telling twice. Despite having no idea what the plan was, Kwah fought harder than he had done at any point in the night so far, and his efforts encouraged those around him to do the same.

Turiel himself wasn't entirely sure what he was planning to do either. There were only a handful of spells among Rachel Goldheart's notes which could deal significant damage, and even fewer which could do so on a scale large enough that it could be useful now. But there was one he knew of, she had simply called it "Ruin."

Turiel took a step back from the fighting. The Spring were doing a good job of holding the enemy at bay now that they had the defensive barricades helping, but he knew that wouldn't last long. The king's soldiers were too well disciplined, too skilled with their blades.

So, he reached out his palms and let the magical energy drift through his body.

He closed his eyes and let the energy worm its way through his arms and down towards his fingertips. With his eyes closed, he could feel the energy of every living being in the battle, he could see as they danced around one another in a game of life and death. He drew on the energy around him and focused his mind on the ones whom opposed him.

He tried to reach out to as many of the enemy as he could, drawing out from his location and spreading into their ranks… and then he was stopped. Not by a lack of power or concentration, but by… someone. He opened his eyes and surveyed the battlefield until he found them. Stood to his left and at the back of the enemy force, a man dressed in a hooded black cloak and with his arms outstretched similarly to himself. Another warlock. Turiel didn't have time to react; his grasp over the energy was slipping away with every second. So he ignited the spell.

• • •

They had never intended to leave their friends behind. Jocelyn had never intended to leave Turiel behind. She couldn't abandon her role of protecting Lyvanne either, but she had been sure that the young girl would not complain once she explained her real plan. Now, the two sat on the outskirts of the woods to the south waiting for a sign that they might be needed.

"Are they going to be alright?" Lyvanne had asked when the sound of fighting from within the woods woke them up.

Jocelyn had told her that they would be, but she knew that the answer was far from simple. The clatter of steel on steel and the cries of anguish filled the night, creating a horrible clamour that rose through the cool air.

Then it came. A bang that ripped through the night sky and a flash of light that momentarily illuminated the woods in their entirety. Heat radiated from within the woods and a shockwave blew Jocelyn's hair from off her shoulders.

"What was that?!" Lyvanne shouted, before immediately holding her hands up to her mouth. Jocelyn had warned her that if they were going to stay here they had to stay quiet. If they were found, they would have thrown everything away.

Jocelyn knew immediately what it was, but she'd never felt it on this scale before.

"Turiel needs me," she said, grabbing her swords from the small fabric floor that they had laid out under the shelter of a wayward oak tree beyond the edge of the woods. "Lyvanne, I need you to stay here. If I don't come back by sunrise then you have to leave, okay?"

"You can't leave me," she argued, "You said we'd help them together."

"You can help them by keeping yourself safe. This is all to protect you."

Jocelyn didn't wait to hear a reply; instead, she grabbed her stuff and darted into the woods, leaving Lyvanne behind. She felt guilty, she knew that she was being irresponsible, but Turiel needed her and right now nothing else mattered.

The clatter of fighting had died down briefly following the explosion of light and sound, but it didn't take long before it filled the air again. Only this time it was more sporadic, less clumped in one direction. Jocelyn soon saw why. Her first sign of conflict was the small fires that had caught ablaze throughout their old camp. There were trees and huts alike caught by the red flowers, with the smoke rising through the canopy and up into the sky. Horses whinnied and scattered into the woods. Soldiers had broken off from any kind of formation and the few who were left found themselves fighting singular battles in every direction she could see.

Where is he? Jocelyn asked as she bounded through the burning camp and out of the other side where the fighting continued.

Seeing a Hemeti caused a number of the king's remaining soldiers to lunge at her as she passed, but she didn't have time to stop and fight back. She had to leave that to the others. Her entire focus was now aimed towards finding Turiel.

• • •

Turiel lay on the ground, embers falling around his face and onto the woodland floor. His ears rang and a constant pain buzzed through his head.

He looked around. The spell had worked, but the impact had been more devastating than he thought it would be. An explosion of magical energy had cascaded from his fingers, aimed firstly at the people whom he had targeted, but the king's warlock had intercepted and before too many of the enemy had fallen his blast had been redirected back into their camp.

Through blurred vision, he could make out the bodies of his enemies. Their armour had been torn open, as if a creature had escaped from the inside, and their blood was scattered across the battlefield. He saw his allies too. Knocked to the floor from the explosion but unharmed. Then the pain started to flow through the rest of his body. The spell had been the most powerful he had ever conducted, and the pain was equally as magnificent. Every bone in his body felt like it was on fire, and his organs felt as though they were withering into nothing.

He screamed, but no one came to his aid. Those who remained standing had started fighting again, and the ones who had been knocked to the floor were slowly regaining their footing. He screamed again. This time someone did pay notice to him. A hooded figure moved in close from beyond the enemy's lines.

The hooded man mouthed something, but with the ringing in his ears blocked out all other sound. Pain seared through his body once more, and this time he knew that it was the pain of a scar being left behind. The pain coursed through his leg and up into his back. His body arched and contorted itself as if with a mind of its own as it tried to shake away the agony. Then it stopped, as swiftly as it had started and Turiel knew from experience that the worst of it had passed. Only this time it hadn't. Instead, the pain resurged into his body, but vastly different in its feel and less precise in its location.

As he writhed on the ground Turiel caught sight of the hooded man again. His arms were outstretched, with the white streams of magic swirling around his fingers.

He's doing this to me, Turiel realised through gritted teeth as he tried his best to hold in the screams. He knew he couldn't withstand the pain much longer; his body was already slipping into unconsciousness.

Then she appeared, cleaving through the air like a griffin through the sky. She was a Hemeti, and in his dazed state Turiel mistook her for Jocelyn, the way she moved, the twin blades… but that wasn't possible, she was safe.

The Hemeti danced with the king's warlock. Each trying to outdo the other, but it wasn't a fight the Hemeti could win. Even with the pain of his most recent spell holding him back the warlock would likely be too much to overcome.

• • •

Jocelyn moved with precision. Her swords glided through the air, but her opponent wasn't playing the same game. The hooded man who had been torturing Turiel danced out of her reach, his every step intent on keeping distance between himself and the opposing Hemeti woman. If he wasn't willing to partake in this battle then she would struggle to win.

The man was tall. His face covered in scars similar to Turiel, but where Turiel's skin was a ghostly white, this man's was red and misshapen, as though terribly burned many years prior. The brown eyes entrenched deep into his skull appeared hollow, as though long devoid of life, but Jocelyn knew not to underestimate her opponent.

There was movement to her left as a man clad in the king's colours darted through a series of trees and shrubbery in her direction. His sword was raised high in the air and was aiming for her. Jocelyn's attention flitted between her assailant and the warlock she was still trying to catch with a lucky swing of her blade.

There was no one in the area that could help; it was just the four of them as the rest of the remaining combatants had drifted off throughout the forest. She wanted to turn towards Turiel, who was still laid out on the floor, to pray that he was in a state where he could help. But she knew that was a fool's hope for now. Instead, she turned her attention to the onrushing attacker. It left her open to the warlock, but she doubted he would have the strength to do any significant damage for a few minutes still after his attack on Turiel.

The soldier was unimpressive. He wore garb different to that of the others, an officer and likely the man who had been put in charge of the company. He was younger than Jocelyn would have expected, not much older than herself, nut she held no sympathy and gripped onto her twin blades as she braced herself for his assault. The officer wielded a rapier instead of the traditional long sword. Jocelyn knew it would give him more movement, and with her severe lack of armour she'd be vulnerable to nicks and small cuts that could steadily wear her down. She didn't intend on giving him the chance.

The man rushed head first into Jocelyn's counter attack. He leaped forward, rapier in hand and aimed directly for her heart, but she had been ready. Jocelyn parried the rapier away with her weaker sword arm and as the man rounded his attack to come back from underneath she brought down her second blade. The fight was over quicker than it had begun as her blade cut through the man's striped shoulder-wear and down into his chest. His life left him instantly.

Jocelyn was about to wrench her sword free of his limp body when a wave of energy bolted into her side and sent her crashing into the nearby trunk of a tree. The bones in her arm that had taken the brunt of the impact shattered on impact, and her swords scattered across the battlefield. She was defenceless as the hooded warlock lowered his hands and approached, dagger in hand.

CHAPTER 34

Lyvanne knew that Jocelyn would kill her, if one of the king's men didn't get to her first. But she wasn't about to let all her friends die whilst she sat quietly on the edge of the woods. She gave Jocelyn a head start and then gave chase.

With Kwah's dagger, tucked inside the pocket of her travelling cloak, she gripped her bow with one hand and an arrow in the other. Her heart was pounding faster than it ever had done before. Everywhere she ran in the trees there were bodies, or the clatter of the final throes of the battle. It was chaos and she wasn't entirely sure how she was convincing her legs to carry on further into it.

The camp was on fire. Smoke billowed into the air and made it difficult to see where she was going. She'd lost sight of Jocelyn as she ran head first through the fire and smoke, but that wasn't about to stop her.

Weaving her way through the battlefield, Lyvanne found a surprising well of confidence that she hadn't known existed within her. She darted out of the path of combatants the way she had done on the streets of Astreya. Passing by many without them even realising she had been there.

The faces of the fighters had all become a blur. She avoided them all, regardless of the colours they wore. She treated every person she came across as dangerous, with the only exception being the green skinned Hemeti who she passed sporadically and with less frequency than she had expected.

As she searched the camp, hoping that Jocelyn would suddenly appear she came upon her hut. It wasn't on fire like some others, and it hadn't been torn down for the defences she could see throughout the camp. But one of the walls had been brought down during the battle, and as Lyvanne crept around the corner she saw why. The battered and bloodied body of a Hemeti had been thrown into the structure.

Her heart skipped a beat as she briefly considered the thought that it might be Jocelyn, but as she turned the body over she was met with the lifeless face of the elder Hemeti who had been rescued on the North Road. She wanted to feel sad, she wanted to cry for him and to tend to his body there and then, but will compelled her on and she darted onwards in search of her friends as the battle slowly died down around her.

• • •

Jocelyn crawled towards one of her swords. The impact with the tree had all but crippled her, and she knew that her chances of making it out of this alive had taken quite a significant downward turn. But she couldn't give up yet.

She could see Turiel lying on the ground just beyond the sword. His body had gone limp and his eyes were closed, but his chest rose steadily with each breath. Saying a silent prayer of thanks to Iridu, she continued her crawl.

"Filth!" The robed warlock shouted as he came towards her. He's over exuded himself, Jocelyn thought as she noticed a limp in his walk. The cost of using magic taking its toll on him.

The insult washed over her, and she took some solace in the fact that this man appeared more intent on throwing emotional barrages rather than just finishing the job. If she couldn't make it to her sword and back up onto her feet then it wouldn't matter much.

The warlock caught up to her. He pressed the full weight of his body onto her bruised back as he trod over her and put his body between her and the sword.

"How dare you attack me, you Hemeti scum," The man said, saliva pouring through his jaws.

Jocelyn didn't cower. She was completely defensceless, but she wasn't going to show any fear. Her eyes peered through the gap between the warlock's feet. She could see Turiel on the other side, still unconscious. She looked around, there was no one nearby, the battle had long since moved on. For all she knew it could be over by now, there was little sound of warfare anymore and it was entirely possible they'd already lost.

"Finish me," Jocelyn snarled at the man towering over her.

She half expected the man to smirk, to be taken over by the same lust and anger that had consumed Drystal. But he didn't. Instead his eyes moved beyond Jocelyn.

"Finish me!" Jocelyn shouted again, sick of the games, sick of the waiting.

The man's eyes didn't move. "You're her…" he said, his eyes still focused beyond Jocelyn.

"Let her go, you've lost," The voice came from behind Jocelyn, she knew it instantly and tried her best to swivel on the floor.

"Lyvanne!" Jocelyn shouted, unable to control her anger. "Get out of here now!"

The young girl stood a few feet behind Jocelyn, her bow raised and an arrow pointed directly at the heart of the warlock.

"All these people have died for you little girl… is it not time you repay them?" The warlock said, goading Lyvanne into action.

Lyvanne stood there rigid in her spot. She didn't break her gaze from the man's eyes.

"They died because of the king, they died because of you."

The warlock finally let out a smirk. "Melruin said you had fire within you. It's almost a shame that I have to snuff it out."

Jocelyn tried to rise to her feet. She used anything and everything she could get her hands on as leverage, but nothing worked. She had been injured too badly and now Lyvanne was facing down impossible odds on her own.

"Run, Lyvanne! He'll kill you," she pleaded. She was meant to stay behind, she shouldn't be here.

"You've lost, consider it a courtesy that I'm giving you the chance to run." Lyvanne replied, as coolly as the adrenaline would allow.

Jocelyn looked at the fire behind Lyvanne's eyes, there was something different about her. Like she had found a well of confidence that hadn't been there before.

"What do you mean I've lost?" The man replied.

He didn't wait for her to answer. His gaze darted beyond their own small plane of battle and into the woods and camp surrounding them. There was no one nearby, but there were figures moving in the distance through the smoke. None of them were sporting the king's colours. The Spring had won the battle.

Jocelyn could see the conflict in the man's eyes. If he stayed then he would die, but he would be able to take Lyvanne down with him before he did. If he ran, then he and Lyvanne would likely survive, but he would have to explain what happened to the king. Jocelyn wasn't sure that cowardice would win out this time and she tried one last time to put herself in the firing line between the man and Lyvanne. Using the last of her strength, she pushed up onto her knees and finally back onto her feet, though she felt like they could give way at any second.

"Your friend is foolish," the man said to Lyvanne, who Jocelyn was now shielding with her one good arm.

Leave, Jocelyn pleaded with Lyvanne internally as she felt her discretely press something into Jocelyn's one working hand. Kwah's dagger she realised as her fingers curved around the smooth ebony handle. At the very least she wasn't defenceless anymore, and the warlock knew it too.

Their opponent surveyed the situation one last time. There were people calling out now, voices in the smoke searching for survivors, no doubt they would find them soon. If they did then it wasn't very likely that they'd let a warlock stick around alive. Self-preservation and exhaustion won the hour. The man pulled his hood tight around his face and began to run for the edge of the woods where the battle had first begun, his cloak whipping in the smoke clouded air behind him.

Jocelyn collapsed. She wanted to go after him—the prospect of letting any of the enemy get out alive, let alone a warlock seemed like a bad idea—but she didn't have any strength left after being blasted by the magic that he had used against her.

"Are you okay?" Lyvanne asked as she knelt down by Jocelyn's side.

"Yes… check on… Turiel," Jocelyn said through gritted teeth as she tried to conceal the pain from her broken arm.

• • •

Lyvanne ran over to Turiel's side. The smoke was beginning to seep into her lungs as it drifted through the woods, so she tore off a piece of her tunic and held it against her face.

"Turiel," she said, using her spare hand to shake him by the shoulder. "Wake up."

She was still scared. Her hands shaking as she tried to revive her friend. She'd dropped her bow by Jocelyn, and she had to keep swinging her head to look through the blurred world all around her to make sure she didn't need it again.

"Wake up!" she said, louder this time.

"Lyvanne?" The reply came not from Turiel or Jocelyn, but from a barely recognisable figure wading through the drifting smoke and feint rays of moonlight.

"Kwah? Over here," Lyvanne shouted towards the man who had now broken into a quick jog in her direction.

Breaking through the line of smoke and into her clear vision Kwah appeared almost unrecognisable. A steady stream of blood trickled down his forehead from a small gash near the top of his scalp and the left sleeve of his gambeson was shredded in multiple places, leaving blood pouring down his arm.

"Are you okay?" Lyvanne asked meekly as she stared at his injuries.

"Never mind me, what are you doing here?" Kwah asked gruffly as he bent down beside Turiel and made to lift him up onto his shoulders.

"I -

Kwah waved her off after he spotted Jocelyn lying nearby. "Answers later. Can you help her walk? We need to get out of this wood."

Lyvanne nodded and ran back towards Jocelyn. "Come on, let's get out of here," she said as she put Jocelyn's arm around her shoulder, picked up her bow with her spare hand and began to follow Kwah out of the forest.

"You saved me, you know?" Jocelyn said through a forced smile.

Lyvanne smiled back. She knew that the telling off would come later, but for now she was content to enjoy the praise. "I guess we're even now."

CHAPTER 35

Lyvanne collapsed on to the grassy floor at the edge of the woods, sending Jocelyn rolling onto her injured arm as she did.

"I'm… sorry!" Lyvanne sputtered through a series of coughs. The smoke had filled her lungs as they tried to escape but she'd managed to get Jocelyn out of there unharmed.

Jocelyn waved off her apology with her good arm as she went into a coughing fit of her own. Lyvanne lay down beside her, the morning dew was cool to the touch and was a refreshing change from the chaos of the woods. The scene around her was less calm. In every direction there were people pouring out of the woods, some carrying their friends over their shoulders and others looking worse for wear themselves. Lyvanne spotted Greyson, but not his brother Davidson, a weary and lost look behind his eyes as he slowly trundled out of the forest and fell down to his knees, exhaustion taking hold.

Tyler the medic was already fast at work, tending to the more critically injured members of The Spring whilst leaving those who appeared somewhat unscathed to look after themselves. Whilst the rest of them had seen out the night, Lyvanne figured that Tyler's night was only just beginning.

"Where are you hurt?" Tyler said as he finally made his way around to Jocelyn's side. The way she was holding her right arm indicated where the problem was, but she was stubborn and didn't want the help.

"Help the others," Jocelyn said, trying to forcefully push him on to the rest of those waiting for his help.

Lyvanne noticed that his left leg had been badly gashed around the thigh, and bandaged up with some torn fabric. "Are you okay Tyler?" she asked.

"I'll be fine, kid," he replied, the usual care in his voice had been replaced by concern for the others.

Lyvanne watched as Tyler tore off swathes of Jocelyn's own tunic and formed a very makeshift sling which he wrapped around her broken arm. It left her side open to the elements, her green skin bruised from the battle. Jocelyn didn't appear to mind the exposure as she felt the weight of her arm being taken away. "Thank you," she said weakly "Now, please help the others."

Tyler nodded. "I can't do much more right now, so stay off the arm and keep it elevated." And just like that, he darted off to the next patient.

Lyvanne looked around. She hadn't seen where Kwah had carried Turiel off too at first, but now that the scene around her was beginning to settle she could see the pair off towards the edge of the cluster. Turiel had thankfully regained consciousness and it appeared as though Kwah was taking the opportunity to rest by his friend's side as they both sat quietly in the grass.

Lyvanne helped Jocelyn to her feet and the pair made their way over to Kwah and Turiel, knowing that it was better to talk to them now before they decided they were rested enough and wanted to get stuck in with helping the others.

"Are you okay?" Jocelyn asked Turiel as they approached.

Turiel met her gaze. "About as okay as I can expect to be."

Lyvanne could see the pain in his eyes as water welled in the corners. She wasn't sure if he was still feeling the effects of whatever spell he had cast during the battle, or whether he had been hurt by a blade, but there was something which still haunted him.

Kwah rose from his position on the grass and walked to meet Lyvanne. "You were supposed to be safe in a far off village by now, Lyavnne! You could have been killed."

Lyvanne's face flushed red. She could see the severity behind Kwah's eyes. "I… I had to help," she tried to argue. "Sorry."

Kwah placed a hand on his hip and sighed. "Don't be. It seems like the two of you have saved our friends life," he said, gesturing back to Turiel who was still sat on the grass. "But unfortunately, we have lost many more friends, and our night doesn't end here."

The survivors spent the next two hours regrouping and tending to the wounded. But the work began in earnest shortly after, as the sun began to cast its rays out over the horizon in the distance, filling the cloudless sky with a blood red haze.

The woods had been ravaged during the battle, and the bodies of their fallen friends were littered throughout. Less than half of their people had survived the battle, and of those who survived another half of them had been declared too badly injured to be of any real use in the clean-up efforts.

"Turiel, Jocelyn… you two stay here with the others. Neither of our are in any shape to help in the woods," Kwah said as he gathered those able bodies who could help. "You too, Lyvanne. Stay with them."

Lyvanne shook her head. "I'm coming, I can help."

Kwah looked down at her, and she made sure not to break her eyes away from his gaze. "Very well, come with me."

When she first broke back through the treeline with the others, she found that the woods had emptied of all living animals or people. The fires were well on their way to dying, the smoke weak and dissipated, no longer filling the lungs of all who entered. It wasn't until they reached the site which had once been their camp did Lyvanne really see the impact of what had happened. Although she had seen the body of the old Hemeti whom they had rescued on the North Road, his body had been largely untouched by battle.

The same couldn't be said about some of the other bodies that they found: soldiers from both sides of the battle who had lost limbs, their entrails spread outwards from their bodies and the signs of carnivorous insects already crawling out of the ground to claim the aftermath of the bloodshed.

The dozen of them who were capable did what they could to gather up the bodies of their friends. It was a dirty job, and Lyvanne was largely relegated to the gathering of supplies and any other material that might be of use in the days and weeks to come.

All in al,l there wasn't much left for her to gather. Making her way through what was left of the camp she tried to salvage what she could. What the battle hadn't crushed, the fire had claimed. Leaving little other than a few stores of food, the weapons of the fallen and what she could find in the Annex. The structure of the Annex itself had collapsed, the wood turned into charcoal. As she rummaged through the ash her fingers brushed the top of a small stone box. Cleaning away the rest of the dirt and ash surrounding the box, she unlodged it from the floor and brought it to Kwah.

"Thank you," Kwah said as she passed the box into his hands. "We're lucky this survived."

"What is it?"

Kwah fiddled with a small stone mechanism on the top of the box. Lyvanne heard a subtle clicking noise and the box swung open. Inside it was filled with parchments and what appeared to be rolled up maps. "This is where we kept all the locations and details of other branches of The Spring. If this had been destroyed we would have had quite the time trying to reconnect."

Everything only grew worse as the group worked their way through the camp and out into the woods on the other side of the clearing. It was evident that this was where the bulk of the battle had taken place. There were bodies strewn everywhere, lifeless husks from both sides who had fallen among the leaves as their blood stained the nature around them. Lyvanne saw Hemeti hung over wooden barricades and fallen trees which had been used to slow the enemy's advances; men in the colours of the king who had been victimised by pitfalls, their bodies impaled on the wooden spikes hidden below. But worst of all were the bodies of the king's soldiers whose remains Lyvanne couldn't explain with reasonable thought. Their armour appeared torn apart from within, and there was little left of their actual bodies except for the immediate splatter of blood and gore that surrounded the ruined armour plating.

Her stomach did summersaults and her breath caught in her throat. She'd never seen anything like it before and her imagination ran wild with what weapon The Spring could have used to cause such an effect. It didn't take her long before she realised what and who the real cause behind the scene would be, and her heart sank as she finally realised just why Turiel had appeared pained back on the outskirts.

"Do not dwell on what has happened," Kwah said walking up beside her as she stared down at the scene of a massacre. "And do not pity Turiel for what he has done. It was his decision to make, and without his actions none of us would be here to tell our story."

Lyvanne wanted to avert her eyes, to move elsewhere and help relocate the bodies of their friends, but she couldn't bring herself to pry her eyes away. "I used to think magic was like a toy, that it was used to bring joy and mystery into the world…" Lyvanne waved a hand at the scene before her. "I didn't ever think it could be used like this."

"I dare say for someone so young you've had a bad experience of magic," Kwah replied. "But yes, I don't know how it was used in ages past, but to be born with it in the world as we know it today is only a burden. One that I must say Turiel carries with great responsibility."

The rest of the morning went slowly. The further into the woods and the closer towards the front line of the battle they worked the more bodies of their friends they found. Tublik had been found by the wooden palisades, his body pierced in multiple locations around his chest. The bodies of three enemy soldiers collapsed around him. Similarly they had found Shri'ook among a scattering of bodies off to the left of the battlefield.

"The left wing of our men fell early into the battle," Kwah reminisced as they moved among the fallen. Their bodies appeared burned in totality, their skin peeling and any hair on their heads gone. "They did not deserve an end like this."

"The enemy had a warlock too," Lyvanne said as she held back the bile in her throat.

"Then we must thank the Goddess' fortune that it was only the left wing who fell in such a manner."

As the sun rose further into the sky, and far off animals crowed the arrival of the morning, The Spring found themselves ready to say their goodbyes to the fallen. They didn't have the manpower to bury their friends and companions properly, so instead Kwah had taken the lead on the construction of a funeral pyre. Tyler and a handful of others had cleaned up the bodies as best they could and then they were placed on a large construction of wood and loose stones that served as their resting place.

The mood was utterly despondent as the flames licked the bodies of the fallen before rising high into the sky. Lyvanne watched as tears rolled down the face of Greyson, his brother Davidson one of the bodies laid across the pyre. To her left, Hemeti were saying a silent prayer for their fallen. The Hemeti man from the North Road whom she swore she recognised had survived the conflict and had joined hands with others nearby as they watched the spirits of their friends move on to the next world.

Oblib was stood on the other side of the pyre, but she could just about make him out through the flicker of the flames. His head was drooped, whilst the other Hemeti had closed their eyes in prayer, Oblib instead struggled to fight back the tears. He had been badly injured during the battle and like Jocelyn part of his clothing had been fashioned into a makeshift sling.

"We can't stay here," Kwah's voice sounded out as the fire slowly began to die. "The king will be back and in greater number than before. We won't survive another attack."

Lyvanne cast her gaze over those around the fire. She was thankful for those who had survived, but what had at first been sorrow for those they had lost quickly turned into a different emotion entirely. As she watched the bodies of the dead burn under the morning sun her mind began to make accusations. This isn't my fault, she told herself, these people didn't die because of her me. They had died because of the king. These people were young. They were optimists who wanted better for their lives and the lives of the people they loved, and they had been killed because of the king's greed and paranoia. The anger swelled inside of her and she knew that without any doubt she had chosen and accepted the path that had been laid out before her. She would fight for the Rive.

CHAPTER 36

There were two dozen of them left alive following the battle, and all of them looked as though they had seen better days. The camp had been destroyed and the horses lost during the attack. So after having gathered all they could, and after saying their final goodbyes to the fallen, Kwah and Turiel gathered everyone together and as one they set off to the South.

Following fields which ran adjacent to a small road that forked off from the North Road the group made slow progress. Many were wounded, some with injuries that made it difficult for them to travel, but Kwah had insisted that they weren't safe if they delayed any longer and that the need to resupply was too critical. The islander had grown into the role of leader Lyavnne noted as she watched him leading the way. His heroics on the battlefield being muttered around like campfire gossip as the gathering of young idealists made their way to a nearby village. Some of the injured had been given the luxury of travelling by horseback and the migration had begun.

Jocelyn had spent the time it had taken the able bodied to clear up and tend to the bodies of the dead informing Turiel of everything that had happened with the warlock. How Jocelyn had fought him and lost, but how Lyvanne and the timing of The Spring's victory had caused the man to flee to save his own life. Turiel had been less than pleased. Not only over the fact that Jocelyn and Lyvanne had come back to the fighting, rather than fleeing to safety, but because they let the warlock go.

"He was too dangerous to let go!" Turiel had said as he walked alongside Lyvanne and Jocelyn through a field of tall grass and chirping insects.

"We had no choice," Jocelyn replied calmly, trying to soothe Turiel's temper so that they didn't attract too many unwanted ears. "It was let him go or push him into defending himself and probably killing Lyvanne."

Turiel furrowed his brows and rested his hands on his hips as he wrestled with the idea. For all his talk about training Lyvanne to defend herself against a warlock, she wasn't sure that before last night he himself had ever faced off with one in such a manner.

Turiel had admitted to still being plagued by the pain that he had suffered during the battle, both as a result of his own actions and the actions of his adversary on the field. She noticed his hands shaking at times as they walked, but Turiel was always quick to hide the quirk away in his travelling cloak or the pockets of his tunic. His eyes darted along the horizon, as if afraid of being watched or attacked by some unseen foe.

"He isn't well," Lyvanne whispered to Jocelyn as the pair walked on ahead, choosing to give Turiel some space as they wound their way down the final stretches of countryside. Gentle columns of chimney smoke were rising into the sky a few miles away, and the small stone and wooden buildings of a village were steadily becoming clearer.

"I know, little one," Jocelyn replied.

"Should we do something?" Lyvanne pressed.

"Not a lot we can do, at least not yet. Let him get some rest once we reach the village and then if it carries on we can try and help. Okay?" Jocelyn asked, looking down at Lyvanne who was walking by her side.

Lyvanne nodded, but in truth she wasn't happy with just watching her friend be like this. A determination had grown within her since the battle and now anything other than a perfect solution felt insufficient.

The tall grassy fields of the countryside began to give way for tended and farmed meadows as the group reached the outskirts of the village. Rolling hills and untamed land gave way for flat farmland and cattle. It felt and looked like some of the places that Lyvanne had seen on their journey down from Astreya. Not the tropical forests or the arid lands surrounding the capital, but the small and peaceful villages that had dotted the riverbanks of the Anya.

As The Spring passed into the boundaries of the village looking like a platoon of soldiers returning home from the front lines of Tyberia, Lyvanne watched in awe as villagers didn't just stand and watch. They instead rushed over and offered aid. Men and women, young and old alike all came rushing over, helping to carry supplies, weapons, the injured. Anywhere they could help, they did. Farmers stopped their work in the fields when they saw them arrive and came over to offer any help where it was needed.

"Thank you," Kwah said repeatedly to every person who approached him. Even the Hemeti among them were being treated with dignity and in some cases admiration. It made her think of the way she had seen and heard the rich of Astreya talk about Hemeti, as though they had been born inferior even to the poor. Yet here, they were equals fighting for the same cause.

"Is it always like this?" Lyvanne whispered to Jocelyn as the pair were swarmed by a gaggle of young children who offered to carry the few belongings they had. Not wanting to part with her few belongings, and in particular the toy soldier Oh had given her long ago, Lyvanne politely declined their aid and ushered them on towards others.

Jocelyn smiled, the first full smile she'd seen since the battle. "Not always, but fighting for a cause that people like this can rally behind often leads to you making new friends."

The reaction brought out a noticeable positive reaction from the crestfallen survivors of the night prior. Oblib who had been travelling towards the rear of the group was back to his usual jovial self as villagers with whom he was apparently well acquainted welcomed him. It was a reception unlike anything Lyvanne had seen in Astreya, a connection that simply wasn't shared between the king's men and the citizens he governed.

The Spring moved across from the fields and joined up with a small cobbled road which led down into the village proper. By now, they were less so being led by Kwah, and more by the rowdy villagers who had joined their numbers.

It surprised her how skinny so many of the villagers were. Some of the children had arms thinner than her own and the way they carried themselves made them appear more fragile than most.

"Are they okay?" Lyvanne asked Jocelyn as the group made their way into the village. More people continuously pouring out of small stone houses and wooden farm buildings as they spied the dishevelled survivors making their way towards a larger building which could be seen down towards the end of the road. Others watched through open shutters, or from the small fenced off gardens filled with decorative flowers that surrounded a number of the houses.

"These people don't have much," Jocelyn replied as a small child bumped into her side excitedly, causing her to wince as a wave of pain shot up her arm. "A lot of people, especially those living so far away from the cities don't have much money, so they can't afford much food. They grow what they can and they breed as much cattle as possible, but it's hard. The king takes so much, for his armies, for his patrons. Not much is left after. I don't know much about what this specific branch of The Spring have been doing day to day over the past few years, but judging by the way we're being welcomed I'd imagine that they've played a large part in helping these people get by."

Lyvanne took in everything that Jocelyn was saying. She found it bizarre that she'd ever doubted wanting to be a part of all of this. During her entire life she'd lived among the rich of Astreya, where every person just wanted what was best for themselves. The Spring were the first people she'd ever seen who actively worked towards making life better for others, and they were loved for it. Everything about it felt right, and she felt foolish for having doubted them.

The building they travelled to was larger than any Lyvanne had seen since leaving Astreya. It was three floors tall, carved from a beautiful grey stone and had wooden stables etched out of the side of one of the lower walls. Hanging above a large pair of thick double doors was a swinging sign which read "The Cat and Dog" and had an ornate painting of the two animals to match. Several members of The Spring who had more severe injuries were rushed inside the tavern by locals and Kwah, who had already made his way inside after handing out some orders to the people nearest him. The orders were relayed back and the more able bodied survivors began to gather up the people carrying what supplies and belongings they had brought with them, and ushered them into the stables.

"Where are they going?" Lyvanne asked aloud.

"Shri'ook had a good relationship with the owner of this place," It was Turiel who answered, appearing from behind Jocelyn and Lyvanne as everyone began to scrunch up as they approached the entrance. "There's a small storage room hidden behind the stables. We store our more exotic items there in case any of the king's men come calling whilst we're here."

Lyvanne looked on and sure enough, she realised that it had mostly been the weapons, spare armour and anything recovered from the wreckage of the Annex which had been taken away through the stables. "Come on, let's get inside," Turiel said, placing one arm around both Jocelyn and Lyvanne's shoulders.

Passing through the double doors and into the tavern was like entering a different world. For the many taverns Lyvanne had walked past during her years growing up on the streets of Astreya, she had never once ventured inside. The room that greeted her was large, the ceiling high with three long wooden tables taking up most of the central area of the room. Along either wall running the length of the room were small wooden booths, made for more private conversations. At the end nearest the doors through which they had entered was a large hearth, and to their left at the other end was a large mahogany surface behind which Lyvanne saw all manner of drinks, glasse,s and large barrels.

"Wow," Lyvanne whispered to herself as she imagined what the taverns back in Astreya's Upper level must have been like on the inside if one so far out into the countryside could be like this.

The room itself was busy. People darted left and right everywhere she looked. Some wore aprons and were evidently part of the staff; they were busy either directing the new comers to rooms up a small staircase which was nestled away in the far corner by the bar, or in the case of the injured leading them through a doorway on the other side of the bar. Then there were the unsuspecting patrons. A travelling merchant who was perched on a stool at the bar, a quartet of well-dressed men occupied one of the booths and a lone Hemeti bard identified by the small string instrument tied around his back sat alone on one of the long wooden tables. All of them stared wide-eyed as two dozen strangers walked through the doors, most of whom looked worse for wear.

"Let's get out of their way," Turiel said quietly to the pair as they watched the chaos unfurl, before leading them towards the stairs and up onto the highest floor of the building where one of the younger waiting staff showed them to one of the rooms. Inside, there were two small single beds, a small wooden chair in the corner, and a basic set of wooden draws with a dusty mirror on top.

"Guess I'm sleeping on the floor then" Turiel said sarcastically as he dumped what few belongings he had to one side of the room and made his way over to a small window on the far side.

Lyavnne joined him after taking ownership of the bed closest to the window. The view was unspectacular, the rolling hills of the distant countryside obscured by the wooden construction below which formed the stables. Regardless, Lyvanne was as close to happy as she believed it possible to feel after what had occurred the night before. But a question was tugging at the back of her mind and had been since they had departed earlier that day. How long could this last? How long could they last during this fight against the king?

CHAPTER 37

That night The Cat and Dog buzzed with life. Whether they were drinking away their sorrow or celebrating their survival, the remaining members of The Spring spent what money they had well and drank into the early hours of the morning. Lyvanne had sat by their side the entire night, sipping on goblets of water and eventually even a small amount of Turiel's ale once he had become drunk enough to share it. It was refreshing to watch her friends unwind for the first time since they had arrived at camp. Greyson had drank until the tears had subsided and then late into the night he drew up a seat beside the Hemeti bard who had been staying at the tavern already and together they sang songs in remembrance of the fallen friends that had been lost.

Kwah had been noticeably quiet throughout the night. Whilst he had remained downstairs for as long as anyone else, he had remained sober and stood by the bar talking to a short woman with curled red hair whom Lyvanne took to be the current owner of the establishment. She noticed that a long dagger hung by Kwah's waist, and it made her wonder how many others in the room had one eye on their drink and another on the door. She had no doubt that many of them would be on edge for a number of days, maybe even weeks. As the bard kept reminding them through song, defeating a company of the king's soldiers in armed rebellion upon soil of The Rive was a first in a long time, and once word reached back to the king he would no doubt come back for a second attempt at quelling the upstarts.

Turiel was the first to retreat back to their room. Claiming that the ale had made his eyes heavy after nearly fifteen minutes of his head continually bobbing against his chest. During which time Oblib, who had proved more than capable of holding his alcohol, had finished off the warlock's drink. After that, the slow trickle of people taking their leave of the communal area downstairs began to increase and tired legs began to clatter up the wooden stairs. Eventually, the only ones left were Jocelyn, Lyvanne, Greyson, the bard stranger, Kwah and the owner. The Hemeti bard, now lacking an audience to play to and to earn money from, said his goodnights and made his way to his own room at the tavern. Lacking a partner to play with and the memories of his brother slowly creeping back to the forefront Greyson also departed.

"Congrats, little one... you beat them all," Jocelyn slurred as she thrust an empty goblet into Lyvanne's hands.

She hadn't really done anything of the sort, Lyvanne thought as she pushed away the goblet. She hadn't been drinking like the others and she hadn't exerted herself in combat like they had, but she decided to let Drunk Jocelyn continue to compliment her.

"We should call you the Heroine... of the Cat and Dog," Drunk Jocelyn continued as she swung her rather full goblet of ale into the air. Lyvanne cringed. Her actions deserved no more praise than anyone else who had fought on the battlefield, but if this helped Jocelyn to cope then so be it.

"To the Hero of the Cat and Dog," Kwah echoed as he slowly walked over to the booth that the pair were occupying. Lyvanne could tell that Kwah's eyes were growing weary and she couldn't blame him, quite frankly given the events of the night before she was surprised anyone had stayed awake as long as they had. "Come now you two, time to get some rest."

Lyvanne half expected Drunk Jocelyn to argue the matter and to order another drink, but logic took hold and the Hemeti dragged herself to her feet and ushered Lyvanne out of the booth ahead of her.

The wooden floorboards groaned and creaked as they carefully made their way up the stairs. The pair made it back to their room without causing too much disturbance, and once inside Lyvanne made sure that Jocelyn was safely in bed before tucking herself in for the night. Turiel shifted on the floor when they came in, but his loud snoring gave away that he was still enjoying a deep sleep. Lyvanne lay in bed and looked towards the window where feint rays of moonlight were beaming down into the room as night slowly gave way to the first signs of sunlight beyond the horizon. Her dreams were plagued with memories of the attack on the woods. She saw the old Hemeti whose body had died on her old hut at camp, the bodies of the ling's soldiers killed at Turiel's command and the warlock who she had let live. Her dreams went back even further. The fires of the camp suddenly became the fires she had seen in her mind as she fought to keep Melruin at bay, and before that the fires that had engulfed the house of an innocent family in Astreya as she watched on from a crowded courtyard.

What felt like seconds passed and the room became filled with sunlight. Lyvanne rolled over onto her side to avoid the bright glare pouring in through the window. Her eyes still heavy and drawn from the late night before.

Turiel was still fast asleep on the floor, a thin blanket draped over him and a makeshift mattress of a worn spare quilt below. Jocelyn, however, was nowhere to be seen. Voices were ringing from the floors below, and deducing that Jocelyn was probably downstairs she crept out of bed, trying her best not to wake up Turiel. Quietly she threw on some spare clothes, which she seemed to be gathering as a collection thanks to various generous members of The Spring, and exited the room.

As she passed along the corridors and down the main staircase the inaudible voices quickly turned into the hustle and bustle of cutlery clattering against plates and the general chatter that often accompanied morning meals. Sure enough, as she reached the bottom floor Lyvanne was hit by the smell of bacon, potatoes and ale, the latter of which made her feel slightly sick after the events of the night. Most of the tavern's occupants were awake and busy eating around the various tables that occupied the main communal area. So many in fact that Lyvanne questioned exactly how long she had been asleep for and whether she should go back upstairs to wake up Turiel. Deciding against it she stepped down into the room and set off in search of Jocelyn, whom she found nestled away in a corner booth with Kwah.

"Morning," Lyvanne said cheerfully as she took a seat beside him. She felt guilty for faking her happiness, the pain of losing their friends still weighed heavily on her shoulders. Everywhere she looked she was reminded of those who hadn't made it to the village. But if her being appearing happy might in some way rub off on the others then it was worth a try.

"Morning," Kwah responded with a forced toothy smile, whilst Jocelyn merely grunted her response.

Lyvanne chuckled as she studied her friend, one hand on her forehead, another around a small goblet of water and a still full plate of food in front of her.

"Are you going to eat that?" Lyvanne asked, nudging her hand towards the plate. Jocelyn shook her head and Lyvanne eagerly snatched the plate away. She still didn't have any money of her own, so since their arrival at the tavern she had been relying on others to pay her way for her, a reliance she wasn't overly fond of. She hadn't asked where they all got their money from, but she'd taken an educated guess early on during her time with The Spring that there had been a fair few convoys of the king's gold that had gone missing along the North Road over the past few years.

"How do they have enough food to feed everyone?" Lyvanne asked curiously as she noted how many people in the room were eating, and how skinny the children outside had seemed.

"This village does better than most," Kwah agreed. "There are a few reasons why. Firstly, the village lies near the North Road, which runs between Astreya and Avagarde, making it a well-travelled location. Secondly, our presence in the nearby countryside has meant that trips here by tax collectors have become few and far between. Lastly, when we come here to resupply people like Jocelyn here often end up spending a lot of money which means that the owner, Rosey, has enough money to stock up when traders come through. These days prices are so high that even a gold coin won't buy you too much from wandering traders, so she's had to spend her money wisely over the years."

Sure enough Kwah nodded in the direction of the redhead who stood behind the bar.

"Is she one of us?" Lyvanne asked, hoping her point was implicit enough.

Kwah considered his answer carefully as he gulped down a large swig of water. "She's sympathetic. There are many people who we've grown close to over the years. Some who would even call themselves friends, but openly associating with us can be dangerous. Many choose just to help in small ways when they can, such as letting us stay at their tavern. The king might not know us by name yet, but there are occasionally local law enforcers who do, and having an open association with us can attract unwanted attention."

Lyvanne thought back to the merchant Trystan who had helped them escape Astreya onboard the Colossal and wondered whether he was in the same situation. It was the first time that she really began to understand the politics of it all, the manoeuvring around the king's grasp and the friends which had to be made if they were ever going to be successful. The game they were playing was much larger than she had ever anticipated it could be, and it was far more complex than Turiel had ever explained.

Jocelyn sat in silence for the rest of breakfast as she nursed her hangover, and it was a long time before Turiel eventually forced himself out of bed and downstairs to socialise.

"Would you like your dagger back?" Lyvanne asked Kwah as the four sat waiting for Turiel's food to arrive from the kitchen. They were some of the last people downstairs. Some had gone back to their rooms whilst others had gone to either help the villagers with work as a sign of good will, or had travelled back to the campsite in the woods to make sure nothing had been left behind.

"No thank you, Lyvanne," Kwah replied. "I fear that if you're going to be as stubborn as you were the night of the battle then you're going to need something by your side to keep you safe."

Lyvanne smiled. It wasn't just the gift that pleased her, but the acceptance that she was in this for the long haul and that she wasn't going to be treated any differently to the others now. If they were putting themselves in danger then she planned on being right there by their sides when they did.

The rider arrived a few hours later. It was Ronnoc, and he had a small rolled up piece of parchment in his hand.

"I found this at the campsite attached to the foot of a carrier pigeon," the Hemeti said as he walked through the double doors of the tavern and straight over to Kwah, handing him the parchment.

"Thank you, Ronnoc," Kwah replied as he took the parchment from the Hemeti's hand and studied it. "Was there anything else worth bringing back?"

Ronnoc took a step back. Lyvanne was still sure she recognised him from somewhere but had long since given up trying to figure out from where. "Nothing else. We cleared out pretty well before we left."

Kwah nodded, a gesture that Ronnoc echoed before taking his leave. Kwah placed the parchment on the table and Lyvanne immediately recognised the seal that had been used. It belonged to Sinjin. All eyes around the table turned to Jocelyn, who quickly snatched up the parchment and undid the wrappings.

"It's a letter," she said as she unravelled the message and began to read.

The parchment was passed around the table, and by the time it reached Lyvanne, she knew that something important had happened.

"We need to discuss this in private," Kwah said as he, Turiel, and Jocelyn all rose in unison, leaving the booth and forcing Lyvanne to play catch up as they walked towards a small door to the left of the bar. "Rosey, don't let anyone in until we return," Kwah asked as the four of them proceeded into the other, smaller communal area. Once on the other side of the door Lyvanne paused to read the letter in her hands.

Dear Jocelyn,

I have said many prayers for you over the past few weeks, and I will say many more in the weeks to come. The searches in the city have been stopped. Whilst that has made life here somewhat easier, I fear that it is because the king knows where you and Lyvanne are. Please do write back now that things appear to be clear and let me know that you are all safe.

Whilst the searches may have stopped I believe that the king has seriously underestimated their lasting impact. The citizens of the lower level are living in a constant state of unrest. Fights between citizens in the lower level and the City Watch are breaking out most nights and more than a little blood has been shed on both sides. I am keeping my head down for now, but it is hard to sit by whilst people we know are dying.

The news grows worse I am afraid. There has been significant movement among the king's army over the past few weeks and it has since come to my attention that an invasion fleet from Tyberia has landed on the Northern shores of The Rive. No one appears to know how it has happened, but the king acted immediately and a retaliation force has been sent to hold them and even attempt to drive them back into the sea. I have not heard if the king's armies in Tyberia have been mobilised to return to The Rive in its protection. I have been contacted by more than a few of our friends who want to use this as an opportunity to take Astreya, as it now largely lies empty of soldiers, but I believe those assumptions to be mistaken and if we strike now we may risk showing our hand too early.

For now, I am delaying any further action within the city until we have heard from the other branches, but I don't know how long I can keep angry mobs at bay on my own.

Please reply as soon as you can.

Look after one another. Stay safe. May Iridu shine upon you all.

I love you,
Sinjin

CHAPTER 38

"We tell the others tonight," Kwah said as the four finally settled down after an hour of discussion and deliberation over what The Spring needed to do next.

It won't matter when you tell them, Lyvanne thought as she watched the others slowly leave the room. *They won't agree on anything either.*

"Everyone's here," Ronnoc said as he reported back to Kwah who was stood by the bar of the tavern, looking out at the remaining men and women of The Spring who occupied the various booths and tables before him.

Rosey had been kind enough to close her doors to any further custom for the night and for want of a better name the tavern had become a temporary headquarters for this particular branch of The Spring. Kwah and Turiel had both offered their sincere thanks to Rosey, who despite her appreciation of what these people had done for her village, was none too pleased about being so openly associated with them. But she was kind and Kwah had easily won her over with some of his Islander charm.

"As I'm sure some of you are aware, we've received news from Astreya," Kwah began, his voice booming throughout the small hall. As he relayed the news brought from Sinjin's letter, Lyvanne watched the eyes of those in attendance. She watched as their emotions rode the same journey that hers had: relief that the searches and torture had been stopped replaced quickly with… a surprising range of emotion in response to news of fighting on the streets. Some of those gathered seemed actively concerned by the news, but others appeared almost proud. Greyson even tried to break out into a rallying song in support of his "brothers and sisters" in Astreya before Kwah calmed him down.

Then those emotions all turned into dread as Kwah finished reading the letter and relayed the news of the invasion fleet from Tyberia arriving in the north. There were audible gasps among the crowd, and Lyvanne noticed Rosey raise a quivering hand up to her mouth. But for the most part faces turned pale, and the room silent.

News of an invasion came as a double-edged sword. On the one hand it provided an opportunity the likes of which The Spring were probably never going to have again. The king would be wholly occupied elsewhere as he sought to protect his own lands from the ravages of war, rather than continuing the bloodshed on far off lands. His gaze would be turned North, and if the various branches of The Spring worked together, then there would surely be victories to claim in the South. On the other hand, an invasion of The Rive was unprecedented and it not only threw any plans into disarray and confusion, but it meant that they now had enemies on multiple fronts.

"The armies of Tyberia won't differentiate between the king's soldiers and an armed group of insurgents if they stood in their way," Lyvanne recalled Turiel's warning. "They're savages! They fight like animals and without mercy. Having the likes of them on The Rive could bring serious trouble if the king isn't able to push them back into the sea quickly."

"What do we do now?" A tall woman with olive skin and short, scruffy brown hair asked from the far end of the room near the hearth.

"That's exactly why we wanted you all here in one place. What we do next is something we all need to decide together," Kwah replied as he tried to look at everyone present in the room.

A chorus of voices rose up as nearly everyone tried to make their own opinion heard. The only people who didn't say anything were Lyvanne, Jocelyn, and Turiel who had taken up residence in the booth nearest Kwah. Instead they exchanged worried glances, even among themselves they hadn't managed to come to any meaningful plan of action and the first signs of how this meeting was going didn't seem any more hopeful. A large man, whom Lyvanne wasn't familiar with, similar in shape and build to what Tublik had been, took to his feet. His voice was deep and he quickly silenced the other echoing voices.

"Our friends in Astreya are right. We need to use this opportunity to take the city!" he said as he balled his fist up and thrust it into the air for effect. As quickly as they were gone, the voices once again rose up in response.

"He's right!"

"We wouldn't survive the night."

Turiel joined the man on his feet. "Listen to me!" he shouted, drawing the eyes of the room onto him as Lyvanne watched on from her seat.

"As some or even many of you will know, we had plans in motion to use Avagarde as a means of finding out more information about the king's armies. Where they are, how many men are left in The Rive and how quickly they can be mobilised," Turiel continued, "but it appears as though the Tyberians have done that for us."

Cheers went up from the crowd, and Lyvanne noticed a discrete smile on the face of Jocelyn as the noose around Avagarde's neck was loosened.

Turiel raised a hand as he tried to continue. "But that doesn't mean that our job is done. The king will be distracted and we have a chance now to win victories that we could have only dreamed of a few years ago. We can't win them on our own and it's too early to strike straight for Astreya. We two-dozen aren't enough to claim more than a few streets of Avagarde, let alone the capital. If we're going to make moves which could really change the landscape of The Rive then we need to bring together the branches, The Spring needs to work as one unit for the first time and we need to begin expanding. We will never truly be enough in numbers or armaments if the people don't rise up alongside us. We need to start being bolder in our expansion, and we need to start spreading our message across the whole of The Rive, regardless of repercussions from the king."

Lyvanne knew he was right. No matter the bravado surrounding them all. After having beaten the king's soldiers, two-dozen insurgents weren't enough to do any real damage to the king even with his armies dragged to the North. But there were other issues she knew would arise.

"What about our friends in Astreya? What about the people who live in the North who are going to be caught in a warzone?" a voice called out from one of the long tables in the middle of the room.

Kwah took his turn to answer. "We do not have the people to split up effectively. Either we act together or everything we've built falls apart and we start again once The Rive has been rid of Tyberians."

The answer didn't please a handful of people sat throughout the room, all of which voiced their disagreement. Including Jocelyn, who took to her feet.

"Sinjin is my brother, and I won't abandon him to a city about to erupt into chaos," she said, as the room grew quiet around her. "It's important that The Spring is stronger than ever over the coming months, and many of you will be needed in the South. But if you have family in Astreya or further North then you're welcome to join me."

There it was, the reason why after an hour of discussions they'd not been able to agree on where they should go and what they should do.

"I won't leave Sinjin to die alone," Jocelyn continued.

"He would understand," Turiel tried to intervene. "This is what we've always wanted. He knows what kind of opportunity this could be."

"That's not your choice to make," Jocelyn said, her voice cold.

"Us three," Turiel said, his voice growing quieter in defeat as the others watched on. "We need to stay together."

"Then come with me?" Jocelyn asked quietly, before in a moment of weakness reaching out and taking his hand in front of everyone. Turiel's head had dropped, the answer already etched in his face.

Lyvanne knew that Turiel loved Sinjin like a brother and that he didn't want to see Astreya descend into chaos any less than the others, but The Spring had been his life's work since leaving the king's palace. He wasn't willing to let the opportunity to establish some kind of foothold in The Rive slip past him.

Tearing her eyes away from her two friends and out over the gathered crowd where small outcrops of people were giving serious consideration to what Jocelyn was saying. She wasn't sure exactly how many had family in the North, but likewise these people had grown so close that they were like a new family all of their own.

"I can't make you stay with us," Turiel said, turning his attention away from Jocelyn and towards the crowd as the clamour died down. "But I do ask that you think this all through before you make a decision. The day after next Kwah and I will be leaving for Avagarde where we're going to meet up with another branch. Once there, we will be sending out letters to all other known active branches of The Spring and we will begin to establish a plan of action for how to take advantage of the situation we have been gifted. I ask that you think of the long-term success of what we're trying to achieve here and join us. But if you do have family in the North who you wish to help, then Jocelyn will be travelling for Astreya on the same day. If you wish to join her then we will send you on with what provisions we can spare."

Turiel shot a sheepish glance towards Jocelyn across the table they shared. It was obvious that Turiel still wasn't pleased that she was leaving them, but he was trying not to let that stand between his feelings for her. Then in a moment of clarity, Lyvanne sat there, looking between her two friends who were about to depart on drastically different paths, and her face grew cold as she realised that she didn't know which one she wanted to follow.

She hadn't given it much thought until now but with things in The Rive being on the brink of collapse, it was hard to tell how long it would be again until they were all reunited. As the voices around the room once again picked up, Lyvanne's mind drifted to thoughts of her friends back in Astreya. The way that she had promised to help them get out of the city and off the streets, the way that none before her had ever come back even if they'd said they would.

Then she heard Abella's voice in her head, and she remembered the way that she had told her how the Angel had granted her a great gift and the opportunity for a better future for not just herself, but for everyone. She didn't doubt that Abella would want her to go with Turiel, to help The Spring work towards the end of the king's reign.

"Take tomorrow to decide," Kwah's voice snapped her back to attention. "If you want to carry on this journey we've begun together then please hold your opinions on what action needs to be taken until we reach Avagarde. The situation has grown beyond us few and a more formal approach will have to be adopted in the coming weeks."

Kwah's voice was firm. Lyvanne felt quite sure that he'd grown tired of people shouting out suggestions for which town or city they should try and liberate whilst the king's attention was being draw elsewhere.

The lively atmosphere of the night before was gone. Shortly after the meeting ,nearly all but a handful of people had already retreated back to their rooms. Lyvanne lay in bed, her mind racing with arguments for and against the two paths she was going to have to choose between. Jocelyn lay in the bed next to her, but with her arm still causing her pain and no alcohol in her system to numb it the Hemeti was tossing and turning unable to sleep. Turiel was still downstairs, not through a longing for alcohol or socialising Lyvanne thought, but through not wanting to have to confront Jocelyn yet.

Lyvanne closed her eyes and imagined a world where none of this had ever happened, a world where she hadn't grown up on the streets, a world where she was free to have a family and make friends who lived in the same small village and weren't constantly on the run. She pictured the future she had always imagined for herself, the one she had started saving for, and the same one that she'd had to give up. It felt like a lost dream now, something that had fallen out of her reach for good. She had chosen to give up that dream when she decided to join The Spring, it wasn't a decision she regretted, but it made the choice before her all the more important. Because whomever she left behind might fall out of reach for good too.

Hoping once again to find an answer as to which path she should follow, Lyvanne said a prayer to the Angel of Destiny.

Dear Angel watching over us, please lend me your sight, please show me what I am to do, show me what is to come.

CHAPTER 39

The next day came and went in a haze. Lyvanne wandered through the village, eager to get out of the tavern and to avoid the deepening split between her friends. Turiel hadn't come to bed until late into the night, and likewise, Jocelyn had been up and out of bed early into the morning. Neither appeared eager to try and talk things through before the time came for them to go their separate ways.

By the time she was out and in the village, there were already people hard at work. She saw Ronnoc riding off along the hills in the distance, scouting their perimeter and watching for any sign of trouble. A few of the other Hemeti in The Spring had gathered with some of the locals in a field nearby and were beginning to help with a day's work among the crops. Lyvanne offered to help as she walked by, but they'd declined, albeit nicely, knowing that her inexperience would only slow down what was already an arduous process. Before long, she was joined by some of the children who she had seen upon their arrival. They danced around her and tried to drag her off in various directions to play their games. Although they were much younger than her, most of them being about Oh's age or slightly older, she enjoyed their company. They made her feel like a child again and given what had happened over the past week, it was a feeling she wasn't eager to dismiss quickly.

She wondered what their future held for them. Open war on The Rive the likes of which Tyberia might bring hadn't been seen since humans invaded what was then the Hemeti homeland. She wanted to protect them the way she had Lira and Oh for all those years, to ask them to come with her when she left on the next day, but unlike her these children had families and homes. They had more safety here in the countryside, isolated and quiet than she could ever offer them.

Dawn turned to day, day turned to dusk and dusk turned to night. Lyvanne spent what felt like hours playing with the other children, she'd walked the perimeter of the village what felt like a thousand times, and as the sun set in the west she had found Jocelyn; sitting under a tree just beyond the village boundary.

"What are you doing out here, little one?" Jocelyn asked as Lyvanne approached, her voice quiet and sad.

Lyvanne shrugged. She didn't really have an answer. Jocelyn patted the ground next to her with her good arm, and Lyvanne took a seat on the grass. Neither said a word, instead they sat there in silence looking out over the countryside beyond them. As the sky turned dark, Lyvanne watched as a number of nocturnal animals took into the sky. Off towards the village Lyvanne watched a pair of owls, flying through the air together before perching on a thatched roof. A rattling from inside the building scared one away and left the other alone, a watchman alone upon the roof.

"I don't know where to go," Lyvanne said, breaking the silence.

"What do you mean?" Jocelyn asked, turning to look at her friend.

"You and Turiel. I don't know who to go with tomorrow."

Jocelyn shook her head. "Lyvanne, it's not a choice you need to make. Tomorrow when Kwah and Turiel leave for Avagarde, you'll go with them."

Jocelyn took Lyvanne by surprise. "Why?" Lyvanne asked, unable to hide her disappointment that Jocelyn didn't want her to come with her back to Astreya.

"Lyvanne, the only reason that Turiel and I are here now is because we wanted to get you out of Astreya," Jocelyn replied, her voice calm but authoritative. "I'm going back to Astreya because that's where I'm needed right now. Turiel doesn't need me by his side whilst he has everyone else there... but he does need you. If you go back to Astreya then everything we've fought for, everything that people died for will be wasted. If the king finds out you're there and captures you then do you really think Turiel will stand aside? No, he'll risk everything to come after you."

"But what about my friends in -

"Don't worry about your friends. I will do everything I can whilst I'm in Astreya to find them, and then when Sinjin and I leave we'll bring them with us. I promise."

Lyvanne blushed, she should have known that all she would have to do is ask. She leant over and wrapped her arms around her friend, being careful not to put any pressure on the injured arm and ribs. Tears welled up in both their eyes. Lyvanne found it surprising how close they had grown in their time together, and now on the verge of being separated it felt like losing Oh, Lira, and Abella all over again—

only this time she wasn't ready.

"I'm sorry I couldn't finish training you," Jocelyn carried on, nodding at the small dagger given to her by Kwah that she now carried around her waist at all times. "You better promise me that the next time I see you you'll be better than Turiel with a sword."

Lyvanne nodded enthusiastically. "I'll ask Kwah to show me how. When will I next see you again?"

"I don't know, little one. Could be a few weeks if I'm in and out of Astreya quickly enough, could be much longer if things don't calm down and they need my help. But don't worry, I'll write when I can, and I'll look for your friends as soon as I can. They can stay with Sinjin and I once I've found them."

Lyvanne smiled as best she could. The concept of being separated from Jocelyn for any long period of time made her stomach churn and her heart ache. "Can you promise me one more thing?"

"What would that be?"

"Go back to the room and talk to Turiel."

Jocelyn looked at Lyvanne and for the first time envied her innocent and youthful outlook on life. "It's not always that simple. Turiel and I we're… complicated. Always have been."

"That doesn't mean you have to carry on like that. If you don't know when you'll next see him then you should clear the air," Lyvanne pressed, unable to understand why two people who clearly liked each other the way they did would allow themselves to go their separate ways at a time like this.

Jocelyn pressed her good arm against the tree and used it as leverage to push herself back onto her feet. "Come on, Lyvanne. It's getting dark, and we should probably head back."

"Promise me…" Lyvanne asked one last time.

"I can't," Jocelyn replied and turned back towards the village.

That night, Lyvanne spent a few hours alone downstairs, sitting quietly in a booth as the rest of the tavern slept. In part, she had wanted to give Jocelyn and Turiel time alone, hoping that they would work things out, but more so she had wanted to delay what was about to happen the next morning. So, she chose isolation and sat near the far end of the room where the hearth was slowly turning into dying embers. Before too long had passed, Lyvanne's eyes grew heavy, but stubbornness won out and despite her bobbing head she forced herself to stay downstairs.

"Are you okay, child?" The voice was quiet, calm, and new to Lyvanne's ears. Opening her eyes, Lyvanne realised that she had fallen asleep in her booth. The dim rays of sunlight breached the windows of the tavern, and Rosey towered over her. "Are you okay?" she asked again.

"Yes… sorry, I didn't mean to fall asleep here," Lyvanne replied groggily.

Rosey smiled. Her red hair was tied back into a bun, and there were a number of freckles dotted across the bridge of her nose. "Don't be sorry, it's alright. Did you at least sleep well?" she asked as she took a seat opposite her.

Lyvanne smiled back and nodded. She felt almost ashamed that she hadn't properly spoken to her before now. "Have you always owned this place? It's lovely."

"Was my pa's before he passed. Went off to fight the king's wars and never came home, so I became the owner. Think I've done alright with the place given that business can be slow at times," Rosey responded, a proud smile spread across her face as she looked around at the stone walls that surrounded them. "What about you though? You seem a little young to be caught up in all of this even for The Spring."

Lyvanne was caught off guard. She realised that until now she'd never had to explain to anyone outside of people who were already involved exactly who she was and why she was suddenly part of the insurgency. "I kinda fell into it I guess. I don't mind though. They do good, and I want to help with that."

Rosey nodded. "They do a lot of good, but it's dangerous you know? Being with them the way you are. I could always do with an extra pair of hands around here... if that interests you?"

Lyvanne's face flushed a bright red. "Do you mean... I could live here?"

Rosey's smile was infectious. "Yes, that's what I mean. You can help me and the other girls out, especially if there's war coming to The Rive then I reckon we'll be seeing a lot more footfall around here sooner or later."

The answer came quicker than Lyvanne had thought it would ever be possible. "No... thank you." She had pictured being with the children again, growing up alongside them and having real stability in her life for the first time, but it wasn't what she wanted anymore; it wasn't how she could best help.

Rosey seemed to understand. "Okay, child, but if you ever change your mind then The Cat and Dog will always have an open door for you."

Rosey placed a warm palm on Lyvanne's cheek and with a sympathetic look in her eyes she said her farewell and went off to tend to the morning prep and cleaning. It wasn't long before others started to join Lyvanne downstairs and soon after that it was finally time for her to fetch her belongings and to say her goodbyes.

The two groups had gathered outside of the tavern entrance. Only two others had chosen to go with Jocelyn. The tall woman with olive skin had chosen to go further North than even Astreya, claiming that she had family near the Northern shores who she needed to help escape before war claimed their land, and an old man of similar descent to Lyvanne who claimed that he couldn't stand by and watch the city he grew up in turn itself into a battlefield.

Everyone had said their goodbyes, ready to depart in their own directions. All but Turiel and Jocelyn who now stood a few feet apart from one another. The others had moved on, opting to make sure that everything had been properly packed as the groups made final preparations, and incidentally giving the two sometime alone. But Lyvanne wasn't feeling so generous and watched on quietly from a nearby stone wall which surrounded the tavern.

"So, I guess this is it for a while?" Turiel asked as the two took a step closer together.

Jocelyn was one of the strongest people Lyvanne had ever met, but right now even she seemed vulnerable to the world. "Just make sure it's not too long okay?" Jocelyn replied as Turiel nodded. "And keep me updated on what's happening. Write to me as often as you can, I'll need to know if you're starting a war without me," she joked.

Not being able to contain himself, Turiel let out a small chuckle and sigh before reaching out and taking Jocelyn's left hand. "I'll write as often as I can. Make sure you and Sinjin stay out of trouble, okay? If Tyberia manages to get off the beaches, make sure you get out of Astreya as quickly as possible. I don't care who you have to leave beh -

Jocelyn broke him off by planting her lips firmly on his. Lyvanne blushed and considered turning away, but it was as if she was trapped in a trance and she remained still. Jocelyn brought him in tightly with her one good arm and Turiel reciprocated by putting both his hands around her waist.

"I'm sorry I have to leave you," Jocelyn said as the two separated.

"I'm sorry too."

Then it was over. The two placed their foreheads against one another for a brief moment before forcing themselves to let go. Jocelyn turned first, but not before blowing a kiss in Lyvanne's direction, which she pretended to catch mid-air. Jocelyn broke into a quick walk and soon caught up to her two travelling companions. Turiel watched her walk away for a quiet moment before turning his back as well, both of them walking in different directions, each of them glancing back one last time to say their last goodbyes.

CHAPTER 40

A vagarde was a two-day journey according to Kwah, but those two days were very quickly beginning to feel like a lifetime to Lyvanne. Wanting to comfort her friend, she had started the journey by riding alongside Turiel. When it became obvious that he just wanted to be left alone, she'd given him the space he needed and drifted off towards the edge of the column.

As their company began to draw closer to Avagarde, Lyvanne found that they were suddenly passing more and more fellow travellers. A merchant rode past in the opposite direction, a mule riding alongside with crates and sacks of cargo hung over its back.

"I have wares if you have coin," the merchant called out as they column of fighters passed him by, but much to Lyvanne's shock he showed an obvious disgust for the Hemeti among the group and was quickly told to carry on travelling.

Others they passed were even less polite. Lyvanne watched as Kwah had to physically hold Ronnoc back as a nobleman spat out of his gilded carriage at the sight of a Hemeti riding on horseback, something unheard of in Astreya. The nobleman's driver had the good sense to speed up the horses when he saw that more than a few people in the column wanted to retaliate.

"We should rest here for the night," Kwah said as he slowed down his horse to come in line with the bulk of the column. Their unelected leader pointing towards a flattened out stretch of land to the side of the road, partially covered by a few isolated trees and a small rocky outcrop towards the edge furthest away from the road itself.

The Spring did as they were asked and slowly began to move over in the direction of their camp for the night. The ground was well trodden and showed signs of travellers making frequent use of the area to rest on their way to or out of Avagarde.

"I'll start work on food before it gets too dark," Oblib boasted as he dismounted his horse with his one good arm and immediately began to unpack some supplies from the saddle across his horse's back.

He won't have much to choose from, Lyvanne thought as she dismounted her own horse and moved to tie it to one of the nearby trees. The Spring had bought what they could from Rosey, restocking on the essentials and resupplying their water rations, but they had been conscious not to leave the tavern owner empty-handed and tried where they could to live off the land. Rosey gave what she could afford to the rest of her village, and she sold goods at a cheaper rate to travellers than most merchants would. The Spring had always respected her for that. Elswhere they had bought from the villagers directly; a handful of horses in return for help in the fields, or what coin they could spare. Tools that would help them rebuild a camp one day, and the silence of those who weren't locals and may let slip the knowledge of their direction.

It didn't take long for everyone to settle down for the night after they'd departed the road, and once a fire had been lit, it didn't take Lyvanne long to realise that whilst many people had seemingly picked themselves up since the battle, there were still a number of people who were struggling with the reality of their new situation.

Greyson had barely said a word since they left The Cat and Dog. He sat alone by the fire gently toying around with his lute. Others were quiet, or even isolated, but it was Turiel who worried her the most. Since they had settled down by the roadside, he had taken himself off towards the rocky outcrop towards the edge of their group and kept entirely to himself.

"He'll be okay," Kwah said as he caught her staring out towards her friend.

Lyvanne turned to face him. "What about you? You sound tired."

She didn't think there was much point in being anything but truthful anymore. Kwah wasn't the only one. They were all tired.

"We're soldiers, Lyvanne. It's our job to be tired, tired until the fighting is done," Kwah replied as he filled his plate with food and moved away.

Lyvanne looked back towards Turiel. Like two souls inter-twined, she felt drawn towards him, a need deep within her to help him in some way. Fortunately Oblib and his insipid meal of brown bread, boiled potatoes, and some cheese that they had bought from Rosey offered her the opportunity.

Grabbing two wooden plates and filling them both with a fair portion of food, she made her way through the darkness of the roadside camp, only illuminated by the flickering flames of the fire behind her and the dim rays of moonlight that were trying to break through a grey cloud overhead. The outcrop of rocks where she found Turiel reminded her of when they had gone out into the countryside together to train her mind to defend itself from a warlock's advances. Unlike then, Turiel wasn't as eager for the company this time.

"I brought you food," Lyvanne said quietly as she approached Turiel from behind. He was sat on top of one of the rocks and with two plates in her hands she didn't hold out much hope of getting up to him. So, instead she waited. "I can wait down here all evening you know? Not like this stuff is going to go cold…"

Turiel didn't move.

"I'll eat yours if you don't come down here," Lyvanne lied as she tried to press her friend into making the first move.

She looked back towards camp, wondering if there was any other way she could entice him back down, but quickly came to the conclusion that unless she could magically conjure Jocelyn from thin air then her chances were pretty slim. Determined not to give up, Lyvanne put down Turiel's plate on a nearby rock and sat at the bottom of the outcrop. She chose to eat the potatoes before they went cold, not that she thought it would matter much if they did. Lyvanne shuffled around until she was comfortable and began to talk to her friend through her chewing.

"She'll be alright you know?" she started, trying to not to be too loud and disgusting as she spoke with her mouth full. "Jocelyn's tougher than both of us combined when she wants to be."

Again, she received no response. She hated seeing Turiel this way, and it made her even angrier that she couldn't do anything to help, not really. So instead, she settled for sitting below him for as long as she could.

Back over in the camp, various people bedded down for the night. Kwah was further off towards the edge of the road, standing over the others, keeping watch as they settled down to sleep. She considered going and asking him for help with Turiel, but again she knew that he couldn't fix the one thing that was bothering him most.

"I'll be okay," Turiel said suddenly. His voice almost made Lyvanne jump, but she managed to restrain herself and quickly looked over her shoulder to see if he had moved. He hadn't, but it was a start.

"You sure?" She could just about make out Turiel nodding in the darkness above. The small gesture was more reassuring than she thought it would be.

"She's hard to let go of," he continued as he stared out into the vacant world beyond. "Every time I think she's going to be around for a while, something comes up and one of us has to leave."

"I'm sure she feels the same way," Lyvanne replied, trying to be reassuring or at the very least somewhat comforting.

"Did you definitely not see either of us in your vision?" Turiel asked.

"I don't think so," Lyvanne said tentatively as she tried her best to recall the scene she had seen before her in the Throne Room. "It's hard to tell because everyone was older…"

Lyvanne trailed off, something had finally clicked. "Ronnoc," She said faintly.

"What about him?" Turiel asked, finally turning down to look at her.

"Ronnoc was in my vision. That's why I recognise him!" Lyvanne said with enthusiasm as she tried not to disturb the rest of the camp.

Turiel swivelled and elegantly jumped down the rocky outcrop and landed beside Lyvanne. "You're sure? He was in the throne room?"

Lyvanne nodded as she tried her hardest to recall exactly what the two Hemeti she had seen in her vision looked like. "I'm pretty certain. I don't know who the second Hemeti was, but one of them was definitely Ronnoc. He was sat around the table with me and the others."

Turiel ran a thumb across one of his facial scars, a habit Lyvanne had noticed him doing more of recently. "Don't mention anything about this. It's probably nothing, but if he's important to The Spring and our future then I don't want to scare him off by telling him you've seen his future."

Lyvanne nodded. It made sense, she thought, even if it was just a possible future it could be daunting to anyone knowing what might be in store. Turiel and her knew that better than anyone else.

"Do you think -

The pain was as crippling as it was sudden. Like a fire streaking outwards from her chest, it coursed all the way through Lyvanne's body until it had entirely gripped her in an endless pulse of agony.

"Lyvanne!" Turiel shouted as she fell limp against the floor "Lyvanne, what's wrong?"

She couldn't answer; all she could do was focus on not passing out from the pain. In the distance the camp was stirring, people rising from their place of rest and Kwah sprinting over in her direction. Then everything was gone and her world turned to black.

"Lyvanne!" Turiel's voice was the last echo of the world she left behind as everything around her turned to flame. She knew where she was and she knew what was happening.

"You're stronger than you were before," the voice rippled through towering flames as the shadowed creature stepped out into her line of sight. "Tell me... what is the name of the one who trained you?"

Lyvanne resisted. She was encircled by flame and stood before her, no more than a few metres away was the same figure encased in shadow that had tried to her invade her mind before. "I won't tell you," She replied as she shifted onto her feet, standing before the enemy where once she had quivered.

"You're foolish to resist," the shadow began to take strides in her direction. "Tell me who it was -

"No!" she shouted, raising a hand into the space between them. "I won't tell you their name... but I know yours."

The figure seemed taken aback by her assertiveness.

"The man you sent to kill me, to kill my friends, he failed... just like you're going to fail... Melruin."

The figure appeared confused, but the confusion was quickly replaced by a sickening grin. "So Kryan betrayed my name to you? It doesn't matter," The figure hissed as it began to circle around its prey. "For someone who has no connection to magic, I've never felt one so powerful. You should be working for the king, not against him."

Lyvanne laughed in the shadow's face. "I would never work for the ling."

"So you seek to overthrow him?"

"It's become a recent hobby of mine, I guess."

"Then that -

"It wouldn't have been the case if the king wasn't paranoid enough to look into the visions of others," Lyvanne interrupted again, this time making Melruin visibly angry but deeming it worth the risk to have her point heard. "I was happy to have a normal life, to just help my friends where I could… but your king pushed me, he chased me away from them! It's his fault that I am where I am now."

"And where would that be?" Melruin growled, his patience lost.

"Among your enemies, and from what I hear… you have quite a lot," Lyvanne growled back at her invader.

Anger possessed Melruin's form. "The king will never stop hunting you," he said with venom. "You will never be safe. Your friends will never be safe. We will kill all who you love." Melruin's shadowy figure roared and soared in her direction. The pain in her chest magnified as the creature drew closer, the heat from the flames licked at her cheeks and the vast space beyond threatened to collapse in around her.

Forcing herself to remember where she was and the power she held in this place, she brought her eyes forward to lock her gaze onto Melruin. "Be gone," Lyvanne commanded calmly. The pain, the fear, none of it compared to the hope of knowing what world waited for them on the other side of war. None of it compared to the strength she felt when she recalled the voices and faces of her friends.

The demon contorted in front of her, rippling like water and gyrating in every direction. The shadows began to fold in on one another, twisting inwards like layers as the flames that had encircled them began to float inwards, mixing with the shadows until all that was left was a chaotic blur. Melruin roared among the chaos as he fought to regain control, but it was too late, he'd underestimated her. An unearthly crack rippled through the air, louder than anything she had heard before and Lyvanne knew that Melruin was being cast from her mind.

Just like that the flames, the invader who had caused her so much pain, the doubt and the worry, it had all gone. In an instant, Lyvanne had sent it all away, and now she was stood there in a void beyond worlds alone and unafraid. Where before there had been uncertainty and fear Lyvanne now found that she stood in the vast emptiness with a newfound confidence and belief. She didn't know for sure, but she had felt how powerless Melruin had been to resist her, and for the first time she really believed that he might not deem it worth the suffering to try and invade her mind for information again.

Taking a deep breath to calm and collect herself, echoes of voices began to filter in from the real world. Kwah asking if she was okay, Turiel explaining what he thought was happening and others further off into the distance. The lure of fresh air tugged at her, the real world was calling her back. She resisted, just for a moment. Tomorrow everything would change, she told herself, tomorrow they'd arrive at Avagarde and together they would take the next steps towards a better world.

Lyvanne took in another breath. She wasn't even sure if she was really breathing or if it was all just some part of the illusion, but it helped.

"I'm ready," Lyvanne said one last time as she cast herself back into the real world.

EPILOGUE

The continuous drip of water falling from the far end of the pitch black room was the only thing keeping Terravin centred. Drip. Drip. Drip. The continuous patter might have driven others into insanity, and if he was being completely honest, he wasn't sure if he hadn't lost all sanity a long time ago. The chaos of having no control over his mind had become the norm.

The stone floor that Terravin knelt on was warm to the touch. The Northern lands of The Rive were hot all year round, and being locked away in a dungeon deep underground - so deep that on certain days he swore he could hear the clatter of the mines below - only added to the unbearable heat.

A distant scream echoed through the corridor beyond the solid metal door that cut off his escape. Not a single ray of light escaped the corridor and into his cell, the vast slab of metal filling the void between the wall in entirety. When the cells had first been devised, the king had wanted to make sure that it was impossible for anyone to try and escape, let alone succeed. Warlocks had always been a handful, particularly when it came to imprisonment. Their magic required specific measures to combat, but it was nothing the king wasn't used to by now. Terravin had dreamed of escaping in his first week or so in the cell, but that hope had quickly faded as he came to accept reality. The king and his minions were experienced at crippling even the strongest warlocks who might entertain the thought of opposing him. Either you conformed to your new way of life, or you would soon find yourself fed to the beasts that lurked the deepest depths of the mines, fiery and accursed.

Another scream. It sounded like the king was working them hard today Terravin thought as he slouched back against the wall behind him, trying his best to let his body drift off into a world of sleep. Rest was rare these days. At first, the strain which his body went through after being put through rigorous shifts of using his magic at the order of the king had exhausted Terravin. Every time he returned, he would collapse in his cell and sleep until the guards came to fetch him for his next shift, his next watch. As time passed, the exhaustion turned into constant pain which turned into agony. His body was no longer left with scars, but instead began to slowly decay.

At times, he had wanted death to take him, for the God of Death to take pity on him and to claim his soul. But the king was good at keeping people alive when he wanted to, even if it took some of the more loyal warlocks to do so.

The sound of footsteps echoed down the corridor outside. His was the only cell down this corridor, he knew. Terravin tried to steady himself, his body already hurting, like a phantom pain travelling through his body as he heard the footsteps drawing closer.

They can't, he thought, it can't be my shift again already.

Terravin had no knowledge of how many years had passed since he had been caught; his only glimpses into the outside world came from the visions that he witnessed at the king's command. Most of which were admittedly dull. He had been able to work out the pattern of shifts, their frequency and when he was due for another. This was too soon.

"No," he muttered out loud, knowing that no one would hear but hoping that it would drive away this nightmare all the same.

The footsteps drew nearer, and he could make out the muttering of people outside his door. Something was wrong; the guards never spoke to each other. Panic coursed through his body like the very blood that kept him alive. A key entered the door and the locks began to unbolt one by one. A guard grunted as he tugged at the handle and slowly pulled opened the door, allowing feint light from flickering torches on the walls of the corridor to fill his cell. Terravin raised a hand to cover his eyes, but through his fingers he could make out four figures standing at the entrance to his cell.

Four? There are never four, Terravin worried. The man closest to the door was a guard, but his armour was red and gold, not the usual black of the guards who work the dungeons and mines.

"I haven't seen those colours in years," Terravin muttered weakly as he tried to use what little strength his body had to raise to his feet on his own. He failed.

"Quiet," the guard commanded. Terravin regarded the man; he was one of the Dauntless, the king's personal men.

Another figure held out a hand across the guard's plated armour, signalling that it was alright.

Blinking against the light Terravin continued. "If he really is one of the king's personal regiment... then that would make you -

"It's been many years Terravin." His voice was as regal as ever Terravin thought as he inspected the king with his own eyes for the first time in what must have been over half a decade by now.

"Your Majesty," Terravin said as mockingly as his current situation would allow. "Forgive me if I've forgotten your face, but you don't appear to have changed much. Just the grey hairs..."

Terravin's eyes quickly fluttered between the other two figures, he didn't recognise either. But then again his mind was no longer what it used to be; he could have met these two a thousand times before he was thrown down here. But the ling, he was one he'd never forget.

"Your king has need of you," The smaller of the other two figures said, his voice was high and full of ceremony.

Terravin never removed his gaze from the king's solemn face, even in the dim light he could make out the displeasure and contempt the king had for being down here. "Why me? I don't think my body is of much use to you anymore."

The king cracked a smile. Not the kind that would put Terravin at ease, in fact quite the opposite. He'd seen this kind of joy from the king before, all those years ago when he used to serve him. It was the kind of joy the king took in causing others great pain and sorrow.

Maybe the God of Death has finally taken pity on me, Terravin wondered before readying himself to ask why again. "Why me?"

To Terravin's surprise, it was the king who replied. "I've been having trouble recently with some insurgents hiding in the countryside to the south."

Terravin hated the guessing game, but he knew the king had been vague for a reason. He wanted him to probe further, and he was happy to oblige. He didn't get to have many conversations these days. "What does that have to do with me?"

"They stupidly let one of my more recently recruited warlocks survive a battle. Between the information he has given me and what my friend here has been able to establish," The king continued, gesturing in the direction of the fourth figure that stood in the doorway, hooded and robed. The scars of magic barely visible beneath his hood. Terravin didn't know what it was, but the fear that the fourth man caused to form in the pit of his stomach was almost as frightening as any the king had induced. "It appears as though your son didn't die in the Anya the way I thought he had all those years ago."

The words sent chills down Terravin's back. His son?

"No," he said weakly, the breath suddenly escaped from his body.

Terravin shook his head. His son was supposed to live a free life away from the entrapments of the king. He wouldn't risk that for some insurgency, he couldn't.

"My son died," Terravin insisted, silently praying to any God who would listen that they had the wrong person and that his son was living a quiet life with a family off on some far off land.

"Wrong Terravin. I had my suspicions, but it all fits together so perfectly," The king boasted. "A boy pale as the moon and gifted with magic. No, Turiel is alive and well. He is committing frequent acts of treason against my crown, and you're going to help me bring him to justice," the king spat with cruelty and venom in his mouth.

"No... I won't," Terravin whimpered as he pushed himself back up against the wall.

The king shook his head. "Look what you've become, old friend."

With a wave of his hand, the guard strode into the cell ready to drag Terravin towards a fate worse than any he had imagined.

Dear Reader,

I can't thank you enough for taking the time to pick up and read my first foray into the world of publishing. *Child of Destiny* has been my passion project for a long time now, and I hope that it has brought some joy to you as payment for your time spent within The Rive.

As a self-published author it really is just down to the readers to keep this dream alive. So if you have any interest in the stories to come, please do sign up to my newsletter, where you can keep up to date with all the latest news from The Rive and all future worlds that my writing takes us to.

Newsletter sign-up: http://eepurl.com/dCGtp9

As my final thank you and to prove my dedication to providing you all with the continuation of Lyvanne's story, I have a parting gift. The first chapter from Book 2, *Betrayal of Destiny*. I hope you enjoy.

"A reader lives a thousand lives before he dies, said Jojen. The man who never reads lives only one."

- George R.R. Martin, A Dance with Dragons.

BETRAYAL OF DESTINY

BOOK 2 IN THE RISING SAGA

CHAPTER 1

The snow fell dutifully against Gromwell's face. The young lieutenant was long since numb to the icy chill of the weather, but the impairment to his vision was still a trouble he wished he could be without. Stood at the summit of a large snow dune, on the creaking wooden flooring of a makeshift parapet, Gromwell was supposed to have a clear view of the surrounding area. He was having no such luck thanks to the recent snow storms. Thankfully, after two years of being stranded in the same bleak location on the very edge of Tyberia, Gromwell no longer needed to be able to see through the blizzards to know what lay before him. At the foot of the dune, he could just about make out the fringes of uniformly placed tents which housed the 501st Legion of the King's Army.

The camp, he knew, occupied an icy plane which stretched out before him before receding into a fresh placement of snow dunes on the opposite side. Those snow dunes were fortified beyond anything he imagined would be possible in such an inhospitable spot of land. Parapets similar to the one he stood on now, wooden palisades and smaller stockades lined the stretch of dunes. The final line of separation between his men and the savage and endless enemy who lived in the ice-tipped mountains which lay in the distance. The thought of their situation had once been a sobering one, but as time grew on and they adapted to this new way of life, it soon became the norm.

The wooden flooring creaked beneath Gromwell's feet and turning he saw one of his seniors making his way up a rickety stairway that crawled up the side of the dune, barely visible through the drifting snow.

"Lieutenant," the man said in greeting as he approached Gromwell's side, one hand raised in front of his face to shield him from the weather.

"Captain," Gromwell replied, his attention half stolen by the sea which lay beyond the dune to the rear. He couldn't see it through the blizzard, but the crash of waves against the small rocky outcrops which lay along the shore was unmistakable.

The Captain lowered his hand as he approached and with a smile clapped Gromwell on the back as he joined his side on the edge of the parapet. Stuck on an icy tundra for two years, the 501st Legion had long since lost the formality so rampant throughout the rest of the king's Army, but Gromwell wasn't sure this Captain would be any different with him in any other scenario either.

"Good morning Grommy," the Captain said.

"You know I hate that name, Landsley," Gromwell replied with a frown.

Landsley smirked. "I know."

The pair had grown up together in the Upper Layer of Astreya, both younger sons of Lording families. Landsley had come from a slightly more well-off family, and had, of course, been given a higher rank of officer. But it wasn't until they decided to draft into the army together that they finally realised that there was more between them than just friendship.

Relationships in the king's Army were frowned upon at the best of times, but during their years fighting against Tyberians alongside the rest of the 501st the two had grown more relaxed about being open around their friends. Fighting to protect the lives of those around you gave you a bond that was hard to shake. Gromwell knew he would give his life for any other man in the 501st and that they would do the same for him. So despite their situation being dire, he enjoyed the freedom from secrecy that being stuck on a foreign continent gave them.

"You eaten today?" Landsley asked.

Gromwell shook his head. They'd been on rations for months now. Their ships had been deconstructed and turned into the barricades which separated them from their enemy, and whilst they had been well stocked upon on arrival in Tyberia they didn't have enough to last for much longer. The ice had helped to preserve what supplies they had brought with them, and smugglers had been sent on regular intervals to help restock what they could. But the dangerous shoreline and weather made it difficult to get much through.

"Make sure you do, you're getting skinny," Landsely joked.

Gromwell knew it wasn't true and waved away the joke. The two weren't just alike in personality, but they looked the same and were built similarly too. Both sported thick beards to protect against the weather, and both were slightly above average in height with broad shoulders and chiselled chests. Skinny, they were not.

"What are you up here for anyway?" Gromwell asked in return.

Landsley reached into one of the deep pockets of his fur coat that he had draped over his uniform to keep warm and pulled out a scroll of parchment. "Smuggler arrived in the night, had news for the Major. We're being called home."

Gromwell's eyes drew wide, and his jaw fell slightly agape. "How? Why?"

For two years they'd held the shore of Tyberia alone, the last legion of the King's Army left from a failed invasion of a foreign continent. The thought of going home was a joy the likes of which he'd never thought he would feel again.

"I don't know, the letter's vague," Landsley replied as he tucked the parchment back into his coat pocket. "Things must be bad back at home if the king wants us to abandon this place completely though."

The jubilation hadn't lasted long. Gromwell knew that Landsley was right. The pair knew that their king was a flawed man; they knew that he could at times be cruel, but they believed in what his Kingdom offered. A stable and secure world, rather than the untamed and wild one which currently lay beyond the borders of his Kingdom. They were happy to fight for his cause in Tyberia, but ever since word had reached them that The Rive itself had been invaded there had been more than one occasion where they had wanted to abandon their invasion in order to return home in its defence. But the King had proved stubborn.

"The ships will arrive -

Landsely was cut off. The unmistakable sound of bells sounded out from across the icy plane. A moment later and the camp below them sprung into life with the clatter of steel and the hurried shouts of men preparing for battle.

"Come on," Gromwell said before scurrying off towards the stairway which would lead him back down from the top of the dune.

The camp was chaotic. Soldiers ran back and forth among the blizzard, some fully decked out in armour, others struggling to piece together what items of protection they had managed to scrape together. The majority of movement, however, was going in one direction, towards the snow dunes which lay beyond the edges of the icy plane. It was there that the bells still sounded out, but they weren't the only sound to echo down into the camp below. The bells had been joined by the sound of whistling arrows, and steel clattering against bone.

Gromwell didn't have his armour with him, but the gambeson and fur coat would have to do, he told himself as he refused to go back to his tent to find greater protection. Landsley was racing behind him, his steel armour joining the clatter of noise.

"Gromwell, you need armour!" he heard Landsley shout, but the noise was drowned out within cacophony that surrounded them.

The blizzard continued to obscure Gromwell's vision as he raced up the stairs laid out across the snow dune, but as he climbed the sounds of battle grew louder. With his palms soaked in sweat, he drew his sword from its hilt and climbed the final few steps onto the dune's peak. The battle was on top of him as quickly as it had come into his vision. His men were pressed up against the various defensive structures, and on the other side were the Tyberians. They were a primitive looking people, their armour was little more than fur and bones, their bodies were thick and covered in hair, their mouths were missing teeth and they fought like animals. He remembered how scared he had been of them when he first arrived on Tyberia. In his first battle, he'd lost three of his close friends from basic training, in his second another two. They were savages of the purest kind, but he was older now, more experienced in combat and when he saw them he felt nothing but the lust to kill.

Hearing cheers of encouragement from other officers who were just now arriving on the scene Gromwell threw himself into the thickest of the fighting. He didn't have the armour to push himself beyond his own men and into the swarms of Tyberians, but he was a confident swordsman, so he took it upon himself to plug the gap of the defensive structure, cutting off the few Tyberians who had made it through, leaving them for his men to deal with.

Fighting in the gap meant that numbers didn't matter, no matter how many Tyberians rushed in his direction it always came down to a one on one fight, something he would always back himself to win. His sword carved through the air as Tyberian men and women, armed with bone hatchets and probing spears hurled themselves foolishly into his reach. Two, three, four he counted as he slew his enemies, leaving a growing pile of bodies blocking the leak in the defences.

An arrow made of bone thudded into the palisade to his left, momentarily drawing his attention. He considered backing up into a safer position, but thought twice as he considered the luck that would be needed to hit him through the blizzard. Gromwell ducked as an onrushing Tyberian man threw his spear at his head, he grunted as a second later the beast had flung himself onto Gromwell, causing both of them to fall flat onto the snow. More Tyberians tried to follow their comrade through the gap, but the 501st were quick to fill Gromwell's place in the wall as he wrestled on the floor with his attacker. The Tyberian was strong, but Gromwell was a better fighter, and after rolling him out of the way of his men, Gromwell allowed the hulking brute to punch him repeatedly in the chest and face, whilst using the time to unhook a dagger from around his belt buckle. Putting as much strength as he had in his arm, he plunged the dagger up into the enemy, causing the Tyberian to slump to the floor, dagger wounds covering his chest and side.

"You alright, Lieutenant?" a passing soldier said, reaching down and offering a hand to help Gromwell back to his feet.

Gromwell nodded his head, despite the blood smeared across his face telling another story. Holding the soldier by his side, Gromwell looked up and down the snow dunes as best as the weather would allow. It appeared as his section were having a harder time of the battle than most, but he couldn't be sure. "What's your name?" Gromwell asked the soldier.

"Holtby, Lieutenant."

"Good name. Holtby, I need you go and find the Major, take note along your way of where the fighting is thickest and have the Major redistribute the men accordingly."

With a nod of his head, and one eye on the battle raging only a few metres away, Holtby ran off along the dunes. Gromwell hated the unknown during a battle, and if sending Holtby to find out where the troops were needed most might help ease his nerves then he was happy to lose a man from the fighting. From what he could tell the Tyberians were attackingg with a relatively large force, not uncommon, especially during blizzards like this. But it worried him all the same. Knowing that they were so close to going home, back to The Rive, made it feel like there was more on the line now than there ever had been before.

Not wanting to waste any more time, Gromwell picked up an iron shield, half buried among the snow, and fought his way back into the bloodshed. Tyberians swarmed over them, climbing the parapets and palisades alike, breaking down the stockades. They were all over them, but his men were brave and as the battle hardened he knew they wouldn't give up. As he cut down one Tyberian after another, he watched as the men around him did the same. Their defences were being torn apart, but as an army they were holding the line.

The attack lasted for nearly two hours. Holtby had returned to Gromwell's side towards the end of the fighting with a group of twenty soldiers at his back. By all accounts, Gromwell had indeed been where the fighting was worst. The 501st had one remaining warlock among their ranks, and by the end of the fighting he too had been killed. He had been the last of three who had originally departed for Tyberia among their ranks. Warlocks had been an unmatchable asset during the first years of the war, but as the Tyberians grew wary of their power they had adapted methods of identifying and killing warlocks early on into battles. Gromwell and other officers had tried their best to reactively find methods through which they could offer the warlocks better protection, but in battles like these things were often thrown into chaos.

As the last of the Tyberians fled from the summit of the snow dunes Gromwell began to take stock of the fallen bodies who littered the ground all around. It didn't take long for him to realise that Landsley was nowhere to be seen.

"Landsley?" he shouted out into the battlefield.

There was no reply. Fear took hold and he found himself pacing up and down the dune's summit.

He was right behind me when the fighting started, Gromwell reminded himself as he searched men both living and fallen.

"Landsley?" he called out again, attracting the attention of his men.

"Over here," a voice which didn't belong to his childhood friend called back.

The man knelt on the floor, hovering over a blood stained body buried in the snow. Gromwell sprinted over to the scene.

"I'm sorry Lieutenant," The man said quietly as Gromwell pushed him out of the way and threw himself on to his knees beside the body.

It was Landsley. Gromwell refused to cry in front of his men, even though he had no doubt they would understand, but he couldn't stop the tears from welling in his eyes. Landsley had wounds across his back and torso, deep enough to kill on impact. His weathered armour pierced and dented beyond repair.

"You stupid bastard," Gromwell whispered as he cupped Landsley's pale face in the palm of his hand.

Sympathetic hands rested on his shoulder as his men passed him by on their way to begin clearing up the summit. Gromwell's thoughts drifted back to the news he'd received just before the fighting had begun, that soon they would be leaving this place behind and that every person who had died had done so in vain. Anger began to pool within him, like a creature being nurtured within his soul. Anger towards the Tyberians, towards the war… towards his king.

Printed in Great Britain
by Amazon